The Choir

By Carol M. Cram

ISBNs: 978-1-963452-28-0 (pb);
978-1-963452-29-7 (hc);
978-1-963452-30-3 (eBook)
978-1-963452-31-0 (audio)

Book Cover Design: The Book Cover Whisperer, OpenBookDesign.biz
Interior Book Design: Inanna Arthen, inannaarthen.com

Library of Congress Control Number: 2025916431

First Printing: 2026
Printed in the United States of America

Publisher's Cataloging-in-Publication
(Provided by Cassidy Cataloguing Services, Inc.)
Names: Cram, Carol M., author.
Title: The choir / by Carol M. Cram.
Description: [Minneapolis, Minnesota] : [HTF Publishing], [2026]
Identifiers: ISBN: 9781963452297 (hardcover) | 9781963452280 (paperback) |
9781963452303 (ebook) |
9781963452310 (audio)
Subjects: LCSH: Working class women--England--Yorkshire--History--19th century--
Fiction. | Women's
choirs--England--Yorkshire--History--19th century--Fiction. | Music--Competitions--
Fiction. | Social
conflict--England--Yorkshire--History--19th century--Fiction. | Women--England--Social
conditions--
19th century--Fiction. | Female friendship--Fiction. | Great Britain--History--19th
century--Fiction. |
LCGFT: Historical fiction. | BISAC: FICTION / Historical / General. | FICTION /
Women. | FICTION /
Literary.
Classification: LCC: PR9199.4.C695774 C46 2026 | DDC: 813/.6--dc23

For Granny & for Mom

Chapter 1

October 1897—Briarstown, East Yorkshire

Eliza

Eliza Kingwell slipped her hands into the wash water to gather up her husband's two work shirts, taking pleasure in leaving them to the last when the water was as dirty as it would get. Nervous excitement squeezed her chest as she kneaded and twisted. The nerves reminded her of how she used to feel singing for people who clapped and cheered and called for more.

In exactly three weeks, Eliza would leave her home and this dreary washhouse forever. In the middle of the night, after Reg was gone to visit his sister in Leeds and all the snooping neighbors were tight asleep, Eliza would gather up the girls and go.

She glanced over her shoulder to check she was alone in the washhouse, although she doubted anyone would come in so late in the day. The other women in the court did their washing and their gossiping in the morning when Eliza stayed away. She opened her mouth to let the delicious hum at the back of her throat escape into the frigid air.

Amazing Grace, how sweet the sound

She'd take the girls to the seaside when they got to Devon. When she'd lived there as a child, Dad and Ma could never afford to take her and her three brothers any farther than Exeter.

That saved a wretch like me

She let her voice rise, imagining the sound filling her with the warmth of a summer sun.

I once was lost, but now am found

Scooping Reg's second shirt from the soap scum, she wrung it hard between her chapped palms and then hung it on the wooden rack.

Was blind, but now I see…

She held the final note for as long as possible before letting it fade to a whisper. Her eyes were well and truly open now.

Eliza emptied the washbasin into the floor drain, then picked up the jam jar containing one sputtering candle and used it to light her way across the yard to her house. She paused on the scrubbed stoop. Candles flickered in the windows of the eight houses in Court Four overlooking the cramped yard where the stink of the privies fouled the air, and people were forever coming and going. The yard was quiet now, with everyone gone inside for their tea.

Another eight houses were built out from the backs of the yard houses and faced the street. Eliza would have much preferred living in an outside house like she had when she'd first come to the North. The wind off the moors battered the thin walls in winter, but at least she'd been able to breathe.

She stumbled over a brick that had fallen from the front of the adjoining house. The state of the dwellings in Court Four were a disgrace. The bosses should be ashamed of themselves. Before his demotion from foreman back to the mill floor, Reg had *promised* they'd move to an outside house or, even better, a terrace house with a garden out back like they'd lived in when they were first married.

It didn't matter now. Squaring her shoulders, Eliza pushed open the door to her house. Reg sat slumped by the coal fire, every muscle slack with exhaustion after his fourteen-hour shift at the mill.

"Girls gone for the pie," he said without looking up.

"Good." Eliza lowered herself onto a stool in front of the scarred table and picked up the newspaper. She searched for any mention of Mrs. Ruth Henton, formerly known as Ruth Kingwell. Beautiful, talented, and adored—Ruth had left Briarstown for London twelve years earlier.

She found it on the second page.

THE PROFESSIONAL BEAUTY. Mr. Andrews is severe upon the "professional beauty," but makes a special exception in favour of Mrs. Ruth Henton. In addition to being exceedingly fair, Mrs. Henton is a charming singer, and the writer has often attended with infinite pleasure her performances at Mr. Johnson's Palladia Theatre. It is therefore perhaps unsurprising that the Prince of Wales has been seen accompanying her to dinner on several occasions.

"Anything about our Ruth in the paper today?" Reg asked.

"No," Eliza said.

"What about them rumors? Do you think they're true?"

"Your Ruth and the Prince of Wales? Don't be daft." Eliza folded the paper and held it in her lap. She hadn't had a letter from her old friend in over nine years, the last time being a note to congratulate her on the birth of Lily May, her second eldest, back in '87. Ruth hadn't bothered to acknowledge the births of Gladys, Emily, and Bessie. Tendrils of resentment wrapped around Eliza's heart, making her despise herself and Ruth in equal measure.

Four-year-old Bessie ran over to Reg and pulled at his pant leg, begging for a ride on his knee.

"Come here, you," Eliza said. "Your dad doesn't want to be bothered with giving rides. He's worked all day."

"She's all right," Reg said as he patted the child's plump cheeks.

"Bessie!"

The child looked up, fear clouding her blue eyes. Eliza felt a pang of remorse for her tone, but it couldn't be helped. Bessie had to learn whose word was law in the house. Reg was too soft on the girls, especially Bessie, whom he coddled more than was good for her. Bessie sullenly crossed the room and joined Emily, who was sitting on the floor cradling a doll. To Eliza's relief, Emily relaxed her grip on the doll and allowed her little sister to sit next to her.

The door crashed open, and Annie and Lily May burst into the room, bringing with them a blast of cold air and the welcome smell of a freshly baked meat pie.

Eliza's stomach churned. She'd not had a moment to herself to eat so much as a piece of toast all day.

"*I'm* telling her!" Lily May said.

"No, you're not!" Annie exclaimed. "I'm the eldest. I'll do it."

"Pipe down, girls!" Reg said. "I've enough to put up with at t'mill without comin' home to more racket."

"You heard your father." Eliza couldn't risk making Reg angry before she could ask him about the photograph. It was the last thing she needed before executing her Plan.

She always thought about it with a capital P. A Plan was much more likely to happen than a plain old plan.

"But Ma!" Annie said. "You'll want to hear this."

"We was talking with Mrs. McKay while we was waiting," Lily May added.

Eliza stood and reached for the warm packet. "I can't imagine anything Hattie McKay has to say would interest me."

"Mrs. McKay asked me to ask you to…"

"For pity's sake, I couldn't care less. Hattie and I've not had a good word for each other since we were girls."

"But Ma!"

Eliza cut a thick slice of the pie and put it on a plate. "Stop your dancing about and take this to your dad," she said, handing the plate to Lily May.

"Mrs. McKay said I was to give you this," Annie said, holding out a scrap of torn newspaper. "She said you'd want to know."

"She did!" Lily May exclaimed, running back to the table after handing her father his pie. "She said it were right up your street."

"What are you on about?"

"Please read it, Ma," Annie said more quietly.

"Put it on the table. I'll look at it later." Eliza held up one hand. "That's enough. You're upsetting Dad with all your carrying on. Where's Gladys?"

"She told me before we went out that she weren't hungry," Annie said.

"*Wasn't* hungry," Eliza corrected her. "Well, we'll not wait."

She sliced equal portions of the pie and then sat down to eat, conscious that both Annie and Lily May were staring at her and that neither had taken even one bite.

"Eat your pie before it gets cold," Eliza scolded. She waited until each girl picked up her fork and started eating before smoothing out the torn scrap of paper. Someone had circled an advertisement with a thick black pencil, partially obscuring some of the text.

But the gist was clear enough.

"You going to do it, Ma?" Lily May asked, her mouth full.

"Going to do what?" Reg called from his place by the fire.

"Nothing," Eliza said, picking up the paper and crushing it into her fist. "Close your mouth when you eat, for pity's sake, Lily May." She frowned at her across the table. "There's more meat and less pastry than usual. Are you sure Mrs. Dorman didn't over-charge you?"

"Of course she didn't," Lily May said indignantly. "We paid her the same as always. I wouldn't let her cheat us."

"That's all right then." Eliza suppressed a smile. Of all the girls, quick-witted Lily May, who bristled at the slightest criticism, warranted or not, reminded Eliza most of herself.

"You 'ave to do it, Ma," Annie said, calm and capable as always. Eliza felt a rush of tenderness towards her eldest. With her over-inflated sense of duty, Annie could be counted on to help keep the four other girls in line. Eliza would need Annie's steady hand when they moved back to Devon.

"I don't *have* to do anything," Eliza said. It would never do to let the girls see her as anything but sure of herself. "I've no time for such foolishness. Help your sisters with the washing up. I'd best get Gladys."

Eliza stuffed the paper into her pocket, then rose from the table and set off up the two twisting flights of stairs to the top floor. Gladys sat on the bed she shared with Lily May, Annie, and Emily. As expected, she was reading. Eliza knew she should scold her for not coming down to her tea. A good mother *never* spoiled her children.

"Why didn't you want your tea?" she asked.

Gladys lowered the book that was almost too big for her small hands. "I'm sorry, Ma. I'd got to such an exciting bit, and I didn't want to stop to eat." She looked up at Eliza. Put her in boys' clothes and she'd be the image of Reg. But where his deep blue eyes flashed contempt, hers shone with wonder.

"What book?"

Gladys held it up—a tattered copy Eliza recognized as a book she'd read and loved when she was Gladys's age. "My teacher let me bring it home."

Eliza held out her hand.

"Can I have it back tomorrow, Ma?"

Eliza saw herself as Gladys must—straight, black-clad—and unloving. *Like her own mother.*

"You can," she said. "And when you're done reading it, I want you to tell me how you liked it."

The relief on Gladys's face rebuked Eliza. She turned away, the book heavy as a brick in her hands. She hated making her girls afraid of her, but what choice did she have? It was her job to keep them safe and teach them how to get on in life in a world that wouldn't do them any favors. They needed to be tough.

"Go down and get your tea," she said gruffly.

After Gladys left the small attic room, Eliza opened the book and read words that were like old friends. How she'd missed falling into Alice's adventures. When she was Gladys's age, she hadn't read books so much as inhaled them. As soon as she got the girls and herself back to Devon, she'd make time to read again.

Closing the book with a snap, Eliza descended from the top to the middle floor and placed the book in the bottom drawer of the bureau next to the trundle bed where Bessie slept. She took a moment to smooth her hand across the worn coverlet on the double bed. At least they'd not yet been reduced to taking in a lodger. Some of the women in the court divided the middle room with a curtain, sleeping on one side with their husbands and whatever children didn't fit in the top room, and renting out a single bed on the other side. Eliza knew of at least three women who had two people sharing the one bed—going and coming at different times of the day and night, so they never met.

Maybe if they had a lodger sleeping so close, Reg would think twice before hurting her.

She carried on down the twisting stairway to the ground floor. Bessie and Emily were quietly playing with Emily's doll, and Reg had fallen asleep next to the fire. While Gladys was finishing her piece of pie, Annie and Lily May sat at the table, their backs straight, and their eyes fixed on Eliza as she entered the room.

"You should do it, Ma," Annie said.

"Off to bed with the lot of you," Eliza snapped.

"But…" Lily May said.

"I said go!" With effort, Eliza resisted the urge to swat Lily May's backside as she headed for the stairs. Her daughters were all that kept her upright most days but keeping them safe frayed her patience and left her irritable more often than she would have liked.

She picked up a stack of washed plates, rattling them as she put them away to rouse Reg. All day she'd been dreading asking him, but there was nothing to be gained by waiting any longer.

"What do you want, woman? You're making enough noise to raise the dead."

Eliza crossed the small room to stand in front of him. "I want us to get a photograph taken," she said. "Of our family. All of us." She let the words come out in a rush before she lost her nerve.

"Why? Sounds expensive."

"It's what everyone's doing these days," Eliza said. "Doris Blair had one taken with her family last month. Her Ed makes less than you at the mill. If they can afford it, we can too."

"I'll say what we can afford," Reg growled.

"I want a photograph taken of our family." Eliza crossed her arms over her chest and stared down at him. She almost always got what she wanted just by asking—at least she had in the years before Reg started drinking again.

Reg sat still, fists curled on his knees. She tamped down a twinge of fear, reminding herself that he only came after her at night when the girls were sleeping, and only if he'd spent the evening at the pub. She held her breath. A fluttering in her stomach—the first with the new child—reminded her that she *had* to have this photograph taken—and soon. She owed it to her girls to have something of their father to take with them when they left Briarstown.

To her relief, Reg's fists uncurled.

"Suit yourself," he said as he heaved himself to his feet. "Happen it can't do no harm."

Eliza knew he'd agreed only because Ed Blair had a photograph taken with his family. Reg hated taking second place to anyone.

For a moment, he loomed over her as if daring her to flinch.

"Thank you," she said, refusing to give him the satisfaction of seeing her cowed. "I'll make the appointment for next week."

"Nothing fancy, mind," he said. "I'm not made of money. Only get the one photograph with me in the center and you and the girls gathered around." He pulled his coat off the hook.

"You're going out?" Eliza tried and failed to keep the dismay from her voice.

"Aye, well, I'm that parched."

"It's awful raw out there," she said.

"You needn't wait up. I'll be back when I'm back."

The door slammed shut behind him.

Eliza sank into Reg's chair, still warm and smelling of his sweat and oil from the machinery at the mill. She fished the ad from her pocket.

Female voice choir of not less than eight and no more than twenty voices.

For a second, she let herself imagine staying in Briarstown and giving Reg another chance—and maybe even singing again.

Real singing for an audience that clapped and cheered only for her.

She tossed the ad into the fire, then turned away to avoid seeing the paper flare across the hot coals.

Chapter 2

London

Ruth

Ruth Henton inhaled the sickly-sweet scent of William's lilies. What a dear he was to send them. She would let him kiss her the next time they met.

Leaning close to the mirror, she wiped the last of the white greasepaint from her chin and neck, then dipped a finger into the pot of rouge and smoothed it onto her cheeks.

Was it her imagination, or did she need more color than she used to?

Of course not. She was at the height of her beauty and her powers. Everyone said so, and if the bloom of youth came from a jar, well, what of it? She glanced down at the folded note delivered with the lilies after she'd returned to her dressing room, flushed with triumph and shaky with exhaustion.

William had sent her lilies because she'd once mentioned they were her favorite. She'd not told him it was because they reminded her of Mother. Ruth thought about the small vase balanced atop the casket on that frosty January day fifteen years earlier. She let the memory settle for a few moments, acknowledging the ache that never eased, no matter how many years passed. If only Mother could see her now!

Ruth had everything worth having in the world——fame, beauty, money, and a voice rewarded every night with roars of adulation from the young men crowding the stalls. She also had William, who was handsome and rich, and called her the most exquisite singer in London. What a wonderful word was exquisite! Nothing in the squalid years she'd spent with Mother before Reg Kingwell came into their lives had ever been exquisite.

Also, William wanted *her*, which her own husband did not, nor ever would.

"These come for you, Miss." Katie held out a massive vase bristling with red roses.

"Put them next to the lilies," Ruth said. She loathed roses with their perfect furled beauty and velvet touch. Mother used to say only men without imagination sent roses. Reg Kingwell had courted Mother with bunches of wildflowers picked from the hedgerows.

"Don't you want to know who they's from?" Katie asked.

"Is there a note?"

"Yes, Miss." Katie handed her a square of plain, stiff paper reeking of wealth and privilege.

Could it be?

Ruth had heard rumors that the Prince of Wales was to be in the audience, but she'd refused to believe it. If she'd known he was watching her, she might have let nerves get the better of her. *That* was something she couldn't afford to do. She was Ruth Henton—darling of the London stage. The public deserved to see her always at her best.

She read the note and blushed. Really, he was going too far.

"Do you like the gentleman, Miss?"

"Oh yes, I suppose I do," Ruth said, laughing. "I could hardly *not* like him, all things considered."

"Miss?"

Ruth waved away the question. The girl was barely grown and still starstruck. Life would take the bloom from her cheeks soon enough. Unlike Ruth, young Katie had no talent and no connections to take her from the dressing room to the stage.

"Help me into my gown, please," Ruth said, not quite suppressing a groan as she rose to her feet and raised her arms. She was exhausted, but resting was out of the question for many hours yet. "I've got more important things to think about than men and flowers."

As the emerald-green gown slipped over Ruth's head and down her body, the feel of silk caressing her skin reinvigorated her. Its soft rustling was a foretaste of the murmurs of admiration that would follow her when she passed through the dining salon to meet with the prince.

There had been a time in Ruth's life when the only silk she saw adorned the dresses worn by the haughty women her mother toiled for.

Now she wore silk gowns every day.

Most of the time, Ruth didn't think about her life before coming to London, before her voice and her face became her fortune. But the note from the Prince of Wales had given her pause. She wondered if he'd have sent it if he'd known about her humble beginnings.

Very humble, she reminded herself with a half-smile. She must take care not to betray herself. The family story she'd manufactured about her life before marrying James would not withstand scrutiny.

"Miss?" Katie held out a bracelet made of interlocking gold rings.

Ruth held out her wrist. If Katie had ever noticed the slight bump protruding from her smooth skin, she'd had the sense to say nothing. Perhaps she suspected what had caused it. Katie came from a rough part of London and was likely no stranger to angry men with loud voices and quick fists.

Like her stepfather, Ruth thought, suppressing a shudder. As always when she let herself think about Reg Kingwell, Ruth felt shame like a slap across her heart. Her old friend Eliza had spent the last twelve years married to Reg while Ruth had fashioned a life that every chorus girl in London would kill for.

The bracelet's smooth rings shone softly in the gaslight. James had given it to her on the day of their wedding—the first and only day of her married life she'd been truly happy.

Sighing, Ruth contemplated spending what little energy she had left entertaining the future King. She'd much prefer dining with William, but turning down the Prince of Wales was unthinkable. If she offended him, he could ruin her career with a flick of one thick finger.

She could not allow that to happen. Ruth needed applause like she needed air. Without it, she'd be less than nothing.

"You look beautiful, Miss," Katie said. "But then you always look beautiful."

"Thank you, Katie. I haven't always been as I am now."

"I can't imagine it, Miss." Katie picked up a pearl necklace and held it to Ruth's throat. "This will go real nice with your gown."

Ruth pointed to a small unopened box next to her hairbrush. "Bring me that one."

She'd wear the gift from her latest conquest, but she'd dine with the prince.

An hour later, Ruth swept into the foyer outside the Savoy Hotel's private dining room. The Prince of Wales stood apart from a gaggle of elegantly dressed ladies and gentlemen. He was resplendent in full evening dress—a tailcoat with shawl collar and a straight-cut waist that emphasized his impressive girth. A watch chain suspended from a white silk waistcoat caught the light. He was shorter than she expected and much wider. She'd read that he was to turn fifty-six in a few weeks, but he looked ten years older—much older than the man she'd prefer to spend the rest of her evening with.

Taking a deep breath, Ruth prepared herself to greet him. If she comported herself well, she could become the next Mrs. Lily Langtry. As a mistress of the Prince of Wales, she'd have fame far beyond what she already enjoyed.

Is that what you truly want?

Ruth shut away the question and dropped into a full curtsy, her eyes fixed on shoes shined so brightly, she blinked. When she rose, she flashed her brightest smile.

"Your performance was magnificent, my dear," he said. "We were enthralled."

"Thank you, Your Majesty. I am honored."

"Quite." He held out his arm for her. "Shall we?"

She took his arm and walked with him into the exclusive dining room. Every head swiveled to follow their progress, William's included. He was seated at a table with three other gentlemen. She wondered whether he'd notice that she was wearing his necklace. Snatches of whispers reached Ruth as she passed.

"She's a singer."

"Very pretty, don't you think?"

"She's also a P.B., but I consider her passable at best."

"These Professional Beauties are no better than they should be."

"I heard her sing last week. Superb voice."

"Look at that skin!"

"Magnificent."

"Quite."

"Bertie loves a pretty face."

"Don't we all?"

Over the next several hours, Ruth endured rather than enjoyed her dinner. The variety and quantity of food brought to their table was truly astonishing. She couldn't help comparing the fine creations with fancy French names to the table scraps she'd lived off as a child before her mother married Reg Kingwell. A dish introduced to her as *Cuisses de Nymphe Aurore* and a favorite of the prince's, turned out to be frog's legs. Ruth's stomach churned.

"You are enjoying yourself, my dear?" Bertie asked. "I must say, this beef has been cooked to perfection, but you've barely touched it."

"I'm enjoying it very much, sir," Ruth lied. "But after a performance, I am rarely hungry."

"Ah, well, that is a shame." He patted his stomach. "And not a problem we've ever been obliged to endure."

Ruth laughed dutifully while keeping her eye on William. He rose from his table and slipped out, leaving his companions talking animatedly. She longed to follow him and spend the rest of the night nestled in his arms. She blushed. How shameless she'd become—dining with one man while imagining herself in another's arms.

She spared no thought for her husband—or William's wife, for that matter.

Another two courses followed the beef. Ruth valiantly managed a few bites of each, but as the evening wore on and the food never seemed to end, she couldn't help wishing she'd declined the prince's invitation. Bertie was known for his charm and wit, but in Ruth's opinion, he talked too much and laughed too loudly. Her head ached with the effort of keeping a smile on her face and her back erect. None of the other occupants at the large table paid her any attention. The women fixed their eyes on the men, who in turn watched Bertie.

A waiter glided over, wine bottle in hand. Ruth shook her head, motioning him to step back. Bertie frowned. "You are unwell?"

"Oh, no!" she exclaimed. "But I confess I am fatigued, sir. Also, too much wine is not good for my voice."

"Ah, well, we can't have that, can we?"

"No, sir."

"But here's something you're sure to enjoy," he said, nodding to the line of waiters entering the dining room. "I ordered the chef to make this dessert especially for you."

One of the waiters set a cut-glass bowl in front of Ruth. It contained one glossy peach sitting atop several scoops of ice cream infused with a red sauce—raspberry, most likely. Ruth didn't even want to speculate how much it must have cost to serve such exotic fruits in October.

"It's a specialty of our chef, Monsieur Escoffier," Bertie said.

"It looks delicious."

"Yes, of course, but you must know the story behind it."

"Sir?"

"A few years back, Escoffier created it to honor Nellie Melba."

"The Australian soprano?" Ruth was impressed. She'd heard Madame Melba sing the role of Nedda in *Pagliacci* at Covent Garden in 1893. That had been in the early years of her marriage to James, when he would sometimes accompany her to the opera. The soprano's voice had captivated Ruth. The next morning, she read in the paper that Melba's performance was "simply delicious in its fullness, richness and purity." Although Ruth had enjoyed her share of glowing reviews, never had she come close to receiving such fulsome praise.

"Escoffier calls his dessert Peach Melba," Bertie said. "Is that not amusing?"

"Very," Ruth said. She picked up her spoon and sliced off a morsel of peach. Although no stranger to good food since marrying James, Ruth had rarely tasted anything so wonderful.

"Perhaps one day, Escoffier will create a dessert in *your* honor. What do you think of that?"

"It would be delightful," Ruth said.

"Eat up, my dear. We hope you've enjoyed yourself?"

"Of course, sir." She took a few more bites of the dessert. Did the Prince of Wales really think she could be famous enough to have a dessert named in her honor? Nellie Melba sang on the great stages of the world in London, Paris, Berlin, and even New York.

Ruth wanted to believe it, but the same small voice that had questioned her earlier whispered the truth.

Chapter 3

Briarstown

Eliza

"I'm off," Reg said, pushing back from the table, scattering crumbs on to the newly swept floor. The one candle flickered and was almost extinguished in the damp morning air.

"Don't forget we're to be at the photographer's studio at two o'clock," Eliza said. She slid past him and picked up the poker next to the grate. The coals sputtered and sparked as she nudged at them, coaxing a few more flames to warm the room before the girls came down.

"I won't."

"I'll bring your good jacket to the photographer's. Are you sure old Jonas will let you off?"

"Of course. I told you already, he's gonna ask Mr. Lewiston to make me foreman again. Says he shouldn't have let Lewiston listen to that hussy, and that I was the best foreman he'd ever worked with."

"That was two years ago, and he's not lifted a finger to help you since. What's he waiting for?" Eliza pushed down the disgust she always felt when she thought about Reg and his goings-on with the mill girls.

"Just like you to go on about money. Can't you be glad for what we got?"

"We have five girls to keep fed and clothed."

Reg rose from the table so quickly he knocked his plate to the floor. "That's enough from you."

Eliza stood still, the poker held loosely in her hand as she watched him blunder around the small room. She wondered if she would have the nerve to use the poker if he came at her.

"The whistle's going to sound in a few minutes," she said, keeping her voice flat. She held his gaze, her chin high. He was a good head taller than she was and twice as broad, but she knew she was safe. He never came at her if there was any chance one of the girls might come downstairs and see. "You'd best get going before the girls get up."

Moments after Reg clapped his cap on his head and clumped out of the house, Eliza braced her hands against the table to quell a ripple of nausea. This pregnancy wasn't going as smoothly as the others. Perhaps she should see the doctor. But doctors cost money, and she didn't want Reg to know about the new baby.

Eliza thought about the advertisement Hattie McKay had given the girls two weeks earlier. She wondered if Hattie had convinced any of the other women in the neighborhood to form a choir. If so, no one had bothered to tell her.

And that, Eliza had to admit, was her own fault. She purposely kept her distance from the other women and would rather die than let on what went on behind closed doors. If people suspected, they'd blame her.

Eliza Kingwell's as sharp-tongued as they come.

She don't deserve Reg Kingwell and that's a fact.

Everyone knows he's a fine sort—handsome as a toff and always with a good word for everyone he meets.

Mind you, there were that bit of bother with Merilee Adams.

Aye, but I don't credit a word of it.

My Frank says he can be a mean drunk.

I've heard he's got a temper.

Aye, but a man like Reg's not the kind to go lookin' for trouble. If you ask me, it were Merilee wanting attention.

Eliza's lucky to 'ave him.

Aye.

Eliza slathered jam across bread for the girls' breakfasts and thought about the work she needed to do to get the frocks and pinafores ready for the photograph. She'd wear the black dress she'd been given years earlier and worn only a handful of times. Even after five children, the dress still molded tightly to her body. Eliza was proud of having kept her figure when so many did not. It was little enough to be proud about, but it was something.

She remembered the first time she'd worn the dress. The applause had been loud enough to tear the roof off the auditorium. She'd felt it like a stiff cleansing wind off the moor. For those few seconds, Eliza had floated high above the dreary town and glimpsed a new future.

The girls tumbled into the room, arguing and jostling. Eliza scolded them half-heartedly while she set to work ironing Annie's pinafore. While her tongue directed the girls, she put the finishing touches on the Plan. She could hardly believe she was about to put it in motion after eight years of saving ha'penny after ha'penny, month after month.

A small part of her wished things could be different. Until he'd started drinking again, Reg had been a decent enough husband. The first time she'd felt the crack of his open hand against her cheek, her only emotion had been surprise.

That quickly changed to rage and then resolve as the drinking got worse and the nights longer. Thank goodness for Granny back in Devon. Eliza thought of the letter hidden under the mattress.

Come as soon as you're able.

What would Ma say? It didn't bear thinking about, which is why Eliza wouldn't tell her. The day after Reg left for Leeds, she and the girls would up and go, and that would be the end of her life in Briarstown.

Eliza looked away from her ironing to hide the tears pricking her eyes. Nineteen long years ago, she'd come to the North from Devon full of dreams. Dad had told her she could go to school and become a teacher, that she was dead clever and could run rings around her two big brothers. Granny always said they had one brain between the two of them. Eliza grinned at the memory. Granny never minced words. Dad used to call her formidable, a word Eliza liked to take out every so often and think about. Did her own girls think of her as formidable? She was stern with them to be sure, but they must know how much she loved them—as fiercely as her own mother had *not* loved her.

Blinking hard, Eliza hung Annie's pinafore over the back of a chair and then reached for Gladys's. The girl was growing like a weed and almost as tall as Annie. Eliza added starch to the frill around the bib, then hung it over another chair and ironed three more pinafores. Absently, she put her hand on her stomach. Would the new one be a boy?

She hadn't told Reg she was expecting. He'd go all soppy and get his hopes up yet again, and then, if a boy didn't come, he'd blame her. But if all went as she planned, Reg would never know about his sixth child.

Eliza opened the cupboard and pulled out a small box from its hiding place at the back. It was so full the coins barely clinked together, and the box was almost too heavy to hold easily in one hand.

The photograph would be ready in time for Eliza to take with her when she left Briarstown. She planned to tell the girls they were going south for a visit to their great-granny and that their father knew all about it. She'd let them look at the photograph and she'd never turn the girls against their father, even though he deserved it.

"Ma!" called Gladys.

Eliza put the box back on the shelf and closed the cupboard. "I'm right here. You needn't shout."

"Annie took the hair brush off me!"

"Oh, for pity's sake." Eliza handed a pinafore to each girl, then lined them up in front of her, youngest to eldest. The pinafores glowed in the dim light, a testament to her morning's work. She dared any woman in the court to do better.

"I didn't, Ma!" Annie exclaimed. "Gladys is telling tales. I gave the brush to Lily May."

"Well, I don't have it," Lily May said. "Ask Emily."

"Come here," Eliza said to Gladys. She sat on a stool and pointed to the floor. Obediently, Gladys knelt with her back to Eliza. "If we're late because of you, your dad will be angry."

"I'm sorry, Ma."

"Sorry won't get us there on time," Eliza said. She took the brush from Emily, placed it against the crown of Gladys's head, and pulled.

"Ow!"

She tugged again, but a little more gently. What kind of mother took her anger out on her children?

"Ma!"

"Hush. I'll be another minute. You don't want to be looking a mess for the photograph, do you?"

The knots seemed to multiply the more she brushed. How could one small child get herself in such a state? Each tangled strand reminded Eliza of how she was failing her girls.

After a few more strokes, Eliza gave up and placed the brush on the table.

"That'll have to do," she said, clambering to her feet and turning away before the girls saw her face crumple like hot coals prodded into flame.

What would Dad think if he could see what she'd become?

She picked up her flat hat and pinned it to her hair, all the while breathing slowly to master the grief that still washed over her, usually when she least expected it. Behind her, she heard the girls chattering as they pulled on their coats and hats.

"Annie," she said, turning around. "You go on ahead with your sisters. I'll catch you up in a few minutes."

"Yes, Ma."

The minute the door closed behind the girls, Eliza let herself sink into a chair. As she stared unseeing at the scarred tabletop, she heard again the rats and mice rustling in the thatch above the small cot where she slept in the rundown cottage in Devon in which she'd spent the first ten years of her life.

She stared out of the tiny window and in the twilight saw Dad sitting on a stone wall, his head bowed into his hands. With the sun finally gone, shafts of the rising moon flooded the yard as bright as day. Dad's shoulders trembled, and with a start, Eliza realized he was crying How could that be? Men didn't cry, and yet here was Dad—big, rough, silent Dad—shaking with sobs.

She thought of the letter Ma had left on the table downstairs. It was from Ma's brother, Bob, who used to live in the next village with his wife, Agnes, and their three boys. A year or two back, they'd moved away, and Eliza remembered Ma saying how she'd never do such a thing, not in a month of Sundays, and didn't understand how Agnes would put up with it.

So why had Dad announced earlier that evening that they were moving to the North? It didn't make sense. Eliza needed to read that letter. Careful not to wake up Ma, who slept with baby Ernie a few feet away, Eliza crept down the stairs, willing the old treads not to creak. Her two older brothers were jumbled together in one corner of the main room like two loose-limbed calves. She paused at the bottom step. Were they asleep yet? But she couldn't risk waiting. Dad would be coming in any moment, and it wouldn't do for him to find her out of bed for no good reason. She darted toward the table and picked up the letter just as the back door opened.

"Here, you!" Dad shuffled forward, his voice a whisper. "What you still doing up?"

"I wanted to read the letter," Eliza said. "Ma asked the boys to, but they wouldn't."

Dad's teeth flashed in a half-smile. "No surprise there." He grasped Eliza's arm. "Come, lass. Bring it outside."

Eliza followed him without a word as he led her into the yard. In the moonlight, she saw his cheeks were wet.

"Read it out loud."

Eliza unfolded the single sheet of cheap paper.

Dear Archie

My best, good wishes to you and Gladys and the littles. We be all fine and miss you. Jobs be going begging here. Come soon as you can. Work in the mill's hard but steady. Good wages for you and the big boys and even your girl. Boss has got houses to let. They be small, but not so cold in winter like what you be used to.

Best to all, Bob

Eliza looked up at her father, too afraid to speak. Good wages for her *and* the boys? She couldn't go to school if she were out earning wages. But she didn't ask Dad because likely he had no more answers than she did. Instead, she handed him the letter and sat next to him.

"You know Mr. Barton? Over at the big house?" Dad said finally. "He be wantin' to pull down the cottages. Build new ones."

"Why can't we live in one of the new ones?"

Dad shrugged. "No point if we don't got work. Barton don't need us next year."

"What about another estate?"

"It be the same everywhere, Eliza. World's changin'. Your Uncle Bob, he be smart gettin' out." Dad crushed the letter between his large hands. "Your Ma don't like it, but she's come 'round, so we be going."

"What will the new place be like?" she asked, to keep him talking. Never had he spoken to her like this, like she was something more than a nuisance to be teased and tolerated.

Dad put his arm around her and pulled her close. She smelled hay and sweat and ale. "Who be to say?"

"Will we like it there?"

"Who be to say?" he said again. And then, to Eliza's surprise, he looked down at her and grinned. Black holes gaped where some teeth were missing. "S'pose we got to wait and see."

"Will I have to go work in the mill?"

"Ah no, lass. You be too young and too clever."

"What?" Eliza pulled away and looked up at Dad. He'd never called her clever. Once, her teacher had said she had brains to burn, but the way she'd said it hadn't sounded like a compliment. Still, Eliza had mulled over and delighted in the words for weeks. Having brains to burn had to be better than having just one brain between two, like her brothers.

Chuckling, he squeezed her arm. "You don't think I sees you read better than both them boys put together?"

"I want to be a teacher, Dad," she blurted before she had time to think better of it. "Can I go to school up north?"

"Aye, 'course you can. Now your Ma's agreed to move after always sayin' she never would, aught's possible."

He pulled her to her feet and turned her toward the door to the cottage, then leaned close and whispered, "Don't be mentionin' our little chat to Ma."

"I won't."

That night, Eliza lay awake long after Dad was snoring fit to blow the rafters off. She stared unblinking into the darkness and began to build, brick by brick, her first ever castle in the air.

Sighing, Eliza dragged herself back to the present. The girls would be halfway to the photographer's by now, and here she was wasting time with memories.

But oh, how she missed Dad—the only person in her life who she knew for certain had truly loved her.

Chapter 4

London

Ruth

Ruth opened her eyes at noon and stared up at the ceiling of her bedroom. Her head throbbed and her mouth felt dry. The events of the night before spun across her mind's eye—the Prince of Wales and his demands for attention, the endless courses of rich food, the barely disguised sneers of the other women, the sweet taste of the Peach Melba.

She should feel elated, but a hollowness filled her chest, as if she were little more than a shell with no compass and no purpose.

Ruth sat up in bed and hugged her knees. For years, she'd dreamed of becoming a serious opera star like Nellie Melba. She wanted to perform the big roles—Aida, Violetta, Mimi. The names of the heroines chased themselves around her mind like the wisps of cotton clogging the air back home in Briarstown.

A knock on the door ushered in Constance.

"Where's Sally?" Ruth asked.

"She's poorly." Constance set down a cup of tea and then opened the heavy curtains to reveal leaden skies. "It's gone noon," she said. "Shall I draw you a bath?"

"Yes, please." A steaming tub perfumed with lavender might help ease the aching of her head, although she wished it was Sally and not the housekeeper attending her.

"Very good." Constance picked up the clothes Ruth had scattered around the bedroom the night before and folded them with the air of a martyr. She was a spare, sour-faced spinster who rarely bothered to hide her disapproval of her mistress. Ruth used to complain to James, but he'd only shrug and remind her that competent servants were not easy to find or keep, and that she needed to make more of an effort. After all, Constance had been with his family for thirty years, which was far longer than Ruth had been Mrs. James Henton. She should be grateful to have such a capable woman running the household.

"Is the master at home?" Ruth asked.

"No, Ma'am."

"When did he leave?"

"He didn't come home last night, Ma'am. Bed's not been slept in." She said the last part with barely disguised relish.

"I see. Thank you, Constance. You may get my bath ready."

Constance shut the door behind her firmly enough to rattle the teacup in its saucer. Ruth sighed. Sally would have cheered her up. Like Katie at the theater, the girl was young, and still full of hope in a world that held few prospects for her.

Ruth was well aware of how close she'd come to sharing the same fate as Sally and Katie and thousands of other working-class girls. A pretty face and a nice singing voice meant nothing without connections.

She leaned back against the pillow, feeling drained and listless. How would she find the energy to perform? A profound loneliness settled around her as she thought about the rest of her day. She had no one to call upon and could expect no visitors. In her twelve years in London, she hadn't made any female friends outside of the theater—and most of them were more rivals than friends.

In less than five hours, she'd again be in her dressing room preparing to perform. Hundreds of people depended on her to sing and flutter her fan and make them laugh, so for a few hours they could forget their troubles.

The week before, a review in *The Times* had described Ruth as "a perfect picture to look at and equally pleasant to listen to...tall, rounded, and graceful, an English rose with a wealth of fair hair and a soprano voice of rare flexibility and power."

A wealth of fair hair. Yes, that much was certainly true. Ruth remembered how fascinated Eliza had been by Ruth's hair when they were girls, how she'd stare longingly at the ribbons Mother tied into bows.

Eliza had never worn ribbons in her hair. Her old friend always looked so serious, her hair plaited into two tight braids the color of coal dust. If she could see Ruth now, would she be green with envy? Anyone who heard the pair of them sing together would know Eliza had the stronger voice. If *she'd* been blessed with Ruth's opportunities, a role like Mimi in *La Bohème* would have been well within her powers.

Ruth stood and held her arms out from her body, then twirled in a slow circle to get her blood moving. It was foolish to think about the past. In a few hours, young men would throw roses at her feet and roar *"encore"*, and maybe the Prince of Wales would again invite her to dine with him. If he did not, then William would.

What did it matter that she'd never have a dessert named after her?

Several hours later, Ruth sat in front of the large mirror in her dressing room at the theater. The scent of lilies and roses still permeated the air, but thankfully, her headache had receded, and she felt ready for the performance.

Katie poked a yellow paper fan into Ruth's black wig.

"Put in another one," Ruth said.

"Yes, Miss." Katie placed the second fan towards the front of the wig and arranged it so it pointed downwards.

"Perfect. Help me up."

Katie grasped Ruth's elbow and pulled her up and then adjusted the wide red obi keeping her kimono in place. The costume was so tight that Ruth could barely walk in it, which, of course, was the point. As a demure Japanese maid in *The Mikado*, she wasn't meant to stride across the stage like a suffragate.

The melody of her first song in Act 1 ran through her mind. *Three Little Maids* was one of the production's most popular numbers. Ruth dearly hoped Helen, the girl who played Pitti-Sing, would stay on key. The night before, her voice had cracked on a high note and almost thrown Ruth off. Thankfully, Vera as Peep-Bo had a good, strong voice that blended pleasingly with Ruth's. But if it happened again, Ruth would go straight to Mr. Johnson and demand that he replace Helen.

A knock on the door was Ruth's signal to shuffle to the wings to wait for her cue. The performance was already well underway. She watched the antics of the actor who played Nanki-Poo, her love interest, interact with the dreadfully over-acting man who played Pooh-Bah. The audience lapped it all up, laughing uproariously and applauding loud and long after every song.

Behind her, she heard the other two "maids" whispering as they awaited their cue. Ruth breathed deeply to quell the nerves that never left her, no matter how often she performed. She'd played Yum Yum in *The Mikado* for six weeks now and had at least another eight weeks to go. After that, Mr. Johnson was sure to give her a starring role in the next production.

Two hours later, Ruth swept into a deep curtsy, her fan fluttering across her face, her eyes downcast in feigned modesty. The applause roared and crested, bathing her with love. She grinned behind her fan, then rose, lowered her fan, and as the audience howled their appreciation, swept again into a curtsy. The noise of the crowd vibrated her very soul. She was beautiful, talented, and celebrated.

The world belonged to her.

"Another triumph!" William said later as he escorted her from the theater. "You never cease to amaze me, my dear."

"I should hope not," Ruth said, laughing. "Thank you for the lilies. You're too good to me. My dressing room is like a garden."

"No less than London's most gifted singer deserves," William said gallantly. "Now, where shall we dine?"

"Somewhere quiet where we won't be gawped at," Ruth said. "I want you all to myself."

"In that case, I know the perfect place."

"Oh? And where might that be?" Ruth reflected that it was fortunate James had his own pursuits and wouldn't notice—or care—if she arrived home late.

"I'm glad not to be sharing you with the Prince of Wales tonight," William said, as he led her to his carriage.

"I'm nothing to the prince. He has plenty of women fawning over him and doesn't need another."

"I'm not so sure about that." William handed her into the carriage and climbed in next to her. He smelled delectable—expensive cologne mingled with a whiff of starch from his collar and the musky odor of his damp cloak.

"What have you heard?"

"He's casting about for a new, ah, companion now that Mrs. Langtry is out."

"The Prince of Wales has been attentive to me, but I doubt I'll be replacing Mrs. Langtry or any of his other ladies. He enjoys his dalliances, but he prefers women of rank."

"Your husband is a wealthy man."

"True." Ruth leaned her head against William's shoulder, sighing. "Let's not talk about my husband tonight."

"He's also a tolerant man."

"He is."

Ruth closed her eyes, the familiar exhaustion after a performance taking hold. She was grateful that Bertie hadn't required her presence at another lavish dinner. For a few minutes, she was glad to rest, knowing she had William all to herself—dear, handsome William, who was smitten by her. He had a wife tucked away at his country estate somewhere in Devon, or perhaps it was Dorset, but that only made their liaison even more alluring.

Ruth enjoyed being able to follow her own desires. She'd been as tethered to the whims of men as a marionette was to its handler for too many years—Reg Kingwell, Uncle Edward, Mr. Johnson at the theater, and finally James.

Thankfully, her husband made few demands upon her time. She was the wife he needed to allay the rumors, and he was the husband she needed to be respectable. He made sure she knew very little about his activities, and certainly nothing about his lovers. She was aware of the gossip about private clubs for men, but this was London. Private clubs were everywhere. She'd even heard it whispered that clubs existed for women who only wanted to be with women.

William took her to his suite of rooms at Claridge's, where he ordered a simple meal and didn't comment when she ate little of it. He regaled her with stories of hunting in the country, and she shared theater gossip. At midnight, she rose to leave.

"You're not going so soon?" he said, rising and taking hold of her hands. "I rather hoped you'd stay the night."

"That would be highly improper," Ruth said with a smile as she pulled her hands away. "And besides, I must get home to my own bed. You know I'm performing again tomorrow."

William looked so crestfallen that her resolve wavered. The prospect of spending the night in his arms in such lavish surroundings was bewitching.

But no.

She might imagine herself in his bed, but she'd never let herself get near it. With all her admirers, Ruth went only so far and then stopped and left, even in the middle of the coldest nights. The moment she gave in was the moment she risked losing her independence.

"Goodnight, William," she said firmly.

"Will you dine with me again tomorrow?" In his well-cut evening jacket and white shirt that looked so much better on him than on the portly

Prince of Wales, he really was ridiculously handsome. Perhaps she should give him what he wanted, just this once. She'd need to be careful, of course. Too many women in the theater saw their careers cut short by unwanted pregnancies and hasty marriages.

At least having children with James was out of the question.

"Goodnight," she said again, kissing him lightly on the cheek. Sighing, he brought her cape and settled it around her shoulders, then escorted her to the door.

When she arrived home, she was surprised to find James sitting in the drawing room, one hand clasping a glass of whiskey.

"You're home early," Ruth said. She untied her hat—an elaborate concoction of bows and feathers she'd bought the previous week. The shop girl had mentioned something about unpaid bills and her credit being exhausted, but she'd waved away her concerns. Such impertinence! But she supposed she ought to mention it to James. He never stinted on her clothes and often complimented her on her good taste.

"And you're late," he said.

She sank into a chair by the fire. "You can hardly complain about the hours *I* keep."

James took a sip of his whiskey, and then regarded her, his expression pensive. "I'm informed that you dined with the Prince of Wales last evening."

"Surprised?"

"Indeed."

"I fail to see why," Ruth said. "He's a charming man, and he admired my performance."

"I don't think you should accept any more invitations from him."

"You must know I can't possibly agree to that," Ruth said. "For one thing, Mr. Johnson would be livid. The good opinion of the Prince of Wales guarantees full houses. If the price I must pay is a dalliance with His Royal Highness, then so be it."

"What about *my* feelings?"

"I think, James, we'd be wise to leave *feelings* out of our discussions. You've never considered my feelings when it comes to *your* activities. But let's not quarrel. I am fatigued. The performance tonight was more taxing than usual."

"You sang divinely."

"You were there? Why didn't you come to my dressing room?" She was surprised to feel a spasm of disappointment. She didn't love James, not anymore, but she did care for him and sometimes wished they could be like other couples.

"I had intended to, but I was waylaid by Lord Randolph."

"Oh, dear. What did the old goat want?"

"Now, now, my dear. Show some respect." But James was smiling, his annoyance about the Prince of Wales already forgotten.

For a moment, Ruth shared a look of mutual amusement with her husband. He may not love her as she wanted to be loved, but at least he had the admirable ability to snap himself out of a bad mood. Within seconds, he veered into smooth waters as if nothing had ever vexed him.

"He's invited us to a party at his country estate," James said.

"That *is* good news. Lord Randolph may be a bore, but Lady Randolph is famous for her parties. His estate is in the North, is it not?"

"Near Leeds. Perhaps you could talk to Mr. Johnson about doing a tour."

"Maybe after *The Mikado* ends. I'll ask him."

"Do that. This is our time, my dear, and we must make the most of it."

Ruth rose from her chair. "Goodnight, James." For a moment, she hesitated. He was looking up at her with such a genial expression that she was almost tempted to drop a kiss on his forehead.

"Goodnight, my dear," he said, dismissing her with a wave of his slim hand.

As she mounted the stairs to her room at the front of the house, she thought about James's idea of a northern tour.

A weekend at a country estate was one thing, but a tour of the towns and cities in the North was completely out of the question. If the tour went to Briarstown, there was the possibility that Eliza and Kingwell would attend a concert.

She could *never* allow that.

Chapter 5

Briarstown

Eliza

The first thing Eliza noticed when they arrived at the photographer's studio was Ruth Henton's photograph prominently displayed in the front window. The eyes were still her most arresting feature, along with her thick blonde hair. It was arranged in an ample pompadour that looked too heavy for Ruth's slender neck. Eliza used to brush that hair down by the canal. The brush always glided so smoothly over the strands, and Ruth would laugh as curled wisps of hair spiraled into the summer air to float with the butterflies.

In the photo, Ruth wore a low-cut gown and held a fan in one gloved hand. The other hand rested against the back of an ornately carved chair. Her lips were parted in a smile that drew the viewer in. Every inch of her shouted wealth and privilege.

Ruth was everything Eliza would never be—beautiful, famous, rich— and able to sing for audiences who adored her.

Eliza glanced back at the girls. Scrubbed, brushed, and sparkling, they were her audience now, her only audience, and she loved them with every ounce of her being. What was done could not be undone. She glimpsed her reflection in the window side by side with Ruth. Eliza was younger by a good six months, but no one would believe it. In her squat black hat, hair pulled into a tight bun, her mouth pursed, she looked worn out, small, transparent. She doubted anyone would miss her if a stiff wind cast her into the canal. The girls might even be relieved to not have her around to nag them.

Eliza looked away.

"Who's the pretty lady?" Emily asked.

"I don't know," Eliza said. "Let's go in and get ourselves settled. Your father's on his way."

Reg wouldn't be happy to see the photograph of his stepdaughter in the studio window. It would put him in a mood so he might even refuse to have the photograph taken. When something upset him, he never bothered to hide his irritation. The handsome face would twist into a snarl, and if he had a few drinks in him, Eliza would receive the brunt of his ire.

At least he'd never laid a hand on the girls.

Yet.

"What's P.B., Ma?" Lily May asked, pointing to the small card next to Ruth's picture.

Ruth Henton, singer and P.B.

"It means Professional Beauty," Annie said importantly.

Eliza stared at her eldest daughter. "How could you possibly know that?"

"Mary at school told me. Her ma said that P.B.s were wicked women full of sin. Is that true, Ma? She looks too beautiful to be full of sin. Shouldn't she be ugly?"

Eliza's lips twitched despite herself. Ruth ugly? There's a laugh. For all the water under the bridge between them, Eliza could never think of Ruth as ugly.

"It's all nonsense," she said. "You don't want to be thinking about P.B.s and such. Here's Mr. Grayson."

"Ah! Mrs. Kingwell! And on time. Delightful! Will Mr. Kingwell be joining us?"

"Of course."

"Good, good. Well, you are a fine-looking family. Five daughters?"

"As you see."

"Charming, charming. Come through to the back and we'll get you all arranged, so we're ready when Mr. Kingwell arrives."

"Thank you."

Eliza followed Mr. Grayson into his studio. She'd never had her photograph taken before and was surprised by the clutter. In one corner were stacked painted scenes of seascapes, mountains, and the like. Next to them were ivy covered tree stumps and large rocks along with clumps of grass and pebbles, and even driftwood. She spied the side of an old boat shoved against one wall.

A single chair had been placed in the center of the room next to a large potted palm.

"Please be seated, Mrs. Kingwell," said Mr. Grayson. "This will be a delightful family portrait. Five girls! And all so beautifully turned out."

He directed each of the girls to their positions surrounding Eliza. Annie stood behind Eliza's left shoulder and Lily May to her right, with a gap in the middle for Reg. A stool was placed at Eliza's feet and Bessie told to perch on it. Gladys stood to the right of Eliza's knee, while Emily stood behind and, at Mr. Grayson's request, placed one hand on Eliza's shoulder.

Mr. Grayson stepped back to survey the composition. "Oh yes, dear me. *So* charming. When did you say Mr. Kingwell would arrive?"

"He should be here by now," Eliza said. Heat crawled up her cheeks, but she kept her back ramrod straight and nudged Emily, who was starting to slouch. "He must have gotten held up at the mill."

"Yes, quite." With his neatly trimmed beard, round glasses, and plain black suit, Mr. Grayson looked nothing like the men who spent their days working in the mill. Eliza wondered if there was a Mrs. Grayson who ironed his shirts and listened to him talk about his customers. She imagined her as cheerful and rosy-cheeked, perhaps still childless, perhaps still in love.

Eliza knew it did no good to imagine other people's lives as better than her own, although sometimes, she couldn't help it. Her imagination was the one thing Reg could never take from her.

Half an hour later, the girls were squirming with boredom, and Mr. Grayson no longer even tried to hide his impatience. He pulled out his pocket watch and frowned.

"Please take the photograph now," Eliza said.

"You could reschedule. I have an opening next week."

"No. Take it now."

"As you wish. Look at the camera, everyone," Mr. Grayson said. "And stay very, very still."

The moment Eliza arrived home from the photographer's, she knew she was in trouble. She shooed the girls upstairs to remove their starched pinafores and then sat at the table across from Reg. In the fading afternoon light, the cupboard hung open and the money from the box was stacked by denomination.

Eight years of savings. Eight years of planning and hoping. Eight years gone.

"Are you going to explain yourself?" Reg asked.

Eliza slowly removed her hat. As her fingers closed over the hatpin, she imagined driving it straight through one of Reg's piercing blue eyes. She saw his mouth opening in a scream, his lips below the meticulously trimmed moustache trembling with rage and pain.

And then she'd hang for the crime, leaving the girls with no one to take care of them.

"No," she said.

"There's got to be five pounds here."

"Six pounds, ten shillings, five pennies, and a couple of farthings."

"What were you planning to do with all this money? *My* money what I earned working my fingers to the bone."

For a few seconds, Eliza considered telling him the truth. She folded her hands on the table, resisting the urge to gather all the money into her skirt and run from the house. She felt a fluttering in her belly, followed by a jagged pain. She bit back a gasp. Something was wrong. She'd never felt pain this early with her other babies.

"Well?" Reg asked, his eyes narrowing.

"I meant it as a surprise for you," she said, gritting her teeth against another bolt of pain.

"What d'you mean, a surprise? I don't much like surprises."

Eliza forced a smile. "For your birthday. You'll be forty come January, and I thought we might celebrate by going to the seaside for the mill trip in July. You've always said you never had much fuss made about your birthday when you were young, and you don't turn forty every day. Besides, we've only ever gone to the seaside for the day, but this year we could go for a full week. I'm sure Mr. Lewiston would agree that you deserve the time off."

"D'ya think I'm daft, woman? You must've been saving for years! You expect me to believe you've been thinking all this time about a birthday at the seaside?"

"It's the truth."

"I don't believe you."

"I can't help that."

Another pain, this one stronger than the other two, bathed her in a cold sweat. She kept her eyes on Reg, biting her cheek to keep her mouth closed.

Reg scooped the money into a large pile. "I'll take care of this."

"The girls would love the seaside."

"That's for me to decide."

"Why didn't you come to the photographers?" she asked. "We waited."

"Jonas didn't want to spare me after all." He held out his hand. "I'll have the money back I gave you for the photograph."

"I had it taken, anyway. Me with the girls." Eliza winced as another pain surged. She'd get Annie to fetch Mrs. Harris from next door. She'd know what to do.

"A family photograph without the father? Don't make sense."

"We'd already taken up so much of Mr. Grayson's time. It didn't seem right to leave without getting him to take the photograph. It'll be ready in a few weeks. Now, I'd best be getting to the butcher before it closes."

He pushed a shilling toward her and put the rest of the money in his pocket. "You can keep that. I'm off for a drink."

Eliza kept her eyes on the small silver coin, the profile of the old Queen facing up. A soft heat between her legs drained what little hope she had left for the new child.

Reg stood and, for a few seconds, loomed over her, one hand resting on the table. Veins like narrow snakes moved under his skin. There had been a time when she'd admired his hands and hadn't much minded them touching her skin.

"You're pale," he said. "Get one of the girls to go."

Eliza's eyes widened at the unexpected tenderness in his voice. Perhaps she'd gotten away with the lie about the money. If she managed to survive the next few hours without him being any the wiser about her condition, then all was not lost.

Chapter 6

London

Ruth

"Evening, Ma'am. Looks to be a rotten day out there." Thomas ushered her in through the stage door and took her dripping umbrella.

"It certainly is," she said. "I hope it doesn't affect the house tonight."

"Not a chance. Every seat's been sold for weeks. No one's going to let a bit of rain get in the way of seeing *you*." As the Palladia's stage-door keeper for over forty years, Thomas knew everything there was to know about the goings-on at the theater.

"You're very kind."

"Not kindness to say the truth." He picked up an envelope and held it out to Ruth. "This come for you. Delivered an hour ago. Woman what brought it said it was urgent like."

Ruth took the envelope and saw it was addressed to Mrs. James Henton. That was unusual. In the theater world, she was known as either Ruth Henton or Mrs. Henton. The envelope was a plain one suitable for every-day letters, so it certainly was not from the Prince of Wales. That, at least, was a relief. After the performance, Ruth was determined to go straight home. She'd dined with Bertie twice more since the first time, and so far, he'd made no improper advances. She'd heard shocking rumors about his predilections in the bedroom, how sometimes he entertained two and even three women at once.

She blushed to think what Mother would say. Her dreams for Ruth had never extended to her consorting with royalty.

"Be happy, my darling," she used to say. *"That's all I ask."*

"Thank you, Thomas."

"My pleasure, Ma'am," he said. "You'll do yourself proud tonight, like always."

"I hope so."

Ruth entered the dimly lit corridor leading from the stage door around the side of the stage to the dressing rooms. The bustle of activity of the theater before a performance always lifted her spirits. The costume mistress edged past, carrying an armful of the kimonos worn by the men in the chorus. Shouting came from the stage, followed by the grinding of huge scenery flats being shunted into place.

She stepped around a box full of paper fans and passed the open door to the dressing room shared by the girls in the chorus. It wasn't so long ago when she'd been one of them—vying for space in front of the mirrors, daubing cheap perfume behind her ears, endlessly repairing holes in frayed stockings. A few of the girls—their cheeks bright without rouge and voices honed by expensive lessons—were warming up with a series of rippling scales. Ruth knew any one of them would kill to take her place if she faltered.

That would never happen.

She reached the relative quiet of her dressing room, where Katie helped her out of her wet coat.

"Evening, Miss," she said cheerfully. "Shall I get you a cup of tea?"

"Please." Ruth placed the letter on her dressing table. She'd look at it after she was dressed and made up. One of her many admirers had probably sent it, although the cheapness of the envelope was unusual. The men who courted Ruth Henton used monogrammed stationery.

The slow bustle of getting ready for a performance consumed her for the next two hours. As Katie fussed and primped, Ruth ran through her lines. Her speech in Act II always made her smile. She began reciting it, much to the delight of Katie, who loved listening to Ruth rehearse.

"Yes, I am indeed beautiful!" Ruth began. Of all her lines, it was probably her favorite, both because it always got a laugh and because she liked to believe it was true.

"That you are, Miss," Katie said, grinning. "Go on."

"Of course." Ruth assumed the simpering look she affected as Yum Yum. She raised her penciled eyebrows and cocked her head to one side to flutter the paper fans poked into her wig.

"Sometimes I sit and wonder, in my artless Japanese way, why it is that I am so much more attractive than anybody else in the whole world."

Katie laughed appreciatively.

"Can this be vanity?" Ruth continued. *"No! Nature is lovely and rejoices in her loveliness."* She paused and winked at Kate in the mirror. "Do you want to say the last line?"

"Oh, yes please, Miss."

"Go on then."

Katie twisted her young face to match Ruth's expression so perfectly that Ruth put her hand over her mouth to stifle a laugh.

"I am a child of Nature," Katie said in a credible imitation of Ruth's accent, honed for years to remove the Yorkshire burr. *"And take after my mother."*

"Bravo!" Ruth said. "If something happens to me, you can be Yum Yum."

"Oh no, Miss!" Katie said, too naïve to realize Ruth was teasing. "I'd never dare do such a thing."

"Ah well, you're wise to stay away from the stage."

"Why?"

"Because," Ruth said with a sigh, "it takes everything you have to give and always demands more."

"But isn't that what you want, Miss?" Katie looked so stricken that Ruth immediately regretted her teasing.

"Yes, of course it is, Katie," she said. "I couldn't imagine any other life."

The first act went smoothly enough, although Helen, as Pitti-Sing, again sang off key. Ruth returned to her dressing room in a fury. She'd talk with Mr. Johnson immediately after the performance and have the girl sacked.

"Are you all right, Miss?" Katie asked, handing her a cup of water. "Your face is red."

"I'm fine. Hurry, please."

"Yes, Miss." Katie removed the heavily embossed kimono that Ruth wore in the first act and helped her into a flowing pink kimono. She removed the paper fans from her hair and fixed in two rows of white wax flowers.

Ruth sat in front of the mirror and picked up a pencil to touch up her eyebrows. Her elbow grazed the envelope she'd left on her dressing table.

"Are you going to open it?" Katie asked.

Ruth finished working on her eyebrows and then put down the pencil. "I suppose I should, although I can't think it's from anyone important."

She slit the envelope open with her fingernail and shook out a single sheet of paper as cheap as the envelope.

Dear Ruth,
Forgive me for being so forward, but it's not in my nature to stand on ceremony. Your husband James is a beast, and I'm determined to make him pay. I thought it only right to give you fair warning. And if that hurts you too, well, I'm not sorry for it.

Ruth stared at the words in horror. She picked up the envelope, but couldn't see a return address, and the letter itself was unsigned. It was from a woman, that much was certain. But what could a woman have to do with James?

"Places for Act Two!" called a stagehand.

The walk from her dressing room to the stage seemed to take forever in her soft slippers and flowing kimono that included a small train. On stage, Ruth needed to walk very carefully to avoid tripping. What a spectacle *that* would make.

She put the letter out of her mind and waited for the orchestra to play the opening melody of the second act. Ahead of her, a girl from the chorus ran lightly onstage, joined moments later by the rest of the chorus entering from both sides of the stage like a flock of exotic birds.

A beat later, Ruth joined them, gliding downstage in her pink kimono with sleeves hanging to her knees.

The chorus surrounded her singing:

Braid the raven hair—
Weave the supple tress—
Deck the maiden fair
In her loveliness—
Paint the pretty face—
Dye the coral lip—
Emphasize the grace
Of her ladyship!
Art and nature, thus allied,
Go to make a pretty bride!

Helen as Pitti-Sing then sang her solo, thankfully staying on key. Ruth maintained a serene expression in her best imitation of a maiden about to become a bride.

The chorus sang the second verse and then swept off the stage, leaving Ruth alone. She picked up the large prop mirror and regarded herself in it, before turning to the audience and delivering her first line.

Yes, I am indeed beautiful!

As always, the audience laughed appreciatively. Ruth delivered the rest of her lines, pausing again after *I am a child of Nature, and take after my mother* to allow for more laughter.

The music changed, and she began her song.

The sun, whose rays are all ablaze…

She never tired of the song in which she compared herself to both the sun and the moon. It was so deliciously arrogant, particularly the lines:

I mean to rule the earth,
As he the sky,
We really know our worth
The sun and I.

Ruth had sung the solo dozens of times and always to rapturous applause. She simpered and smirked and hit every note like it was a sparkling drop of crystal.

Just as she was about to sing the line, *We really know our worth*, comparing herself and her beauty to the sun, the words in the hateful woman's letter flashed across her mind.

And if that hurts you too, well, I'm not sorry for it.

She reached for the highest note on the word *worth*, confident it would be there for her as it always was. And then, to her horror, she felt her throat constrict. As if separated from her body, Ruth heard the note flatten a semi-tone—more than enough to be noticed by even the most unmusical members of the audience.

In a frantic attempt to recover, she affected a giggle as if to say the wrong note was intentional and rushed to complete the song. She glanced down at the pit, saw the conductor's white face, his baton adjusting to her faster tempo. Thankfully, he kept up, so she and the orchestra ended together.

A smattering of applause trailed off so quickly that she had to start in on her lines earlier than usual. Heat crawled up her neck and she felt the prickling of sweat under her heavy costume. She giggled again with what she hoped passed for girlish modesty and then paused for the usual laughter, only to be met by silence. Hastily, she rushed through the rest of her lines, then turned with relief to greet the chorus returning to the stage.

The rest of Act II passed in a blur, and when she took her final bows, there were no cries for an encore.

Chapter 7

Briarstown

Eliza

Eliza stared out the one small window in the bedroom at the leaden sky. She imagined the cold air blowing away the blood and the sadness that flowed from her body, thick and sluggish like the wake of a barge sliding slowly down the canal. Dimly, she was aware of Mrs. Harris's stubby fingers prodding at her private parts, her tongue clucking with concern.

"A boy," Mrs. Harris said.

Her first boy. Her son. She'd have named him Ernie after her little brother. Eliza lay back, remembering how she used to soothe Ernie by singing to him. She thought about the long day she'd spent on the train that had taken her and Ma and Dad and Ernie and the two big boys to the North. What would her life had been like if she'd stayed in Devon?

She remembered the grinding of the wheels and the screech of metal on metal. The noise had made her feel like she was being crushed in one of the massive new threshing machines that Dad said was driving families like theirs out of Devon. She hated feeling so frightened, so out of control. All she could do was sit still and watch the other passengers laden with suitcases and bundles crowd onto the rows of backless wooden benches.

On the bench opposite Eliza, sat a man and his wife with their three children. They all had scrubbed red faces, and the woman's smile was cheerful and gap-toothed. A boy about Eliza's age pressed his nose to the grimy window. A pair of twin girls that Eliza judged to be about five years old sat so close together they almost looked like one girl. Eliza wondered how it would feel to want to stick so close to another person. Most of the time, she wished her little brother would leave her be.

Eliza wanted to sit next to the window like the boy so she could watch England hurtle past at what seemed an impossible speed, but she was squeezed between Dad and Ma, who was holding Ernie. Her two big brothers hung off the end of the bench, their legs tripping people in the narrow aisle.

"The wages be enough to keep a family," said the man who'd introduced himself as Mr. Callahan.

"And what of the work?" Dad asked. "My wife's brother says it's hard, but that don't tell me much. You heard anythin' more?"

Mr. Callahan shook his head. "Nah. I expect it won't be easy, and the hours will be long, but I doubt you're a stranger to hard work."

Dad laughed. "When I can get it. I'll not miss having nuthin' to do in the winter."

"From what I gather, there's enough work to carry a man through all the year." Mr. Callahan leaned forward, pressing broad, hairy hands onto his knees. "And there be plenty to do in the off hours."

"Oh?" Dad asked. Jack and Billy stopped pushing each other and listened.

"Aye. My sister went north two years back with her man and she writes us about all sorts of activities put on by the mill owners. That is, if you get a good'un. They ain't all good."

"What activities be they?" Jack asked.

"Some lads play on football teams, and then there be lectures and concerts and, I dunno, lots."

"Concerts?" Dad turned to Eliza. "You hear that, my girl? You'll be singing with one of them concerts before long, I wager. Won't that be somethin'?"

"That's enough of such talk," snapped Ma. "Eliza's got better things to do than go to concerts." She shoved Ernie onto Eliza's lap. "Here, you, make yourself useful. He's been fussing so as I can't get a moment's peace."

As soon as Eliza took Ernie, Ma pulled her black bonnet low over her eyes, then folded her arms across her stomach and ignored any attempt by Mr. Callahan's wife to engage her in conversation.

Eliza gathered Ernie onto her lap and bounced him to stop his whingeing so she could listen to the men talk more about the North. Mr. Callahan appeared to know so much! But Ernie wasn't for being soothed. She looked around the crowded carriage. Most of the women held babies, all of whom were peacefully sleeping. Nearby, a little girl Ernie's age sat quietly on the filthy wooden floor, one thumb stuck in her mouth, her eyes wide and curious. *She* wasn't making a fuss. Sighing, Eliza stood and, with Ernie squirming and crying in her arms, began pacing back and forth between the narrow benches. One of the women glared at her, but she ignored her. It wasn't her fault Ernie wouldn't settle.

She supposed she loved her little brother, but she wished Ma hadn't had him and wasn't always making her take him.

"Shhh," she whispered. "People be lookin'."

Ernie twisted his body to get out of her arms. His crying took on a frantic edge, his breath coming in great gulps that made him sound like she was torturing him. Her eldest brother Jack looked up. "Sing to him 'Liza," he said. "He likes it."

"I can't sing here! Not with all these people about."

Jack shrugged and turned back to listen to Mr. Callahan.

Eliza sighed and walked with Ernie to an empty section of bench. She started humming *Over the Hills and Far Away* and then sang the words.

Tommy was a Piper's Son
And fell in love when he was young
The only tune that he could play
Was Over the Hills and Far Away.

She sang quietly at first, but as Ernie stopped crying and softened into her arms, she realized that the low hum of chatter all around her had also stopped. She let her voice trail off.

"Go on then, love," said the woman who had glared at her. "Don't stop."

Several women nodded their encouragement, although Eliza noticed that Ma still sat in the corner, her head down. She'd be angry at Eliza for making a spectacle of herself, but for once Eliza didn't care.

She shifted Ernie's weight, so he leaned back against her chest. Now that he'd cried himself out, he'd soon drift off. She sang another tune. At the chorus, some of the women joined in, their voices rising above the sound of the wheels clattering over the train tracks.

Something shifted inside Eliza. The North was new and might even be frightening, but moving there was an adventure.

And Eliza had never been on an adventure.

Mrs. Harris's voice brought Eliza back to reality. Close to twenty years later, the adventure had become a nightmare and now another little boy named Ernie was dead. She let a low moan escape.

"There now, dearie," she crooned. "You've been through the wars with this one."

"I'll be fine."

"I don't doubt that. But you go easy on yourself. No getting up and about for at least two days."

Eliza felt a rough cloth being dragged across her skin. She winced.

"Sorry. I won't be long."

"Can I?" Eliza asked.

Mrs. Harris shook her head. "Best not."

Eliza propped herself up on her elbows to better see the cloth-covered basin that Mrs. Harris placed on the bureau. "I want to see him."

"No, dearie, you don't. Should I get one of your girls to fetch your husband?"

"No!" Eliza cried. "I mean, thank you, Mrs. Harris. I'll speak to him later."

Mrs. Harris's eyes widened with understanding. "Ah. As you wish, dearie."

Eliza sank back against the pillow and stared straight up at the brown-stained ceiling. She hadn't wanted this child, so why did she feel so profoundly empty, as if a hole had been scooped out of her, leaving behind a black void? There would be no new life, no new mouth to feed, no tiny body to dress in Bessie's cast-offs.

"I just need to sleep awhile," she whispered.

"You do that. I'll go down and talk to the girls. Your Annie's kept them quiet all this time. What a fine girl she's growing up to be. I remember well the day she were born."

Eliza remembered too. What had been the happiest day of her life now seemed like a dream belonging to someone else. Reg had been kind to her, except when she'd refused to name the baby Bertha after his mother. He'd stomped out of the room, leaving her alone with Annie, who had opened her eyes and gazed at a point beyond Eliza's head.

Reflexively, Eliza had turned, expecting to see something behind her apart from the faded wallpaper. When she'd looked again at Annie, Eliza had the eerie sensation the baby was searching for something or someone she'd left behind before coming to this world. The large gray eyes—so like Eliza's—had shone with a kind of wisdom that belonged not to a newborn child, but to a child of the angels.

And now her Annie was growing up too fast in a place where her prospects for a better life were all too dim. Eliza lay back against the stained pillowcase and sighed into the pain of her loss. A warmth filled her chest as she remembered the births of Lily May, then Gladys, then Emily, and finally little Bessie four years earlier. Each baby had been as perfect as Annie, each one wrapped in a cloak of love as comforting as a shaft of sunlight on a winter's day.

Her girls were everything to her, her blood, her body, her soul. They were all that made the days worth greeting, and all that stood between Eliza and darkness.

Heavy feet trudged back up the stairwell and Mrs. Harris stepped into the room. "I'll make the tea for your girls and Mr. Kingwell," she said from the foot of the bed. "Don't you worry. I'll tell him you're suffering from women's problems. Men never ask questions when I say that."

"Thank you, Mrs. Harris," Eliza said. "There's a shilling on the bureau. Please take it for your trouble."

"That's kind of ye, Mrs. Kingwell."

As soon as Mrs. Harris headed back down the stairwell, Eliza spread her hands across her belly and breathed into the emptiness. With all the money she'd saved gone, her Plan lay in ruins. There'd be no leaving Briarstown the day after Christmas, no shepherding the girls on and off trains on the journey south to Devon, no reunion with Granny.

How long would it take to again save enough money? Two years? Three? By that time, Annie and Lily May would be working at the mill, with Gladys not far behind.

Eliza blinked into the gathering darkness and gave in to the rare comfort of tears.

Chapter 8

After the performance, Ruth dressed and left the theater as quickly as possible so as not to risk running into Mr. Johnson. While she didn't think he'd let her go on the strength of one missed note, she knew he'd be angry.

She arrived home to again find a light burning in the drawing room.

"Ruth?" James appeared at the door leading to the drawing room. "Please, come sit with me. I need to speak with you." He walked back into the room and settled into his chair by the fire, not bothering to wait to see if she followed. His collar was undone, and his jacket tossed carelessly over the sofa. He waved toward the settee—an ornately carved concoction he'd recently purchased on a trip to Paris. He'd pompously told her it was an example of the new Art Nouveau style. James loved to be at the forefront of all things fashionable.

Ruth lowered herself onto the midnight blue velvet seat. Before James could say anything, she said, "I received a letter this evening. At the theater."

"Ah! She's made good on at least one of her threats."

"You know who it is?"

"Oh yes, my dear. I know."

He stared into the fire, his face haggard in the dim light. Gray touched the hair at his temples, and the beginnings of a double chin marred his once sharply etched profile.

Ruth ran her fingers over the twists and swirls of the carved wood making up the back of the settee. The solidity grounded her in a world spun upside down.

"What does she want?" she asked.

"Five thousand pounds."

"And if she doesn't get it, then what?" Ruth dropped her hand and straightened her spine to move away from the massive carved snake coiling upward from the middle of the seat.

"She will go to the police and have me arrested for corrupting her son. I'll be convicted and sent to jail." He managed a small smile. "Like Oscar Wilde, who I believe was recently released." His smiled faded. "He's a broken man and has left England for Paris."

"Her son, did you say? What did you do, James?"

"Her son is a man of twenty-two, in full possession of his faculties and his preferences. I did not corrupt him, if that's what you're thinking."

"It hardly matters what *I* think. What will you do?" Ruth asked again.

"I suppose I must find five thousand pounds," James said. "If she goes through with her threat to report me to the authorities, we'll lose everything."

"But surely you have the funds." Ruth looked around the richly furnished room. The house in Grosvenor Square that James had inherited from his father was large and must be worth a great deal. Money had never been something they'd discussed, and Ruth had taken their wealth for granted.

"Yes, well, it's complicated." He paused, rubbing his palms across his thighs. "Can you ask your Mr. Johnson for a raise?"

"He increased my salary a few months ago. The theater is doing well, but I doubt he'll give me more." She'd rather die than tell James what had happened to her voice that evening.

"You could threaten to go to another theater. Mr. Johnson won't want to lose you."

"I can't do that, James."

"Why ever not? Everywhere I go, I hear about Mrs. Henton's charming portrayal of Yum Yum. Any theater would be happy to have you."

"What about your business interests?" she asked to turn the subject. "You spoke a while ago about purchasing a factory in the North."

"Yes, my dear. *Purchasing.* Not selling. But now all my assets are currently tied up."

"Can't you sell another one of your factories?"

"No."

Ruth had never seen James look so diminished, as if he'd lost half his weight. Even his clothes looked too big for him. This was not the confident, suave man she knew. James had always been so dependable and good-tempered. More importantly, he let her do as she pleased, so long as she was discreet.

"Who is this woman?"

"I doubt you are acquainted."

"You can't give in to her! Your position in society, your connections—"

"Will mean nothing. I'm afraid, my dear, that we must prepare ourselves. And I should say now, before it's too late, how grateful I am that you've always been sensible about the limits of our marriage. Another woman might have made a fuss, but you never have. I do appreciate it. You've been a good wife to me."

"What do you mean, before it's too late?"

"Forgive me. I'm giving in to melodramatics, which is unforgivable at any time of the day, but particularly at one o'clock in the morning. I suggest you go to bed. We'll not solve this tonight."

"Has this person given you time to get the money, or can you find some other way? Who is she? Can she be reasoned with?"

"Reasoned with?" James barked out a laugh. The effect was to rouse him, so he seemed to grow back into himself. His expression hardened.

"Let me speak with her," Ruth said. "Woman to woman."

"I doubt it would help."

"I'd like to try."

James shook his head. "I appreciate the offer, but no. I can't drag you into this mess."

"I'm already in it. She contacted me, remember?"

"Yes, and that is regrettable." James stood and came towards her, holding out his hand to help her up. For a moment, they stood face to face. He was the same height as she was but stockily built. She remembered a time when she'd longed for his touch, and then how shocked she'd been when he told her on their wedding night that relations between them would not be required.

"I'm sorry this has happened to you, James," she said. "You don't deserve it."

"Thank you. Now, off to bed with you. You look tired."

Ruth mounted the stairs to her bedroom at the front of the house. In the darkness, the coals of the dying fire glowed eerily, casting huge shadows of her body onto the ceiling as she undressed and eased herself into bed.

James was surely exaggerating the danger of exposure. Ruth would find out who this woman was and persuade her to leave them alone. After all, James couldn't help what he was.

There had been a time, early in her marriage, when Ruth believed James capable of conquering his unnatural tendencies. But as weeks became months, she was forced to realize that James would never love her the way she wanted to be loved.

Then, when months became years, she learned to find her pleasures elsewhere.

In every other way, James had proved himself to be an excellent husband. Few other men would have allowed Ruth to pursue her career on the stage and have so enthusiastically supported her triumphs. Most women in the theater who married left within months when the arrival of child after child wiped out any hope of returning to the stage.

Ruth reached over and turned down the gas lamp. The light glinted off the tiny diamond chips embedded on each side of the single ruby in her mother's ring, the only valuable thing Mother had ever owned.

"This ring will be yours, my dear," she often said. "When I'm gone, I want you to wear it to remember me."

"Where are you going?" Ruth was only eleven. Who would take care of her? Not her new stepfather. Mother said she liked him, but Ruth did not.

"I'm not going anywhere for many more years," Mother said, smiling. "I meant one day. Promise me you'll never sell it."

"No, Mother. I'd never do that."

Ruth curled her fingers around the ring. She'd had it appraised once and was staggered to find out its worth. Mother could have saved the two of them so much pain if only she'd sold the ring years earlier.

Outside, a horse clopped past, and in the distance, church bells tolled two times. The front door below her window opened and then closed. James must be going out for some air. Perhaps a walk would help him put things in perspective.

She would *not* let some random, aggrieved woman destroy the perfect life that she and James had built together.

Chapter 9

Briarstown

Eliza

By the time Reg came in from the pub and stumbled up the stairs, not a trace remained of Eliza's hours of agony apart from a faint smell of blood. Reg flopped down next to her, breath stinking of beer. After several minutes of silence, he said, "Y'awake?"

"Yes."

"I heard Mrs. Harris came to the house. Yer not sick, are ye?"

"Women's troubles. Nothing for you to worry yourself about."

"The girls need you well."

"I'm fine." Eliza closed her eyes. All she wanted now was to descend into the blessed darkness of sleep. Perhaps Dad would come to her and lay his hands on her head like he used to when she was small. Over the years, he'd come to her a few times in her dreams. She'd sense him as a solid mass that gathered her into his arms and held her so close that she sensed his heart beating. For a few moments, a profound contentment such as she'd rarely known in her life would envelop her.

And then the arms would loosen, and she'd find herself alone on the edge of the canal, wailing into the wind while the dream burst into wisps of cotton and twisted down into the murky waters.

"I've been thinkin'," Reg said into the darkness, his voice clear despite the beer. "We could use some of the money for a day or two by the sea. Not a week, mind. But a day or two."

"The girls would like that."

"There'd be money left over."

"The girls need new shoes."

"Aye."

He rolled over and pushed his back against her shoulder. She shifted to the edge of the bed, her mind reeling with the upheavals of the day—two losses, two futures dashed.

Was this the life Granny had wanted to save her from? Eliza hadn't seen her grandmother for nineteen years and yet she could still hear her voice like she was standing in the dark room inches from her head.

"Marry a kind man like your father," she'd said the last time Eliza saw her before leaving Devon. "Someone who will treat you and your children right. You'll be away up north, and I won't be around to meet him, so you need to have your wits about you."

When Eliza asked what she was supposed to do if her husband wasn't kind, Granny merely shrugged and told her to get on with her life and not make a fuss.

Below the thin mattress supporting both her and Reg lay the single sheet of Granny's letter telling her to bring herself and the girls to Devon. Eliza wasn't sure what Reg would do if he found it. He'd been easy to do with lately, not drinking too much nor taking his fists to her if she talked back. They'd even occasionally shared a laugh about something one of the girls said or a goings-on at the mill. Absently, Eliza laid her hand across her breast to touch her upper arm. The latest bruise was long gone now, and if she was careful, she'd never get another.

Sighing, she closed her eyes, dropping immediately into a blessedly deep and dreamless sleep that not even memories of Dad could penetrate.

The next morning, Eliza slipped from bed at her usual time. Ignoring the dull ache that filled the hole in her belly, she stepped into the thicker of her two everyday dresses. It rose easily over her slim hips. With cold fingers, she buttoned it to her neck. She supposed it was wrong to have named the child Ernie after her little brother, but she couldn't help it. She wished Mrs. Harris had let her see him.

Shivering in the morning chill, she wrapped a shawl around her shoulders and crept down the stairs. This child should have been the last with Reg. Now, how many more times would her belly swell and the pains come?

Eliza lit the coal fire, then stood a moment in front of it, warming her hands. The day stretching before her would be another day like the hundreds, thousands gone before and yet to come. She breathed back the tears she'd shed the night before.

"Stop this foolishness," she scolded herself. "You've got five girls to care for. Leave off your bellyaching."

Smiling ruefully at how much she sounded like her mother—and Granny, come to that, Eliza set about preparing for the day. She filled the kettle with water from a jug and set it on the grate. Reg would be down before she knew it, and she still needed to get buns for his breakfast from the bakehouse. She pulled on her coat and went out into the yard.

"Mornin', Eliza!" Hannah called. "Off to the bakehouse? I'll walk with ye."

Eliza would have preferred to walk alone, but there was no denying Hannah. A large woman with a booming voice and a perpetually sunny smile, Hannah always had a good word to say for everyone. For a moment, Eliza thought of confiding in Hannah about her lost child and then decided against it. Hannah had her own memories to contend with. It wouldn't be kind to burden her.

"Did you see the advert about the choir?" Hannah asked. "Hattie McKay told me she gave it to your girls to show you."

"I saw it," Eliza said.

"Seems like it's something you'd be interested in."

"I've enough to do taking care of five children."

"But you're our best singer! I've heard you in the washhouse when you think no one's listening. You're as good as you were when we was girls."

"I haven't sung in public for years, Hannah, as you well know."

"Please join us. It'll be a lark."

"I can't." Eliza wished Hannah would leave her alone. She quickened her pace and entered the narrow passageway leading from the yard out to the street.

"Can't or won't?" Hannah said, coming up behind her.

"I'm sorry." Eliza reached the curb and turned to look back at Hannah. "But good luck to ye."

She crossed over and joined the queue outside the bakehouse. Thankfully, Hannah hooked up with another woman, leaving Eliza in peace.

She refused to think about making time for singing with the other women, most of whom didn't even like her. She needed every ounce of energy to get the money to leave Briarstown. Maybe she should take in sewing. Plenty of women did. The pay was low, and she risked damaging her eyes, but anything was better than nothing. If only Reg would spend less money on his beer. She couldn't shave anything more off what he gave her to run the house without him noticing.

She paid for a packet of fresh-baked buns, then holding them close to her chest, ran back across the road and down the passageway to the yard. Fancy the women wanting to get together to sing in a choir! What did they hope to accomplish? Who would want to listen to them?

But Eliza knew she'd not been honest with Hannah. She would have loved to join the new choir.

Chapter 10

London

Ruth

The clock struck three and Ruth still stared into the darkness. Despite her exhaustion, her mind wouldn't stop whirling—bouncing from the blackmailer's letter to the missed note in her solo to William to the cold and joyless years in Briarstown.

Finally, she slipped from her bed and relit the lamp. With James gone from the house and the servants all asleep, she couldn't afford to wait. Feeling like a criminal in her own home, Ruth padded down the corridor to James's room. They lived such separate lives that she rarely had cause to enter it. When she did, it was only for a few moments to remind him of a rare social engagement that required them to attend together.

Appearances must be maintained.

That refrain had underscored her marriage for six years.

She set the lamp on his desk and picked up a small stack of letters. To her surprise, all of them were from tailors, milliners, dressmakers, and more. She recognized several of the shops as ones she frequented. Each letter was a plea to be paid, with many couched in strong wording indicating the request was not the first. James had never once said anything about financial difficulties. He took what she made at the theater every month, thanked her, and then encouraged her to spend as much as she wished on clothes and hats.

"I want my wife to be fashionable," he liked saying. "It wouldn't do for people to think James Henton can't give London's most alluring P.B. everything she deserves."

Ruth shuffled through more papers in her search for a clue to the woman's identity.

"You won't find it."

The voice in the darkness made her jump. For a second, she was back in the cramped terrace house in Briarstown, her body vibrating with fear. She breathed deeply and turned around. "You startled me."

"Forgive me." James reached into his jacket pocket and pulled out a scrap of paper. "Here."

"I thought you didn't want me to contact her."

"I'd rather you didn't, but I'd also prefer you didn't go through my things." James sighed. "I suppose it can't do any harm. As you said, you *are* an actress. Perhaps you can convince Mrs. Greenwood to leave us alone. After all, she must realize that if my relationship with her son becomes public, she will also suffer."

"She must be in a great deal of pain to have resorted to blackmail."

"You'll forgive me if I don't share your opinion. *You* accepted me."

"I wasn't given much of a choice," Ruth said. "Also, my circumstances differ greatly from this Mrs. Greenwood. For one thing, she's a mother." She took the paper from James and glanced at it. "I shall call upon her this afternoon."

"What will you do if she refuses to listen to you?"

"I have no idea."

An hour before she was due at the theater, Ruth alighted from a hansom cab outside a fashionable address in Mayfair. She told the driver to wait. As she walked to the front door, nerves sparked across her chest like Roman candles on Guy Fawkes Day.

A maid answered the door, took the card Ruth held out, and ushered her into a small parlor at the front of the house. Taking pride of place on the mantle was a photograph of a young man wearing a straw boater, a jacket that looked too big for his slight physique, and white trousers. A shock of wavy hair, artfully tousled, framed smooth cheeks and pensive eyes.

A woman in her forties entered, holding Ruth's card between two fingers like it was something she'd plucked from the gutter.

"I didn't expect him to send his wife," she said without bothering with a greeting.

Ruth inclined her head. "Good day to you, Mrs. Greenwood. My husband didn't send me. I came of my own accord. James would prefer that I stay out of his affairs."

"Quite right. So why are you here?"

"I hoped we could talk. What you are doing to my husband is, ah, unnecessary."

"I believe I can be counted upon to know what is *necessary*. Your husband seduced my poor Alexander." Mrs. Greenwood glanced adoringly at the photograph. "He's a good boy."

"My husband told me your Alexander is a man of two and twenty."

"To me, he's still a boy. I take it you have no children."

"I do not," Ruth said.

"Then you can't understand."

"I understand that you wish to protect your son, but surely blackmail isn't the way to do it."

"Blackmail? Such an ugly word." Mrs. Greenwood lowered herself onto a hard chair and motioned for Ruth to sit. "I intend to teach your husband a lesson. Then, maybe he'll think twice before corrupting other young men."

"My husband didn't corrupt anyone."

"We disagree."

Ruth took it as a good sign that Mrs. Greenwood hadn't yet asked her to leave. Clasping her hands in front of her, she leaned forward in what she hoped was a confidential manner.

"The truth is that we do not have five thousand pounds, or anywhere close to it," she said. "If you go to the authorities, your son will be dragged into court and made to testify. Have you considered that?"

The pause before Mrs. Greenwood answered told Ruth that she had not. She sensed an inroad. Before the woman could reply, Ruth asked, "You have heard of Mr. Oscar Wilde, I presume?"

"That degenerate playwright? Yes, of course."

"Then you know he was accused of corrupting several young men, including young Lord Alfred Douglas. It was Douglas's father who started the proceedings against Mr. Wilde."

"I am aware."

"Thanks to his father's actions, young Mr. Douglas's name is now forever paired with Mr. Wilde's. Guilt by association. Is that what you want for your Alexander?"

"Of course not. But you leave me no choice. I will report your husband to the authorities and make sure my son's name is never brought up.

"And I will make very sure that your son's involvement remains front and center," Ruth said sweetly. "My husband is acquainted with several excellent lawyers. If there's a trial, he may share Mr. Wilde's fate, but your son's name will most certainly be dragged through the mud." Ruth had no idea if James was connected with any lawyers, but she trusted Mrs. Greenwood couldn't know that.

"You wouldn't dare!"

"No? Two can play this game, Mrs. Greenwood. I'm as determined to protect my husband's good name as you are to destroy it."

To Ruth's surprise, one fat tear appeared in the corner of Mrs. Greenwood's eye and slid down her powdered cheek.

"You don't need five thousand pounds any more than you need to fly, do you?" Ruth asked gently.

Mrs. Greenwood daubed at her eyes with her handkerchief. "I want my boy back," she said. "Ever since my dear husband Everett passed, I've been alone. Alexander never comes to see me anymore."

"This isn't the way to get him back."

"I suppose not. I don't know." She twisted the damp handkerchief between her hands. "I thought that threatening your husband with exposure would be enough for him to break things off with Alexander. You're right that the money isn't important, and besides, I thought your husband was wealthy."

Ruth thought so too, but after seeing the pile of unpaid bills on James's desk, she was beginning to have doubts.

"What will you do now?" she asked.

"I wish I knew." Mrs. Greenwood regarded Ruth thoughtfully. "How do you bear it?"

"I have my life on the stage," she said. "And James is a kind man. I can't wish for more."

"Don't you think you deserve more?"

The directness of the question startled Ruth. She rose quickly. "I must get to the theater. Will you promise me that this matter is at an end?"

"I suppose I have no choice."

"My advice to you, although you didn't ask for it, is to talk with your son and remind him that you love him. He won't change. It's best for you if you stop hoping."

Mrs. Greenwood nodded. "I'm a foolish old woman," she said. "My Everett used to say that I see the world as I want it to be, not how it is."

Ruth laughed. "I suppose we're all guilty of that. Good day to you."

Chapter 11

Briarstown

Eliza

"Well, well, if it isn't my daughter, come to visit at last," Ma said. "Look here, Agnes. Eliza's gracing us with her presence."

"Now, Gladys," Aunt Agnes said. "Don't be like that. You know how busy Eliza is, and besides, she visited us a few weeks ago."

Ma sniffed. "Sit down, then. I see you've brought our Bessie." She extended her hand to the little girl, who clung to Eliza's skirts. "What's wrong with her?"

"She's shy."

"She don't need to be afraid of her granny." Ma grabbed hold of Bessie's arms and pulled her close. "You've grown." The child tried squirming free, but as Eliza well knew, Ma had a grip like iron.

"She was four in September, Ma. Don't you remember?"

"She favors her dad."

"I suppose."

"Your husband's kept his looks, I'll say that for him. So, what brings you to see your old Ma?" To Eliza's relief, Ma let go of Bessie, who ran to where Agnes was holding out a tin of thin biscuits, a treat Bessie rarely saw at home.

Eliza bit back a sigh. She wished she didn't dread these visits with Ma. Other women her age got along fine with their mothers. Some even had them living in the same house and talked about how grateful they were to have another pair of hands to help with the housework and watch the children.

Eliza shuddered at the thought of Ma living with her.

"We're happy you've come," Aunt Agnes said. "Are you keeping well? You look a little peaked."

"Peaked, is it?" Ma barked. "She's pale as a ghost. Are you ill?"

"No, Ma. Only a little tired."

"You've got plenty of girls to help you with the housework. More than I ever had."

"You had me, Ma."

"Most of the time, you was off at school or at the mill. Fat lot of good that did me, 'specially when your dad got sick."

"Yes, Ma." Eliza turned to her aunt. "Annie tells me your Bella's doing well as a pupil teacher at the school."

She knew it was disloyal, but sometimes Eliza wished Dad had married a woman like Aunt Agnes. Where Gladys Treleven was all hard angles and sour looks, Aunt Agnes—wife of Gladys's brother—was round and smooth and cheerful. She always had a smile for everyone and never complained, even when she had to take in her sister-in-law and spend her days listening to her moaning.

Eliza wished she had half Aunt Agnes's patience and good humor. Most of the time, she felt like screaming to the wind about the injustices of her life. Perhaps she'd be as soft and easy-going as Agnes if she'd married a man like her Uncle Bob, who doted on her. On the other hand, Dad had doted on Ma, and it hadn't made her any easier to do with.

"Aye, that she is. Bella loves it, says she wants to be a proper teacher one day."

"How can you afford that?" Ma asked.

"We'll manage," Agnes said. "I don't want to hold the girl back. She's got the brains to go far."

"She'll be getting notions," Ma said. "So, Eliza, your Annie's almost of an age to get work at the mill."

"I want to keep her in school for another year or two. Maybe she'll take over from your Bella."

"Perhaps she will," Agnes said. "She reminds me of you when you were her age—serious beyond her years."

Eliza laughed. "I don't know about that."

"I should say not," Ma said. "Annie's as responsible as they come, what with the way she keeps all her sisters in line. *She'd* never let one of them drown in the canal."

Eliza stiffened. Even after almost twenty years, Ma could still find and pierce with surgical precision the tender core of Eliza's guilt.

"We've had a letter from Devon," Aunt Anges said hastily. "You can read it if you like." She rose and retrieved the letter from the sideboard, then handed it to Eliza.

"Your granny's been unwell," Ma said.

"She has?" Fear twisted through Eliza's body like a sapling in a hurricane. She scanned the short letter.

My dear family,

The doctor tells me I've got to take it easy. He says if I don't, I might not live to see another Christmas. I don't believe him, but my husband's gone and got all worried and made Mr. Barton relieve me of most of my duties. I don't suppose I can do much about it. The weather's been terrible dreary.

Write me when you have time.

"What's wrong with her?" Eliza asked.

"She's getting on, dear," Aunt Agnes said. "She was seventy on her last birthday. We can't expect her to live forever."

"Knowing Mother, she'll live another twenty years to spite us," Ma said. "She's been dangling her legacy in front of me and Bob for years. What are the chances we'll see a shilling of it, 'specially since she up and remarried a few years back?"

"Now, Gladys. You wouldn't deny your ma a bit of happiness? Bob told me your dad weren't always good to her."

Ma shrugged. "Aye, he be a bully, and she was well shot of him. But she's *my* mother. I got a right to that legacy, same as your Bob, and I ain't ashamed for wanting it. Mother's led a good, long life."

"We should be praying for her to get well."

"I suppose." Ma shrugged. "So, Eliza, I heard some of the women are thinking of putting together a choir. I'm guessing you're the ringleader. You always did like putting yourself forward."

"Who told you that?" Eliza asked.

"Mrs. McKay dropped by the other day and barely talked of anything else."

"Hattie's mother-in-law? What did she say?"

"Only that her Hattie's keen to be part of a choir and enter some kind of competition. Sounds harebrained to me."

"I think it's a lovely idea," Aunt Agnes said. "And didn't Mrs. McKay say there's cash prizes to be won?"

"What's that?" Eliza asked.

"Oh yes," Aunt Agnes said. "I don't know how much, mind. But I've heard about other towns putting choirs together and going in competitions. I think the women of Briarstown could give any of them a run for their money."

"Eliza's got no time for such nonsense," Ma said.

"You're right. I don't," Eliza said. She stood and held her hand out for Bessie.

"On your way so soon?" Ma asked. "You never have more than ten minutes to spare for your mother."

"The girls will be home from school in half an hour. Thanks for the tea and biscuits, Aunt Agnes. You're both welcome to come visit us any time."

"What? Walk all the way over to Court Four?" Ma huffed. "I should say not. Well, off you go, then."

Instead of heading straight home, Eliza detoured to the canal and led Bessie to the edge of the moors. The rain had stopped, and the sun's rays were carving apart a low bank of purple clouds on the horizon, flooding the landscape with a vivid, eerie light.

"Pwetty." Bessie pointed a pudgy finger at the view.

"It is," Eliza said. As she watched the clouds play with the light, she felt fractured and whole at the same time. In the immensity of the moor, Eliza and Bessie were mere pinpricks. Witnessing such beauty made Eliza want to put bits of herself back together—pieces lost through the years of bearing children and living with Reg and working all the hours God sent.

Cash prizes.

She repeated the words over and over. How much cash? Any amount would be better than nothing. Any amount would bring her closer to reviving her Plan. And now, with Granny feeling poorly, there might be an opening for Eliza to take over her duties as housekeeper at Mr. Barton's manor. Almost without realizing, Eliza began singing one of her favorite hymns from church. She started low and thoughtful.

Come down, O Love divine,
Seek Thou this soul of mine,
And visit it with
Thine own ardor glowing

She liked the line "seek thou this soul of mine." Some days, she felt like she no longer had a soul, that Reg had taken it along with her happiness, her dignity, her hope—and even her voice. As for love divine—she sometimes wondered if even God loved her.

But singing the words comforted her, and when Bessie clapped her hands, eyes shining, Eliza sang with more volume and energy. By the time she reached the last line of the first verse, her voice soared out over the wild, wide moor.

O Comforter, draw near,
Within my heart appear,
And kindle it,
Thy holy flame bestowing.

She sang the last note as loudly as she could and then laughed and swung Bessie in an arc around her before pressing her close.

"Oh Bessie," Eliza whispered into the soft curls, "What's going to become of us?"

Chapter 12

London

Ruth

Ruth rarely saw James over the next several weeks. His gratitude for her handling Mrs. Greenwood hadn't extended to his wanting to spend more time with her. The few times they met—usually in the afternoon before Ruth left for the theater—he spoke only pleasantries. No matter how late she came home, he was out.

She was surprised to realize that she missed him. Mrs. Greenwood's threat had joined them in a common purpose. For a while, she'd meant more to James than an ornament hanging off his arm to stave off gossip.

She shook off the regrets. After the performance that evening, she'd dine again with the Prince of Wales. Everything was back to the way it should be. Her voice had wavered a few times since that dreadful night when she'd failed to hit the high note in her solo, but she doubted anyone noticed. The applause was as rapturous as ever, the dear boys in the front rows still throwing roses at her and calling for encores.

She stood in the wings next to the girls playing Pitti-Sing and Peep-Bo. Thanks to Ruth's complaining, Helen, who'd played Pitti-Sing, had been replaced by a new girl named Joyce. She was a harmless enough girl with an adequate voice. She'd not be a threat.

Vera, who played Peep-Bo leaned close to Ruth and whispered, "Mr. Johnson said I'm to have the lead in the next production."

Ruth whirled around. In the darkness backstage, Vera's eyes glinted, giving her a demonic look.

"You're lying," Ruth hissed.

"Ask him yourself."

At that moment, the orchestra played the notes signaling their cue. Ruth snapped open her fan and glided onstage between Joyce and Vera. She needed every ounce of self-control she possessed to hit all her notes while her mind reeled. The spiteful witch *must* be lying. Mr. Johnson would never replace Ruth.

She glanced up to the royal box where the Prince of Wales sat, his back to the stage. He appeared to be conversing with two elaborately coiffed women seated behind him and not paying any attention to Ruth.

After her last curtain call, Ruth returned to her dressing room to find Thomas standing in the doorway, his grizzled face stricken.

"What are you doing here?" she asked, her voice sharper than it needed to be considering old Thomas had always been good to her.

"It's Mr. Johnson, Missus. He wants to speak with you."

"Tell Mr. Johnson I'll talk with him tomorrow." She turned to Katie. "The red dress for this evening, please. His Majesty has not yet seen it."

"He don't want to wait," Thomas said.

Ruth glanced back. "For goodness' sake, I'm dining with the Prince of Wales." Her irritation returned. "Tell him that."

"But…"

Ruth sat at her dressing table. In the mirror, she saw Thomas open his mouth as if to say something more. She frowned. "Good night, Thomas."

"Yes, Missus."

Ruth removed her stage makeup and lightly rouged her cheeks. She wasn't looking forward to spending another tedious evening with the prince, but it couldn't be helped, and she was grateful for the invitation.

A knock sounded, and moments later, Katie handed her a folded note. "This come for you, Miss."

Sighing, Ruth unfolded the stiff paper. It was likely William asking for her company. She hated turning him down yet again in favor of the prince, but she had no choice.

She scanned the words—elegantly penned, obviously a woman's hand.

His Royal Highness, the Prince of Wales, regrets he must forgo the pleasure of your company this evening. He sends you his best wishes.

"What is it, Miss?"

Ruth refolded the note and placed it on her dressing table. "Nothing. Bring me the dress I wore to the theater. I've changed my mind about going out."

"Yes, Miss."

The prince had many demands on his time, Ruth told herself. Perhaps the old queen had summoned him. It was well known she disapproved of her heir's love for fine dining and married mistresses. A worry that the prince might hear about James's troubles surfaced briefly. She dismissed it.

"Miss?" Katie held out Ruth's cape. Made of finely spun cashmere in a deep forest green with a high collar in the latest fashion, the cape had been a gift from James. He'd told her it brought out her eyes and had even kissed her cheek when he'd draped it around her shoulders.

The door opened and James himself burst in. He glanced at her, his eyes wild. "You're wearing my cape? I suppose that's one thing to be pleased about." He flung himself into the only other chair in the small room.

"What are you doing here?" Ruth asked, surprised to feel a rush of pleasure. Perhaps they could dine together like they had in the early days of their marriage. She opened her mouth to suggest it, then noticed his pale cheeks and a sheen of sweat on his brow. James never sweated. "Is something wrong?"

"I'm sorry," he said.

"Whatever for? What's going on?" She heard the mounting fear in her voice.

"Something terrible has happened," he said. "I must leave London. Tonight."

She stared at him. "Leave London? What are you talking about?" Ruth saw Katie standing by the door, still holding the cape, her eyes wide. "Leave us!"

The girl dropped the cape and scurried out. James lowered his head to his hands. His shoulders began shaking, and Ruth realized he was crying.

"You're frightening me! What's happened? Why do you need to leave London?"

"That woman…" James gulped and then looked up. The urbane gentleman with the beautiful clothes and impeccable accent looked like a scared little boy.

"Mrs. Greenwood? What did she do?"

"You told me that she'd leave me alone. But tonight, Alexander came to me and said his mother's determined to go to the authorities."

"Why? Doesn't she realize that her precious Alexander will be called to testify?"

"Please don't talk about him like that," James said miserably. "He's not to blame for any of this."

Ruth rose and knelt in front of James. She took both his hands in hers and looked up into his tear-stained face. "Listen to me, James. You're overwrought. I'm sure things aren't that bad. Mrs. Greenwood is a bitter old woman who misses her son. She'll not do anything to harm him."

"She will. She has." James pulled his hands back. "I've no choice but to leave England."

"And go where?"

James stood and offered his hand to Ruth to help her up. "Paris. Alexander and I are taking the first train in the morning."

"You can't do that! What about me?"

"You have your position here. And I've already talked with your Uncle Edward. He'll help you get settled."

"What are you talking about, James? Settled where? This is ridiculous. You can't leave England. I'm your wife."

"And you've been the most patient, most beautiful wife any man could ever want. I've never deserved you."

"This is all nonsense. What about the house? The servants?" Ruth paced around the small room, her arms wrapped around her chest. The situation would be ridiculous if it were not so horrible. What had she done to deserve such treatment?

"The servants must be let go."

"And the house?"

"Will be sold. I've appointed an agent who has promised to get a good price."

Ruth stopped pacing, only just resisting the urge to slap him. Instead, she sat again at her dressing table and picked up her brush. The fine blonde hairs trapped in the brush did not look as bright as they used to. "You've decided all this without saying a word to me?" she asked quietly.

This couldn't be happening.

"I'm sorry…"

"You've said that already." She put down the brush and folded her hands in her lap in a vain attempt to calm herself. "How long have you been planning this?"

"For some weeks now. Alexander wasn't convinced his mother would stay silent even after she spoke with you. We thought it wise to prepare."

"And not once did you consider consulting me?"

"What could you do? As I've said, I've made arrangements. My agent has promised to find you suitable lodgings. With what Mr. Johnson pays you at the theater, you should have sufficient funds for a small flat in a respectable neighborhood. I imagine somewhere close to the theater would suit you."

"You want me to move into a tiny flat in Soho like I was some kind of kept woman?" Ruth rubbed her thumb across the raised shells and flowers crusting the surface of her wedding band. It was solid gold and had cost James a small fortune. "How can you even think such a thing?"

"As I said, my dear…"

"You're sorry. Yes, I know."

"I suppose you might come to Paris…"

"With you and your lover? Yes, that would be a fine situation. And what do you suppose I'd do in Paris? I don't speak French."

"I, well, I don't know, but Paris has many delights. I'm sure you'd find plenty to keep you amused."

"Stop it," she snapped. "You've never once thought about me when you were making your plans. All you care about is yourself—and Alexander."

"That's not fair. I told you, my agent, a fine fellow by the name of Mr. Braithwaite, will help you find suitable lodgings. I'm afraid I can't promise you more than a maid. Funds are rather strained at the moment."

Ruth remembered the stack of unpaid bills on James's desk. "You're not leaving London only to escape the law, are you?"

James puffed himself up, and Ruth prepared herself for more lies. Then, he seemed to deflate before her eyes. "I've had some bad luck lately."

"Gambling," Ruth said flatly. She'd known for years about James's fondness for horses and cards, but he'd always kept his spending under control. Never had she been given any reason to suspect they were living beyond their means.

"Please, Ruth, I never intended for any of this to happen," James said, his voice plaintive. "Is it my fault that horrible woman won't leave me alone? And as for the gambling, the losses aren't my fault. I had a sure bet on a horse that went lame. You can't blame me for that."

Ruth stared at her husband as if seeing him for the first time. She'd been used to thinking of James as a good man. He had his flaws like any man, but he was always kind to her and supported her career on the stage which many men would not. Now, contempt triumphed over the sympathy she'd always accorded him. And from contempt, it was a short step to anger.

"You don't particularly care what happens to me, do you?" she asked.

"So long as you're safe in Paris with your lover."

"Of course I care, my dear."

"Don't call me that."

He reached for her, but when she stepped back, he dropped his arm, his expression twisting from bewildered to ashamed. "You're right," he said, eyes downcast like a chastened child. "I don't deserve you."

"Get out," Ruth hissed. "Now. Go to Paris and leave me here. I can stand on my own two feet. I don't need you."

James paused a moment. He seemed to shrink before her eyes, leaving nothing except a shell dressed in a fashionable suit.

"Ruth…"

"Goodbye, James."

She turned her back on him. Moments later, the door opened and then closed with a muted thud.

Ruth sank onto the dressing table chair, keeping her face averted from the mirror. She didn't want to see herself—an abandoned wife, a woman cast adrift. All she wanted was to climb into her soft bed and sink into the blessed comfort of sleep. Tomorrow, she'd find her way out of this mess. She could *not* allow James to ruin her life. She'd go to Mr. Johnson and make him promise to give her the starring role in the next production. So long as she had the theater, she could survive.

Ruth picked up her cape from where Katie had dropped it and fastened it around her shoulders. She didn't need a big house and servants and carved settees from Paris. She was Ruth Henton—Professional Beauty and star.

She'd worked far too hard for too many years to be cast aside like an old slipper while an upstart like Vera, who barely got two words out before betraying her Cockney roots, took her place.

Chapter 13

Briarstown

Eliza

Eliza stifled a smile as she watched thin, sallow-faced Hattie McKay, her lips pursed as if she'd swallowed vinegar, try without success to tame her thick Yorkshire accent into posh tones.

"Female voice choir of not less than eight and no more than twenty voices," she read.

"There's only the four of us," Josie said.

Hattie waved the objection away. "For pity's sake, we can easily get another four women to sing with us, maybe more. There's plenty 'round here who'd jump at the chance to get out the house for somethin' other than goin' t'mill or shoppin'."

"It's been weeks since you showed me the ad," Hannah pointed out. "So far, there's only us."

"We got Eliza now," Hattie said.

"You haven't *got* me," Eliza said. "I only came by to ask what it was all about. I haven't sung for years."

"That's an untruth. I've heard you singin' myself, down by the canal and in the washhouse when you don't think anyone's around. You got a lovely voice, and I ain't one for givin' compliments when they're not owin'."

That was true enough, Eliza thought. Hattie McKay was the last person to say something nice if she could come up with a mean-spirited alternative. She hadn't changed since they were girls together in the mill school.

"The prize money is ten pounds," Josie said. "Happen people don't know that yet."

So, her aunt had been right about the cash prize. "The ad said nothing about prizes," Eliza said. "How do you know?"

Hattie held up the newspaper folded over to frame the advertisement. "See? This here's a new ad put in today. Says right here. The winning group in the Ladies choir category gets ten pounds. The male choir gets thirty pounds but there's not much we can do about that. Ten pounds is still a good sum."

"Ah, well," Eliza said. "That's nice for those who win." She did her best to keep her tone neutral. The money wouldn't be nearly enough—especially when split—but it would be something.

"It could be us," Hattie said. "That kind of money divided eight ways is…" She paused. Numbers—or any kind of book learning, come to that—had never been Hattie's strong suit. "Well, it's a lot."

"Twenty-five shillings each," Hannah said. "That's enough to pay for new boots for my Cliff *and* a dress for me, with some left over."

"I'd put it away for a rainy day," said Josie. "For when I'm old." As usual, she was smiling. Smiles came as easily to Josie's open face as smirks did to Hattie's. With a twinge of envy, Eliza watched Josie carefully set down her teacup on the immaculately pressed and starched tablecloth. With no children or husband to mess up the place, Josie's house that she shared with her parents was always clean and well-ordered—a state of affairs impossible in Eliza's house.

"I'm all for trying, so long as we can get four more women to join us," Josie continued. "I'll ask Minnie again. She said no before, but I reckon she'll change her mind once she finds out Eliza's joined us."

"I haven't joined yet," Eliza said, frowning. "Where did you say this competition was?"

"Over on the coast, at Whitby," said Hattie. "It'd be a long day, but we could go out early and be back after tea."

"Who's going to lead us?" Hannah asked. "We can't do it on our own."

"Miss Donahue, of course," Hattie said. "She did all right with us back when she was our teacher and takin' us to competitions. 'Course, Eliza was down at mill by the time we was competing." She glanced at Eliza as if to gauge the effect of her words. Eliza kept her expression blank. Not for the world would she let Hattie see the hurt her words caused.

"Yes, but we was nippers," Hannah pointed out. "This is a proper competition. We'll have to be first rate to even get close to winning."

"You don't think we can be first-rate?" Hattie asked.

Hannah laughed. "Wantin' summat ain't the same as gettin' it."

"How about Mr. Skinner?" Hannah asked. "Him what leads the Briarstown Choral Society?"

"No!" Eliza exclaimed, louder than she intended.

"He used to say *you* had a fine voice," Hattie said.

"We don't want a man leading us," Eliza said. "And besides, Mr. Skinner would probably think we're beneath his notice."

"I agree with Eliza," Josie said. "We should ask Miss Donahue. If she says no, then we get a group together and enter the competition anyway. Hattie, you ask her."

"Oh, no!" Hattie exclaimed. "Miss Donahue never liked me. Obviously, Eliza's the one to ask her."

"Why me?"

"You was always her pet, and there was that time you sang at the Christmas bazaar before you left school."

"Hattie!" Josie exclaimed.

"What about you, Hannah?" Eliza asked, ignoring Hattie.

"Miss Donahue barely knew I existed," Hannah said.

"That's 'cause you was never one to make waves," Hattie said.

"Do you think she'd want to lead us?" Josie asked.

"Well, we won't know *that* until we ask her," Hattie said. "I'll wager she'll be glad to have some time away from that mother of hers. And just because *you* don't need the money, Eliza, don't mean the rest of us couldn't use a few extra shillings. *I* ain't too proud to admit it."

"What's that supposed to mean?"

"I saw your Bessie prancing around in brand new shoes at church last Sunday."

"And why shouldn't our Bessie have new shoes?" Hattie had it all wrong, but Eliza wasn't about to correct her. Bessie's shoes weren't new, not even close. Eliza had spent an entire evening blacking and polishing a pair that had been handed down from Emily after being well worn by both Gladys and Lily May. No one would ever accuse Eliza Kingwell of letting her girls look sloppy.

Hattie sniffed. "No reason, I suppose, 'cept that for most of us, gettin' new shoes for what, the sixth child? It looks a lot like spoilin'."

"Fifth." Reflexively, her hand strayed to her empty belly as she sensed grief passing like a shuttle between big, blowsy Hannah who'd lost her only child and Josie who didn't even have a husband, never mind children. Hattie was always so intent on wounding Eliza that she never stopped to consider how her words hurt others. She lorded it over Eliza that she had three boys and no girls, as if this were an accomplishment she'd had something to do with.

"Oh, give it a rest and ask her," Hattie snapped. "In t' meantime, I'll see if I can drum up some interest. Minnie for sure, and then Doris, Gert, and Kitty."

"Not Kitty," Hannah said. "She's got a voice like a foghorn."

"How about Maisie?" Josie said. "When we was children, she sang almost as good as Eliza here."

"Maisie's only just had another bairn, so I'd say she has her hands full," Hattie said.

"How about that new girl what's started at the mill?" Hannah asked. "Lottie? She looks a lively sort."

"Can she sing?" Eliza asked.

"Only one way to find out." Hattie looked around at the group of women, her small eyes snapping with triumph. "So, it's settled? Eliza, you're to ask Miss Donahue if she'll conduct us, Josie will ask Gert, Hannah will talk to Doris, and I'll ask Lottie and, of course, Minnie." Hattie rose to her feet and smoothed her skirts. "I'd say that was what you'd call a productive meeting, girls. Now, I'd best be off home. Andy's been good enough to watch the boys for me this afternoon. He's a gem is my Andy." She turned to Josie and bobbed her head. "Thanks for the eats and the tea, as always, Josie. Your Ma outdid herself with them scones."

Eliza took the newspaper from the table. Excitement stirred within her at the prospect of once again singing with a choir. She peered at the list of categories. *Small female groups* was one, but there was also a competition for the best female vocalist. The prize money for that was almost what she'd lost and exactly what she needed to get the girls and herself away from Briarstown.

She thought about the letter from Granny. What if she died before Eliza could gather enough money to go south? Eliza shook her head. No use looking for trouble. Upright, no-nonsense Granny would probably outlive them all, and she'd *promised* to help Eliza.

Granny wasn't the kind of woman to go back on a promise.

Chapter 14

London

Ruth

Ruth woke the next day to a shaft of sunlight streaming through a gap in the curtains. After days of rain, she welcomed the prospect of a bright day. Stretching her arms above her head, she decided to take the sunshine as a good omen. James had been ridiculously over-dramatic at the theater the night before. Of course, he wouldn't desert her to go to Paris with Alexander. James had his faults, but he'd always been generous with her. He'd find a way out of this mess, and all would be well.

She should take advantage of the fine weather to go for a stroll in the park. She'd then pop into Whiteley's to browse the latest fashions. A new hat was exactly what she needed—something with satin bows and a cluster or two of cherries. One more bill added to James's collection would hardly make a difference.

Idly, she wondered if James had made it home and was at that moment sleeping off the effects of too much brandy. The house had been dark when she'd returned from the theater. She'd gone straight up to her bedroom, deciding not to rouse Constance. The pleasure of a hot drink before bed couldn't compensate for the housekeeper's long-suffering sighs and resentful looks.

Ruth decided she must insist that James let Constance go. It was the least he could do, considering everything he'd put Ruth through over the last several weeks. With a good reference, Constance would easily find another situation. Ruth could then train Sally to take over the housekeeper's duties. It would be gratifying to give the girl a leg up in the world. She was young and eager to learn.

Ruth rang the bell on the table next to her bed and then curled like a cat under the blankets.

A loud knock on the front door, followed by two more, startled her. She sat up. The knocks came again, even louder and more urgent. No one respectable called before noon, and tradesmen always went around to the back entrance.

The front door opened, and heavy boots struck the wood floor in the hallway. A deep male voice spoke, but she couldn't make out the words, only that he sounded official.

Light footsteps mounted the main staircase, and moments later, Sally burst into the room.

"Ma'am!"

"Who's making all that noise?"

Sally stood at the foot of the large bed, her face as pale as her apron. "Constance sent me up to fetch you, Ma'am." Tears welled in the girl's eyes.

"Is the master at home?"

"No, Ma'am. His bed's not been slept in."

Ruth pushed back the blankets and climbed out of bed. "My dressing gown, please."

"Yes, Ma'am." The girl appeared relieved to have someone tell her what to do.

Ruth wrapped herself in the heavy brocade gown and stepped into a pair of slippers. "Bring me my tea, and for heaven's sake, light the fire."

"I can't, Ma'am."

"Why not?"

"It's the police downstairs, Ma'am. They say they've come about the master."

Ruth sat down hard on the bed. Had James tried to escape after all and been caught? How could he do this to her? She took a slow deep breath, like she did to calm her nerves before a performance. If James had truly left her, she needed to be strong. She thought back to the day that Mother died. Although only sixteen, Ruth had found the courage to continue, even after Kingwell broke her wrist and told her it was her fault.

No one was breaking her wrist now.

"Open the door, Sally," she said. With her head held high, Ruth descended the staircase.

"Mrs. James Henton?" With his tall black helmet and black uniform, the policeman looked like a giant in the small foyer. A row of medals on his chest provided the only color. Three stripes on each arm denoted his rank as sergeant. Behind him stood another police officer, an anxious-looking younger man with blotchy skin.

"Yes," Ruth said in her most imperious voice. "What's going on?"

The policeman removed his helmet and tucked it under one arm. "It's your husband, Ma'am." The man's stolid features were unreadable, his lips a small pink slash in the middle of a full black beard.

"He's not at home," she said. She pushed down a rising sense of panic.

"We are aware." The sergeant drew himself up, so he looked even taller. "I regret to inform you, Ma'am, that your husband is dead."

Ruth gripped the banister to keep herself upright.

What was this? Impossible! James was still a young man.

"I don't understand," Ruth said. "My husband can't be dead."

"I'm sorry, Ma'am, but there is no doubt, although we will need you to identify the body."

"The body?" Ruth's knees gave way, and she collapsed onto a stair. Dimly, she was aware of Constance gliding forward and whispering something to the sergeant, who nodded.

"Of course," he said. "Your housekeeper will help you into the drawing room. We will be more comfortable there."

"What? No! I'm fine where I am. You must be mistaken. James dead? How? Where?"

"I believe we'll be more comfortable in your drawing room," the officer repeated.

"Come, Ma'am." With surprising tenderness, Constance put her arm around Ruth's waist and helped her to her feet, then guided her across the hall and into the drawing room.

Ruth leaned against her, comforted by the homely scents of cooked food and soap. The horrid policeman should be ashamed of himself for disturbing her with such lies. Any minute now, James would bound up the front steps and into the house. He'd kiss her cheek and ask about her performance. He always loved hearing her talk about the theater.

Constance lowered Ruth onto the Paris settee and stood aside. Both policemen entered the room, the young one positioning himself next to the mantle and the sergeant sitting in James's chair next to the fire.

"No!" Ruth said, rousing herself. "That's my husband's chair."

Ignoring her, the officer leaned forward, hands on his knees. "I'm afraid, Ma'am, that your husband, Mr. James Henton, has taken his own life. He was found this morning floating in the Thames."

"That's impossible! James would never do such a thing. You must have the wrong man. He should be home any moment now. Sometimes, he stays at his club, you know." She affected a laugh. "He has a large social circle and enjoys good company. I would accompany him, of course, but I am engaged at the Palladia Theatre. Do you know it?"

"Yes, Ma'am. Please get dressed, and we'll take you down to the mortuary."

"Is that necessary? As I said, you must have the wrong man."

"I assure you, Ma'am, we are quite certain. There is a note."

"What does it say?"

"All in good time, Ma'am."

Ruth twisted her mother's ruby ring around her finger. Surely, this was a nightmare. She'd wake up soon and all would be well. James would never abandon her like this.

Not true, she told herself. He'd been all set to leave her to fend for herself while he sailed for Paris with Alexander.

Constance stepped forward and helped Ruth to her feet. "Come upstairs. Ma'am." She turned to the policemen. "She won't be long."

Ruth wanted to protest, to launch herself at the policeman with the unreadable expression, to claw at his black beard and demand he leave her in peace. Constance's grip was gentle, but insistent. Ruth let her guide her back to her bedroom where Sally, with eyes red and hands trembling, helped her out of her nightclothes, and then brought out a plain black dress.

"Bring me my new ensemble," Ruth said. "The gray one."

"Don't you think the black is more suitable?" Constance asked.

"Do as I say." Ruth was still mistress in her own home. She stood in the center of the room, her arms bare and corset undone. When Sally returned from the closet holding the dress, Ruth leaned over and gripped the bedpost.

"Tighter!" she commanded as Sally pulled on the cords to tighten her corset. No matter what happened, Ruth refused to go out into the world looking anything less than her best. The new dress was made of tweed spun in a factory up north. Ruth had worn it only once before. She loved the fineness of the wool, and the way the full skirt draped from her cinched-in waist to brush the ground.

Sally tied off the corset and then helped Ruth into the skirt and the fitted jacket with gold piping and navy silk insets. Ruth felt detached, her eyes dry. Everything was going to be fine. Obviously, there'd been a terrible mistake. James would never take his own life.

Chapter 15

Briarstown

Eliza

The last time Eliza had spoken with Miss Donahue, she'd been only eleven. She still remembered sinking for a few blissful moments into Miss Donahue's embrace.

Her teacher had come to the house to convince Eliza's parents to let her stay in school. She'd meant well, but she hadn't a clue. As the vicar's daughter, Miss Donahue had been insulated all her life from the harsh realities of the mill workers' lot. Not for the world would Eliza tell her how Ma had put her foot down and insisted that she go to work in the mill. It was Ma's way of getting revenge for what had happened to little Ernie. Even Dad hadn't been able to convince Ma to let Eliza stay in school.

Eliza stood at the door to the small cottage that Miss Donahue shared with her mother. Through the front window, she glimpsed her former teacher placing a shawl around her mother's plump shoulders. Thankfully, the old lady appeared to be asleep. Eliza didn't think Mrs. Donahue would be keen on her daughter conducting the women who lived in the courts and terraces. It was common knowledge she'd made Miss Donahue leave off teaching at the mill school when the vicar died so she could stay home and take care of her.

Eliza rapped softly on the front door.

"Eliza Kingwell!" Miss Donahue said, opening the door wide. "Goodness! It's been far too long!"

"Hello, Miss Donahue."

"Come in, come in! It's shockingly raw out today. Come through to the kitchen. Mother is sleeping, and I don't want to disturb her."

Eliza followed Miss Donahue down a narrow corridor to a small sitting area next to the kitchen. She perched on the edge of a worn settee and watched as Miss Donahue picked up the kettle.

"Tea?" she asked.

Eliza nodded. She was burning with impatience to state the reason for her visit but was worried about appearing too forward. She kept silent and watched Miss Donahue fill the kettle with running water from a tap in a deep sink and then place the kettle on a large range. With a clanking sound, Miss Donahue pried open a door at the front of the range. The acrid smell of burning wood filled the small kitchen.

Eliza had heard about these modern wood stoves, how they had surfaces large enough to cook four dishes at once. In her small house in the court, Eliza could do little more than boil a kettle or warm up a pot of stew on the grate above the coal fire. Most of the food her family consumed came from the bakehouse across the road.

While waiting for the kettle to boil, Miss Donahue slid several slices of lemon cake onto a china plate and placed it on the table next to Eliza. "Is your family well?" she asked.

"Yes, thank you." Eliza felt awkward in her serviceable woolen dress with its narrow sleeves. She tucked her heavy shoes under her skirt.

The kettle boiled, and Miss Donahue poured the water over tea leaves she'd measured into a teapot adorned with blooming red roses. Eliza couldn't help comparing it to the cracked brown pot she used at home. She accepted a brimming cup and took a tiny sip. The aroma filled her senses with a pleasant sharpness.

As Miss Donahue sat down opposite her and took a sip of her own tea, Eliza realized with a start that her former teacher was only about seven years older than she was. Miss Donahue had been eighteen when she'd started teaching at the mill school but had seemed so much older and wiser to eleven-year-old Eliza. Now, Eliza saw a woman not that much different from herself—skin pale, eyes weary, the promise of youth long faded.

Like Eliza, Miss Donahue had never been beautiful. Some unkind souls would call her plain, and certainly she'd never managed to attract a husband. To her surprise, Eliza felt a twinge of sympathy for her. Being the vicar's daughter may have shielded Adelaide Donahue from the drudgery and hardship of a mill worker's life, but she'd still had to resign herself to a fate she hadn't chosen, just as Eliza had.

"So, what can I do for you?" Miss Donahue asked, leaning forward, her expression earnest like she was about to lead the children in chanting the times tables.

"I have a favor to ask, Miss Donahue," Eliza began.

"I haven't been your teacher for a great many years, Eliza. Please, call me Adelaide."

"Oh, no, Miss Donahue. It wouldn't seem right."

"As you wish."

"Some of the women and I want to put together a choir," Eliza began. She took the ad from her pocket and handed it across the table. "We need a conductor."

Miss Donahue picked up and read the ad, then placed it back on the table and took a long sip of tea. "I see the competition's being held in Whitby."

"Yes. In April. We're hoping to go out and back in a day. Will you help us? You know most of the women from when we were girls. They all remember you teaching us singing in school."

"The competition will be stiff," she said. "Do the women know that?"

"You don't think we stand a chance?"

"I didn't say that."

"Then what?"

"Honestly, I don't know," Miss Donahue said. "Turning a group of women who have never sung together—or at least not since they were children—into a choir worth listening to will require a considerable amount of practice. Are you sure the women can spare the time?"

"We can practice one evening a week and on Saturday afternoons when those who work in the mill get their half day."

"What about your children?"

"We'll manage. We've friends and family to call on, and my Annie's almost twelve. She can watch her sisters for a few hours."

"You'll be up against choirs that have been singing together for years. I don't want to discourage you, but a group assembled only five months before a competition has little chance of succeeding."

"Do you remember the first time you asked us children if we wanted to sing?" Eliza asked.

"Of course. But that was years ago."

"If it hadn't been for you getting us all started, teaching us to like singing and all, we'd never even be thinking about this competition lark."

"I know and I'm sorry I can't help."

"It would mean a lot to the others." Eliza paused, sucked in her breath. "And to me."

"I wish it was possible," Miss Donahue said. "Truly I do. But Mother can't spare me."

"I see," Eliza said. *So that was that. Well, she wasn't about to beg.* "I'll not trouble you further." She stood and held out her hand. "Please give your mother my best wishes."

Miss Donahue rose too. "Perhaps you could find someone else. Mrs. Walker at the church?"

"The organist? No, I don't think so. Thank you for your time, Miss Donahue."

"I'm sorry, Eliza. But my hands are tied."

"I understand." Eliza tried hard to keep the resentment from her voice. She'd been a fool to think her old teacher would care to associate with women like her. Teaching children at the mill school was one thing, but spending time with the rough, often brash women they'd grown into would not be proper for a woman like Miss Donahue. But without her, the choir didn't have a ghost of a chance of winning.

Hastily, Eliza bade Miss Donahue a good day and escaped into the damp November air. Squaring her shoulders, she opened the gate to let herself out to the road. Well, if Miss Donahue wouldn't help them, they'd have to find a way to manage on their own. Eliza had the most training of all of them put together, and so it would be up to her to lead them.

Doubt slowed her pace for a moment. She remembered being back in school and overhearing the school inspector, his voice dripping contempt, tell Miss Donahue that the mill children couldn't be taught, that the best she could do was to keep them quiet and teach them to recognize their letters and do simple sums.

The shame Eliza had felt all those years ago turned to anger, a burning fist that lodged in her chest. Mr. Wharton was *wrong*. She and the other children had not been a waste of time. And neither were the women they'd become.

Chapter 16

London

Ruth

Ruth went directly to Mr. Johnson's office the minute she arrived at the theater after identifying James's body at the mortuary.

She told him what happened in as few words as possible and with no mention of James's last letter. God willing, no one would ever know *why* James had ended his life by throwing himself into the stinking Thames.

"Lover's spat," the sergeant had said, his voice dripping with distaste. "His note explains everything. It was found tucked inside his jacket, which he'd left by the side of the river before he, ah…"

"Thank you, sergeant," Ruth said. It had drizzled the night before, so the paper was damp. She unfolded it carefully.

Dearest Ruth,

I won't say I'm sorry yet again. It's an absurd affectation in the circumstances. We never should have married. I see that now. None of this is your fault. I am a coward, but I see no other way out. Alexander refuses to come with me to Paris, and with him goes my soul. Do one thing for me, please. Never give up on music.

He'd not bothered signing the note.

Ruth had ripped it to shreds right there in the mortuary next to James's body resting on a marble slab and covered by a threadbare sheet.

"I need to work, Mr. Johnson," she said. "Word will not have gotten out yet, but when it does, I'm sure people will be sympathetic. My husband was ill."

"Your husband was a criminal," Mr. Johnson said. "You do know that suicide is illegal?"

"I'm aware, but who is to pay for the crime now? I've done nothing wrong. Please, let me perform."

"I can't have my theater embroiled in a scandal," Mr. Johnson said. He stroked two fingers on either side of his moustache, dyed jet black in a futile attempt to make him appear younger.

"The police promised to keep it out of the papers," Ruth said.

"I'm afraid that will be impossible. By tomorrow, the news will be all over London."

A sickening dread filled Ruth. She'd been a fool to think she could swan back into the theater and perform as if nothing had happened.

"Will you at least allow me to perform this evening?"

"Very well, Mrs. Henton. You may perform…tonight." He walked to the door and opened it, standing aside to let her pass.

She wanted to ask him what he meant but feared his answer.

Ruth entered her dressing room to find Katie brushing Ruth's black wig. Tears streaked her cheeks. "I'm so sorry, Miss," she said, jumping up and coming to Ruth to remove her cape and get her settled in front of her dressing table. "Thomas told me."

"Thank you."

Katie looked at her expectantly, as if waiting for her to dissolve into tears. Ruth waved her away and set to work applying her make-up for the performance. The familiar movements calmed and centered her. Perhaps grief would come later, but for now, all Ruth felt was a terrible, burning rage.

She'd be damned if she'd let the fact that James had thrown himself into the Thames take away everything that she'd worked so hard to achieve. She'd sell the house and all its fancy furnishings and move to more modest lodgings. Her career onstage didn't need to end. Her adoring public would never desert her.

And William! Yes, of course. William would help. He loved her! After a decent interval for mourning, she'd pour every ounce of her considerable charms into convincing William to divorce his frumpy wife and marry her. Of course, he'd allow her to continue her career.

An hour later, dressed and ready to perform, Ruth shuffled in her tight kimono along the dark hallway backstage. Vera and Joyce were already waiting. Both girls stared at her in the darkness, but neither said anything. Ruth imagined the dressing rooms buzzing with news of James's death. Well, let them talk. She'd give the performance of her life tonight, and then agree to a short break, so long as Mr. Johnson promised her the lead in the next production. Rehearsals would start in six weeks. Propriety demanded a much longer mourning period, but Ruth didn't have the luxury of worrying about propriety. James had chosen his path—a cowardly one—but that didn't mean Ruth should suffer.

She was *not* a coward.

At the end of the evening, Ruth floated off stage, the applause ringing in her ears. To her relief, the dreadful events of the day had not affected her performance.

"This come for you, Missus." Thomas waylaid her in the wings and held out a folded piece of thick, white paper.

She unfolded it.

I regret I shall not be able to see you this evening. I am otherwise engaged and ask that you refrain from contacting me in future.
Sincerely, William Eaton

Ruth crushed the paper between her hands. She thought back to the first time in her life when she'd been left alone.

Flecks of white had slivered the edges of her mother's grave, and *he* had stood next to her, his cheeks wet with crocodile tears. After the service, she'd made the mistake of telling him she wouldn't quit the Academy to be his housekeeper. The moment she'd said the words, Ruth had realized she'd done what Mother told her to never do.

Don't upset Father.

Faster than she thought possible, Kingwell crossed the hall and pinned her wrist with one broad forearm against the door frame. The sound of the bone snapping had taken Kingwell from rage to blame so quickly that Ruth almost believed him when he chided her.

"You shouldn't o' pulled away so sudden," he said. "Now look what you've done."

Worse even then the pain was the feeling of helplessness. She stared at him and understood for the first time how Mother must have felt.

"You'd best see the doctor," he said, his eyes softening with what Ruth realized was concern. "I'll take you."

She turned away without responding and, with her good arm, slung her coat over her shoulder. It would be enough to keep the rain off for the short walk to the doctor. She clenched her jaw against the stabbing pain. She wouldn't give him the satisfaction of seeing her wince.

"Ruth."

He'd never said her name in such a gentle tone. Ruth hesitated. Perhaps she should let him take her. The street was slippery with rain, and she didn't want to fall, and it was true that she'd jerked her arm away.

"Fine," she murmured, then stood aside to let him open the door. He pulled her coat more firmly around her shoulders, then put on his own coat and followed her into the wet afternoon.

"The doctor will 'ave you fixed up real quick," he said. "And I meant to tell you, Mr. Lewiston's promised to give me a pay raise." The pride in his voice reminded Ruth of a child looking for approval.

"That's good," she said, keeping her voice neutral.

The doctor examined Ruth with eyes narrowed. "It's broken," he said. "How did it happen?"

Ruth hesitated. Telling the truth might cost Kingwell his job, maybe even the house. Before she could leave Briarstown for good, she needed to pass her exams, and that was still two years off. Also, Dr. Easton had treated Mother several times for bruises and broken bones. He'd never spoken up then, so why would now be any different?

"I tripped and fell down the stairs," Ruth said. She glanced at Kingwell, who sat so close she smelled his nervous sweat. "Are you sure it's broken?"

The doctor lightly pressed her wrist, making her yelp.

"I'm afraid so, my dear. I will set it, and you must be brave."

She nodded, letting the white-hot pain stoke her anger. She'd lie for Kingwell this time because to do otherwise would not serve her.

But she'd never let him touch her again.

Ruth returned to her dressing room and stood mutely while Katie removed her costume. Reg Kingwell hadn't succeeded in cowing her when she was fifteen, and she'd not let this new tragedy get the better of her.

Stripped to her corset, she sat at the dressing table and slowly wiped away the layers of make-up. Her wrist twinged, the pain a dart of heat, dulled now after so many years, but still sharp enough to make her breath catch. She glanced anxiously in the mirror to make sure Katie hadn't seen, but the girl was busy hanging up Ruth's costume from the third act. Relieved, Ruth patted on some rouge to highlight the famous blooming cheek of the Professional Beauty.

Mother had died before she'd found a way out of the life she'd accepted with Kingwell. Ruth would find a way to make her own life worth something.

Chapter 17

Briarstown

Eliza

Eliza stood a little apart from the other women, watching as they chatted and laughed. After all these years, she still felt like an outsider.

"Sorry we're late!" The door to the church hall banged shut behind Hattie and Minnie. "Our Daniel's come over funny after tea. Got the colly wobbles, he did," Hattie said cheerfully. "I had the devil's own time getting away."

As she spoke, Hattie peeled off her damp coat and threw it over a chair. Minnie followed suit. The pair of them had been best friends since they were children and had worked side by side at the mill until they married, Hattie at eighteen and Minnie at twenty. Eliza hated feeling the tiniest bit envious of Minnie. With both her children now in school, Minnie had gone back to work at the mill. Although Eliza had hated working there—the long hours, the noise, the boredom—she'd relished the independence that came with getting a pay packet at the end of each week. She'd given most of it to Ma to help with the household expenses but had been allowed to spend what was left any way she liked. Usually, she'd bought music.

A few days earlier, Eliza asked Reg if she could go back to work when Bessie started school. He'd laughed and told her she was daft.

Sometimes, his laughter hurt more than his fists. *But only sometimes.*

"We'd best get started," Eliza said, swallowing the nerves that threatened to strangle her resolve. "Minnie, I remember you as having a good, strong voice. Why don't you stand over here next to Gert? Hattie and Doris, you two have lower voices and should stand to the right."

"Who made you the boss?" Hattie demanded. "Where's Miss Donahue?"

"Miss Donahue said she doesn't have time to lead us," Eliza said.

"Well, that's a shame," Gert said. She was a tall, gangly woman who was raising three children on her own after her husband died in a mill accident. She and Lottie were the only ones who hadn't sung with the others at the mill school.

"Her mother can't spare her," Eliza said.

"I doubt that," Hattie said. "More likely, she don't want to be seen helpin' women like us."

"That's unfair, Hattie," Josie said mildly. "Miss Donahue were always good to us."

"When we was small, yes, but things are different now we're grown."

Looking past Hattie, who seemed determined to be contrary, Eliza said, "We're fortunate that Mrs. Walker here has offered to play for us during rehearsals. It's thanks to her we're meeting in the church hall." Eliza smiled tightly at Felicity Walker, who sat bolt upright at the piano. "How about I get us started with the singing while she accompanies us?"

"Oh well, I suppose you're as good as any," Hattie said. "Beggars can't be choosers."

Eliza noticed Mrs. Walker's spine stiffen even more. A slight breeze would send her keeling headfirst over the piano keys.

"Eliza has the most experience," Josie said. "With singing, I mean."

"I didn't think you meant anything else, Josie," Hattie said. Glowering, she wedged herself between Hannah and Doris. Eliza had been surprised to see Doris Blair—Doris Clarkson that was—but then reflected that she likely appreciated any excuse to get away from her husband. Everyone knew Dan Blair was a miserable old sod.

No one would believe that Reg Kingwell was no better, and Eliza intended to keep it that way.

Eliza faced the women, thankful that Josie and Hannah were smiling encouragement. Young Lottie bounced with excitement, and Minnie and Gert both looked hopeful. For a moment, the trust in their eyes made her want to run back into the rain-soaked night to her crowded house. At home, she was Mother and her word—at least with the children—was law.

Who was she to lead a group of women her own age?

"Well, come on then, Mrs. Kingwell. Tell us what to do, since you're so keen on it," Hattie said.

"I've been reading up about the competition," Eliza said. "We have to sing two songs, one that they give us—they call it a set piece—and one we choose ourselves. And then there's something called sight singing. We'll worry about that later. I guess we should start with the set piece. I got my Annie to write out the words, and Mrs. Walker's got hold of the music." She started handing out the pages.

"Ahem."

"Yes, Mrs. Walker?" Not for the first time, Eliza wished she'd been able to find a different accompanist. Felicity Walker was a cut above most of the women in the area, being both the church organist and married to a man who owned a shoemaking business.

"It is customary to start with a warm-up, Mrs. Kingwell," Mrs. Walker said.

"Oh yes, of course. I, ah…" Eliza's voice trailed off, and her cheeks flushed as if Mrs. Walker's gaze had burned them. Every exercise she'd ever known from her days with the Briarstown Choral Society flew from her memory. It was as if she'd never sung a note in her life.

"Oh, for pity's sake," Mrs. Walker muttered as she struck a C chord. "Allow me."

For the next fifteen minutes, the group warbled up and down the scales—notes flying off in all directions like bobbins disconnected from their looms. Even the most charitable of listeners would cringe at the sound and question whether these eight women could ever become a choir worth listening to.

"Thank you," Eliza said finally. She saw her own dismay reflected on the faces of the others. The competition was in April, and it was already coming on to the end of November. If they couldn't make it up and down a scale without croaking like a load of frogs, how did they expect to compete? She should go back to spending every evening at home with the girls and squirreling away a few pennies here and there without Reg finding out. At the rate she was going, the girls would be grown and married before she'd saved enough to leave, and by then, what would be the point?

With that cheerful thought, she directed the women to look at the words that Annie had so carefully copied out.

"It's a fine bunch of words, but what do they all mean?" Hattie asked. "We ain't never sung owt like this before."

"It's from Shakespeare," Eliza said. She knew that because Mrs. Walker, dripping condescension, had told her. "From a play called *A Midsummer Night's Dream*."

"Who's this Shakespeare fella when he's at home?" Doris asked.

"William Shakespeare lived over three hundred years ago," Mrs. Walker said, turning from the piano to face the group. "He is considered the greatest playwright who ever lived."

"I'm not so sure about this," Doris said. "I thought we was going to sing songs, not do plays."

"It's only the words that come from Shakespeare," Eliza said. "The music was made up by someone else."

"*Composed*," Mrs. Walker said. "The music was *composed* by a man named Felix Mendelssohn. He was German and died about fifty years ago. His music is extremely famous, and he once even met our queen."

"Well, *I* ain't never heard of him," Gert said. "And what's this first line about spotted snakes? It's daft."

Secretly, Eliza had thought the same when she first read the words they were to sing.

Ye spotted snakes with double tongue,
Thorny hedgehogs, be not seen;
Newts and blindworms, do no wrong,
Come not near our fairie queene.

It made little sense, although at least the piece was in English. When she'd sung with the Society choir, most of the songs had been in foreign languages like Italian and German.

"It's right strange," Minnie said. Then, to Eliza's relief, young Lottie stepped forward.

"When I lived in Sheffield, the choir I sang with entered a few of these competitions," she said. "There was always what they called a set piece by one of them dead composers. We sang this one by Mendelssohn a few times. It's very nice once you get used to it. The fairies are singing about protecting their queen from nasty things like snakes and spiders and the like."

"We're supposed to be *fairies?*" Hattie asked.

"Aye," Lottie said. "And why not? It's pretend, and the music's beautiful."

"Did you ever win any of them competitions?" Hannah asked.

"Once or twice," Lottie said, her smile bright.

"That's as may be, but I ain't interested in singin' songs I don't like," Doris said.

"How do you know you don't like it?" Josie asked. "I say we give it a chance."

"It was loads of fun, competing," Lottie said. "But it were hard at first, like now."

"Yes, but I'll wager you had someone who knew what they was doing leadin' you," Hattie said.

"That's enough from you, Hattie McKay," Hannah said. "It's far too soon to talk about giving up. Quit if you want to, but I'm staying."

"Me too," Gert said.

"Yes, well, I never said nowt about quitting," Hattie said sullenly. "I just asked a question."

"How about I sing the first verse while Mrs. Walker plays?" Eliza asked. She'd long ago learned that the only way around Hattie was to look through her as if she didn't exist. "I'll be singing the soprano part, but remember, we'll sing it in three parts."

"I thought we was singing a whole song," Hannah quipped. She looked around to see if the joke had landed. Everyone except Hattie and Mrs. Walker smiled, and Lottie laughed out loud. The tension in the drafty hall stretched and broke.

Eliza sighed with relief. "Most of us are a bit rusty with part singing, but it should come back soon enough. Mrs. Walker? Will you play the introduction?"

With a barely concealed huff, Mrs. Walker turned back to the piano and began to play.

The long warmup had paid off. When Eliza sang the first bars of the solo soprano part, the notes came out pure and clear. She barely knew the song herself, having sung it only once with Mrs. Walker, but she'd been struck then with the beauty of the melody. Once the women got comfortable with it, they'd learn to love it too, even if the words were a little cracked.

Well, perhaps not Doris and Hattie, but one couldn't expect miracles.

Eliza stopped after her solo and pointed to the next word. "Now you all sing this bit together, like this." She sang the next few lines. "We'll eventually sing it in parts, like I said, but for now, let's all sing the melody. That's the top part." She sang it again. "If it's too high for you, just hum along."

Mrs. Walker struck a chord, and slowly the women sang the next few bars. "That's right," Eliza said in what she hoped was an encouraging tone. "Don't worry about what it sounds like. We want to get a feel for the words and the rhythm."

For the next hour, the women sang and made mistakes and sang some more and bickered a bit and then laughed. Once or twice, Eliza caught Mrs. Walker's eye and guessed what she was thinking. They'd need hours and hours of practice to blend the eight voices into a pleasing whole good enough to perform in public, never mind in a competition.

But for the first time in years, Eliza went to sleep that night seeing glimmers of hope in a future that before the rehearsal had looked as murky as a foggy winter's day. She'd arrived home with time to spare before Reg came in. On Tuesdays, he always attended one of the lectures put on for the workingmen at the mill. Thankfully, he'd come straight home instead of detouring to the pub and then dropped immediately to sleep without reaching for her.

Annie, Lily May, and Gladys wouldn't say anything to Reg about their mother being out, and Eliza had to trust that six-year-old Emily and little Bessie would also keep quiet.

If Reg found out about the choir, he'd put a stop to her taking part. She knew exactly how he'd do it. Most of the time, he hit her where no bruises showed, but if he really wanted to hurt her, he'd go after her face. He knew that her pride would never allow her to let others see her shame.

Chapter 18

London

Ruth

Ruth was almost to the stage door on her way home after the performance, when Mr. Johnson emerged from the shadows.

"I need to speak with you," he said. "Now."

Her heart pounding, Ruth followed him into his cluttered office. Stacks of paper covered most surfaces, and the stink of stale cigar smoke thickened the air. She remembered the first time she'd entered Mr. Johnson's office as a girl of eighteen. With her head full of dreams, she'd been as green as the leather covering the one good chair in the room.

She was no longer that girl. Before Mr. Johnson had a chance to speak, she said, "You must see I'm not to blame for what my husband did."

"I am aware," Mr. Johnson said. He sat down behind his desk without waiting for Ruth to take the other chair. She remained standing in the futile hope he'd feel ashamed of his rudeness.

"Then you agree to my returning in six weeks?" she asked.

"There's no longer a place for you at the Palladia Theatre," he replied. "Not now, and not in six weeks or any other period of time. Tonight was your final performance."

"But you've said yourself many times that my performances have increased ticket sales. The word you used was *significantly*."

"That was true at one time, but lately, your performances have been somewhat lacking. I've been thinking about replacing you, which you'd have known if you'd come to see me when I asked."

"My performances are as good as they've ever been." A cold sweat prickled down her spine. This couldn't be happening. She'd done nothing wrong! The phrase kept repeating itself in her head.

Nothing wrong. Nothing wrong.

"Your performances have been lacking," he repeated.

"I'm sure another theater will be happy to employ me." Ruth needed every ounce of her training to keep the desperation from her voice.

"I wish you luck, my dear." He stood and came around his desk, looming above her. She smelled stale breath and gin.

"Please, Mr. Johnson." She inhaled deeply. "I'll return to the chorus. I'll take whatever bit parts are available. I don't mind. But don't make me leave. The theater is everything to me."

"You really don't know, do you?" he asked, almost genially.

"What are you talking about?"

"Your husband came to me several weeks ago and begged me to give him an advance on your earnings. I confess I was foolish enough to give it to him in the belief that he'd pay it back."

"How much?" Ruth asked.

"More than you can work off in the chorus," he said. "As for being the star, that is out of the question now. I'd rather take the loss than let you stay one moment longer under my roof. You and your disgusting husband are a liability, my dear, and I can't afford liabilities." He none too gently ushered her to the door.

"I must be allowed to gather my things," she said, mustering as much of her shattered dignity as she could.

"Thomas will clear out your room in the morning and send the boxes to your home."

Ruth steadied herself on the doorframe. "You can't do this."

"I can, Mrs. Henton. And I have." He stepped back and slammed the door in her face.

Chapter 19

Briarstown

Eliza

"You goin' out tonight, Ma?" Annie asked. "It's Tuesday."

"Yes," Eliza said shortly. She didn't want to admit to Annie that after three weeks of rehearsals, the choir sounded dreadful, and Eliza had no clue how to fix it. She wondered if she should tell the women that it was hopeless, that they'd never be good enough to win a competition. They'd be lucky not to humiliate themselves in front of choirs that had sung together for years.

Doris almost never sang the right notes at the right times; Josie's voice was as sweet as she was, but she often got the words wrong; and Hattie sang loudly, but off-key. On the other hand, Hannah and Gert both had strong voices; Lottie held her own; and wispy little Minnie, who still followed Hattie's lead in everything, sang on key in a rich contralto voice that blended well with Eliza's soprano.

Even so, Eliza worried that the strengths of some were not enough to counteract the weaknesses of others.

"Martha at school told me her ma's heard folks saying the mill ladies' choir is showing real promise," Annie said. "Her ma says it's a wonder, considering you haven't been singing together for long."

"Martha's mother has heard about the choir?"

"She told Martha that Mrs. Kingwell was doing a fine job with a lot of sow's ears. What does she mean by that, Ma? You ain't pigs."

"Aren't," Eliza said automatically. She wouldn't have people calling the Kingwell girls untutored savages. "Making a silk purse out of a sow's ear means to make something valuable out of something that's useless."

"I don't understand," Annie said. "You're not useless."

Eliza suppressed a smile. "I don't suppose Martha's mother meant we're useless so much as she's surprised women like us can sing."

"Why wouldn't you be able to sing?" Annie asked. "That's an awful thing to say. You got a beautiful voice. Granny told me you used to sing with the big choir in town."

"She did?"

"'Course. Granny's always going on about how good you are and how we should mind you because you're the best ma and we're lucky to have you."

"Oh!" Eliza was so surprised she almost dropped the plate she carried from the table to the sink. "Your granny said all that?"

"Oh aye. And more."

"Yes, well, your granny does like to talk. But about the sow's ears, I don't think Martha's mother means any harm. We may be sow's ears now, but we won't stay that way. How did Martha's mother find out about our choir?"

"I asked Martha that," Annie said, a touch of pride in her voice. "I thought you'd want to know, seeing as how Martha's ma's not in the choir herself."

"And?"

"She said her ma got it from Mrs. Walker. She's the one what plays piano for you, ain't she? I mean, isn't she?"

"She is." To think Mrs. Walker was telling people the choir had potential! Perhaps things weren't as dire as Eliza feared. "Make sure the littl'uns are in bed by seven, and if Dad comes home before I'm back, say I've gone to attend to a sick neighbor."

"Yes, Ma."

"And Annie? Thank you for telling me what Martha's ma said." Eliza reached out and touched Annie's cheek. "You're a good girl."

Annie's eyes widened with surprise, and Eliza knew it was because she almost never complimented her girls.

"I'd best be off," she said, turning away and busying herself with putting on her coat and hat. She knew she was often too strict with her girls, but wasn't it her job to keep them firmly in line? They needed to be strong to survive in the world. She couldn't have people saying the Kingwell girls couldn't hold their own.

Impulsively, she turned back and kissed Annie's cheek before hurrying out the door.

The rain drenching the yard had let up. Eliza skirted the worst of the puddles on her way through the passageway leading from the yard to the road. Up ahead, she saw Hannah waving to Josie, who emerged from one of the terrace houses. When Josie saw Eliza, she put her hand on Hannah's arm to stop her walking and waved.

An unfamiliar warmth spread across Eliza's chest when she realized that Josie and Hannah were waiting for her to join them.

"I've been practicing all afternoon," Josie said.

"Me as well," Hannah said. "Here's to givin' Mrs. Walker a run for her money tonight. What about you, Eliza? Do you think we'll ever impress her?"

"Probably not," Eliza said. "But my Annie's just told me that Mrs. Walker's been telling folks we've got promise. I suppose we should be pleased."

"Of course we should!" Josie exclaimed.

"You don't think we sounded rough at the last rehearsal?" Eliza asked.

"Not a bit of it!" Josie said. "We're not polished, I'll grant you, but we're not terrible. What do you say, Hannah?"

"I don't really care what we sound like," Hannah said. "So long as we keep practicing. I like the chance to get out of the house. And my Cliff says he's real proud of me."

Eliza couldn't imagine how it would feel to have a husband who was proud of her.

"What about the others?" she asked. "Do you think they want to carry on?"

"Of course they do!" Josie said. "Why would you even think such a thing?"

"You don't want to get put off by Hattie and Doris," Hannah said. "They like stirring things up, always have, ever since we was bairns."

Eliza nodded, the memories of Hattie's taunting still vivid enough to wound her even after so many years. On her first day at the mill school, horrid Miss Lane had made Eliza point to China on the map. Eliza had never seen a map before and had pointed to Canada. Hattie hadn't let her hear the end of it for weeks.

Remembering her schooldays brought back the image of George Ledbetter as he was back then—all arms and legs and soft brown eyes that always looked at her with such longing. When he'd tried taking her side against Hattie, Eliza had shooed him away rather than be seen consorting with a boy. The meanness of her actions—making her no better than Hattie—still made her feel ashamed of herself. George hadn't deserved her scorn. He also hadn't deserved her choosing Reg over him when she was seventeen, but that was another matter, and she couldn't dwell on it.

"Eliza?" Josie said, touching her arm. "You comin' in?"

"What? Oh, yes, of course." Eliza realized she'd been so caught up with remembering her school days—and George Ledbetter—that she'd not noticed they'd arrived at the church hall. Mrs. Walker was already seated at the piano, and most of the women were assembled.

Hattie McKay was over in one corner, gossiping with Minnie. The years hadn't changed Hattie. From a skinny, sharp-tongued girl, she'd become a spare and strident woman who still acted like she was better than everyone else.

Eliza took her place at the front of the group and nodded at Mrs. Walker to begin the warmup. Starting on an A before middle C, Eliza sang "Mee, Mo, May." The women repeated the phrase back to her. Then, to Mrs. Walker's accompaniment, they slowly progressed up the scale. By the time they reached a high F, several of the voices had trailed off, leaving Eliza and Lottie to carry the final notes.

Was it her imagination, or did the women sound more unified? Hattie had managed the high C without her voice cracking, and Minnie's tone was round and full at the high E. Doris's voice was mellowing, and Josie's volume was improving.

Mrs. Walker struck a low chord again, and Eliza sang "Mee, Mo, MAH." The women sang two bars, and then Eliza gestured for them to stop.

"Try that again," she said. "Let the AH expand." She demonstrated, opening her mouth wide and letting the sound come from the back of her throat. "AHHHHH."

The women nodded and started again. To Eliza's delight, a full, rich sound filled the hall, each voice blending as one. She glanced over at Mrs. Walker. A small smile played across the woman's usually dour face.

Maybe there was still hope for them.

Chapter 20

London

Ruth

Ruth raised her gloved hand and knocked firmly on her Uncle Edward's front door. He'd helped her once before; surely, he'd do so again.

"My condolences," he murmured once she was seated in his over-furnished parlor. "What James did was…unfortunate."

"Is that what you call it?" Ruth didn't bother keeping the anger from her voice. If it hadn't been for Edward, she'd have never even met James, never mind married him.

"He was always an impulsive man."

"Yes, well, not anymore." Ruth held fast to the anger. It was all that had sustained her during the week since she'd left the theater. Day by excruciating day, she watched her life fall apart.

"You will have already heard that I'm no longer at the Palladia."

"I did. Mr. Johnson is a pragmatist. I never liked him."

"It was you who introduced me to him."

"That was a long time ago. Much has changed."

Ruth had rarely seen her uncle in recent years. When she'd first married James, Edward had been a constant fixture in their lives. They'd often dined together, and she had much to thank him for.

"I'm not ready to stop performing," she said.

"Maybe not, but while you *are* talented, your charms will soon fade." He chuckled ruefully. "I know a little something about *that.*"

As always, Edward was stylishly dressed with a fresh flower in his lapel and thick hair perfectly waved. But Ruth noticed strands of gray in his hair and fine lines furrowing his brow. He'd be close to fifty now, and three decades of living well were taking their toll.

"I've only just turned thirty," Ruth said.

"Which means your ingenue roles will soon end. I suspect Mr. Johnson has decided to, what is the vulgar expression? *Cut his losses?*"

"What can I do?" Ruth asked. "James left considerable debts."

"Hardly surprising. He had expensive tastes."

"The house must be sold, and the servants dismissed."

"That sounds like a sensible solution." Edward studied his hands, his expression unreadable. Ruth felt as if she was standing on an empty stage singing her heart out to an empty auditorium. Her uncle was her only living relative, and yet he was acting like they were little better than strangers.

"Before he died, James told me that his agent—a Mr. Braithwaite?—would find me lodgings," Ruth said, keeping a tremor from her voice. "He was planning to go to Paris with his lover. Did you know that?"

Edward flinched, then recovered himself and looked up at her. "As I said, James was an impulsive man with a heart too easily bruised."

"There's no money left. If you won't help me, I'll be thrown into the streets within the month."

"I doubt your situation is quite so dramatic, my dear."

Ruth's breath caught. She straightened her back. "I assure you it is. I have no money and no way to earn a living. I've gone to a dozen theaters, and none of them will take me on." Despite herself, her lips quivered. She blinked to force back the tears.

"You could leave London," Edward said. "The provincial theaters are not so particular. They'll be happy to have you."

"My life is here."

Edward said nothing for several long moments. He shifted his gaze to the fire, his shoulders softening. He blinked rapidly, and for a moment, Ruth saw a spasm of pain ripple across his face. She wanted to remind him how he'd taken her in and helped launch her career, how she'd never have come to London if it hadn't been for his letter.

When she'd first met Edward, she'd expected to see a man long past his prime, but the man who had looked up at her from an overstuffed armchair couldn't have been older than thirty-five. He'd told her the sordid truth about her father—how he'd seduced her mother and left her high and dry when she was carrying Ruth.

"Do you remember telling me about my father?" Ruth asked.

"Of course."

"You told me that he'd known about my birth and had even gone to my mother and offered his assistance."

"Yes, and she'd sent him packing. Your mother was a headstrong woman."

"She could be." Ruth paused, blocking out the memories of the bruises, the broken arm, the protestations that all was well with Kingwell, and that they should be grateful he'd given them a roof over their heads.

"He should have married her."

"Yes, well, the less said about those days, the better."

Ruth's chest tightened at the memory of her mother scrubbing floors, knees rubbed raw, hands bleeding with chilblains in the winter.

"My brother made amends, don't you think?" Edward asked. "Thanks to the money he left, you had a good education at that Academy, did you not?"

"It was sufficient," she said stiffly. The Briarstown Ladies' Academy had been a gloomy old pile filled with snobby girls and sour-faced teachers. Ruth had hated being pulled out of the mill school and away from Eliza to spend her days with girls who looked down their noses at her. The only good to come out of her five years at the Academy was a posh accent and excellent musical training.

Ruth stood abruptly. At eighteen, she'd been eager for the future Edward had dangled before her. She'd worked so hard at the voice lessons he paid for that within two years, she was good enough to join the chorus at the Palladia Theatre. Four years later, she was married to James and on her way to becoming a star.

If her uncle refused to help her again, then she'd not stay to be further humiliated. Edward had obviously decided that he owed her nothing.

"I won't trouble you further," she said.

Edward rose as well. "I'm sorry, Ruth. Truly. But James hurt me as well."

Ruth turned to go and then paused and turned back. "I know you loved him," she said, a pang of sympathy softening her voice. She'd rarely allowed herself to dwell on why Edward had arranged for her to marry James. When, a few years later, Edward had disappeared from their lives, she'd been so preoccupied with herself and her career that she'd asked no questions, nor made any attempt to contact him herself.

"I did," he said.

"I'm also sorry that James hurt you," she said, keeping her voice steady. "But obviously, I shouldn't have troubled you." She started for the door.

"Wait."

"Yes?" Ruth didn't turn around for fear he'd see the desperation on her face.

"I have an idea for something that may suit you. I'm not sure you'll like it, but the pay is adequate, and you can employ your skills to good effect. It's also respectable, which I suppose would please my late brother."

Chapter 21

Briarstown

Eliza

Although Eliza was relieved the choir was making progress, she knew they'd soon need a proper conductor. She was the only one with a voice strong enough to take the soprano solo, and she couldn't sing and conduct at the same time. Most of the women were keen, but Eliza suspected they cared more about getting away from the crushing routines of their daily lives than winning a competition.

For them, the choir was little more than a lark.

"What's this I hear about you singing again?" Reg asked one evening as he flopped into bed. Bessie was asleep in her cot at the foot of the bed, and the four eldest girls were settled in the attic room.

Eliza's heart froze. She'd been fooling herself thinking that in the cramped courts and streets of their world, Reg wouldn't find out about the choir. Most of the husbands worked with Reg at the mill, as did Minnie and Lottie.

She kept her voice light. "Some of the women have gotten together to form a choir, and they asked me to join. I couldn't think of any reason not to. You remember how I used to love singing."

"I remember how you liked making a spectacle of yourself." To Eliza's relief, Reg folded his hands across his chest and stared up at the ceiling. He didn't sound angry—not yet.

"You used to say I had a beautiful voice. Remember when I sang with the choral society?"

"Aye, and I wasn't sorry you stopped."

"I didn't have much choice," she said, although quietly so as not to provoke him.

"Folks are sayin' there's to be some sort of competition in Whitby," Reg continued as if she hadn't spoken. "What makes you think you can traipse all the way out there? Who's goin' to watch out for the girls?"

"Annie's perfectly capable of staying home with them. And she has Lily May to help. Gladys and Emily won't give them any trouble and even our Bessie doesn't need looking out for so long as she has her sisters close by."

"I don't like it."

"There's no harm in it."

"I don't want you singing."

"Hattie McKay's in the choir," Eliza began. She pushed her hands under the blanket and clasped them together to keep them from shaking. "Doris Blair too. Don't their men work with you?"

"Aye," Reg conceded. "They're good blokes."

Eliza needed to tread carefully. With Reg, she'd learned that stating the obvious and letting him believe he'd made the decision usually worked so long as he was sober, which fortunately he was. That evening, he'd come straight home from the mill and spent the hours before bed dozing by the fire.

"Hattie's real keen," Eliza continued. "Getting the choir together was her idea."

"I thought you didn't get on with her."

"That was years ago when we were girls. Hattie's all right. Seeing as it was her who asked me special, do you think it right for me to drop out?"

Reg yawned and stretched his arms above his head. Although stocky, he was still straight-backed and lean, unlike many of the men who had worked in the mills since they were children. He stroked his moustache—an impressive growth he maintained with meticulous care.

"I suppose it wouldn't do to get on the outs with Andy McKay. When I was foreman, he was one of my best workers. I'll ask for him soon as Mr. Lewiston gives me back my job."

"Is he considering it?" Eliza asked. "It's about time he saw sense." She thanked God for the change of topic. Get Reg harping on about his grievance with Mr. Lewiston and he'd quickly forget any objections to her singing.

"Aye, we agree there." He patted her shoulder. "Put out the candle, lass."

When she reached the church hall the next afternoon for the Saturday rehearsal, Eliza was surprised to see all the women clustered around the piano. Normally, they stayed as far away from Felicity Walker as possible. The pianist might have said good things about the choir to Martha's mother, but during rehearsal, she almost never cracked a smile. All the women, except Eliza, were afraid of her.

A well-dressed woman wearing a hat adorned with a single feather stepped forward.

"Miss Donahue?" Eliza said. "What are you doing here?"

"Good afternoon, Eliza. I've changed my mind about conducting the choir. I spoke with Mother, and she agrees it's something I should do."

"Oh! Well, that's wonderful," Eliza said. She looked around at the other women. They were all smiling, even Hattie McKay. A heavy weight lifted from Eliza's shoulders. With Miss Donahue conducting the choir, and Reg not getting in her way, her Plan sprang back to life.

"Shall we begin?" Miss Donahue said. She positioned herself next to the piano and motioned to the women to gather in front of her.

"Sopranos on the left, second sopranos in the middle, and altos to the right," she instructed.

Eliza slipped between Minnie and Hattie, the only other women with voices almost capable of reaching the highest notes.

"Thank you," Miss Donahue said. "I'm honored that you're willing to put your faith in me." She nodded toward Eliza. "But first, I believe a round of applause is in order for Mrs. Kingwell."

Eliza blushed and looked down at the floor as all the women clapped— even Hattie and Doris. The first time she'd heard applause directed at her was the first time she'd sung in public at the Christmas bazaar when she was eleven. She'd never forget the muffled sound made by the hundreds of gloved hands of the posh ladies and gentlemen clapping for her. Some of the gentlemen had even called out *Brava*, whatever that meant.

Ruth had been there—smiling broadly, her soft cheeks pink with excitement and pride in her friend. Eliza remembered thinking that for the first time in her life that she might have something special to contribute to the world.

Eliza looked up at the women clustered around her. "Thanks," she mumbled, and then smiled. Maybe she still had something special.

"Now, let us begin with our warmup," Miss Donahue said. She raised both hands. "When you're ready, Mrs. Walker."

Eliza fixed her eyes on Miss Donahue and let her mind go blank to everything but the music.

"Za, Za, Za, Za, Za," Miss Donahue sang in a five-note pattern up and down. She paused and motioned for the choir to repeat the notes. Her expression was inscrutable as Mrs. Walker played progressively higher notes until only Eliza's voice achieved the required pitch without cracking.

"Ze, Ze, Ze, Ze, Ze," Miss Donahue sang, starting again at the lower notes.

Up the scale they went, and then with Zi, Zo, and Zu followed by more consonant-vowel combinations, and then arpeggios, intervals, and nonsense songs. Eliza's chest expanded with pride as she sang. The women were comporting themselves beautifully. To be sure, there was room for improvement, but Miss Donahue couldn't fault their enthusiasm.

They then sang the Mendelssohn set piece. Most of the women knew the words and had some grasp of the melody, although their timing left something to be desired. Eliza took the soprano solo, while Minnie did her best with the contralto.

"Thank you, ladies," Mrs. Donahue said after she signalled an end to the last note. "That was, ah, commendable. Shall we do it again? And this time, please keep your eyes on me, so we're all singing in unison. Ready?"

After the rehearsal, Eliza hung back, waiting until all the women and Mrs. Walker left the hall.

"Well?" she asked.

"It's difficult to say after only one rehearsal," Miss Donahue said.

"Can we be ready for the competition in May?"

"To be honest, I'm not sure. So much depends on how important the competition is to the other women. I can see it's important to *you*, Eliza, but it seems like more of an excuse to get out of the house for the others."

"What can we do to get better?"

"First of all, you need more voices."

"The competition is for female choirs from eight to twenty voices. We have eight."

"Yes, but the chances of winning any competition with eight voices, particularly if the other choirs are larger, are slim," Miss Donahue said. "Eight voices, even eight strong voices, can't get the depth of sound that a dozen or more voices can."

"The women of Briarstown don't need to take a back seat to anyone," Eliza said, smiling. "Do you remember?"

"Oh, yes. I remember it well. The *children* of Briarstown—I used to say that to motivate them."

"And it worked, didn't it? They won every trophy going."

"They did indeed. I'm sure even today there's a teacher somewhere in Yorkshire telling her students to follow the example of the Briarstown children."

"After all this time?"

"Perhaps not, but it's nice to think it, don't you agree? And it's true our little mill school choir turned a few heads for a year or two."

"That they did." Eliza's own smile faded, the pain of being left out still rankling even after seventeen years. Eliza had been long gone from the school by the time the children's choir was entering and winning competitions. "I'll find more women," she said. "Will another eight be enough?"

"If you can do that, and they can carry a tune, then you might have a chance," said Miss Donahue. "The competition at these festivals gets fiercer every year."

"I'll do my best."

"I know you will."

Chapter 22

London

Ruth

Ruth stood on the steps of the house she'd shared with James for all six years of their marriage. She'd come to him when still a chorus girl at the Palladia—full of dreams and convinced she was in love. As she watched the last of the furniture being carried out, she reflected that her life had been a series of letdowns by the people she'd loved.

Mother. Eliza. James.

"Ma'am?" Constance joined Ruth. She was dressed in her coat and hat and carried a large carpetbag. "Do you have somewhere to go?" she asked.

Ruth was surprised to hear the concern in her housekeeper's voice. "Yes, thank you, Constance. That's good of you to ask."

"It's a rough go you've had," she said. "I'm sorry for it."

"I appreciate that. Is your new situation to your liking?" Ruth was at least able to congratulate herself on finding places for all the servants. None of them would be turned into the streets.

"Yes, Ma'am."

"Then, I suppose this is goodbye." Ruth held out her hand. "James always thought highly of you, Constance. You served this family well."

"May I say something, Ma'am?" Constance asked, ignoring Ruth's outstretched hand.

"Of course."

"I'm sorry if I sometimes weren't as respectful of you as I should have been. I served the master's mother, you see. She was a difficult woman who never understood the master. She wanted him to marry someone in Society."

"I'm well aware of *that*," Ruth said. "It's perhaps just as well she died before she met me." She fixed her gaze on the hard angles of a face that had always reminded her of a chipped anvil. "I don't blame you for your loyalty, Constance. You were with James's mother much longer than you were with me."

"Since I was twelve." Constance sucked in her breath, her expression softening. "But I think she was wrong, Ma'am. You've had to put up with a great deal."

"That's kind of you to say."

"And begging your pardon for speaking out of turn," Constance continued, "but, if you ask me, you're going to do all right. You're made of sterner stuff than I gave you credit for at first, and I'm not ashamed to admit it." She bobbed a curtsy. "Goodbye, Ma'am, and God bless."

Before Ruth had a chance to reply, Constance pushed through the wrought-iron gate and started down the street.

In a few more hours, the house would be empty of all its furniture, leaving only Ruth's trunk packed with three of her most serviceable dresses, some linens, and a few hats. The hansom cab would then arrive to transport her and the trunk to the station, and from there, she'd catch a train back to the North.

Most of the time, Ruth never thought about what she'd left behind in Briarstown. The past belonged in the past and had no role to play in the brilliant London career she'd forged for herself. But as she stood on the steps of her former home and contemplated the weeks and months to come, she wondered what Mother would have said if she could see Ruth now.

Mother had believed that Reg Kingwell was their savior, and it was true he'd saved them from the workhouse. But no matter how hard her mother had worked to keep the house clean and cook the meals, she couldn't save herself from Reg's fists.

Sighing, Ruth returned to her empty house. A new life awaited her, and it was up to her to save herself.

Chapter 23

Briarstown

Eliza

"Where on Earth are we going to find another eight women?"

"And good morning to you too, Hannah," Eliza said, smiling up at her friend. Hannah never wasted words. It was one of the things that Eliza appreciated most about her.

"How did you hear? I haven't told the others yet."

"My Cliff sometimes helps out over at the vicarage, bringing in the coal and such. He told me that he got to talking with Miss Donahue about the choir, and that she told *him* we needed more voices."

"Miss Donahue's right, and I guess it makes sense," Eliza said.

Hannah fell in step next to her. "You off to the shops? I'll walk with ye. It's awful nippy out today."

"Aye." Eliza didn't want to be rude, but cheerful Hannah was the last person she felt like seeing as she mulled over the question of where to find eight more singers. Hannah meant well, but she wasn't likely to know anyone suitable.

They stopped in the middle of a bridge spanning the canal and watched a barge loaded with cotton bales slide beneath. The water looked almost solid, the smell rank.

"Have you found anyone yet?" Hannah asked.

"No," Eliza admitted. She turned her back on the canal, pushing memories of a similarly raw day almost twenty years earlier into the darkest recesses of her mind. "But we have to try."

"Some of the lasses over at Elmbridge Mill used to sing together."

"Used to?"

"They sang in pubs a few times, but I don't think they ever went to a competition."

"That's excellent news, Hannah!" Eliza exclaimed. "Maybe we can convince some of them to join us. Do you know anyone who works at Elmbridge's?"

"My cousin's in the carding room. I'll ask her. And I could talk to George."

"George?"

"George Ledbetter? He left our mill getting on, oh, twelve year ago now, not long after my accident? He went over to Elmbridge's. Weren't he sweet on you back when we was young? I remember him helping you move when you and your ma had to go live with your aunt."

"I don't remember," Eliza said shortly.

She turned away from Hannah and fixed her gaze on the chimney of the nearby mill. Every detail of that day was clearly etched in her mind— the humiliation, her mother complaining, the rain drenching their meagre belongings as George loaded them into his cart.

"So, you've kept up with him? George?" Eliza asked, staring straight ahead and hoping her voice sounded casual.

"He lived with us for a few years after his parents died. He were always kind to me. Likely he's a foreman by now so he should know plenty of women, maybe even some as sang in the choir. Why don't me and you go see him come Saturday?"

"What, waltz over and ask if he knows of any lasses who might want to sing with us?"

"Why not?" Hannah asked, practical as always. "We've nowt to lose, and even if you say you don't remember much about George Ledbetter, I'll wager he remembers you well. You know, he's never wed."

"That's nowt to do with me," Eliza said sharply. As a matter of fact, Eliza did know that George Ledbetter had never married. But that past was as dead as the black water of the canal.

"That's as maybe," Hannah said. "On Saturday, we can go over to his house before choir practice. He lives out on the edge of town."

"Fine," Eliza said. "As you say, what've we got to lose?"

Years ago, Eliza had vowed to leave George Ledbetter firmly in the past, and for many years, he'd stayed there.

Even so, as Eliza made her way home through the December dusk, she let herself think about the first time she'd seen George as anything other than a pleasant enough fellow who worked at the mill. Big and gangly, but also quiet and unassuming, George was Reg's opposite. People rarely paid attention to him, not like they did Reg, who was everyone's best friend until they got to know him.

Eliza had just endured her first disastrous rehearsal with the Briarstown Choral Society during which Mr. Skinner, the conductor, had humiliated her. She could still hear the contempt in his voice.

"Miss Treleven? You're a bar behind. Please endeavor to keep up." His tone reminded Eliza of Mr. Lewiston, the mill boss. Why did these posh men think they could talk to her like she didn't have the wits of a fly?

She'd emerged from the rehearsal feeling defeated when she heard a man call her name.

"Eliza Treleven! What are you doing in this part of town?"

Eliza turned to see George Ledbetter coming towards her, smiling broadly.

"I'm on my way home," she said. Perhaps if she didn't answer his question, he'd take the hint and move on. She was in no mood for small talk.

"Can I walk with you? I saw you coming out of the hall. What was you doing there?"

Eliza sighed. She supposed everyone would hear about her singing with the choir soon enough, that is, if she managed to survive another rehearsal.

"I've been accepted into the choir."

"The Briarstown Choral Society?" George whistled. "Impressive!"

"Why?" Eliza didn't care that she sounded hostile. Even mild-mannered George seemed to think she didn't belong.

"I meant *you* are impressive. There's not many as gets into one of the Society choirs. My sister tried a few years back, but she got turned down."

"She did?"

"Oh, aye. My sister—name's Florence? She's got a beautiful voice, she does, and even though she's not posh like most of 'em in the Society, she decided to audition. But they sent her packing. So, what I'm saying is good for you, getting taken on, like. Happen they think you're something special." He grinned. "And they'd not be wrong."

"Oh, well, thank you." Eliza didn't know where to look. No one in Eliza's life ever complimented her. Even Reg Kingwell never said anything nice about how she looked or what she did. He mostly talked about himself when they were together.

"So, I've been wondering," George was saying. "I mean to say, I know you're walking out with Reg Kingwell and all…"

"How do you know that?" Eliza asked sharply.

"Everyone knows," George said, surprised. "Kingwell's made no secret of his interest in ye when he's talking to the lads at the mill. But I don't mean to speak out of turn."

Eliza didn't know what to say, so she said nothing.

"Anyways, I'm wonderin' if you'd like to, maybe, you know, go walkin' out to the country with me come Sunday. The weather's supposed to keep fine. I thought seein' as it's been so sunny and that, you might fancy a turn on to the moors for a bit. I goes up there every chance I get."

"You do?"

"'Course. After spending all week inside t'mill, I can't wait to breathe some fresh air."

Eliza smiled. "I've only ever seen the moors from the towpath."

"We must fix that, then! How about I call for ye mid-morning come Sunday? After Church if ye're goin'? We could make a day of it? That is, if you'd like. Or are you spending the day with Kingwell? I don't want to step on no-one's toes if you're already spoken for."

"No, no, nothing like that. Mr. Kingwell and I are not that well acquainted."

Eliza wasn't sure why she said that. They certainly were well acquainted, but it wasn't as if he'd proposed to her. She thought about spending a breezy Sunday afternoon striding across the moors with affable George by her side. He was looking at her with such hope. Where Reg reminded her of a panther—sleek and with a coiled energy that threw her off kilter— lanky George Ledbetter was more like a slightly bemused giraffe. She'd seen one a few years back when a menagerie had come to the town, and she'd gone with Dad. The impossibly tall animal had peered down at the gaping people with huge brown eyes. George's eyes were also brown and shone with soft kindness.

"So, you'll come?"

"Yes," Eliza said. "I'd love to." She smiled up at George. "And thank you for asking me."

"Thank *you!* Well, here we are at yours already. Thanks for letting me walk with you."

"Ledbetter?"

At the sound of Reg's voice, Eliza stopped, surprised to feel her heart pounding, like she'd been caught doing something wrong. She turned to see him striding across the street towards them. He stopped in front of George. "What're *you* doin' 'ere?"

"Taking a walk," George said mildly. "It's a fine day."

"You'd best be getting on home," Reg said, glancing at Eliza and then back up at George. He didn't say anything more, but his meaning was clear enough, and George appeared to understand.

"Aye, Kingwell. I'm on my way." He touched his cap with two fingers. "Afternoon, Eliza."

"What did *he* want?" Reg asked as soon as George walked away.

"Nothing. He was walking my way, and I stopped to say hello. I've known him since we were in school together."

"I don't like you talking with him."

"I can talk to whoever I want," Eliza said.

Reg stared down at her, his eyes narrowed. For a moment, she felt as if a brisk wind had blown a black cloud across the sun. She shivered.

"Happen I got a bit of time," he said. "Fancy a walk?

Before she could think of what to say, he took her arm and steered her toward the canal. His grip was harder than she expected—not painful exactly, but also with a strength that made it impossible for her to pull away without hurting herself.

On Saturday, Eliza spent a few extra minutes smoothing her hair and brushing every speck of mud from her skirts before setting off with Hannah to a detached cottage far enough away from the mills to seem remote. Eliza wondered if the long walk that George would have to make every morning and night to and from the mill was worth the isolation. After a few minutes of gazing out at the wild expanse of moorland spreading to the horizon from George's doorstep, she realized that any amount of walking would be worth it to live in such a place.

"Eliza Treleven!" George's wide smile tripped something in Eliza's heart. Reg never smiled at her like that. "Ah, sorry. Mrs. Kingwell, I should say. Come in out o' the wind! And Mrs. Shipley too! I'm a lucky man today."

He ushered them straight into the main living area of the small house, where a fire burned in the grate. "Excuse the mess. A bachelor's house. I have a girl come in once a week, but she's not been these five days." George bustled around the room, picking up a half-full teacup and a plate of toast crumbs. "Please. Sit down. Can I get you tea?"

"We don't want to put you out, Mr. Ledbetter," Eliza said. "We won't take up much of your time."

"Mr. Ledbetter, is it? You used to call me George! And with today being my half day, I've got nowt but time."

"We'll have tea, then," Eliza said. "Thank you."

He flashed her another broad smile. "I'll 'ave it ready in no time." He put the kettle on the grate and then laid out cups that needed a good wipe. With an effort, Eliza restrained herself from reaching for the cloth on the sideboard.

When the tea was made and poured, George sat opposite the two women and listened intently as Hannah told him about their choir and how they needed more women who could sing. He hadn't changed much, Eliza reflected as she watched him cross and uncross his long legs and wrap thin fingers around his cup. He'd still never win any prizes for his looks.

"That sounds like a fine project for you women," George said. "Happens I do know some lasses who might be interested in joining you."

"How many?" Hannah asked.

"Oh, well, let me think."

Eliza almost laughed out loud as she watched George carefully put down his cup and place one fist under his chin. He frowned, looking all the world like a little boy. A softness bloomed in her chest.

"We're hoping to find another eight women," Hannah said.

"Aye." George relaxed his fist. "Eight? Well then, I'd say start with Mary Denholm. She'll know who else would want to join. She lives over on Spring Road, number three, back of four? You call on her and tell her George sent you. She's a character is Mary, but she'll help you out. A few years back, she lived in Manchester, where it's said she sang in one of them big city choirs with men and all."

Eliza imagined he rested his gaze a little longer on her than he should, but that was nonsense. And even if he had, what could be done about it? A woman with five children from another man? Impossible!

"Ta, George," Hannah said. "You're a lifesaver."

"Ah, well, I wouldn't go that far," he said. "I reckon you ladies would have found a solution without me." He looked again at Eliza, and this time there was no mistaking his admiration. "But I'm glad you stopped by. It's a right treat to take tea with old friends."

For a split second, Eliza let her eyes meet his. Her stomach flip-flopped as she imagined his hands gently stroking her body. He'd go slowly with her, not climb on top of her like she was little better than a hobby horse to be ridden and discarded. She turned away quickly, her cheeks flaming.

Later, in the bustle of leaving, George briefly placed one hand on the small of her back to usher her to the door. She stiffened her spine and didn't turn around to acknowledge his goodbye. The past was the past, and she was a fool to wish for anything different.

"That went well," Hannah said as they walked back towards Briarstown. "George hasn't changed a bit, has he?"

"I wouldn't know."

"I guess he never had a chance with you once Reg Kingwell started comin' around. You got married soon after your dad passed, didn't you?"

"You've a good memory," Eliza said. She wished sometimes she could go through life like big-hearted, generous Hannah who had known her share of tragedy and yet never showed it. Everyone knew *her* husband doted on her.

As they walked back to the town, Eliza noticed Hannah starting to limp.

"Is your leg bothering you?" she asked sympathetically.

"It does sometimes if I walk too far in a day." Hannah grinned. "But I mustn't complain. I'd not be walkin' or doing anythin' else if it weren't for what you done."

"Ah, well," Eliza said, pleased that Hannah hadn't forgotten. "Someone was bound to have come along."

"By then it would have been too late."

In her nightmares, Eliza sometimes still heard Hannah's screams. It was the day after Eliza's seventeenth birthday, and she and Hannah were working at the mill in one of the rooms on the second floor that contained three scribblers and three condensers.

From a hole in the center of the small room protruded an upright shaft enclosed in a tin casing, save for an opening at the bottom that allowed for oiling. Hannah caught her skirt in the space between the rim of the opening and the rotating shaft. Within seconds, she was swept off her feet, her head banging back against the shaft, her arms flailing. The inexorable rotation of the shaft swung her around the room, her heels skidding against the oiled floorboards, the terror in her eyes boring into Eliza like hot pokers.

Hannah clasped her hands to her pregnant belly in a futile attempt to protect the life growing inside her as her head jerked back, leaving a smear of red against the tin casing.

Eliza leapt forward and wrapped her arm around Hannah's thick waist. She pulled, digging her heels into the floor, grunting with effort, but nothing budged. She was forced to let go, scuttling back as Hannah whipped around for another revolution.

And then from somewhere deep within her came the certainty that she had the strength to save Hannah. She lunged forward again and gripped the material trapped in the rotating shaft and with every muscle screaming pulled.

"I'll never know how you got the strength to get me free," Hannah said as she linked her arm through Eliza's and leaned against her to take some weight off her leg.

"I don't know either," Eliza said. She doubted she'd ever forget the sound of tearing fabric and the relief that had washed over her when Hannah, her face dead white and her arms still cradling her pregnant belly, fell back into Eliza's arms.

"Them were hard days, to be sure," Hannah said. "But ain't we blessed to be grown now and singin' together of all things?"

"Yes," Eliza said. "I suppose we are."

At least the singing part, she thought to herself.

The second Eliza laid eyes on Mary Denholm, she realized she'd met her match and then some.

"George Ledbetter sent ye? Lovely man. Bit peculiar, mind. Living alone in a cottage like he does."

Tall, lean, and loud. Those were the three words that popped into Eliza's head as she was led into an immaculate sitting room. Every surface groaned under the weight of china figurines, while pictures cut carefully from magazines papered the walls. The prevailing theme was sheep.

"So, y'need women for your choir. Well, you've come to the right person. I've been thinking about putting a new choir together myself with some girls from the mill, but I wasn't sure how to go about it. You say you've got a conductor?"

"Miss Adelaide Donahue," Hannah said. "She used to teach at the mill school. Most of us were in her class when we was girls."

"For a few years, she entered the children into choir competitions." Eliza said. "They won a fair number."

"Then she's got experience. Good. I can't work with them as don't know what they're doin'."

"Miss Donahue knows what's she's doing," Eliza said stiffly. *Who did this Mary Denholm think she was?*

"Good to know. So, how many girls did you say you needed?"

"At least eight."

"Competing in the Whitby festival, are ye?"

"Yes. How did you know?"

"Let's say I have my ways." Mary laughed out loud. "Don't look so surprised. Briarstown's not Manchester. Word travels. I've known about your choir for some weeks now, and I'm glad to help. When d'you practice?"

"Tuesday night at half seven and for two hours on Saturday afternoons."

"Sounds like you're serious."

"We are."

"I'll come Tuesday with six girls. With me, that makes seven, which should be enough to fill out your sound, and give you a fighting chance of winning the competition. Stranger things have happened, eh?"

Chapter 24

Manchester

Ruth

Ruth settled into the train compartment for the five-hour journey from London to Manchester. Thankfully, the compartment was empty, saving her the humiliation of weeping in front of strangers. Edward had used his connections to find her a position as an adjudicator of music competitions. It was a far cry from starring on the London stage, but at least it was respectable, and the salary included most expenses.

Ruth dreaded the prospect of sitting for hours in drafty halls listening to amateurs sing set pieces. Most of the competitors would likely be abysmal. But what choice did she have?

"We expect you to maintain the highest of standards," Mr. Gordon from the Music Association had said while interviewing her for the position of festival adjudicator. He looked like a dyspeptic stork—long-necked with skin the color of congealed paste. When he shook her hand, Ruth needed every ounce of willpower not to wipe her fingers on her skirt.

"The music competition movement currently sweeping our great nation is attracting entrants from every county and from all walks of life," Mr. Gordon intoned. "You'll interact with choirs at every level—village choirs, amateur groups of mill hands, semi-professional choirs from the big cities and, of course, a fair number of church and cathedral choirs."

Mr. Gordon then asked Ruth a series of demeaning questions that made it clear he didn't consider her career on the London stage an asset. Obviously, she lacked experience with traditional repertoire. The songs she sang on stage were so far beneath his contempt that he barely acknowledged them as music.

The day after her interview, she received a letter.

Dear Mrs. Henton,

Thank you for speaking with me yesterday about your willingness to offer your talents to become part of the adjudication team for the music competitions sponsored by the Music Association. As we discussed, the classical repertoire we require of our competitors encompasses a broad and serious range of classical styles in keeping with our commitment to bringing excellent musical offerings to people in all walks of life across our fair country. Maintaining our superior standards is, of course, our very first priority.

That said, the opening we currently have for a junior adjudicator has not yet been filled. Your esteemed uncle was recently introduced to me and spoke highly of your talents and your readiness to work hard. I do hope this is true.

As a favor to your uncle, we are prepared to offer you the position on a six-month trial basis. You will be paid a stipend for expenses in addition to your salary and expected to stay in modest lodgings and to travel second class.

Please be so kind as to reply to the sender at your earliest convenience to indicate your acceptance of this offer.

I remain, yours respectfully,
Stanley L. Gordon

Ruth had to laugh at the contents of the letter, which she needed to read twice before realizing she'd been given the job.

In Manchester, she was to attend a short training course before going farther north to co-adjudicate the singing competition at the Blackpool Music Festival. After that, she was scheduled to preside at competitions in Leeds, Scarborough, and Whitby.

Ruth spent the journey staring out at the passing countryside, brown and brooding under a light blue February sky. As they neared Manchester, dreary tenements replaced hedgerows, and dung-colored clouds crowded the sky.

A young man with a shock of curly hair the color of new pennies met her at the station.

"Mrs. Henton?" He grabbed hold of her hand and shook it vigorously.

Instinctively, Ruth reared back, snatching her hand from his grasp so quickly that he was left holding air.

"Oh!" he exclaimed, his expression stricken. "Forgive me. I didn't mean…"

"No, no," Ruth said, recovering herself and holding her hand out again. "I was merely startled." She nodded at her hand. "Please."

He looked down at her outstretched hand as if it was a rare and exotic flower. Carefully, he touched palms and then drew back quickly. "Delighted," he said, his exuberance subdued. "I'm Silas Gallagher? You've been assigned to me."

"Thank you for meeting me."

"Of course!" He blushed a deep red that clashed with his hair like a lurid sunset. "I'm so sorry if I offended you."

"No offense at all," Ruth said, amused despite herself.

"If I may say so, you're even more beautiful up close."

"Have we met?"

"Oh no! No!" He laughed, showing a mouthful of large teeth. He wore spectacles and towered a good ten inches above her. "I would never presume…Oh no!" He squirmed with embarrassment. "Dear me, I'm making a thorough botch-up, aren't? Ever since I found out I was assigned to you, I've barely slept I've been so excited to meet you."

"I don't understand."

"I've seen you perform. In London? You were marvelous!"

"That's kind of you." Ruth bit back a sigh. Just what she needed— another fawning sycophant like the boys in the stalls who stared at her like lovesick puppies. She should never have left London. "Will you help me with my trunk?" she asked. "I believe the porter has unloaded it already."

"Oh yes! Of course! Yes! This way!"

Ruth followed him off the platform and waited while he paid the porter, who loaded her trunk into a small cab outside the station.

Her first impression of Manchester was of dirt and noise and smoke. She was used to the clamor of London, but there was something even more aggressive about England's second largest city. A light rain started falling, and she shivered in her light coat.

"We'll go straight to the presentation," Silas said as he handed her into the cab. "I hope that's all right? It's being put on at the Town Hall, and Miss Wakefield is speaking. Of course, you *definitely* don't want to miss her! Afterwards, I'll take you to your lodgings. You'll be very comfortable there, I think. Mrs. Patterson runs the place, and she's been hosting Music Association folks for years."

"Thank you." The headache that had started halfway through the journey intensified in the wake of Silas's constant chatter. He seemed incapable of saying one thing when he could say three.

In the cab, he settled himself across from her and grinned. "You're in luck."

"Why?"

"Miss Wakefield rarely has time to come speak with the new adjudicators. She's a legend is Miss Wakefield." He waited expectantly. "You've heard of her, of course?"

"I have not."

"Ah, well, you're new to this, of course."

If he said 'of course' one more time, she was going to strangle him.

"As you already know," she managed to say. "I was recently performing in London."

"Yes!" he said ecstatically. "I've seen you as Yum Yum, of course, and before that in *Pirates of Penzance*, and you were a *superb* Josephine in *HMS Pinafore*. I know it's not the thing among festival adjudicators to admit, but I *love* Gilbert and Sullivan."

"We agree on that score at least," Ruth said, thawing slightly. Mr. Gordon's dismissal of her musical background still rankled. He appeared to think that anyone who sang anything written after 1835 was a musical heretic. He'd quizzed her for a good five minutes about the Handel repertoire until finally giving up when she had to admit she was only familiar with *The Messiah*. The look he'd given her would have frozen a falcon in mid-flight.

"Who is this Miss Wakefield?" Ruth asked. "I gather she has something to do with music competitions?"

"Something to do with them? My word, yes. She practically *invented* the festival movement ten years ago way up in the Lake District. Oh look! We're here. I'll let her tell her own story."

Silas scrambled out of the cab and then took Ruth's hand to help her descend. He had the firm, long-fingered grip of a musician.

She glanced down. "Do you play an instrument?"

"Clarinet and piano," he said, grinning again. "And I sing, of course. Or more precisely, sang. But choral music is my passion, so I made that my specialty. In this game, you're sometimes called upon to judge orchestras and solo instrumentalists, even brass bands on occasion, although not often, thankfully." He leaned close, and she smelled soap and starch. "I'm not a fan of brass, truth be told. Usually, if the competition includes instrumental classes, we judge pianists and violinists. Do you play?"

"Only sing," Ruth said. She paused. Mr. Gordon had said nothing about judging pianists and violinists. And brass bands? She frowned.

"Don't worry," Silas said cheerfully. "You'll get the hang of it fast enough. Music's music, eh?"

He ushered her into an imposing-looking building that he said was the Manchester Town Hall. Its pointed gables and arches reminded Ruth of the Parliament buildings in Westminster, complete with a clock tower that she learned later was the twin of Big Ben.

"Why are all the buildings so black?" she asked.

"Coal dust and smoke mostly," Silas said. "You'll see that a lot in the cities in the North. This way." They crossed a large foyer and entered a room on the ground floor where several dozen young men and women were already seated facing a platform. Most of the women were dressed in plain skirts and shirtwaists. Ruth suddenly felt self-conscious in her flower-trimmed hat and her dress with its fashionably wide sleeves.

"Here's two spots at the front," Silas said. "Come on."

They took their seats as a smattering of applause ushered a man on stage, followed by a sturdy-looking woman in her mid-forties. She had a no-nonsense air about her that Ruth found appealing, despite her determination to endure rather than enjoy the coming days and weeks. *And months*, she thought ruefully. Who knew how long she'd have to toil in drafty rehearsal halls before an opportunity presented itself for her to return to the stage?

Chapter 25

Briarstown

Eliza

With a chorus of goodbyes and good-humored jostling, all the women except Eliza left the hall after the first rehearsal that included Mary Denholm and her friends.

Eliza approached Miss Donahue, who was gathering up her music, her back to the door. Her normally ramrod straight shoulders sagged, and Eliza heard a deep sigh.

"We're terrible, aren't we?" Eliza asked. "Even with the new girls?"

Miss Donahue turned, the unguarded expression on her face revealing the truth. She quickly recovered herself, but her smile was thin and unconvincing. "I wouldn't say terrible, exactly," she said.

"Can we win?"

"To be perfectly honest, I'm not sure. There's no doubt the women are willing. And you sing your solo beautifully, Eliza."

"But?"

"The set piece is extremely difficult. Even trained choirs that have sung together for years are challenged by it."

"Much less a group of working-class lasses who have only sung together for a handful of weeks," Eliza said. "Is that what you're thinking?"

"I want to help, Eliza, I really do. But we need to be realistic. We should consider this first competition as our practice run. There are plenty more competitions."

"We can't go gallivanting to competitions all over the North. Even getting to Whitby will be a challenge for most of us." Eliza tried and failed to keep the desperation from her voice. "We're a lot better than when we started. Everyone knows the words now."

"Knowing the words is good, but it's the notes that really matter."

"Please don't give up on us yet."

"I wouldn't dream of it!"

The surprise in Miss Donahue's voice reassured Eliza. Maybe she needed to be working with the choir as much as they needed her to conduct them. Everyone knew her mother was difficult. The chance to get away from her twice a week was likely as welcome for Miss Donahue as it was for the women to escape the dreary predictability of their own daily lives.

"I have a favor to ask," Eliza said quickly, before she lost her nerve. "Will you give me private coaching?"

"Why? You're the best singer in the choir."

"I've entered the solo category."

"Oh?"

"Aye." Eliza ploughed on, her voice breathless with nerves. "I've picked out my song and I've been practicing, but…" She paused. *What if Miss Donahue said no? Well, there was no going back now.* "I need your help."

"Of course I'll help you."

"You will?"

"Did you think I wouldn't? Dear me, Eliza, you must know that you have an exceptional voice. It's high time you started using it again."

"Thank you!" For a moment, Eliza considered telling Miss Donahue about her Plan to get herself and the girls away from Briarstown. But no, that would be foolish. She didn't want Miss Donahue's pity.

"You'll need to work harder than you ever have in your life," Miss Donahue warned.

"I'm no stranger to hard work." Eliza reflected that Miss Donahue meant well, but she really had no clue. She'd not last ten minutes on the mill floor.

"I believe it. And, Eliza, you *do* have a chance. Meet me here an hour early on Saturday. What song did you choose?"

"*An die Musik*?" Eliza said. "It's what I sang when I auditioned for the Briarstown Choral Society when I was sixteen. It was good enough to get me into their mixed choir so I figured I couldn't go wrong singing it again."

"I remember your doing very well with their mixed choir. For a time, you and Ruth were quite the duo."

"That was a long time ago," Eliza said shortly. "I'll see you Saturday."

On her way home, Eliza was obliged to jump out of the way of a trio of girls clattering past on bicycles. Instead of feeling irritated, she felt only envy. How wonderful to be young and pretty and free with hair escaping its pins and cheeks flushed with laughter and wind. The girls looked to be shop assistants or maybe some of the new female office workers. Either way, they were a step above mill hands. In their hiked-up wool skirts and tight bodices that showed off tiny waists, they faced lives bursting with possibilities unknown to Eliza. While many would be married within a year or two, some would go on to own their own shops or manage other girls in an office.

Eliza imagined Lily May careening past on her way home from her job in a smart shop. Annie would balance books in the bike basket as she pedaled back from a day of teaching, and Gladys would likely follow in her eldest sister's footsteps. And as for Emily and Bessie, they'd grow up to become sturdy, capable young women with jobs that gave them far more independence than Eliza could have dreamed of when she'd worked at the mill and answered to Ma.

The new century was coming, and Eliza was determined to do everything possible to make sure her girls thrived.

Chapter 26

Manchester

Ruth

"Good afternoon, ladies and gentlemen. On behalf of the Music Association, I'm delighted to welcome you. For those of you who do not know me, my name is Thomas Harrison, and it is my distinct pleasure to prepare you for your new duties as festival adjudicators. You'll find me a fair but demanding instructor."

Ruth wondered what he meant by demanding. In his plain tweed suit, Mr. Harrison looked more like someone who ran a haberdashery shop or worked as a bank clerk, than an experienced music festival adjudicator.

Silas nudged her and whispered, "Demanding is right. But don't worry. I'll help you."

Ruth kept staring straight ahead. Silas was very wrong if he expected her to seek *his* help. What could he teach her about singing that she didn't already know?

"You have chosen to embark upon a noble pursuit," Mr. Harrison continued.

Noble pursuit? Ruth almost laughed out loud. What could be noble about judging amateur singers from the provinces?

"Each of you has been chosen because you've demonstrated your skill as musicians. My job over the coming days is to instill in you the expertise you'll need to judge and encourage the work of others. I know of no other person more qualified to inspire you than our special guest." He beamed at Miss Wakefield. "I'm sure there's not a person here who doesn't know about the enormous contributions that Miss Mary Wakefield has made to your new profession. She needs no introduction."

To Ruth's amusement, Mr. Harrison then embarked upon a long description of Miss Wakefield's career and accomplishments, how she'd been a singer of some renown before turning her attention to encouraging local, amateur musicians. After starting a choral festival near her family home in Kendal in the Lake District, Mary Wakefield had worked tirelessly to inspire a national movement.

"It is no small thanks to Miss Wakefield that you are sitting here today. Her efforts to bring music to the masses has resulted in the steady growth of her festival and others like it. Massed choirs now perform some of the greatest works in the choral repertoire in every corner of the country. Ladies and gentlemen, I give you Miss Mary Wakefield."

Loud applause greeted Miss Wakefield as she made her way to the podium. Ruth glanced over at Silas. He was clapping wildly, his lips parted and eyes shining.

"Thank you for that very kind introduction, Mr. Harrison," Mary Wakefield said. "I am honored to stand before you, a new generation of judges. It is you who will fulfill my dream of bringing music to people in all corners of our great nation. In your role as judges, you can and you will shape the musical tastes and skills of thousands of people, young and old. Your words will have a lasting impact on the people you serve. Yes, I said serve. Do not forget that in your role as a festival adjudicator, your first responsibility is to encourage and celebrate people who make music."

Ruth stifled a yawn. She wondered how much longer she'd be obliged to stay before Silas took her to her lodgings. She hoped there'd be someone there to make her a cup of tea.

"There are three pillars upon which the festival movement is built," Mary continued. "First, I strongly believe that competition is a necessary stimulus to the study and practice of music. Every choir, from the smallest collection of children in a rural school to a group of ladies and gentlemen in one of our largest metropolises, benefits from working towards a common goal. A competition provides them with incentive to perfect their craft and by so doing, win the respect and appreciation of their peers."

Mary then proceeded to decry the growing practice of awarding money prizes to competition winners, before sharing her conviction that every festival should end with all competing choirs forming one massed choir to sing together.

"Competition is forgotten in the pursuit of a common goal which, of course, is the making of beautiful music," Mary declared. "My hope for you is that when you listen to the choirs come together as one, you'll feel the same sense of joy and accomplishment that I do."

People all around Ruth were nodding their heads in agreement.

"Thank you for the dedication, the skill, and above all, the love of music that I know you will bring to your new duties. Always remember that music is a fair and glorious gift from God."

The applause went on for so long that Mr. Harrison had to wait several minutes before he was able to again address the audience.

"We will reconvene here tomorrow morning at nine o'clock sharp," he said after thanking Miss Wakefield. "Good evening to you."

In the bustle of leaving, Ruth was surprised when Mr. Harrison descended from the platform and walked purposefully towards her.

"Mrs. Henton? Miss Wakefield wishes to speak with you."

Mary stepped forward and held her hand out to shake Ruth's. "It's an honor to meet you," she said.

Ruth only just stopped herself from asking why. Next to her, she felt Silas practically vibrating out of his skin as he watched her shake Mary's hand. "I enjoyed your speech," Ruth said. "It was most inspiring."

"Thank you," Mary said. "I had the privilege of attending one of your performances in London some months ago. The association is exceedingly fortunate to have you."

"I hope to return to the stage before very long," Ruth said.

"I understand, but I wanted to tell you, my dear, that the joy you will get from helping others reach their potential is a hundred times more fulfilling than singing only for yourself."

Ruth smiled politely. She thought about the adulation of the London audiences, the sound of their applause, the cheers.

Nothing was better than that.

"I see you don't believe me," Mary said. "There was a time in my life when I thought as you do."

How dare she? Ruth wanted to tell this earnest woman to keep her platitudes to herself. The new life Ruth was being forced to accept would keep her from the workhouse, but it could never be better than what she left.

"I'm sure that has been your experience," Ruth said icily. "But as I mentioned, I'll be returning to the stage as soon as an opportunity presents itself."

Mary Wakefield looked at her intently. She had slightly prominent eyes that seemed to bore into Ruth's soul. "If that is what you truly want, Mrs. Henton, then I wish you luck."

Before Ruth had a chance to reply, Mary turned away to greet several students who clustered around her, all asking questions at once. They all looked so earnest, so excited to be a part of Mary's vision for bringing music into the lives of the masses. It was a laudable vision, Ruth supposed, but it was not, nor ever would be, *her* vision.

"Shall we go?" Silas asked. He had a soft Welsh lilt to his voice that, despite her resolve to dismiss him, Ruth found appealing. She and Mother had spent some of the happiest days of her childhood in Cardiff. It was one of the few periods in their lives together when Mother had a secure situation in a home where both she and Ruth were treated kindly. Then the mistress of the house had died and they'd been again left to fend for themselves. Her mother's next situation was in Sheffield, where she met and married Reg Kingwell.

"I'm ready," Ruth said.

"Wasn't she *wonderful?*" Silas asked as he escorted her from the hall. "I've heard her speak several times, and she *always* inspires me."

"She's certainly passionate," Ruth said. "Are my lodgings close by?"

"Yes, of course. We can walk there if you like. I've already had your trunk sent on."

A soot-speckled drizzle began to fall as they made their way along the crowded sidewalk. Ruth's headache bloomed as she listened to Silas chatter on about the festival movement and Mary Wakefield and the joys of judging choral competitions.

Ruth was more certain than ever that she'd made a mistake taking this job. What had her uncle been thinking? She didn't belong with these people.

"Mrs. Henton? Here are your lodgings." With a sweep of one arm as if showing her a palace, Silas indicated a four-story brick building with narrow-paned windows and a general air of utilitarian dreariness.

Ruth thought of the creamy white façade and neat iron gate of the home she'd left behind in London and suppressed a sigh.

"How long will I be here?" she asked.

"Two weeks while you complete your training, and then on and off throughout the season. Didn't they tell you that Manchester's your home base while you're working for the association? At the beginning of March, we'll be off to the festival in Blackpool, and after that, we go to Leeds."

"Where will I stay when we are at the festivals?"

"The association finds us lodgings," he said. "You don't need to worry, Mrs. Henton. Most of the time, they're comfortable enough, considering we're rarely in them for longer than a few days at a time."

"Most of the time?"

"Here's your trunk already come," Silas said, ignoring her question and pointing to Ruth's trunk outside the front entrance. "Come in. I'll introduce you to Mrs. Patterson, who runs the place. She's extremely strict, so make sure you don't stay out beyond eight o'clock. I've heard stories of her locking girls out."

"She sounds charming," Ruth said, but irony was lost on Silas. He grinned and stood aside to let her pass into her new home.

Chapter 27

Briarstown

Eliza

"Again!" Miss Donahue said. "You're not concentrating, Eliza."

Eliza wanted to protest that she was doing her best and that Miss Donahue was making her feel like she couldn't sing at all. She took a deep breath and sang the phrase again.

"Again. Louder, please."

Eliza repeated the phrase.

"You sang it exactly the same way. I can't help you if you won't do as I ask."

"I'm sorry," Eliza said.

"No one won a competition by being sorry," Miss Donahue said. "I realize I sound harsh, but you can do better. Now, please, sing the phrase again, and this time, imagine that your voice is powerful enough to blow the walls out."

Smiling at the image, Eliza opened her mouth and sang the phrase as loudly as she could.

"Better. Now, sing it again, but this time focus on tone."

Eliza tried again, imagining the sounds coming from her mouth as billows of silk. She'd never owned a silk dress and barely knew what silk felt like, but the image seemed to work.

"Open your mouth wider. That's it. Now again from Bar 32 to Bar 35."

Eliza sang the four bars again, and then three times more until finally Miss Donahue lifted her hands from the piano and rested them in her lap.

"It's coming," she said. "Keep practicing."

"Can I win?"

"That depends entirely on you," Miss Donahue said. "You have the ability, Eliza, but as I've warned you, the competition will be intense. You'll be competing against singers who have trained for years."

"What should I do?"

"Apart from working on your breathing and your tone, remind yourself *why* you are singing."

"I need the prize money," Eliza said.

"I understand that, but if that's your only reason for singing, then you're not likely to win against more experienced singers."

"What reason should I have?" Eliza asked.

"Only you can answer that." Miss Donahue rose and faced the door. "Here come the others."

Eliza followed her gaze and couldn't help rolling her eyes at the sound of Hattie's brassy voice dominating as usual. The woman would never change, but at least she was proving herself to be a staunch supporter of the choir.

"I told her to mind her own business," Hattie declared.

"She's just jealous we didn't invite her to join us," Doris said.

"That don't give her the right to tell folks we're wasting our time."

"Who are you talking about?" Josie asked. "Has someone been saying unkind things about our choir?"

"Mrs. Conroy, the butcher's wife? She said we're foolin' ourselves thinkin' we can win in Whitby."

"Ladies!" Miss Donahue called. "That's enough talk. May we begin our warmup?"

Eliza took her place next to Hattie who was still glowering. "You don't want to be minding what Mrs. Conroy says," she whispered.

"There's plenty who think different," Hannah said, who stood behind them. "Folks are saying we should be proud of ourselves for what we're doin'."

At a nod from Miss Donahue, Mrs. Walker played a chord on the piano. "*Mee, Ma, Mo, Mah*, please."

Eliza lifted her chin and began to sing. Her hour of rehearsal with Miss Donahue had loosened her vocal cords. The cares of her daily life, her worries for the future, her plans for her girls melted away as she lifted her voice and let the sounds pour forth, clear and pure.

Mrs. Walker modulated from a major chord to a minor. Eliza felt her heart expand as a quiet joy suffused her. Win or lose, this was what she was meant to do.

Eliza practiced every day when all the girls except Bessie were away from the house. She spread the music for *An die Musik*, Schubert's achingly poignant tribute to the soul of music, on the worn tabletop and pored over every note. Miss Donahue insisted Eliza had the range to do justice to the piece, but sometimes progress was so slow that Eliza wanted to cry.

Today was one of those days. She heard the door open behind her, and for a moment, a chill ran through her. Had Reg come home early? Had he been demoted…again?

"You sound nice, Ma. Don't stop."

Letting out a sign of relief, Eliza sent up a small prayer of thanks before turning around to greet Annie. "You're home early," she said.

"Sing it again, Ma."

"I don't think so, Annie. I sound like a croaking frog." Eliza pointed to the bar that was giving her trouble. "See these black marks here? They're called notes."

Not for the first time, she lamented that Miss Donahue no longer taught the children at the mill school. That mother of hers had made her quit teaching when the vicar died, not long after Grace was born. Eliza realized that she and Miss Donahue had more in common than it would seem, given their different stations in life.

Neither were free to do as they pleased.

"Are they like letters?" Annie asked.

"You could say that. Each note corresponds to a different sound."

"So, they *are* like letters."

"I see what you mean. Yes, notes are like letters." Eliza smiled. Annie was too smart for her own good. She'd turned twelve in January, and Reg had already put his foot down and insisted she leave school in June and start working at the mill. Since he'd been demoted for that business with the mill girls, the family needed the extra shillings that Annie's work would bring in.

Eliza hated that Reg had put them in such a position—and all because he couldn't control himself. The latest girl he'd interfered with had gone so far as to complain to Mr. Lewiston. She'd been let go and Reg only demoted and docked a week's wages. Eliza hated the unfairness, but she was torn. On the one hand, Reg deserved to be punished, but on the other, her family would suffer if Lewiston fired him from the mill. As it was, she'd had to scramble to feed them that week. Of course, as always, she'd managed.

"Show me," Annie said. She sat down and pointed at a bar of notes. "Sing these ones."

"I should be getting the tea on. Your dad will be home soon."

"Please, Ma. I want to learn."

Eliza picked up the score and started to sing.

Du holde Kunst, in wieviel grauen Stunden,
Wo mich des Lebens wilder Kreis umstrickt,
Hast du mein Herz zu warmer Lieb entzunden,

"Is that a foreign language, Ma?"

"It's German. A man called Schubert wrote the music about eighty years ago, way back in 1817. Fancy that!"

"What's it mean?"

"Well," Eliza said, "It's all about loving music, and how music can take us to a better world. This first part? Miss Donahue said that in English it means something like:

Beloved art, in how many a bleak hour
* when I am enmeshed in life's tumultuous round,*
have you kindled my heart to the warmth of love,
and borne me away to a better world.

Annie's eyes widened. "What's enmeshed?"

"It means to be trapped in something, like being trapped in a busy life. Tumultuous means wild and chaotic. Like the mill. You've heard what it's like when the machines are all running. Wouldn't you say it was tumultuous?"

Annie nodded. "Some of my friends can't wait to work there." She looked up at Eliza. "I don't want to."

"I know." Eliza longed to tell Annie that she'd never work in the mill, but she didn't dare, not until she'd won the prize money. She put her finger on the German word *lieb*. "This word means *love*. Music makes our hearts love."

"That sounds nice."

"And music also takes us to a better world, even if only in our minds. That's a good thing, don't you think?"

Annie nodded. "Sing some more."

Eliza glanced at the door. "Where are the others?"

"Miss Samson let us out an hour early on account of the school inspector stopping by. The others stayed to play a while, but I run home to see if you needed any help."

"That was good of you."

Annie flushed at the compliment. "Thanks. Will you sing some more?"

For the next hour until the other girls came home, Eliza sang to Annie, stopping every few bars to explain the words and talk about the parts she was having trouble with. Annie drank in the new knowledge like clean water gushing from the pump. She learned quickly, soon naming the notes Eliza sang and repeating the German words, her strong Yorkshire accent mangling the vowels, but Eliza didn't correct her.

A rare surge of happiness filled Eliza as she sang and talked with her eldest daughter, almost like they were equals. She loved her girls and would give her life for them, but she never really saw them as *people* separate from herself. They were bodies she was responsible for feeding and clothing, for reprimanding and supervising, and most importantly, for not spoiling. Her job was to mould them into respectable, well-behaved girls who would be a credit to her.

In Annie, she discovered a keen mind and a wry sense of humor that she'd never taken the time to notice. Her Annie would make a fine teacher.

"Annie?" Eliza asked as she folded away her score and began setting out bread and butter for the family's tea. "You like school, don't you?"

"Oh yes, Ma! I love it! Miss Samson made me a monitor. Did I tell you?"

"I don't think so," Eliza admitted. "When did this happen?"

"A few months back. She lets me help the littl'uns with their reading."

"Do you like doing that?"

"I really do! They're so sweet. They sit in a circle around me and listen to me read. It's nice, Ma."

Eliza hesitated. Perhaps she should tell Annie about her plans to get them away from Briarstown. Annie would be such a help to her, and what a comfort it would be to have someone to talk to about her plans, her fears, and her hopes.

The door burst open, and Lily May flounced in, her face red.

"That Robbie McKay is *horrible!*" she cried.

"What's he done now?" Eliza asked. She wasn't surprised to hear that Hattie McKay's eldest boy was turning into as big a bully as his mother had been.

"He called me names!" Lily May exclaimed.

"Ignore him." Eliza resisted the urge to ask what names. "Bullies only want attention."

"But Ma!"

"That's enough. Go and wash your hands and then help me with the tea. I've got enough on my plate without worrying about Hattie McKay's son."

"Ma!"

"You heard me."

That evening, Eliza waited until Reg was asleep and then crept downstairs. She lit a candle and went over to the battered bookcase, the one piece of furniture she'd brought from her parents' house. Smiling, she remembered George Ledbetter loading it carefully onto his cart.

She pulled out a book and opened it. The newspaper clipping from the *Briarstown Chronicle* she'd saved since before her marriage slid out. She needed to read again what had been written about her, to remind herself that what she was doing wasn't a waste of time.

Miss Eliza Treleven's solo was the highlight of the evening. No one who had the pleasure of hearing her could fail to appreciate the purity and sweetness of her voice. Mr. Skinner is to be commended for his conducting, and we look forward to many more performances by Miss Treleven with the Briarstown Choral Society.

Eliza had sung with the Society for two wonderful months—the happiest months of her life, even with the grueling schedule she'd kept up— long days at the mill followed by night after night poring over the scores, practicing her singing every waking minute she could get free of her duties.

The last time she'd read the review was the night after the concert when she'd read it aloud to Dad.

He sat in his usual place by the fire, his coughing mercifully stopped, although his face was as white as marble. Eliza had begged the company doctor for medicine, for anything to stop the terrible coughing and bring him peace. Dr. Easton had merely patted her arm and said she was a good girl and a blessing to her father. When she asked him if there was any hope of recovery, he looked away and mumbled something about *byssinosis*.

Eliza knew the word. Everyone did. It was the scourge of the textile mills, a death sentence for anyone unlucky enough to get it. Cotton fibers lodged in the lungs and bloomed there, causing the victim to cough day and night, keeping the family from sleep, and shredding the nerves of workers already irritated by the relentless clamor of the mill.

She remembered when Dad had worked in the fields back home. She still thought of Devon as home and wondered if she always would. In her mind, she saw him striding across the fields at harvest time, his scythe slicing cleanly, his smile brighter than the summer sun.

"You're a credit to me, you are," he croaked.

"Thanks, Dad. I wish you could've heard me at the concert." Eliza smoothed her hand over her skirt. It kept getting tighter, which was a surprise since she barely choked down her food these days. But then, she'd always been thin. A few extra pounds would give her more of a presence in the choir.

Dad didn't reply, only stared at her, his expression almost quizzical. "Dad?"

His mouth slackened and his head slumped sideways.

"Dad!" Eliza grabbed hold of one of his calloused hands.

He's just tired. He needs a good hot cup of tea.

She started to rise and then sat back down with a thump. The hand she held was limp, like a length of rubber hose.

"No!" Her voice fell to a harsh whisper. "Dad?" She clutched his hand, willing her own life to flow into him, to revive him and bring him back to her.

"Dad?"

He was completely and utterly still, like a statue—a body that took up space, but with no spark, no soul. He was Dad, and yet he was not Dad. Before her eyes, he seemed to melt into the chair. She wanted to spread her palms across his cheeks and press them until blood pumped into his colorless skin.

She lifted his scarred hand to her lips. He couldn't be gone. It was too soon. His fifty-second birthday was in a few weeks. Eliza had planned to ask the baker to make him a special cake, a sponge with jam in the middle. They'd have a lovely party. Her big brothers, Billy and Jack, along with Jack's wife and their two boys would come. They'd talk and laugh, and for a little while, they'd be a family again.

She sat back on her heels in the silent room.

How could Dad leave her?

He'd never again smile at her and take her side against Ma.

"Oh, Dad," she whispered. "I'm so sorry, Dad. So very, very sorry."

The beginnings of a sob caught in the back of her throat but went no further. If she let herself cry out loud, she'd never stop. Something shifted in her as she looked at him, so motionless and quiet, his breath no longer labored, the coughing stopped. After so many long months of pain, Archie Treleven was free.

Eliza carefully folded the clipping and placed it back inside the book—a worn copy of *Great Expectations* that Miss Donahue had given her the first winter she'd replaced horrid Miss Lane at the mill school. Sighing, she mounted the narrow stairwell and slipped into bed next to Reg, who was snoring loud enough to shake the walls. As she closed her eyes, she thought of the coming weeks, of winning the prize money, and then leaving Reg forever.

Great expectations indeed.

Chapter 28

Blackpool

Ruth

"Thank you. Next, please," Silas said. As one choir shuffled off the platform to be replaced by another, he glanced over at Ruth. "What did you think?"

"Average," Ruth said. "Vowels were well-rounded, but the blend and balance were only fair. And the diction! I can't give them more than twenty-eight."

"We agree exactly," Silas said, his smile widening. "See?"

Ruth glanced at his form and saw that their marks were almost identical. Only one point separated their final marks, putting the men's choir from Lancashire firmly in the middle of the pack.

"The choir from Leeds are last year's winners," Silas said. "I have high expectations."

"I certainly hope they're better than the ones we've heard so far. I wouldn't like to award the trophy to any of *them*."

"You're right, as always."

To Ruth's surprise, his approval sent a small shiver down her spine. After almost a month of sitting next to him and judging hundreds of anxious singers, she'd become cautiously accustomed to his cheerfulness. She supposed having a cheerful partner who saw the good in everything was better than spending every day with some dried-up old codger who hated the world.

Silas always kept a respectful distance between them and still insisted on calling her Mrs. Henton, although she'd asked him to use her Christian name. He'd looked aghast at the mere thought of taking such a liberty.

The men in the next choir were much less formally dressed than the men in the previous choir.

"The Mavensbridge Mill Choir," Silas said.

Ruth looked down at her list. "It says here this is their first competition."

"Which means they will probably be dreadful."

"Let's hope not."

"Regardless, we shall endeavor to say something positive about their performance."

Ruth nodded her agreement. Despite her intention to like nothing about her new position, she had to admit that she enjoyed the opportunity to encourage competitors with helpful praise.

"We will," she agreed.

The choir consisted of eighteen men. With their scrubbed faces and slicked-back hair, each man looked uncomfortable wearing what was likely his only suit.

At a nod from Silas, the accompanist struck the opening chords of the set piece. Called *Warrior's Song*, it was a popular choice for male choirs, and Ruth was curious how the men would manage it.

"Impressive," Silas whispered as the men sang.

Ruth nodded. The voices blended remarkably well, the balance between the bass, baritone, and tenor voices as smooth as any city choir. She noted carefully mended patches on elbows and knees and imagined wives toiling for hours to make their husbands as presentable as possible on their meager incomes.

Wives like Eliza.

The men finished the piece and bowed self-consciously to the wildly clapping audience. A few audience members shouted their support. The broad, flat vowels and dropped consonants reminded Ruth of her girlhood.

Silas showed her his marks.

"A forty-five? That's very high," Ruth said.

"They earned it, don't you think?"

She studied her own mark sheet, then jotted numbers next to each of five categories: Tone/Intonation, Technique, Musicianship, Interpretation, and Ensemble. She glanced up and met the eye of one of the singers, a tall fellow in the front row, who winked at her. He had a carefully trimmed mustache and piercing blue eyes—a dead-ringer for Reg Kingwell.

She shuddered. When was the last time she'd written to Eliza? She didn't even know how many children she had.

"Mrs. Henton? Are you unwell?"

"What? Oh, no, thank you, Mr. Gallagher." She tallied her marks and handed him her sheet.

"You're right," she said. "They should get the top prize."

Chapter 29

Briarstown

Eliza

Eliza loaded Reg's shirts and the girls' pinafores into her basket and stepped out into the yard. For once, she was doing her washing at a time when she might run into some of the other women who lived in the court. The prospect didn't bother her anymore. She smiled as she walked toward the washhouse. The early spring day was unseasonably warm, the air filled with the squeals of children too young for school. Bessie was settled in one corner of the yard playing with another girl her age.

To Eliza's surprise, the washhouse was empty. She suppressed a small feeling of disappointment. Maybe it wouldn't be so bad to have someone to talk to while she did her washing. On the other hand, she needed to get the washing done as quickly as possible so she could work on her piece for the solo competition. The phrasing in bar ten was still not right. As she poured water into the tub, she hummed the choir's set piece. In front of everyone at the previous night's rehearsal, Miss Donahue said the piece was coming along—high praise after weeks of grueling practice.

Eliza switched from humming to quiet singing, trusting that the noise of the children would prevent anyone from hearing her. Her shoulders relaxed as she let the notes spill forth like the water trickling through her fingers. The music filled her up the way nothing in her life ever had. She closed her eyes, and before she knew it, she was singing at full volume, the sound bouncing off the dripping brick walls.

Another voice joined hers and then another—three voices singing at first in unison and then breaking into parts. Eliza opened her eyes to see Hattie and Minnie, each carrying a laundry basket, entering the washhouse.

She acknowledged them with a nod and continued singing. Hattie, her pinched face flushed and eyes bright, set down her basket. Gone were the usual sneers and sour looks. Minnie followed suit, but singing a third lower and perfectly in tune. Eliza lifted a dripping hand and gestured to bring up the volume, imitating Miss Donahue conducting.

A line of children appeared at the open door. They stared at the singing women, dirty mouths agape.

Three women fractured by years of cares and responsibilities that often took them to the edges of poverty sang together as one. Old rivalries and hurt feelings dissolved like the harsh lye soap frothing the wash water.

They finished the song and burst into laughter. The children clapped and called for them to sing some more.

"Go on with you!" Hattie said good-humoredly, shooing them back into the yard. She turned to Eliza. "We couldn't resist, you sounded that fine. I reckon we have as fair a chance as any of winning. I have to say, Miss Donahue's done wonders with us."

"I hope so," Eliza said. "There's only a few weeks left now."

"I'm that excited," Minnie said, her normally dour face split into a grin. "My Frank's been real encouraging. He says I sing like an angel!"

"My Andy's the same," Hattie said smugly. "Say, you know what I think?" She looked at Minnie and Eliza expectantly.

"What?" Minnie asked.

"We should put on a concert after we get back from the competition. Folks around here would love to hear us sing."

"That's a wonderful idea!" Minnie exclaimed.

"What do you think, Eliza?" Hattie asked. "You haven't sung in public since you was sixteen. I remember thinkin' at the time that you could have had a future."

"You did?" Eliza was so surprised she dropped the pinafore she'd been about to hang up.

Hattie stooped to pick it up and shake off bits of grime. "You'll want to be washing that again."

"Thanks." Eliza took the pinafore from Hattie's wet hands.

"Anyways, as I were saying," Hattie continued, "a concert would give us a chance to show off what we done."

"We'll need more than two pieces for a concert," Eliza pointed out.

Hattie waved away the comment with one damp hand. "Now that we've learned two songs, it's bound to be faster to learn some more. You ask Miss Donahue."

Eliza couldn't think of an excuse that would satisfy Hattie, so she just nodded and carried on rewashing Gladys's pinnie. She had no intention of staying in Briarstown after competing—and winning—in Whitby. She'd miss the choir and the feeling of camaraderie that had developed between the women, but it couldn't be helped.

"Here comes Doris!" Minnie said. "I hope she's not planning to do her washing now. We're using all the tubs."

"I'll be finished soon," Eliza said. She hung up Gladys's pinnie and reached into the dirty water for the first of Reg's two shirts.

"I heard you singing from across the yard," Doris said, filling the doorway.

"Did we sound good?" Hattie asked.

"Made me proud," Doris said.

Eliza busied herself with the shirts to hide her smile. To think that stolid Doris, who never had a good word to say about anyone, was proud of them.

"Hattie here says we should get a concert together after we get back from Whitby," Minnie said.

"You mean sing in front of our friends and families? In public like?" Doris asked.

"Why not?" Hattie asked. "Even Miss Donahue said we's coming along. Eliza here's going to ask her to teach us some more songs."

"Then we'll have a program," Minnie said importantly. "I think it's a smashing idea."

Doris crossed her heavy arms across her chest. "This right, Eliza?"

"I suppose it is," she said. "I'll talk to Miss Donahue."

"Well, that's fine, then," Doris said, cracking a rare smile. "It's about time we women blew our own horns."

"That's what I was thinking," Minnie said.

"Make sure you tell Miss Donahue it was my idea," Hattie said.

Eliza finished hanging up Reg's shirts and then poured the dirty water into the floor drain. "I'd best get the tea started." She left the washhouse and crossed the yard to her house. She'd only joined the choir and entered the solo competition to get enough money to take the girls away from Briarstown. She certainly never expected to make friends.

She imagined standing in front of everyone she knew and performing like she had before marrying Reg. Fancy Hattie thinking she'd had a future back then! Ruth had been the one with the future. The Briarstown Choral

Society had been the training ground for her brilliant career in London.

Eliza called for Bessie to get washed up and then went inside to start the tea. She hadn't read anything about Ruth in the newspaper for a good six months, and the last time she'd passed the photographer's shop, Ruth's picture had been removed from the window.

Emily, Gladys, Lily May, and Annie all crowded into the house, laughing and jostling each other. At a look from Eliza, Emily settled down to play with Bessie, while Gladys picked up a book and sat at the table, Lily May laid out the cutlery, and Annie began cutting thick slices of bread for their tea.

Peace descended.

Eliza's heart swelled with love and pride as she watched her girls. This was her future—the only one she needed. Ruth Henton might have all of London swooning at her feet, but Eliza had her girls, and very soon they'd be free of this cramped, cold house.

An hour later, Reg pushed open the door and sauntered in. He patted Gladys on the head before flopping into his chair in front of the grate.

"Take your dad his tea," Eliza told Gladys.

"Thanks, pet," he said, taking the cup from his middle daughter. He raised it in Eliza's direction. "Yer ears must be burning today."

"What do you mean?"

"Out in the yard, I got talking to Mrs. Jones."

"You mean Minnie? She's in the choir with me."

"So's she said. Seems you and her were singing this afternoon in the washhouse with Andy's wife. She said you're the star of the choir."

"What of it?" Eliza asked warily.

"Minnie also said there's talk of you lasses putting on a concert when you all get back from Whitby."

"Hattie thought it might be a good idea for us to perform for folks. Lots of people are curious about what we've been doing."

"I don't like it."

Beside her, Eliza felt Annie stiffen and put down the half-piece of bread and jam she was about to eat.

"It's only talk," Eliza said hastily. "There won't be any concert."

"I don't want you making a spectacle of yourself," he said. "Bad enough you're involved in this competition nonsense. You pulled a fast one on me there. Seems I got no choice but to let you go."

"Now, Reg, I did no such thing," Eliza said, keeping her voice mild.

"Lily May? Put another spoonful of jam on that bread and then take it to your father. He's worked hard all day."

"That's true enough," he said, smiling as he took the plate from Lily May. "There's a good lass."

When everyone had eaten their tea and the dishes were cleared away, Reg thankfully fell asleep in front of a weak fire. Eliza shooed the girls upstairs and sank into a chair at the table. She wished she could get out her music and practice, but she daren't wake Reg. At least he was sober. Soon enough, he'd rouse himself and climb up to his bed.

She watched him sleep, his mustache ruffling slightly when he exhaled. When had love become hate, she wondered. Was it the first time he'd hit her after Gladys was born? Or even earlier, when he'd interfered with one of the girls at the mill and got himself demoted? Or after Emily was born and he'd taken to belittling her because she'd given him a fourth daughter instead of a son?

And yet she couldn't deny that he was a good father to the girls, with Bessie his favorite even though her birth had disappointed him for a fifth time.

Absently, she placed her hand on her flat belly, her chest tightening as she remembered the first time it had begun to swell. She'd been so young, so impossibly innocent. It wasn't until Mrs. Harris heard Eliza vomiting into the communal privy for the third time in as many days and told her she was in the family way that she'd known.

"Ten weeks gone, I reckon," Mrs. Harris had said. "You'd best get yerself married quick before people start noticing."

Eliza had thought then of George Ledbetter, of his kindness after Dad died in helping her and Ma move into her uncle's house, of how Reg hadn't even stopped by to express his condolences. If she could get George to marry her, she could let him believe the child was his. Mrs. Harris would back her up.

No. She couldn't lie to him. She *wouldn't.* George hadn't done to her what Reg had—fumbling with her underclothes, crushing her with his weight, making her cry out in pain, and then grunting and groaning like a stuck pig before rolling off her. He'd looked down at her then, his eyes soft.

"Good lass," he'd said, patting her shoulder before swinging his legs off the bed and pulling up his trousers.

She'd felt so horribly ashamed.

A few days after Mrs. Harris told her she was expecting, Eliza agreed to go out walking with Reg. She hadn't seen him since *that afternoon* when she'd gone to his house to see Ruth and been told she wasn't there but to come in anyway.

What a fool she'd been.

And yet, he'd not forced her, not really. She hadn't known what was happening until he was on top of her and by then it was too late.

George Ledbetter would never have done such a thing to her—leastwise, not like that.

"What do you say to us making a go of it?" Reg asked, taking her hand as they walked alongside the canal in the golden light of an evening in June.

Say yes, she told herself. *You have to say yes.*

The words wouldn't come. People said they admired Reg, although so far as she knew, he didn't have any friends. Some of the girls gossiped about his first wife—Ruth's mother—declaring that he'd not always been good to her.

But Ruth had never said anything, and surely, she'd tell Eliza if her stepfather was a brute.

A wave of nausea hit her. Eliza looked around for somewhere to sit, but the only support was Reg's hand in hers. If she held on, her future was secured.

"Eliza?"

Mrs. Reg Kingwell.

Her throat loosened, and she found her strength. "Of course, I'll marry you, Reg," she said briskly. "I'd like nothing better."

"Well, that's grand!"

Reg swept her into his arms and twirled her in a circle. The bottom of her skirt brushed the fresh new grass at the side of the towpath. The swell of her belly pressed into Reg when he stopped twirling to gather her against his chest. He glanced down, but said nothing, only lowered his lips to hers. She smelled tea mixed with beer.

Her stomach tightened again, and then she closed her eyes and kissed him back.

Reg Kingwell was the ticket to her own household and to respectability for the child growing inside her. She could only hope she was doing what Granny had told her back in Devon.

Marry a kind man, like your father.

As Reg held her close, a fluttering deep within her belly startled her.

Eliza had never felt anything like it before. To her surprise, a soft calmness descended, and along with it a resolve unlike anything she'd ever felt before. For the first time, the child inside her was real, and no matter what happened, she'd protect it with her life.

In the corner by the fire, Reg stirred and opened his eyes. He stared blearily at Eliza. "What yer doing sitting there like that? Are you watchin' me?"

"Can't I sit still a moment after a long day?" Eliza asked, careful to keep her tone light. "I've been on my feet since five."

"Aye, well, count yerself lucky that you're not at t'mill these days. Old Jonas is workin' us like slaves."

"Have you talked to Mr. Lewiston? Got him to see sense and make you foreman again?"

Reg heaved himself to his feet. "Nah. But he's sure to give me my old job back soon enough. Come on then, let's to bed. Tomorrow will be here afore we know it."

Eliza put her two hands on the table and pushed herself up, then followed her husband up the narrow staircase. Regrets were useless now. The competition in Whitby was in less than three weeks. She'd waited twelve years to finish what she'd started with the Briarstown Choral Society.

This time, she'd see it through.

Chapter 30

Yorkshire

Ruth

Ruth woke to the sound of a cock crowing. For a few moments, she was taken back to when she and Mother had lived in a country house near Cardiff. She never would have guessed that one day she'd spend most of her days sitting next to a soft-spoken man from Wales.

"We'll be judging the children's choirs this morning," Silas said at breakfast. They were staying in an inn in one of a dozen northern towns and villages they'd visited over the past two months. Ruth had lost track, happy to let Silas, with his customary cheerfulness, take charge of their travel arrangements.

"That's fine," she said. Most of the choirs they judged blended together into one cacophony of sound. A mixed choir from one town wasn't much different from a mixed choir from the next town. Some sang well; some did not. Some choirs were composed mostly of ladies and gentlemen and some were made up of singers that came mostly from the lower orders—mill hands, laborers, a sprinkling of shopkeepers. Every so often a choir stood out from the rest, like the Mavensbridge Mill Choir had, which made the job much more bearable than Ruth had expected.

She had to admit that the children were particularly entertaining to judge even if sometimes the sounds they made gave her a headache. Ruth had pushed aside any thought of having children herself years ago. Her life in London never brought her in contact with them, apart from the ragged mites who roamed the streets of the West End. She'd scatter a few pennies in front of them when she thought about it, but most of the time she'd been far too preoccupied thinking about the evening's performance.

"The children mostly come from small rural schools in the area," Silas said. "For some, this will be their first time singing in front of strangers."

Ruth nodded, then took a final sip of tea and stood.

Silas hastily put down his last spoonful of porridge and scrambled to his feet. "We don't need to be at the hall for at least thirty minutes," he said.

"Please, don't get up," she said. "Stay and finish your breakfast. I can find my own way to the hall. It's not a very large town, and I fancy a walk this morning."

"Oh, well, of course." He sat back down. "I shall see you at nine."

She escaped the stifling breakfast room and strolled out into the chilly morning. Here and there, clusters of daffodils shivered in the March wind, and white buds clustered along the branches of some of the trees.

The coming of spring brought back memories of when she and Eliza had been inseparable. After school, they'd scamper down to the canal and run as far as they could into the countryside, talking and singing and laughing.

The inn overlooked a river with running water that sparkled in the sun. Ruth breathed in the fresh smell of new grass and walked to the edge of the river. Unlike so many other towns she'd visited in the North, this town was free of smokestacks and factories. Silas told her it was a market town that had served the villages and smaller towns in the area for centuries. An old stone church dominated the central square while on a nearby hill, the remains of a medieval castle loomed. Ruth walked to the center of a small bridge spanning the river and leaned on the railing to watch the water below flowing towards her.

At that very moment in houses big and small for many miles around, dozens of people were getting ready for the day's competition. Mothers dressed children in their best clothes; soloists practiced their scales; people who had sung together for months and years greeted each other as they walked together to the hall.

"Ah, there you are!"

Ruth turned to see Silas approaching. His tie was slightly askew, and his hair was a mass of bronzed curls ruffled by the breeze. For a moment, she was tempted to reach out and straighten his tie.

"It's a beautiful day," she said instead, fixing her gaze again on the river.

"It is that." He held out his arm. "Shall we go? The children will be arriving soon."

They entered the silent hall that smelled of dust and floor polish and took their places at the table arranged in front of a platform. Overhead, heavy dark beams spoke of the hall's long history of hosting country dances and festivals and town meetings.

"Before I left the inn," Silas said, "Mrs. Boyle waylaid me. She's the festival organizer?"

"I remember."

"Mrs. Boyle says that the choir mistress who was to conduct the massed choir this evening has been taken ill."

"That is unfortunate. Will we cancel the performance?" Ruth felt a pang of disappointment. She'd started looking forward to the coming together of all the choirs as the end of a multi-day competition. There was something wonderfully stirring about the sound of hundreds, occasionally even thousands, of voices singing in unison and in harmony. Relieved of the necessity of judging, Ruth enjoyed the opportunity to listen to the music. In London, she'd rarely had time to attend concerts.

"I was rather hoping you'd agree to step in and conduct," Silas said.

"Oh no! Surely not. Isn't that your job as the senior adjudicator? I couldn't possibly."

"I understand why you'd think that," Silas said. He picked up a pencil and tapped it on the table. "It's just that… I mean, of course, I'd like to, but…" His voice trailed off and he looked at her miserably.

"What's wrong?"

"It's silly, I know, but the reason I'm a judge and not a performer is that I suffer from terrible stage fright."

"What do you mean a performer?"

"I once trained for a career as a singer," Silas said. "Back home in Wales? I even competed a few times in the Eisteddfod."

"Did you win?"

"Twice."

"You've never told me that," Ruth said, impressed. The Eisteddfod in Wales was Britain's most prestigious music festival, attracting thousands of participants every year. To win there, a performer needed to be top-notch.

"I didn't think there was much point," Silas said. "Any hopes I've entertained of continuing to perform have long since been dashed."

"What happened?"

"I was competing at the first Westmoreland Festival, and I choked. Right in the middle of my aria, my voice stopped."

"Oh dear!"

"Ever since then, I haven't been able to get up on stage in front of people." He shuddered. "I'm sorry, Mrs. Henton, but I can't do it."

"But you'll be conducting, not singing," Ruth pointed out.

Silas shook his head. "I can't. Please, you have so much experience performing. This will be easy for you."

Ruth could see further argument was useless. Silas looked like he was about to cry. A surge of tenderness overcame her own qualms.

"Fine," she said. "I shall do my best, but you must know I haven't conducted a choir for years."

"So, you do have some experience?"

"A little. When I first went to London, I joined a ladies' choir and sometimes took over from the conductor."

"Did you like it?"

Ruth couldn't help smiling. Silas had such an artless way about him that her resolve to always keep herself aloof from his relentless cheerfulness was lately showing signs of weakening. "Yes, as a matter of fact I did."

"Splendid!" he said, eyes shining with admiration. He reached out to touch her hand and then, seeming to remember himself, drew back. Ruth was surprised to feel a small pang of disappointment.

"Thank you," she said, then picked up her pencil and smoothed open the score sheet.

Don't be ridiculous, she told herself. Silas was a perfectly lovely man, but he could have nothing to do with her future.

Ten hours later, Ruth walked out onto the platform, her heart hammering. She bowed to the standing-room-only audience and faced the massed choir. A hundred children were arranged in two rows at the front. Behind them, two hundred adults stood on four rows of risers—women to her right and men to her left. A few hours earlier she'd been given one hour to turn the dozens of different choirs of all ages and backgrounds into one unified voice. While she hadn't quite succeeded, she felt confident that their performance would be pleasing enough for an audience mostly comprised of friends and family.

Ruth picked up her baton and nodded at the accompanist to begin. Three hundred pairs of eyes stared at her as three hundred pairs of ears listened for their notes in the introduction. Ruth glanced down at her score and then back up at the choir. Pasting on a bright smile, she raised her eyebrows and her baton and then struck the down beat.

Her drilling during the afternoon rehearsal had paid off. A powerful sound shook the ancient roof beams. Ruth's heart swelled with the music as she swayed and gestured to keep the voices together and in tune. The sound was sometimes ragged and the pacing off here and there, but none of that mattered. Three hundred people who, days before, had been strangers, were coming together to make music.

As the final notes died away and the audience behind Ruth exploded with applause, an unfamiliar emotion suffused her. In London, she'd bowed to the applause in triumph, accepting the ovations as her due.

Now, she stood aside and gestured for the choir to bow. A sob caught in her throat and her eyes grew hot as she watched the singers, many with self-conscious grins on their faces. Some of the children laughed and waved to their parents in the audience. She inhaled sharply as in her mind, she saw two little girls running along a towpath—Eliza with dark hair pulled into two tight braids, Ruth with blonde curls caught into bows that bounced as she ran. For the first time since those innocent days, Ruth felt something she'd never expected to feel again.

Joy.

Chapter 31

Briarstown

Eliza

A shiver of nervous excitement was the first thing Eliza felt when she woke up and realized that in exactly two weeks, she'd be competing in Whitby for the title of Best Female Vocalist. Finally, she was close to realizing her Plan.

She slid out of bed, taking care not to wake Reg, and padded down the twisting staircase. The chill in the air would soon dissipate as the day slowly warmed. Eliza had always loved the beginning of spring, but this year more than ever. She set about getting ready for the day—lighting the fire, putting out plates for breakfast, sweeping the floor. In a few minutes, Annie and Lily May would be down. One would go for the water and the other for bread from the bakehouse oven down the street. Eliza hummed as she worked.

If she won—*when* she won, she corrected herself—she'd need to decide when to leave.

What if Reg came after them?

Let him try.

She'd take a dozen different trains if she had to. He'd *never* find them.

Her three eldest girls emerged from the stairwell. While Annie's hair was already neatly pulled into two braids tied with bows, both Lily May and Gladys looked like they'd fed their long hair through a threshing machine. Sighing, Eliza picked up the brush and beckoned Lily May over.

"Come here," she said. "I'll get the tangles out and then you can go for the bread."

"Ma!"

"Hush. It won't take a minute." Eliza tried to be gentle, but Lily May still yowled like a cat in heat. Finally defeated, she pulled the brush one more time through Lily May's hair and then tied a ribbon at the crown of her head. There were still knots, but they'd have to wait. She motioned for Gladys, who reluctantly took Lily May's place.

Eliza reflected that one day she'd cut the hair off all five of her girls and be done with this ridiculous morning ritual.

As usual, Gladys's hair was one huge knot. It would take an hour to untangle it, an hour Eliza didn't have.

"What have you done to get yourself in such a state?" she asked.

"I'm sorry, Ma. I didn't do owt."

"Anything. You didn't do *anything*. Well, it can't be helped. I'll do what I can, but I only have five minutes before Dad's up. Now sit still."

While she worked on Glady's hair, the two youngest girls came down to join their sisters. They buzzed around the room like wasps. Bessie tugged at Emily's dress, while Annie and Lily May argued about who should be first to read a book Annie had brought home from school. The noise made Eliza's head pound, but for once, she didn't scold them. Except for Bessie, they'd all be off to school soon enough, and she'd have peace to practice her song.

Miss Donahue would be pleased to hear her progress.

Eliza hardly stopped singing in the hours when she had only Bessie to watch out for. Thank goodness she could sing and do chores at the same time. An image of George Ledbetter's cottage popped into her mind as she brushed Gladys's hair. It was small, certainly, but surrounded by country-side, and only needed a woman's touch to make it into a comfortable home. A room for the girls could easily be added on.

She stopped brushing Gladys's hair mid-stroke. What was she think-ing? George Ledbetter was nothing to her. As soon as she won the prize money, she'd take the girls to Devon, and that would be the end of her life in Briarstown.

At ten o'clock, with Bessie in tow, Eliza made her way to the church hall to meet Miss Donahue. She found her standing next to the piano and holding a letter in one hand. Tears spilled down her cheeks.

"Good heavens! Miss Donahue? Whatever is the matter?"

"I'm sorry. I've received some news that…" Miss Donahue stopped, gulped.

"Can I help?"

"No one can." Miss Donahue wiped her eyes and then sat at the piano. "Shall we start with a warmup?" she asked shakily.

"Not until you tell me what's wrong," Eliza said. "I wouldn't be able to concentrate knowing you're upset."

Miss Donahue shook her head. "I don't know if *upset* is the right word. Perhaps hopeless would be more fitting."

"Please, Miss Donahue. Tell me." Eliza fetched a folding chair from a stack near the door and set it down next to the piano. She sat and put her hand on Miss Donahue's shoulder. "The burden will be less if you share it." She smiled to herself at the truth of her words. If only she could do the same for herself.

Miss Donahue sighed. "All right. But please, promise me you won't tell anyone."

"Of course not."

Miss Donahue held out the letter to Eliza. "It's from the detective I hired to find my son."

Eliza stifled her surprise as she read the letter and then handed it back to Miss Donahue. Although shocked to find out that upright, self-contained Miss Donahue had a son living in Canada, she was hardly entitled to pass judgment.

"You must miss him very much," Eliza said. She couldn't imagine being so far away from her girls.

"I was twenty-four when he was born. It was a few years after you'd left the mill school."

"He was taken away from you?" Eliza asked.

Miss Donahue nodded. "I wasn't given a choice. Afterwards, Mother took me back, and I kept teaching until Father died."

"What will you do now you know where he is?" Eliza asked.

"What can I do?" Miss Donahue cried. "Mother can't be left alone. It's impossible for me to even think of going to find him."

"I'm sorry," Eliza said. "I wish there was something I could do."

Miss Donahue placed her fingers on the keys and softly played a chord. She smiled up at Eliza, her eyes bright. "You can sing for me, and you can win in Whitby. At least then, I'll feel like I'm doing something important with my life."

"Oh, Miss Donahue, of course you are. Look what you've done with the choir! Just a few months ago, no one would have believed a bunch of local lasses like us could sound so good."

"That's kind of you to say."

"It's the truth."

"All right, then." With more energy, Miss Donahue struck a C chord and nodded at Eliza to stand and begin her warmup.

As she sang, Eliza reflected that everyone had secrets, even Miss Donahue. She wondered about sharing her own secret and then thought better of it.

If Eliza had learned anything in her thirty years, it was that she needed to be strong and depend only on herself.

Chapter 32

Yorkshire

Ruth

Ruth felt as if she were floating off the platform at the end of the massed choir's performance. Silas rushed toward her.

"That was marvelous!" he exclaimed. "I knew you could do it!"

"I'm glad it went off well." She placed her hand on the back of a chair to steady herself. Never in her life had she been so exhausted and yet so elated.

"Well, of course it did! Mrs. Boyle is ecstatic. She's already asked me if you'll conduct at next year's festival."

"Next year?" Ruth sank into a chair. "That's a long way off." She shook her head. "I'd like to go back to our lodgings now. It's been a very tiring day."

Silas held out his hand to help her up. For a moment, they stood close, the pressure of his hand in hers a comfort. He was a head taller than she was, but slightly stooped. When they'd first met, he'd reminded her of a crane with a bobbing head and anxious eyes.

"Mrs. Henton?"

Ruth dropped Silas's hand and turned to see a well-dressed man coming towards her.

"I thought that was you," he said. "Permit me to introduce myself. I am Morris Anderson."

"Pleased to meet you," Ruth said. "Have we met? Is there something I can help you with?"

"We have not formally met, no," He smiled, showing even teeth. Ruth judged him to be in his late forties. He looked over Ruth's shoulder at Silas. "May I borrow Mrs. Henton for a moment?"

"Oh, yes. Of course." He leaned close to Ruth. "I'll meet you at the entrance?"

She nodded and waited for Mr. Anderson to continue. In his dove-gray suit and patterned waistcoat, he looked out of place in a gathering of mostly local people dressed simply.

"I saw you perform many times in London," he said. "You were wonderful."

"That is kind of you to say. But as you see, I'm no longer performing."

"Evidently." He looked around at the crowded hall, his expression scornful. "You've chosen a new profession."

"Yes." She hoped he'd get to the point. The elation was fading as quickly as the sun on a winter's day. If she didn't get to bed soon, she was in danger of fainting.

"Have you positively decided against a return to the theater?" he asked.

"What do you mean?"

"I have a proposition for you, Mrs. Henton, that I very much hope you'll seriously consider. A talent such as yours must not be kept from the public. May I give you my card?"

Before Ruth could answer, he pressed a card into her hand. She looked down at it, her heart racing.

Morris Anderson, Manager, Buckland Theatrical Troupe, Manchester.

"You have a theater in Manchester?" she asked, looking up.

He waved away the question. "We perform there, yes."

"And what is your proposition, Mr. Anderson?" she asked.

"I should think that is obvious, Mrs. Henton," he said. "I'd like you to join us as our principal soloist."

Chapter 33

Briarstown

Eliza

On the first balmy day in April, with one week to go until the competition in Whitby, Eliza strode to the Saturday afternoon rehearsal, smiling and nodding at everyone she passed.

She'd never felt so confident. The choir had learned both its songs, and in Eliza's opinion, they sounded wonderful. When all the voices sang together as one, she felt weightless. One gust of the mild April breeze and she'd float high above the smokestacks of Briarstown, as free as the wisps of cotton perpetually swirling through the air. Snatches of song bubbled from her lips as she walked.

She arrived at the church hall and nodded hello to Miss Donahue, who was at the piano talking with Mrs. Walker. She then turned to watch the rest of the women stream into the hall. They looked so different from the group that had first come together five months earlier. Instead of heavy coats and boots, they wore light-colored blouses and small straw hats.

But more than their dress had changed. The women walked with their heads held higher, their movements more agile and self-assured. Eliza greeted them like the friends they'd become. They laughed and chattered as they got into position.

Miss Donahue stepped forward and folded her hands across the bodice of her navy dress. She looked more at peace than she had at their last rehearsal. Glancing over at Eliza, she nodded as if to reassure her.

"Good afternoon, ladies," Miss Donahue said. "In one week, we'll be competing in Whitby. How are you feeling?"

"Terrified!" Josie said.

"And excited!" Lottie chimed in. "You've done wonders with us, Miss Donahue."

"So do you think you're ready?" she asked.

A chorus of yesses dissolved into laughter.

"Good. Now, today I want you to forget everything you've learned and sing the music, not the notes."

"What do you mean?" Hattie asked. "I thought you said we was to learn the notes."

"Yes, and you have learned them. You can sing them in your sleep. But to win in Whitby, you need to tell a story to the audience. You want to share with them the emotion of this music—the joyfulness of it. Do you understand?"

A few heads nodded.

"Don't think any more about notes and intervals and breathing. You know all that. Now come together to make music." She raised her baton.

Mrs. Walker played the introduction to their set piece *Ye Spotted Snakes*. It was a jaunty, rhythmic melody meant to convey the lightness of the fairies. Eliza breathed in, remembering how Miss Donahue told her that singing should begin before she made any sound. The baton lowered, and she began her solo.

When, after several bars, the rest of the choir joined in, Eliza's heart expanded. From mothers and wives and mill hands, they had transformed themselves into a choir, united in a common purpose.

After the rehearsal, Eliza returned home to find Reg already sitting by the cold grate in an empty house. The girls—her protection—were scattered outside in the yard, playing with their friends.

"Fire's not lit," he said.

"So, light it," Eliza said without thinking. Moments later, he jumped up from his chair and came at her.

She twisted away and backed toward the door. If she could get outside, she'd be safe. Several of the women from the choir were still out there, and plenty of the men too, what with it being Saturday and a half-day. Reg would cool down soon enough. The girls would come back in the house and all would be well. He'd be rough with her that night, but there wasn't much she could do about that.

"Stay still," he growled. "I'll not be sassed in my own house." He wedged himself between her and the doorknob, then closed one hand over her forearm. He yanked her towards him, crushing her small frame against his chest. "I don't like the way you're gettin'," he hissed.

She kept her eyes on his face, determined to show him she wasn't afraid, resisting the temptation to look down at his hand encircling her arm. She wouldn't give him the satisfaction of wincing as he increased the pressure, grinding bone on bone. "I'm not getting *like* anything, Reg."

"Yer changin'."

She knew better than to argue. The window was open a crack, letting in the sound of children playing yards away. Any moment now, one of the girls could come in and see her trapped like a fly under glass.

"Let me go, Reg," she said as steadily as she could. "I'll get the fire lit and the tea made in no time."

"I'll not put up with it, you hear?" He squeezed until finally she gasped. Then, to her astonishment, he threw her to the floor.

She landed on her shoulder, the jolt as startling as the sound of all the looms at the mill turning on at the same time. For the first time since the first time he'd hit her, Eliza felt fear crawling up from the darkness she kept buried deep inside her—as loathsome as the stinking waters that had taken her little brother.

For the first time since the first time, she wondered if he'd kill her.

She lay very still, hearing only his breathing above her, imagining the rage on his face. Usually, it dissipated quickly and then he'd say he was sorry, and it was her fault for provoking him. She kept her eyes closed against the humiliation and the fear.

Then, the thought that one of the girls might come in gave her the strength to pull herself up to sitting. She could not let them see her like this. Opening her eyes, she stared at the cold grate. Would he push her back down? What if she hit her head on the brick hearth and died?

For a few moments that felt like years, Eliza imagined making the final escape. She'd see Dad again, and little Ernie. She'd be free.

A memory of the first time Annie smiled up at her when she was just four months old swam past Eliza's fear and into her heart. Annie's whole face had radiated with such purity, such trust. Her first born had grown so tall now and so capable. She'd be a woman soon and would need Eliza more than ever.

What of Lily May, brassy and with an innate self-confidence that Eliza both envied and admired? She'd need someone to channel her energy, to help her grow into a woman who could take on the world.

Eliza thought of studious, serious Gladys who was so like Reg in her looks, but nothing like him in personality. Who would help her choose good books?

And Emily—quiet and kind, she welcomed in the harsh world around her without question, content to play in a corner with her baby sister, content to follow the bigger girls around in the hopes they'd sometimes notice and include her.

Finally, with a half-suppressed sob, Eliza remembered twirling Bessie at the edge of the moor, of her round cheeks glowing, her blue eyes crinkled with laughter.

If Mother faltered, what would become of her girls?

At least Reg had never yet laid a hand on them. On the other hand, he'd also never thrown her to the floor.

Eliza scrambled to her feet and turned to face him.

"I'm sorry…" he stuttered. "I didn't mean for you to fall. You're always so clumsy."

"No harm done," Eliza said through gritted teeth. "Must have tripped." She slid past him. "I'll light the fire now." She forced herself to keep moving, to not look back at him. "Won't take a minute, and then I'll make your tea."

Chapter 34

Yorkshire

Ruth

Ruth waited until after breakfast the next morning to tell Silas. They stood together at the entrance to the inn, watching as their cases were loaded onto a cart to take them to the train station. They were returning to Manchester for a week off before heading for a competition in Sheffield.

"You can't quit!" Silas exclaimed. "The association won't allow it."

"I'm sure the association will easily find someone to replace me. And you must have known I'd return to the theater as soon as I got the chance."

"I don't know," he said. "I never thought about it. You've settled in so well, and last night, your conducting was wonderful. You can't tell me you didn't enjoy yourself."

Ruth pushed aside a pang of remorse. "Mr. Anderson has offered me a starring role with his company. I can't turn him down."

Silas crossed his arms over his chest. "You're sure this is what you want?"

"It is."

"Then I wish you well, Mrs. Henton."

"Will you not finally call me Ruth?" she asked, trying to put a playful note in her voice. "We may not be colleagues any longer, but we can still be friends."

"Friends?" Silas turned away quickly and signaled for the cart driver to pull up in front of the inn. He helped her into the cart and climbed in after her. They sat side by side facing backwards, momentarily touching shoulders when the cart lurched forward. He shifted away.

During the short drive to the train station, the cart passed the hall where

Ruth had spent three days with Silas adjudicating festival participants. All that remained of the concert the night before were a few programs scattered across the grass. Two children emerged from a small terrace house and began running alongside the cart.

"Sir! Miss!" they called and waved. They began singing their part from the concert. Ruth felt a lump in her throat as she returned their wave.

"We do good work," Silas said quietly, his case fixed on the road. "You must see that."

"I do."

"Then why leave? Do you really think you'll get as much satisfaction performing with Mr. Anderson's troupe? You know nothing about him."

"I'll be performing again," Ruth said. "I never wanted to leave the stage. There were, ah, circumstances."

"I don't wish to pry," Silas said. "You have your reasons, I'm sure. But what we do *helps* people. We bring music into their lives. That's got to be worth something."

Ruth stayed silent. If only the cart would move faster. The sooner she got to Manchester and away from Silas, the better. Who did he think he was, telling her how she should live? Mr. Anderson had promised her a share of the profits in addition to an admittedly meagre salary. But she'd be back on stage! When she'd asked which parts she'd play, Mr. Anderson had been vague, only assuring her that he looked forward to her enchanting every audience who came to see her perform.

At the station, Silas jumped out of the cart as soon as it came to a stop. Instead of helping Ruth out, he spoke a few words to the driver and then busied himself with the luggage. Ruth was left standing until the driver lumbered around the cart and offered his hand to help her descend. Feeling both chastened and annoyed, she followed Silas into the station.

When they reached the platform, she turned to him. "I've truly enjoyed our time together," she said in what she hoped was a mollifying tone.

"I'm happy to hear it."

"Please, Mr. Gallagher…Silas. I belong on the stage. You've said it yourself."

A great hissing and creaking signaled the arrival of the train. By the time they'd boarded and were seated opposite each other in a compartment, Silas would no longer meet her eye. She kept her gaze on the passing landscape and resolved not to explain herself. He was being unreasonable.

She'd been given a second chance. Silas should be happy for her.

Chapter 35

Briarstown

Eliza

"Everyone's depending on me! I have to go!" Eliza knew it was foolish to let Reg see her desperation, but she couldn't stop herself. Her arm still ached from where he'd grabbed her, but at least her sleeve hid the bruise. No one would know.

"Our Bessie's poorly," Reg said. "You said it yourself. Your place is here with the girls."

"Bessie's fever broke yesterday. I'll ask Mrs. Harris to check on her, and you know Annie's very capable."

"I don't like Mrs. Harris. I'll not have her in the house."

"She brought all five of our girls into the world. Besides, you promised."

"I said no, Eliza." Reg walked around her to the door. "You'll stay here with our Bessie and there's an end to it." He placed his hand on the knob. "I'd best get to work. There's a lecture I've a hankering to go to after my shift and then I'll stop by the pub. I should be home by nine or ten."

Eliza's heart sank. In the past few days while Bessie had been feeling poorly, Reg had reined in his drinking to such an extent that he'd come home drunk only once. Fortunately, he'd not tried to hurt her since grabbing her arm and throwing her to the floor. But there was no guarantee it wouldn't happen again. She felt as if she were invisible, without will or purpose. What would the other women say? She was the soloist. The choir needed her!

"The whole town's depending on us," she said. "Do you want everyone knowing it was you who stopped it?"

"The choir can do very well without you," Reg said. "And no one will think the worse of you for staying home to take care of Bessie. They'd be much more likely to talk if you *didn't* stay home. What kind of mother leaves her sick child?"

"Bessie will be fine. It was only a cold," Eliza said. "I wouldn't leave her if I didn't think so."

"Last week, a bairn died of fever. He was only a wee lad, just two years old. His dad worked with me. Poor bugger was a wreck. D'you want that on your conscience?"

Bessie cried out, and moments later, Annie appeared at the foot of the stairs. "Bessie's asking for ye, Ma," she said. "You'd best come."

Eliza ran up the narrow stairwell, almost toppling forward in her haste to reach Bessie. She'd rather die herself than be the cause of another child's death. What if she was wrong, and Bessie was really ill? She'd had a fever for a few days, but it had broken, and the child had slept peacefully for the past two nights. Eliza laid the back of her hand against Bessie's forehead. It was dry and cool. Tears of relief welled in her eyes, dripping down and off her chin to the worn coverlet.

"Don't cry, Ma," Bessie said.

"Hush, girl. Go back to sleep."

"Where's Dad?"

"He's gone off to work. When he comes home, he'll come up to see you."

"I want to see Dad!"

Eliza stood and beckoned for Annie. "Stay with Bessie a while. I'll make tea."

"Are you going to Whitby now Bessie's better?" Annie asked. "I heard Dad say he wanted you to stay, but I don't think that's fair, Ma. You've worked so hard."

"Bessie might take a turn."

"She won't," Annie said. "And I'll be here to watch out for her. Lily May will help, and there's Mrs. Harris next door."

"You heard your dad."

"You'll be long gone by the time he gets home, and then there won't be much he can do about it."

Eliza almost laughed at the earnest look on her eldest daughter's face. She shouldn't encourage disloyalty, but wasn't she planning to take her daughters away forever? Loyalty had taken a back seat to rage since the first time Reg hit her.

Eliza cupped her daughter's bonny cheeks between her two hands and kissed her forehead. "Thank you, Annie. You're a good girl." She quickly folded her best dress into a small bag, along with a hairbrush and a change of linens. She'd need to stay overnight in Whitby to compete in the solo category the following day.

"You'd better hurry, Ma," Annie said. "You don't want to miss your train."

Chapter 36

Manchester

Ruth

"Ah, Mrs. Henton. You've come at last. I was starting to despair." Mr. Anderson welcomed Ruth into a small office on the ground floor of a nondescript building on a narrow street in the center of Manchester.

"My apologies," Ruth said, her breath catching in her chest after a climb up two sets of rickety stairs. "I was looking for a theater at this address and got myself turned around. The cab driver insisted this was the place, but I directed him to drive to the end of the road and back."

"Understandable, but in this instance, incorrect." Mr. Anderson gestured to the one other chair in the office, then hastily stepped forward and removed a stack of playbills. Ruth noticed the words *Halifax Fairground* in large letters.

In the scruffy office on the second floor of a building in a rough area of Manchester, Ruth felt like a peacock in a barnyard. She'd spent some of her wages from the Music Association on a new hat and pair of soft mauve gloves that perfectly matched the one good day dress she'd brought to the North. The chair wobbled under her weight as she sat. A small prickle of doubt lodged itself in the pit of her stomach, but she pushed it aside. Mr. Anderson was respectably dressed and had a gentlemanly manner about him. She shouldn't jump to conclusions.

"In my experience, managers have their offices backstage at their theaters," Ruth commented.

"That would be the normal way of it, I agree," Mr. Anderson said cheerfully. He settled into a wooden revolving chair that squeaked under his weight. She noticed that much of the oak finish had rubbed off.

"I don't understand," she said.

"The truth is, Mrs. Henton, that I may have given you the wrong impression about my little enterprise."

"You said you wished me to perform with your troupe," Ruth said, keeping her voice calm. "I took that to mean you had a theater here in Manchester."

"That is not precisely the case, although we have on occasion performed in Manchester."

"Are you saying that you *don't* have a theater?"

"Not in the traditional sense, no." His smile widened. "We are a traveling troupe, Mrs. Henton. From May through October, we go from town to town, mostly here in England, but occasionally as far north as Edinburgh. The Scottish audiences are most enthusiastic. And you, Mrs. Henton, will be our new star."

"A traveling troupe?"

"You'll find us a jolly lot. We travel with our own theater, which measures a good seventy by forty feet. We also have five scenes on rollers, all the ropes and pulleys we need to change them, and of course a respectable array of props and costumes."

"What do you perform?"

"Our repertoire varies. Usually, we put on at least one scene from Shakespeare. Lady Macbeth's sleepwalking scene is always popular. Your predecessor did an admirable job, as I'm sure you will, too."

"My predecessor?" Ruth asked weakly.

"Oh yes. Miss Gleeson was a cherished member of our troupe."

"What happened to her?"

"Ah, well," Mr. Anderson demurred. "An unfortunate accident took her from us."

"An accident?"

"A fluke, I assure you. We were performing in a field near Leeds and there was an atmospheric disturbance." He paused. "A hailstorm. Regrettably, Miss Gleeson was standing too close to a piece of scenery that detached."

"She was killed?" Ruth asked, stunned.

"Oh no, no, no, nothing so dramatic," Mr. Anderson said, smiling again. "But she was, I am sorry to say, rather badly injured."

"When did this happen?"

"Not long ago. But please, let us not dwell upon such unpleasantness.

You're here now, and I'm sure you're anxious to meet the rest of the troupe. I've scheduled a rehearsal for this afternoon. You will perform three songs. Can you also do the Lady Macbeth scene? It's not essential, but as I said, it's very popular."

Ruth stared at him in disbelief. Her dreams of returning triumphant to the stage, even if it wasn't the London stage, disappeared like wisps of smoke on a windy day. What Mr. Anderson was describing was no better than a traveling music hall. She wouldn't be surprised if his troupe included a fire eater, a magician, and acrobats.

"I think there's been a mistake," she said finally, her throat tight.

"No mistake, I assure you."

"In London, I was the principal female star at the Palladia Theatre. The Prince of Wales regularly came to watch me perform."

"Yes, you were quite charming. But I'm afraid, Mrs. Henton, that you are fooling yourself if you think you'll get a better offer. I'm giving you star billing."

"I am not so bereft as to need to stoop to such a level."

"You think yourself too good for my theater?" Mr. Anderson no longer looked so genial. His brow darkened and he gripped the edge of his desk.

"I don't wish to offend."

"But?"

Ruth thought about Silas, his gentleness, the admiration in his eyes when he looked at her. It wasn't the fervor of the boys who crowded into the stalls, whistling and calling *brava*, but nor was it the calculating admiration of men like the Prince of Wales or even William. *They* only wanted her because she was a star.

Silas looked at her like she mattered because of who she was, not because of what she could do.

She stood. "Good day to you, Mr. Anderson. I wish you all the best with your theater, but I won't be able to join you."

His lip curled with disdain, reminding her of how Kingwell had looked the one time he'd grabbed her wrist with enough force to snap it. The pain had been nothing compared to the humiliation.

Mr. Anderson rose from his desk. "You're making a mistake," he said. "I saw you perform many times in London. If you'd stayed, it wouldn't have been long before you'd be begging the music halls to take you on."

"Good day, Mr. Anderson."

Chapter 37

Briarstown

Eliza

"Take care of your sister," Eliza said. "If something happens, fetch Mrs. Harris."

"I know, Ma," Annie said. "You've told me three times. But nothing's going to happen."

"Here's some money to buy sausages for your dad's tea, and some sweeties for yourself and your sisters."

Annie looked down at the coins nestled in her palm and then up again at Eliza. "Thank you."

The door banged open. "Here you!" Reg said to Gladys, who was sitting at the table reading. "Fetch me my lunch pail." He looked over at Eliza, who had stepped away from Annie. "You forgot to give it me."

"It was there on the table," she said. "I can't be looking out for you every minute of the day." Her heart clenched. Reg coming home now might well prevent her from getting to the train in time.

"Well, now I'm here, I'll stop a moment and have another brew," Reg said. "Mr. Lewiston's off to London this morning and he'll not miss me if I'm a few minutes late getting back." He settled himself into his chair. "And I'll have another slice of that bread and jam."

Eliza glanced over at the small black bag in the corner of the room, all packed and ready for her journey to Whitby. Almost as if she could read her mother's mind, Annie edged over to the sink and grabbed a towel off the rack. When her father's attention was fixed on the slab of bread Eliza was cutting, Annie dropped the towel over the bag. Eliza marvelled at the quickness of her daughter, not to mention the steadiness of her own hands. The train would leave in twenty-five minutes, and she needed ten minutes to get to the station.

Reg stretched his legs out in front of him and sighed with pleasure at the unexpected break in his morning routine. "Good lass," he said to Gladys as she handed him a cup of milky tea. "I'm a lucky man to have such a helpful daughter." He beamed at Eliza. "All is forgiven about the lunch pail," he said. "Don't be stingy with the jam, love."

Eliza crossed to the sink to keep her back to Reg. The day that moments before had held such promise now faded to the relentless sameness of every day she spent in that house. She closed her eyes and clutched the side of the sink to keep from slumping. She hated letting down Miss Donahue and the women in the choir. They'd all worked so hard. But what she hated most of all was losing her only chance to make enough money to get away from Briarstown for good.

Behind her, Reg droned on about the mill and how Mr. Lewiston still wouldn't give him his old job back. She'd heard the same litany of complaints for years and could recite them herself.

I'm in the right and everyone knows it. That hussy who went over my head to complain about me should be ashamed of herself. It was only a bit of fun. And as for you—aren't I always the very best of husbands? A devoted father? If I sometimes lose my temper with your nagging, then who could blame me? I'm only human, and so much is expected of me. You know I had a hard go of it when I was young. I deserve better.

"I'd best be off," he said finally. When Eliza heard him stand, she forced herself to turn around, her face impassive. A smile would make him suspicious. Reg was many things, but stupid was not one of them. She suspected he'd left his lunch pail on purpose so he could return and prevent her from joining the others at the train station.

"Off you go, then," she said. "There'll be chops for your tea, so don't spend too long at the pub after your lecture."

"I'll be home when I'm home," he said.

As the door closed behind him, Eliza glanced at the small clock on the wall. 8:20. The train departed in ten minutes. She'd never make it in time. Her knees weakened, so she had to sit down quickly to avoid falling. Annie and Gladys stared at her.

"You've gone all white, Ma," Gladys said.

"I'm fine," she snapped. "You've got chores. Off you go." She closed her eyes against the clatter of Emily bursting in from the courtyard carrying water from the pump and going on about a fight that had broken out between two boys. Moments later, Lily May came down the stairs like a ton of bricks to add her perspective on the fight, which she'd seen from the top-floor window.

To Eliza's relief, Annie shushed Lily May and Emily and sent them out to the yard, saying Ma had a headache and needed some quiet. She then took Gladys's book from her and shooed her out as well.

"Stop your bellyaching," Annie hissed to her little sister. "Go play outside with the others." She then turned to Eliza. "Ma?"

Eliza didn't respond. She'd never get her girls away now. Each one of them would end up in the mill, any hopes they might have for a different life sucked into the unrelenting clatter of the looms.

"Leave me be," Eliza said wearily. "Go upstairs and check on Bessie."

"You can still go," Annie said. "I'll handle Dad."

"The train's gone already; I'll never make it."

"You got to try, Ma. And there's the solo singing tomorrow, right? I've heard you practicing, and you sound wonderful. Get your bag and run to the station. You can catch the next train."

"I'll be late."

"If the choir isn't singin' first, you'll have time."

"Maybe? I don't know." Eliza looked up into Annie's determined face and sensed their roles shifting. The hard shell she'd cultivated in front of her girls began to crumble, leaving her feeling bewildered and out of control. Annie sensed the shift and seemed to grow taller.

"Go!" She picked up Eliza's bag and thrust it at her. "Now!"

Pride in her daughter propelled her to her feet. If Annie believed so much in her, then she had to try. Eliza gathered Annie into a hug and briefly rested her cheek against her hair.

"Thank you," she said. "Take care of your sisters."

"I will, Ma."

Eliza left the house and crossed the courtyard to the narrow passageway leading to the street, then turned toward the station.

"Mrs. Kingwell!" George Ledbetter came alongside her, matching her quick pace. "You're in an awful rush. Aren't you supposed to be on the train with the others?"

"I've been detained," she said. "And now I'm in a hurry to catch the next train."

"But it's not until one o'clock! You'll not get to Whitby until four, and surely that's too late for the competition."

"There's a train at ten."

"Been cancelled."

"What?"

George shook his head. "Sorry to be the bearer of bad news, but I've just come from the station, and the stationmaster told me there's been a problem down the line." He took her arm and steered her toward a pony hitched to a small cart. "I've got old Meg here with the cart. I can give you a lift."

She pulled back. "I couldn't put you out!"

"It's no trouble. I can take you to Middlesbrough, and from there you can catch the fast train. You'll be in Whitby by two, I promise."

"But…"

"Please, Mrs. Kingwell, Eliza, let me help you. I'm off work this morning and got nowt to occupy my time. The whole town's depending on the choir to bring back a trophy."

"I can't."

But even as she protested, she let George help her into the cart. She glanced around, afraid of prying eyes. What would people think if they saw her going off with another man? Fortunately, the street was quiet.

George climbed up next to her and moments later was steering them out of Briarstown and up the hill to the main road. Eliza looked back at the mills clustered around the river in the valley below. Smoke belched from every chimney, and even from a distance, she could hear the clash of machinery. And then they passed over the ridge, and the moors spread before her, splendid in the April sunshine.

At the station, George took Eliza's elbow to help her from the cart. The heat of his hand seeping through the thin material of her summer dress took Eliza by surprise. She felt a stirring she hadn't experienced since early in her marriage to Reg, and even then, only once or twice. She pulled away.

"Thank you, Mr. Ledbetter. You are a lifesaver."

"Come now, Eliza. You know it's George, and I'm always happy to help." He was much taller than Reg and yet standing close to him didn't frighten her. He leaned towards her, his breath warm, "I've a mind to get a train ticket myself and come watch you."

"I'd like that," she said, momentarily caught off guard.

"You would?"

The tenderness in his voice soothed her heart and for a moment, she imagined softening into his arms, of bending without breaking.

But there was no room in the Plan for George Ledbetter.

"Suit yourself," she said stepping away. "I'm obliged to you for the lift, but I'd best get inside. The train goes in ten minutes."

Before he had a chance to say more, she almost ran into the station, her face burning with a mixture of shame and pleasure.

Chapter 38

Manchester

Ruth

Ruth hurried along the street, her eyes blurred with tears. What a fool she'd been to accept Mr. Anderson's offer! His cruel words echoed in her ears—*you were on your way down, my dear. I'm offering you a chance to redeem yourself.*

Redeem herself? She'd rather never sing again than spend months traveling around the country like a common tramp.

She stopped and looked around, conscious that she had no idea where she was and how she'd get back to her lodgings. Fortunately, Mrs. Patterson had let her keep her room for another week while she got settled with the new theater. Her disapproval had been cold enough to freeze the watery porridge she served at breakfast.

The April day swirled with a damp, cold fog that held no promise of spring. Ruth wondered if sunny days ever came to this gloomy city. The shops she passed were mean-looking, with many windows boarded up, and the people she passed on the street were roughly dressed.

She came even with a young woman sitting on a stone step in front of a two-story house. She wore a coarse knitted shawl around her shoulders and was singing to the small child she held in her arms. She stopped singing when she saw Ruth.

"You look lost, ma'am."

Another woman came towards them, also carrying a child. "You comin' tonight, Mabel?" she asked the woman sitting on the step.

"Wouldn't miss it." The woman gestured to Ruth. "This lady here's lost."

"Do you know how I get to Warren Road?" Ruth asked.

"It's a ways off, but aye, I know it. If ye like, I can get my Harry to show you."

"That would be very kind," Ruth said. "Thank you." To her surprise, she felt a kinship with these women who looked like they lived hard lives yet had no qualms about helping a stranger. "I heard you singing just now. You sounded lovely."

"That's good of you to say, ma'am. I was practicing as it happens." The woman nodded toward her friend. "Me and Ruby here sing in a choir if you can believe it."

"Do you like it?"

"Oh, aye," said Ruby. "I never thought I'd do such a thing, but now we got started, I can't imagine doing without."

Mabel nodded agreement as she beckoned at a young boy who was playing in the street. "Go get your da for me." She looked up at Ruth. "Harry will see you to Warren Street. You needn't be afraid. He's a good sort."

"I'm sure he is." Ruth smiled. "While I'm waiting, would you sing again?"

"'Course. Ruby? Let's sing her the song by that Schubert fella." The two women launched into a spirited rendition of a song often performed by the choirs that Ruth judged. The two women's voices harmonized, with one taking the soprano and the other the alto.

Ruth's heart swelled and when the women reached the chorus, she joined in, harmonizing a second soprano part. For a few moments, their voices faltered, and then both women grinned and sang louder. A few windows flew up and heads leaned out, while passersby stopped to listen.

When the women finished singing, the people in the street and looking out of the houses clapped and cheered.

"Happen yer quite the singer yerself," Ruby said.

"I suppose you could say that," Ruth replied. Suddenly, she felt lighter, as if shedding the weight of a dream that no longer served her.

A man wearing a flat cap and in shirt sleeves despite the damp cold crossed the street and stopped in front of them.

"Here's my Harry," Mabel said, standing and bouncing the baby against her shoulder. "Nice meeting you, miss. Yer all right."

"Keep singing," Ruth said.

"Oh, aye, you can count on us doin' that."

Two days later, Ruth stood before Mr. Harrison at the Music Association office in Manchester and asked for her job back.

"It's highly irregular," he said. "And most inconvenient."

"I'm sorry for it," she said as humbly as she could.

"I should say so."

"I promise I won't let the association down again, sir."

"Humph, well, I suppose you may return, but only because I wouldn't want it getting back to Mr. Gordon that I wasn't accommodating enough to your whims. He was very particular that I take you on, although knowing your background, I had my doubts."

Ruth remembered Mr. Gordon as the man who had written the grudging letter of acceptance. She hid a smile. "He was very kind to accept me," she said.

"See to it that you don't up and get married and leave me in the lurch again," he said. "That keeps happening with the young women. It's why I'd rather we didn't accept them. No sooner do I get them trained, then they meet a man and off they go." He looked her up and down. "Although I suppose you're past all that now."

With an effort, Ruth kept quiet. *How dare he?* She was not yet thirty-one.

He scribbled a note and handed it to her. "The train for Whitby leaves tomorrow at nine. The festival's only in its second year and the association's anxious for it to build. Make us proud."

"I will," Ruth promised. She knew Silas would be one of the judges at the festival. At least *he* would welcome her back with open arms.

Chapter 39

Whitby in Yorkshire

Eliza

By the time the train pulled into Whitby station, Eliza had only a few minutes to get to the auditorium. She ran, dodging holidaymakers—men decked out in boaters, women sporting hats, some the size of roasting platters. When she entered the auditorium, she saw the Briarstown women already assembling near the stage. She pushed past the people crowding the aisles until she stood behind a table facing the stage. A well-dressed lady and a gentleman were seated there, their gazes fixed on the choir perform-ing—a group of young women wearing matching white lace blouses and black skirts. Eliza took in the lady's thick swirl of blonde hair, the long neck and blooming cheek.

She stopped so abruptly a man coming up behind her almost knocked her over. "Watch where you're going, love," he whispered.

"Sorry." She stepped aside to let him pass, her heart pounding. She thought of running out of the auditorium before Ruth saw her.

The choir finished their piece and bowed. Miss Donahue took advan-tage of the applause to rush towards Eliza, her arms outstretched.

"You made it! We're on next. Come!"

As Eliza followed Miss Donahue to the stage, she glanced over at Ruth, who at that moment turned her head and saw her. Eliza's throat constricted as the old anger surfaced but tinged now with regret. Her former friend looked as beautiful as ever, while Eliza knew the years hadn't treated her kindly. No wonder she'd read nothing about Ruth in the papers for months.

"Are you prepared?" Miss Donahue asked when they reached the stage. "Can you sing?"

"I'm ready," Eliza said firmly.

She couldn't think about Ruth. Nothing could change the past, and her first allegiance now was to the women closing in around her, clucking with relief and excitement.

"Thank God!" Hattie said. "We can't do without *you*."

Moments later, the fifteen women mounted the platform and faced the packed hall. Eliza reached out and squeezed Minnie's hand. "Breathe," she whispered.

Minnie nodded, her face as pale as a bolt of unbleached linen.

Miss Donahue raised her baton. Eliza remembered her words at the last rehearsal.

Sing the music.

She imagined the hearts of the women all around her beating time together, each breath fusing into one breath. The hours and weeks of practice had come down to this moment.

Eliza fixed her gaze on Miss Donahue, who mouthed the words *Good luck* and smiled. She, too, had been transformed by her work with the choir. She stood taller and with more confidence, reminding Eliza of the teacher who had first introduced her to singing. There was still a sadness about her, which Eliza now knew was because of her son growing up so far away in Canada. She imagined Miss Donahue as a young woman, frightened and alone as she gave birth to a child she hadn't been allowed to keep.

At least Eliza had not experienced that kind of loss. The ache for baby Ernie never left her, but she didn't have to live with the pain of knowing he lived but was lost to her.

Behind her, Eliza sensed the collective intake of breath, the nervous energy of fifteen women who had dared step out of their lives for a few hours a week to sing together. They'd prove to the world that lasses who toiled in the mills and mothers who brought up their children in dingy back-to-backs and pinched each penny until it bled could make music that touched the soul.

The pianist played the introduction, and Eliza began to sing.

Chapter 40

Whitby

Ruth

Ruth sat forward in her seat, her eyes fixed on Eliza, who stood at the front of the choir and to the right of Miss Donahue. When she'd seen the entry for the Briarstown Ladies' Choir in the program after arriving in Whitby a few days earlier, Ruth had presumed it was one of the choirs in the Briarstown Choral Society. She'd never expected women whom she'd known as girls to form a choir with Eliza taking the soprano solo. She studied the faces of the women. Hattie had changed little, although the sneer Ruth remembered as a perpetual feature on young Hattie's face had been replaced by an expression of total concentration as she waited for Eliza to finish her solo.

Little Josie had also not changed—still looking fresh-faced and kind-hearted, while Hannah appeared as stolid and cheerful as ever. Ruth wondered if she still walked with a limp because of the accident at the mill, and if she'd ever had a child to replace the one she lost. The presence of mousy little Minnie was a surprise. She stood next to Eliza, ready to take the contralto solo. Ruth remembered Minnie only as Hattie's loyal side-kick—a pale, timid little girl with faded ribbons in her hair.

Minnie was still pale, to be sure, but with her hands clasped in front of her and her chin held high, she no longer looked timid.

"This is the first competition for the Briarstown Ladies' Choir," Silas whispered. "We must be encouraging."

Ruth nodded. She couldn't let on that she knew half the women in the choir, and that the choir mistress had once been her teacher. Silas was a stickler for the rules. If he found out, he'd ask her to step aside to avoid any whiff of favoritism.

Since Ruth's return to her Music Association duties, he'd been distant, only speaking to her when they sat at the judges' table. The evening before, he'd left the auditorium first, so she'd had to make her way back to the hotel on her own. Whitby was small, and the hotel was a short walk from the auditorium, but his inattention pained her. He should be happy she'd come back.

The pianist played the opening bars of *Ye spotted snakes*. A perennial favorite as a set piece for the ladies' choirs, Ruth had heard it performed dozens of times. It was a demanding piece, particularly for the two soloists, and, more often than not, poorly executed.

Ruth realized she was holding her breath in anticipation. Had Miss Donahue managed to turn these women into a choir worth listening to? Although each one wore what must be their best dress, they looked shabby and care-worn next to the women from the other choirs, with their well-cut dresses and elegant hats. The choir from Halifax even sported matching blue silk sashes, and each lady in the Leeds choir wore a cameo brooch at the throat of their high-necked lace collars.

Miss Donahue's baton lowered, and Eliza's voice rang out into the auditorium. Ruth allowed her shoulders to relax. The tone and pitch were perfect, the choir sounding as musical as any Ruth had yet heard in the competition. And the expression! Eliza sang so passionately about keeping snakes and hedgehogs away from the faerie queene that Ruth's heart quickened. She could almost see the fairies rushing to protect their queen.

When the choir took up the stirring refrain, tears pricked her eyes. With an effort, Ruth kept her gaze steady. Next to her, Silas was scribbling notes, but she couldn't move. Minnie chimed in with the contralto part. While not as polished as Eliza, Minnie's voice held a sweet richness. When the two sang together, the effect was mesmerizing.

Loud applause that went on longer than the applause for the other choirs rewarded the Briarstown Ladies Choir. Some of the women in the choirs waiting to go on looked dismayed, and Ruth couldn't blame them. She also wouldn't have wanted to follow that performance.

After the last of the five competing choirs finished performing, Silas turned to her. "The Halifax choir had a wonderful tone. What did you think?"

"They sang well," Ruth said.

"But?"

"Their articulation was a bit lacking."

"It was perfect!" Silas exclaimed.

"And the tempo was too slow."

"Surely not! I don't think we were listening to the same choir. Their tempo was perfect."

"The Briarstown Choir had a more comprehensive grasp of the piece. I liked their interpretation," Ruth said. "And their tone was crisp and balanced. I've rarely heard better."

"What mark did you give them?"

"Forty-eight."

"Impressive! I've never known you to mark a choir so high. But I agree they sang well." He looked down at his scorecard. "I gave them a forty-seven."

"What about Halifax?"

"Also, forty-seven."

"I gave them a forty-five."

"Then I suppose we must award the prize to the Briarstown Ladies Choir," Silas said. "Quite an achievement for a first-time choir."

"It is," Ruth said, suppressing a smile.

Chapter 41

Whitby

Eliza

The Master of Ceremonies bounded up to the stage. He smiled genially and bowed to each of the five choirs assembled around him.

"Charming!" he said. "So much impressive talent has been displayed here by the ladies' choirs. May we have a round of applause for them all?"

As the audience clapped, Eliza studied the faces of the women in the other choirs. The elegant ladies in the Halifax choir looked particularly hopeful. According to Miss Donahue, they'd won first prize at last year's festival and were a fixture on the competition circuit with wins at festivals in Westmoreland, Morecambe, and Blackpool.

Eliza discreetly rubbed her damp palms against her skirt. Even if they didn't win, she was proud of herself and the others.

The Master of Ceremonies cleared his throat. "I have a special announcement. The winner of the Ladies' competition will be asked to compete at the Morecambe Festival in July."

Eliza noticed the Halifax ladies smiling and nodding complacently. Her heart sank. Even if they won, they'd never have enough money to travel all the way from Briarstown to Morecambe in Lancashire.

"And now, it is my very great pleasure to announce that the winner of the Ladies' competition at the Second Annual Whitby Music Festival is…" he paused for dramatic effect. "The Briarstown Ladies' Choir!"

Eliza felt like she'd been struck by lightning. They'd done it! They'd won!

She turned to the other women. They were all looking as stunned as she felt. Then Hattie let out a whoop, while Hannah and Lottie hugged each other, and Mary Denholm's smile was as wide as her face.

As the hall erupted with cheers and applause, Eliza caught the eye of the soloist from the Halifax choir. She looked like she was about to cry.

"You're our soloist," Hannah said. "You go."

"I can't!" Eliza tried to hang back, but several pairs of hands pushed her forward. She crossed the platform to stand before the Master of Ceremonies. He held out a small trophy and an envelope. She took them and faced the audience. Ruth was clapping wildly, her face alight with happiness. As their gazes met, they were girls again, friends again.

Eliza bowed and then gestured for the choir to join her. She felt as if she were floating a foot above the stage. The name of the Briarstown Ladies' Choir would be forever etched in the annals of the Whitby Music Festival! Eliza thought about how proud people would be back in Briarstown.

After the Master of Ceremonies congratulated them again, the women filed off the stage and out through the auditorium to the street, where they clustered around Miss Donahue like blackbirds to a birdbath, all talking at once.

"Did you hear? They want us to go to the festival in Morecambe!" Mary Denholm exclaimed. "Fancy that!"

"I've never been farther than Leeds," said Josie.

"Me as well," said Minnie.

"I've never even been *that* far," Gert said.

"How do they think we'd get there?" asked Lottie.

"Take the train, I suppose," Hattie said.

Everyone laughed.

"Ladies," Miss Donahue said, gesturing for them to stop talking as if she was about to conduct them again. "First, congratulations! You've achieved something truly remarkable. I'm so very proud of you."

"What do you think, Miss Donahue?" Hannah asked. "About this Morecambe business?"

"The Morecambe Festival is one of the largest music festivals in England," Miss Donahue said. "To be asked to compete there is a great honor."

"It's not much of an honor if we can't go," Doris said.

"And why can't we go?" Mary asked. "What's wrong with all of you? This is the most exciting thing that's ever happened to me. We *have* to go."

"What are we to do for money?" Minnie said. "I had enough trouble finding the money for the train fare to Whitby."

"There's the prize money," Lottie pointed out.

"It's not nearly enough," Doris said. "Besides, since my Ed got injured, I need my share."

Several of the women nodded.

"Eliza, what do you think?" Josie asked.

"I'm not sure," Eliza said. "Morecambe's a lot farther away than Whitby, and Doris is right about the money."

"Let's not give up so easily," Mary said. "What about that posh choir that came back from London in '79 with a gold medal? People went crazy. That could be us!"

Eliza smiled at the memory of Dad taking her to the train station to greet the members of the Briarstown Choral Society. The choir had come together right on the platform and favored the crowd with a song. Eagerly, Eliza had looked from one to another, at their red lips forming perfect O's when they were singing and then relaxing into smiles when they were not, their eyes fixed on the conductor. Each voice had blended into one glorious voice that shook the rafters of the train station. Eliza remembered thinking that nothing in the world could sound more heavenly.

"That was years ago," Hannah said. "Besides, everyone in that choir had money to spare."

"Not everyone," Gert said. "My Ma was in it, and my aunt. They managed and so can we."

"Miss Donahue?" Lottie said. "What should we do?"

"The festival is three months away," Miss Donahue said. "I think if you all put your minds to it, you'll find a way to raise the money."

The women murmured, some skeptical, others like Mary still proclaiming they'd find a way. Hattie turned to Eliza. "Good luck tomorrow," she said. "We'll be rooting for you."

The rest of the women chimed in with their good wishes until Hannah said, "We'd best get a move on if we're to catch the train. We'll see ye back in Briarstown, Eliza. We know you'll do us proud."

As Eliza watched the women walk away, the sound of their excited chatter fading into air that smelled of the sea, she wished she could go with them. A terrible loneliness replaced the isolation she'd spent years cultivating like armor to keep herself separate and alone. If she made sure she had no friends, then no one could know the truth about Reg.

"I was surprised to see Ruth judging the competition," Miss Donahue said. "Did you know about her new position? Mother and I used to love reading about her performances in the paper."

"We haven't kept in touch."

"You two were such good friends when you were girls."

"That was a long time ago," Eliza said. "If you don't mind, I'm going back to my lodgings. I'll see you tomorrow?"

"Of course. Get plenty of rest, and I'll meet you here at ten. And Eliza? Today, you proved that you belong here."

"Thanks."

Eliza set off toward her lodgings. Many hours stretched in front of her until bedtime—hours she had no idea how to fill. Back home, she never needed to think about how to spend her time. There was always something to do—a smock to mend, tea to make, clothes to wash, quarrels to settle, a husband to mollify.

She stopped and turned back towards the auditorium. People were spilling out into the street. One man came up to Eliza and tipped his hat. "Congratulations, missus," he said. "You were marvelous."

"You were and all," said another man. "Are you singing in the solo competition tomorrow?"

"I am."

"Good luck to ye!"

The two men walked off. A well-dressed lady nodded and smiled, and several more people offered their good wishes. While the praise buoyed her spirits, Eliza had never felt so alone.

She waited until the crowd thinned to a trickle of people and then took a deep breath and re-entered the auditorium.

Chapter 42

Whitby

Ruth

By the time the last of the choirs had left the stage, Ruth's head felt like it was being crushed under a thousand-pound weight, and her emotions were in turmoil. For ten hours, she'd endured Silas's long silences and reproachful looks. When he spoke to her about the competition, a scrupulous politeness replaced the charming deference he'd always shown her.

"Good evening," Silas said, standing. "We start again tomorrow at nine with the solo competitions. Please don't be late."

"I won't be," Ruth said. She wanted to grab hold of his arm and *make* him listen to her. She knew she'd made a mistake going to Mr. Harrison in Manchester. If Silas valued their friendship, he should at least *try* to understand why she'd done it.

His footsteps sounded hollow as he hurried through the empty auditorium. Ruth sighed. All she wanted was a hot cup of tea and the solace of sleep. The lodging house in Whitby was close to the seafront. The walk there in the fresh sea air would do her good.

"Hello, Ruth."

She looked up to see Eliza, looking pale and drained. Ruth's heart went out to her. She well remembered the crushing fatigue that followed the elation of a performance. "You sang beautifully," she said.

"I was wondering if maybe we might talk a minute."

"I'd like that." Ruth stood and gestured toward the door.

As she'd hoped, the fresh air eased her headache as she walked in silence with Eliza to a bench. It was directly in front of a large whalebone arch that framed a view of the town and the evocative ruins of the medieval Whitby Abbey rising high above the River Esk on East Cliff.

"It's beautiful here," Eliza said as they settled onto the bench and gazed out at the view.

Ruth wanted to say something, but she didn't know what. After so many years apart, how could they be anything more than strangers?

"I didn't expect to see you here," Eliza said. "What happened to your life in London?"

"My husband died, leaving behind so many debts that I lost my position at the theater. This job was available and so I took it." Not for the world would she tell Eliza the whole sordid truth.

"I'm sorry."

Ruth nodded. "As am I. But what about you? I was thrilled to see you singing again. You never should have stopped."

Too late, she realized her mistake.

"You know why I had to stop," Eliza said, her voice tight.

Ruth looked away, her heart racing as she replayed their last conversation by the canal all those years ago.

"I thought you *wanted* to marry him. You wouldn't promise me not to."

"I had no choice," Eliza said. "After Dad died, Ma and I had to go live with my aunt. Then your dad came along and got me in the family way with Annie. What else could I do?"

"He's not my dad," Ruth said.

The hurt simmered between them, dimming the bright day and twisting Ruth's heart with regret and guilt. She should have stopped Eliza from marrying Kingwell, should have told her that charming Reg Kingwell was not all he seemed.

"We were good friends," Eliza said. "Do you remember the day we met?"

"I can't forget it. You were down by the canal, twirling, of all things."

"It was the first time I'd walked so far along the canal that I came to the edge of the moor. It was so lovely there. I couldn't help myself."

"And so, you twirled. When I saw you, I thought, there's a girl who isn't afraid."

"You thought that?" Eliza asked.

"Oh yes! It's why I wanted to be your friend."

"I don't understand."

"I guess maybe I wanted to learn from you how not to be afraid. I loved all the times we met after school and sang together."

"I thought you had the most beautiful voice," Eliza said. "It's because of *you* I wanted to sing."

"You never told me that."

"I never got the chance. You went to that fancy academy, and I thought you wanted nothing more to do with me."

"You were wrong. Don't you remember when I came to see you after we sang at the Christmas bazaar?" As soon as she asked, Ruth wished she could take it back. How insensitive of her to remind Eliza of that terrible day! She saw Eliza's eyes widen, the hurt sparking for a second and then mastered.

"Not much use talking about it now," Eliza said tightly, regarding Ruth with that direct manner she'd had since she was a girl. "You said you were afraid in those days. Why?"

Ruth sighed. "I was terrified of Mother dying. She was never strong. When she married Kingwell…" Ruth paused. "I'm sorry. I suppose I should say your husband."

"Call him what you like. It makes no difference to me." Eliza laughed, a sound so harsh that Ruth recoiled. For years, she'd convinced herself that Kingwell had changed for Eliza, and that she had nothing to feel guilty about. "Tell me about your mother," Eliza said more gently. "Didn't she die of the pneumonia?"

"She did," Ruth said. "Kingwell wouldn't send for the doctor when I asked him to. She couldn't breathe, and yet he just stood there." Ruth looked up miserably. She'd carried the secret for so long that it had become a part of her. "He was drunk, Eliza, and he wouldn't help her."

"When I married Reg, he told me he'd sworn off the drink. Now I know why."

"And did he keep that promise?"

"No."

The word hung between them like a drop of blood too thick to fall. Breathing slowly to steady herself, Ruth asked, "Is he good to you?"

"If you have to ask, then you know the answer."

"I'm sorry."

For a moment, Eliza said nothing, only kept staring out at the water, her small face pinched and pale from years of hard work and despair. Finally, she looked at Ruth. "You should have told me."

"I wanted to."

"So why didn't you?"

"A letter came from my uncle, and I had to go to London. You were working at the mill, and there wasn't time." Ruth reached for Eliza's hand.

"I convinced myself that he'd change for you."

Eliza pulled her hand away. "He didn't." She stood abruptly and walked a few steps toward the railing. Keeping her gaze on the sea, she said, "I used to wonder what I'd say to you if we met again. If I could forgive you."

"And can you?"

Eliza inhaled sharply and turned around. "Eight years ago, after my third girl was born, Reg started drinking again. He'd gotten himself tangled up with a lass at the mill—the first of many." She rushed on before Ruth could say anything. "Eight years, Ruth."

"I'm sorry."

"So you said."

"Please…" Ruth stood up. "I've suffered too, knowing what I did to you."

"Suffered?" Eliza barked out a laugh. "What could you know of suffering?" Before Ruth could respond, Eliza turned on her heel and hurried away, the thin ribbon encircling her flat hat trailing behind her like a smudge of coal smoke.

Ruth slumped back onto the bench. Yet again, she'd made a mess of things. She thought back to the icy day in December when she'd gone to see Eliza. All the girls in Ruth's class at the Briarstown Academy for Young Ladies couldn't stop talking about the death of the little mill baby. That's what they called Eliza's little brother, like he was less worthy of sympathy because he was the child of a mill worker. Ruth longed to snap at them that the mill baby had a name and that it was Ernie Treleven and that he was the brother of the girl who had once been her best friend.

But she didn't want to bring attention to herself from girls who already considered her an outsider. Most of them came from much wealthier families and looked down upon the *foreman's girl* as they delighted in calling her.

Darkness was falling quickly, and Mother would worry if she was late home. Ruth arrived at the court on Hillcrest Road to find Eliza emerging from her house. She carried an empty bucket in one hand and with the other, she pulled the edges of her coat together. It was too small for her, barely reaching her knees that shone red and raw in the December cold.

When Ruth ran up and reached for the bucket, Eliza looked up, startled.

"What are you doing here?"

"I wanted to tell you how sorry I am about your little brother. Are you going to fetch water? I can help."

"You'd best not," she said.

"Why?"

"I don't think we can be friends anymore."

"Why not?" Ruth asked. "I was thinking maybe we could go walking again after school when it starts getting light again in the afternoon. Maybe practice singing."

Eliza slowed her pace a fraction and then sped up again. "I don't have no time for singing now. Everything's about to change."

"Why?"

"You'd not understand."

"Is it because of what happened?"

"Yes." Eliza said shortly. She reached the pump and set to work filling the bucket with water, working the pump with hands as red and raw as her knees. Ruth winced.

"I miss you," she said.

Eliza stopped pumping and glanced up. Her face crumpled in on itself, her large gray eyes misting. Abruptly, she turned her back to Ruth and began pumping the water again, this time so vigorously it splashed onto Ruth's smart leather boots.

"We can't be friends," Eliza said finally when the bucket was full. "We be too different now."

Without looking at Ruth, Eliza started back toward her house. Ruth wanted to follow her, to *make* her be friends again. This was her fault for neglecting Eliza all autumn. Suddenly, Ruth felt very small. She was older and taller than Eliza, and yet she felt younger, untested by the grief that settled around Eliza like an iron shroud.

Ruth saw herself standing in the middle of a vast and desolate moor, alone and bereft. She had no one. Even Mother was not really hers anymore. Ruth had to share her with Kingwell and then stand by and watch Mother be hurt.

A hardness had crept into Ruth's soul that freezing afternoon. If she was to be of such little use to anyone in her world, then she may as well be of use only to herself.

As Ruth gazed out to the glittering North Sea, her cheeks warm in the summer sun, she thought of Silas. He was a good man. He'd not hurt her like her stepfather nor neglect her like James.

But now even Silas had turned away from her, leaving Ruth alone again.

Chapter 43

Whitby

Eliza

Eliza clenched her fists as she walked away from Ruth. How dare she try to apologize now? After all these years! She turned away from the seafront and walked inland for several blocks to her lodgings for the night—a neglected-looking house set back from the street.

She felt a quiver of remorse. Even if Ruth had tried to tell her about Reg all those years ago, would Eliza have listened?

What's past is past, she told herself as she raised her hand to knock.

"You must be Mrs. Kingwell," said the woman who opened the door. "Come in! I'm Mrs. Sheridan. Your room's upstairs."

Eliza followed her up a dusty staircase to a room overlooking a yard littered with rubbish. A faded beige counterpane that had seen better days covered the single bed and patches of damp darkened the peeling wallpaper. But for one whole night, every inch of the room belonged only to Eliza. No one would ask anything of her, and for the first time since she was a young girl in Devon, she wouldn't need to rise at five.

"Will you be needing anything tonight?" asked Mrs. Sheridan. "Cup of tea?"

Eliza put her bag on the bed. A cup of tea that she didn't have to make herself while six people clamored for her attention?

"Thank you," she said. "That would be lovely."

"Come on then. The kitchen's quiet now with all the men down the pub. You'll hear a racket when they come back around ten, but don't be frightened. They're a rough lot, but harmless enough."

Eliza followed Mrs. Sheridan back down the stairs to the kitchen at the back of the house. "Have you been running this place for long?" she asked.

"Oh, dear me! These fourteen years, ever since my Bert died. He left me with nowt, God rest him. I had to make me own way."

"How did you manage?"

Mrs. Sheridan laughed. "A lot of hard work and a bit of luck. I took a job cleaning this place and worked my fingers raw for three years. The woman who owned it was a proper old hag. But in the end, she did all right by me. She had no family, so when she died, she left the place to me."

"And you've been running it ever since?"

"Aye, for me sins. But it's been a godsend, I can tell you. I take in long-term boarders—men working on the railways. Most are Irish, but I don't hold that against them." She guffawed. "Men is men. They're all the same. Feed 'em, give 'em rules to follow, cut 'em some slack on a Saturday night, and they'll be right as rain."

Not all of them, Eliza thought.

"And you can make enough money to keep you?" she asked. "I'm sorry to be rude, but I'm curious. It might be something that would interest me." A ghost of an idea, so faint as to be a mere pinprick at the bottom of a deep well, nudged her.

"It's not for everyone, I can tell you that, but it's not a bad life. And during festival season, I rent out an extra room to people like yourself." Mrs. Sheridan smiled, her teeth black. "I heard you sing today."

"You did?"

"Sang like an angel you did. I had tears listening to ye."

"That's kind of you to say."

"It's the truth. Have you got a family of your own?"

"Five girls."

"What a blessing. I never had no children. It's the great sorrow of my life."

"Unfortunately, I also have a husband."

"Ah! I take that to mean he's not good to you?"

Eliza nodded.

"I'm that sorry to hear it. My Bert was the same."

"He was?"

"Oh, aye. The day he died was one of the best of me life, except for him leaving me only debts." She poured herself another cup of strong tea. "But as you can see, I've landed on me feet and then some. This place ain't a palace, but it puts food on the table, and I'm glad to be helping the men.

Most of 'em are pining for home."

"How would I go about getting a place like this?"

"You?" Mrs. Sheridan's eyes narrowed. "That bad, is it?"

"If I win the solo competition tomorrow, I'm taking my girls and leaving."

"What's your plan?"

"We'll go to Devon. My grandmother's there, and she'll help us."

"She got a place for you to stay?"

"For a while. I reckon something will turn up once we get settled. I thought I'd look for work as a housekeeper. My grandmother's getting on and I'm hoping I can take over from her."

"Not much of a plan, is it?"

"It's better than staying put."

"Aye, well, I can't argue with that. I suggest you look in the papers when you get to the South, get yourself a position in a boarding house in one of the seaside towns down there. Work hard, and you never know. Are your girls old enough to fend for themselves?"

"My two eldest can work if they have to, but the other three are still too young to leave school." Eliza thought of little Bessie. Of all the girls, she'd miss her dad the most.

"You've got your work cut out for ye, I'll say that." Mrs. Sheridan heaved herself to her feet. "Right then, I'm off to bed. See as you're down by eight at the latest for your breakfast. The men don't come for theirs until nine on a Sunday, so you'll have the place to yourself."

Eliza went to bed that night with her head full of ideas. If she were to take charge of a place like this, she'd fix it up nicely, get new wallpaper, clean the stairwells. She'd noticed roils of dust in the corners, and that kitchen was a disgrace. Mrs. Sheridan was friendly enough, but she wasn't much of a housekeeper. Eliza imagined opening her doors to men who would pay well for a hot meal every night and clean lodgings. She'd run the place with an iron hand. The girls would help.

She fell asleep imagining Annie staying in school long enough to become a teacher and Lily May getting set up as a shop assistant. Any amount of hard work would be worth it to see that.

Eliza woke at five the next morning, as usual. Feeling deliciously extravagant, she stretched and lay in bed until the sky lightened, the promise of a brilliant sunrise painted in the clouds. She got up and dressed quickly, then hurried downstairs and let herself out the front door. In the cool damp of the morning, the smell of the sea sharpened her resolve.

Today, she would win.

She walked to the promenade and descended a flight of steps to the shingled beach to watch the sun emerge over the horizon, its rays piercing the clouds and then lighting them on fire. The song she would sing later that morning played in her mind. She looked around and saw that the beach was deserted. Marvelling at her boldness, she opened her arms wide like she had as a girl and sang to the rising sun.

She couldn't wait to stand on the stage. And perhaps with Ruth as the judge…

Eliza didn't like to think she'd win because of it, but at this point, she didn't care. She *knew* she was good, and if knowing Ruth gave her a bit of a leg up, then what of it?

It was her turn to shine.

Later, she joined Mrs. Sheridan in the grubby kitchen for a breakfast of dry toast and lukewarm tea. If Eliza were in charge, she'd serve porridge laced with brown sugar and always make sure the tea was fresh and hot.

"I imagine you're excited," the landlady said.

"Terrified more like."

"Ah well, me hat's off to you. I'd never have the nerve to stand up in front of all them people. But if you sing as well as you did with the choir yesterday, me money's on you."

"Thank you." Eliza beamed.

At nine, Eliza was dressed and ready. Her insides were churning like a spinning room running full tilt, gears clacking, threads whirring and break- ing, girls toiling.

"Good luck," Mrs. Sheridan said, walking her to the front door. Behind her, five roughly dressed men tramped down the stairs and headed along the hallway to the kitchen. None of them so much as glanced in Eliza's direction, their eyes fixed on their heavy boots, their shoulders hunched.

Eliza left the boarding house and hurried toward the auditorium, every nerve on fire with anticipation. Elation warred with fear. All the months of hard work, the planning and the scheming were about to end in triumph or in failure.

There was no middle ground.

"You look pale," Miss Donahue said when Eliza arrived. "How do you feel?"

"Nervous," she admitted.

"That's totally natural," Miss Donahue said. "If you weren't nervous, I'd be worried."

"Really?"

"Oh yes. You should always be nervous before a performance. It means you'll do a good job. Do you remember my first day at the mill school?"

Eliza nodded. "You were so much nicer than Miss Lane."

"Well, that morning, I'm not ashamed to admit I felt so sick that I barely made it out of bed."

"Oh, dear!" Eliza smiled sympathetically. "That's terrible."

"Don't you even think about being sick. Use the nerves to give you strength."

"How?"

"Breathe deeply and imagine that all those bothersome butterflies flapping around your insides are nothing more threatening than wisps of cotton in the air. And then breathe out and imagine them all blowing away." Miss Donahue breathed, held her breath, eyes bulging for several seconds, and then exhaled with a loud whoosh. "You try it."

Eliza couldn't see how it would help, but she followed Miss Donahue's lead, breathing in slowly, imagining her insides filling with soft wisps of cotton instead of a giant hawk flapping its wings in a windstorm.

"Hold!" Miss Donahue said. "That's it. Now, let it go. Blow everything out."

As Eliza blew out, her shoulders softened.

"Better?"

"I think I'm ready."

"Good. They're announcing your category now."

Eliza was the last to perform. She listened with dismay as singer after singer took the stage and performed with such accuracy and brilliance, she was sure she'd be laughed at when her turn came. Fortunately, Miss Donahue didn't agree. At the end of each performance, she whispered all the reasons the singer should lose points.

"She slurred her notes in the third bar. Shocking sloppiness."

"Oh no, that one should *never* have been allowed out of the practice room."

"Dear me, she's off by a full semi-tone. I don't know how the judges can keep straight faces."

A wave of affection for her teacher shooed away the nerves. The auditorium contracted to the space between her and the stage. The noise receded, replaced by a peaceful, blessed silence.

All she could do now was sing.

"Mrs. Eliza Kingwell."

Eliza walked to the center of the stage. The hawk wings opened again, rocketing around her stomach so that for a terrible moment, Eliza was sure she'd be sick all over the polished wood of the stage. She swallowed hard.

She didn't belong here. She could never belong here.

"Whenever you're ready," the male judge sitting next to Ruth said.

Eliza knew she was supposed to nod at the pianist to play the introduction when she was ready to sing, but she couldn't move.

Ruth was sitting forward in her chair, her elbows folded on the table, her lips parted as if she were about to speak.

Eliza closed her eyes for a second. She couldn't let Miss Donahue down, not after all she'd done to help her prepare.

She opened her eyes as a wave of nausea surged and ebbed. Ruth was nodding now, her eyes boring into Eliza's as if she could send all her energy and encouragement to her old friend.

Why hadn't Ruth warned her about Reg?

No. That was in the past.

This was the future.

Eliza looked over at the accompanist and nodded. The first bars of her song sounded too loud in the vast space, but Eliza kept her focus and hit the first note with absolute precision.

As she sensed her feet fusing with the wooden stage, grounding her and giving her strength, she lifted her chin and sang to Dad and her girls, to the past and most importantly, to the future.

This was what she was born to do. *This* was what she was good for.

Chapter 44

Whitby

Ruth

Ruth's spirits rose within seconds of Eliza opening her mouth. She really had the most remarkable voice. If Eliza had been given the opportunities Ruth had enjoyed, she'd have easily eclipsed her.

"Very nice," commented Silas when Eliza finished and the hall erupted with wild applause, louder than for any of the other competitors.

"It was more than nice," Ruth said as she totalled her marks and showed them to Silas.

"I think Mrs. Dawson was better," he said, barely glancing at her paper. He shifted in his seat and wouldn't meet Ruth's eye. "Mrs. Kingwell was sharp in bar ten."

"She was not, and you know it."

"I do *not* know it." Silas was holding himself so rigidly Ruth imagined he'd shatter if she so much as nudged him.

"Mrs. Kingwell is the clear winner," Ruth said. "You heard the audience."

"I am not in the habit of letting the audience's reaction affect how I judge a performance," Silas said stiffly. He beckoned for the Master of Ceremonies. "I've made my decision."

"But I don't agree!" Ruth said.

"As you've said, but may I remind you that I am the senior adjudicator? In the event of a disagreement, my opinion takes precedence over yours."

"Silas!"

He shook his head and then whispered the name of the winner to the Master of Ceremonies, who looked surprised.

"Of course. I shall announce it," he said.

Ruth sat in miserable silence. On the stage, she saw Eliza's pale face flushed with triumph. Her performance had garnered the largest ovation by far. Ruth turned to Silas. "Why are you doing this?"

"I told you. She was sharp."

"That's not true! Mrs. Kingwell deserves to win."

"Lower your voice," Silas said.

Ruth pushed back her chair and stood. "Forgive me," she said. "I am unwell." Without another glance at Silas, she started walking out of the hall. She could *not* watch Eliza lose.

But when the Master of Ceremonies announced the winner of the Ladies' Solo category, she couldn't help turning back. Eliza had a smile fixed on her face and was clapping for Mrs. Dawson, a florid woman wearing a green and white checked straw hat topped with an enormous yellow bow.

Ruth wondered if Eliza would blame her for the loss. She wasn't to know that Silas had over-ruled her. As she stood at the back of the auditorium and watched her only friend be passed over, Ruth felt loneliness wrap itself around her like an ice-soaked cloak. Over the years, she'd kept the emptiness at bay, even early in her marriage when she'd lain night after night alone in her bed. Then, she'd at least had the theater and been able to fill the emptiness with the sound of applause, the accolades of the press, the adoration of her admirers, the flowers filling her dressing room with their cloying perfumes.

A hand closed over her arm. She gasped and tried to pull away, the memory of the first time Kingwell had hurt her as sharp as if it had happened yesterday. And then she turned to see Silas.

"Forgive me," he said, his expression stricken. "I didn't mean to startle you. We have a short break now before the men's competition."

"What do you want?" She didn't care if she sounded rude. It was thanks to Silas that Eliza had lost.

"Please don't be angry."

"You *knew* Mrs. Kingwell was the better singer. Why did you vote against her?"

"I was trying to protect you," Silas said. He looked around nervously. "Come away from the crowd. I need to speak with you." He gestured for her to follow him outside.

The April air was still chilly, but Ruth was too angry to notice. She put her hands on her hips. "Well? What do I need protecting from?"

"Please, Mrs. Henton. Ruth."

It was the first time he'd used her Christian name, and Ruth couldn't help liking the sound of it in his soft Welsh accent. A tremor of pleasure ran up her spine. She pushed it down.

"Mrs. Kingwell was the better singer. She deserved to win."

"If I'd voted for Mrs. Kingwell and awarded her first place, your relationship with her might have been discovered."

"What do you mean?"

"You are related."

It wasn't a question.

"How can you possibly know that?"

"Your maiden name was Kingwell, correct?"

"Kingwell is not an uncommon name."

"Perhaps not, but you told me once that you lived in Briarstown as a girl. That's enough of a connection to raise eyebrows, but I…" He paused, looking sheepish. "Yesterday evening? I saw you and Mrs. Kingwell sitting together on West Cliff. Even if you're not related, you're obviously acquainted. If the Music Association discovers you had a prior relationship with Mrs. Kingwell—even as a friend, much less a relation—you'll be let go. There can't be even a whiff of nepotism associated with our judgements. It's bad enough that we awarded first prize to the choir, considering it featured Mrs. Kingwell."

Ruth hesitated. She could lie and say she didn't know Eliza. The meeting on West Cliff could be explained as a casual chat between strangers who had the festival in common. But the damage was already done and Ruth wanted to be free of lies. She'd spent far too much of her life either lying to men or telling them what they wanted to hear.

"Mrs. Kingwell is married to my stepfather," she said. "And we were friends when we were girls. Good friends."

"Ah, so I was right to vote against her."

"I suppose," Ruth said wearily. "But at least admit she was the best singer."

"Without a doubt," Silas said. "You should encourage her to enter other competitions—ones at which *you* are not a judge."

"Mr. Gallagher?" An usher tapped Silas on the shoulder. "They're ready for you now."

Ruth looked around for Eliza, but she'd already slipped out and would soon be on a train back to Briarstown, her hopes dashed. She'd let her friend down again. Twelve years had passed since Kingwell had announced he was marrying Eliza just moments before Ruth left his house forever to catch the train south to London. She could have gone to Eliza then and told her. She should have missed the train and taken another one.

But she hadn't.

Ruth directed her attention to the stage where the first of the male competitors—a young man with a wispy beard—was making a meal of his solo. He should never have been allowed to humiliate himself. She totalled her marks and showed them to Silas.

He nodded agreement and then provided the lad with such gentle, sensitive advice that against her better judgment, a softness bloomed in Ruth's chest. Silas always found something positive to say about every competitor, no matter how challenging.

At the end of the competition, she pushed back from the table and stood. "That's the last of them," she said. "Have a pleasant evening."

"You don't need to rush away," Silas said. "I was rather hoping we could dine together." He struggled to his feet and put his hand on her arm.

A peculiar sensation rolled through her stomach like a wave surging onto Whitby's shingle beach.

"I am fatigued," she said, her voice unsteady.

"You won't forgive me for Mrs. Kingwell?"

Ruth shook her head. "No, I mean, yes." She pulled away. "I don't suppose there's anything to forgive. You did what you thought was best."

"I wouldn't for the world have you think badly of me."

This time, Ruth's stomach flipped over. "Of course, I don't," she said. She wished he'd stop looking at her with such a tender expression. No man had ever looked at her like that.

She turned and hurried through the thinning crowd and out into the late afternoon sunshine.

Chapter 45

Whitby

Eliza

Eliza stared out the window at the fields and hills passing by the train window. Now, in the cold light of failure, the flaws in her Plan were revealed. How did she expect to start a new life with five girls in tow even if she had won the prize money? She'd been a fool. The best thing to do now—the only thing to do—was to go home and be Mother to her girls and a wife to her husband. She'd keep quiet and stay out of Reg's way. He was easy enough to deal with so long as she didn't anger him when he'd had a few too many pints at the pub.

Briarstown station heaved with people, the air heavy with coal dust and reeking of wet stone and urine. Eliza left the station and crossed the busy road, hoping to make it home without running into any of the women from the choir. She felt weary to her bones and wanted only the solace of a cup of tea and some quiet, although that wasn't likely to happen. The girls would be on her the moment she walked through the door, and she didn't even want to think about Reg.

"Home at last," he said when Eliza walked in the door. He was sitting in his chair by the cold grate. "I hope you've gotten all this foolishness out of your system. You'll not pull a stunt like that again. I've a mind to teach you a lesson."

Eliza froze. She'd been a fool to think she'd get away with going to Whitby. How would he make her pay this time?

Slowly, he rose from his chair, as if wanting to make her wait as long as possible before he came at her. She looked around for something to defend herself with, but the table was bare and the poker too far away for her to reach.

205

"The choir won," she said.

"So's I heard. They got back last night," he said. "But you stayed on. Why?"

Eliza knew there was no point in lying. He'd probably already heard about the solo competition. Hattie McKay was not known for keeping quiet.

"Miss Donahue thought I was good enough to compete in the solo competition and so I did."

"Did ye win?"

"No."

"Hmph. Just as well." He took a step closer, his fists flexed.

Eliza swallowed hard but refused to back down. Let him hit her. Let him show the world he was a monster.

He pulled back his arm and was about to smash his fist into her jaw when the door burst open.

"You're back!" Annie cried.

The other girls crowded in behind her.

"Everyone's talkin' about the choir winning," Lily May said, eyes shining.

"People say you're goin' to Morecambe," Gladys said. "Is that right, Ma?"

"What's this?" Reg asked, hastily lowering his fist.

"Nothing," Eliza said automatically.

"It's not nothing, Ma!" Annie said. "Mrs. McKay's tellin' everyone. She wants to put a concert on to raise money so you can all go."

"What are they on about?" Reg asked. "Most of the women have families. They can't be goin' off to Lancashire."

"Ma?" Annie asked.

"Your ma won't be going there or anywhere else," Reg said. "She belongs here." He wrenched open the door and burst into the yard, not bothering to shut the door behind him.

Firmly, Eliza closed the door. "You heard your father," she said, her voice tight. "I'll not be going to Morecambe."

"But Ma," Annie said. "You have to."

"I don't *have* to do anything. Off you go with Lily May to get the bread. Gladys, you stay here with your sisters. I'm going upstairs for a few minutes."

Without waiting for the girls to reply, and with her back rigid with shame, Eliza mounted the stairs to the middle floor. Only when she heard the younger girls chattering and the door close behind Annie and Lily May did she allow her face to crumple.

Tears were for the weak, but she couldn't help it. She let out a sob, and then gulped in air, anxious to stifle the sound so the girls wouldn't hear.

Her life stretched before her with tedious predictability—more pushing out babies until she got too old, more washing and cleaning and cooking, more being the axle around which her family rotated.

She was Mother.

She was also not the only woman in her neighborhood saddled with a husband who wasn't good to her. She could have done worse.

And then she thought about George Ledbetter and realized she could have done so much better.

Chapter 46

Durham

Ruth

R uth was again called upon to rehearse the choirs before they performed together at the festival finale. This time, she was in Durham, and the final concert was being held in the ancient Norman cathedral.

She breathed in the dusty smell of old stone as she walked slowly up the nave. Risers had been added to accommodate the choirs that couldn't fit into the carved choir stalls. As always, the children were arranged in the front, scrubbed faces expectant. Several of the choirs had come from colliery towns in the region. Men with faces gray with coal dust that never quite washed away and women in shabby best dresses stood next to smartly dressed ladies and gentlemen. The conventions of class were forgotten when the choirs came together to perform at the end of the competition.

"Good afternoon," Ruth said. The enormous cathedral both humbled and inspired her. The massive round pillars rising along both sides of the nave held up a procession of round arches. Elegant vaulting soared high overhead. These stones had witnessed more than a thousand years of history. With her help, the massed choir would gladden the hearts of everyone who heard it. She breathed deeply to steady her nerves.

"Let us go slowly through the piece," she said, projecting her voice like she used to do on the London stage. "You need to get a sense of how your voices blend." She raised her baton and nodded at Silas, who stood close by facing the organist. At his signal, the organist struck the first chord.

As Ruth expected, the choir sounded rough and unfocused.

"Let's try that again," she said, smiling. "Look up and out and let your chests expand. Remember your vowels."

The choir began again, and this time, the raggedness smoothed out. She mouthed the words they sang, making sure she didn't join her voice with theirs.

"Excellent," she said after the fourth time through. She then rehearsed each of the parts separately and together, male and female, adult and child voices weaving around each other and echoing through the ancient space.

At the end of the hour, she thanked the choirs and turned to Silas. "What do you think?"

"Beautiful," he said. "The performance tonight will be perfect."

He regarded her with such naked admiration that she took a step back. His anger had fizzled out to such an extent that she frequently caught him looking at her with a soft expression in his dark eyes that had nothing to do with their discussions of competition scores.

"They'll do very well. Thank you for your help with the organist," she said, gathering up the score and starting down the nave. She pulled open the heavy door leading from the cathedral to the clipped green. Buildings from many periods—ancient to recent—enclosed both sides of the space with the round keep of Durham Castle rising at the far end. Ruth veered to her right and descended steps to a street paralleling the green. Her lodgings were in an old building now housing one of the colleges of Durham University. She retrieved her key from the porter and then stood aside as a stream of gowned students—all men—passed by. They looked so young, their faces clean-shaven and skin smooth. She wondered what it would be like to have a son—or perhaps one day a daughter—attend a university.

Silas sometimes talked to her about his student days at Cambridge. She'd listened with envy as he described going to lectures and exams, singing in the university choir, and spending weekend afternoons punting on the Cam. He'd laugh and tell her how he was teased for his Welsh accent.

"I wanted to be a teacher," she'd once confided.

"Why didn't you become one?"

"My uncle sent for me to come to London. I believe I've told you about him? He had me trained for the stage."

"Is that what you wanted?"

"At the time, yes."

"And now?" The hopefulness of Silas's smile unnerved Ruth. She'd cut the conversation short, turning away to avoid seeing the hurt in his eyes.

The performance of the massed choir in the cathedral that evening went off smoothly, much to Ruth's relief. The voices of the men, women, and children of County Durham filled the cathedral to the delight of everyone present. When the piece finished and Ruth stood aside and gestured to the choir to bow, she saw Silas's eyes glowing.

The next day, she and Silas were to return to Manchester, where they'd enjoy a full two weeks of rest before adjudicating a competition in Leeds. She looked forward to spending time well away from him.

Chapter 47

Briarstown

Eliza

A few days after returning from Whitby and with the choir's win still the talk of the courts and terraces, Eliza opened her door one afternoon to find Hattie McKay tapping her foot impatiently.

"There you are!" Hattie exclaimed. "Come outside. A few of us are havin' a meeting."

Eliza followed Hattie into the yard. Josie ran forward, eyes shining. Minnie and Gert joined Josie, while Doris stood to the side, large and gloomy as always.

"We've all decided that we have to go to Morecambe," Hattie began. "Which means we'll need to raise the money for the fares and staying there and all. You've got to talk to Miss Donahue about teaching us new songs so we can put on a concert."

"Reg doesn't want me going to Morecambe," Eliza said. "And as for me singing in a concert…"

"Rubbish!" Hattie said. "He'll come round soon enough. Everyone's talking about us. My Andy says he's never 'eard the like."

"You can sing without me," Eliza said.

"Not a ruddy chance!" Doris rumbled. "You're our soloist."

"That husband of yours needs to see sense," Hattie said. "I'll have my Andy talk to him."

"No!"

But the women weren't listening, distracted by the sight of Miss Donahue emerging from the passageway.

"Miss Donahue?" Hattie said, for once nonplussed. "What can we do for ye?" She smoothed her hands over her apron. The other women did the same. Meeting Miss Donahue in the church hall was one thing, but Eliza imagined they were all thinking that the crowded yard with its noxious smells and piles of rubbish and fallen bricks was no place for a lady like Miss Donahue.

"We was just talkin' about you," Doris said.

"Oh?"

"Eliza here was going to ask you about helping us put on a concert," Josie said. "You know, to raise funds so's we can go to Morecambe?"

"Oh, dear!" Miss Donahue said. Eliza noticed she was trying very hard not to wrinkle her nose.

"What's wrong?" Gert asked.

"Forgive the intrusion, but I wanted to come tell you right away before you heard it elsewhere."

"Heard what?" Doris asked. "It ain't like we travel in the same social circles."

A few of the women tittered nervously.

Miss Donahue clasped her hands in front of her waist. "Before I left Whitby, I was offered a post with a large choir from Newcastle. They've invited me to go on tour with them to Canada."

"Oh, Miss Donahue!" Josie exclaimed. "That *is* exciting. Congratulations!"

"Thank you. Unfortunately, I'm to leave by the middle of May."

"What about Morecambe?" Gert asked.

"I'm very sorry."

"We can't be a choir without you!" Hattie exclaimed.

"I really am very sorry," Miss Donahue said again. "Conducting you has been a wonderful experience, and as I told you in Whitby, I'm so very proud of you. I do hope you'll keep singing together."

"Can't see how we're goin' to do that," Doris said.

"Shut it, Doris," Gert said. "We appreciate all you done for us, Miss Donahue," she said. "Ain't that right, girls?"

Josie and Hannah both said *yes* immediately. Minnie looked at Hattie, who was frowning, then stepped forward and kissed Miss Donahue's cheek. "You take care of yerself, Miss," she said. "We won't forget you."

"And I won't forget you," Miss Donahue said. "Goodbye." She bit back a sob, then turned and hurried back across the yard, leaving the women to stare at each other in astonishment.

Before anyone spoke, Eliza broke away and followed Miss Donahue through the passageway to the street.

"You're going to Canada?" she asked when she caught up with her. "Does that mean you'll find your son?"

"I don't know," Miss Donahue said. "At least for now, I barely dare to hope. Canada's a very large country, although the choir's itinerary includes Vancouver. That's where the detective said my son lives."

"I'm very happy for you," Eliza said. "But what about your mother?"

"You won't believe it, but I finally convinced her to move in with her sister in York. Conducting the choir has helped me too, Eliza."

"How so?"

"It gave me a sense of purpose. I realized my life could be bigger than it was, that I didn't need to disappear because of one mistake."

Eliza stared. So, she'd been right. Miss Donahue, with her comfortable cottage and respectable social standing, wasn't so very different from herself. Both of them were searching for something more in the life they'd been given.

"You're not angry at me for leaving?" Miss Donahue asked.

"Of course not!" Eliza said in what she hoped was a reassuring tone. The truth was that Miss Donahue leaving was a terrible blow. The choir needed her. But she couldn't begrudge her a chance at freedom, and to find her son.

"Please promise me you won't stop singing, Eliza."

"I don't know if I can do that."

"Speak with Mrs. Adams. Do you remember her running the Christmas bazaar that you sang at when you were a girl? She's very active in Briarstown society and had a hand in forming the Briarstown Choral Society some years ago. She's sure to know someone who can take my place." Miss Donahue put her gloved hand on the worn sleeve of Eliza's dress. "You *have* to keep singing."

"Ah, well, I don't know about that," Eliza said. "I lost at Whitby."

Miss Donahue gestured impatiently. "Put it out of your mind. You have a gift that you must share with the world."

Eliza smiled sadly. "It's not so easy as all that."

Miss Donahue enfolded her in a hug. "I have every faith in you, Eliza," she whispered. "You have to try again."

Eliza laid her cheek against Miss Donahue's and inhaled the subtle scent of her face powder. Perhaps Miss Donahue was right.

She had to try again—both for herself and for the other women in the choir.

Eliza stood in front of one of the grandest houses she'd ever seen. Her resolve wavered. She should have worn her best dress which, even after five children, still fit. If only the women hadn't insisted that Eliza be the one to find Miss Donahue's replacement.

"You know people in the Choral Society," Hannah had pointed out. Several of the other women nodded.

"They'll remember you," Josie said. "And everyone knows it were your solo that helped us win."

"We all sang well," Eliza said.

"Don't be so modest," Hattie said. "You're not foolin' anyone."

"I told you that Reg doesn't want me going to Morecambe."

"He'll come 'round," said Hattie dismissively.

"Now that we can't do a concert what with Miss Donahue gone, folks been chippin' in money to help us," Gert said.

"We've almost got enough," Josie said. "We *have* to sing at Morecambe."

Eliza pushed open the small iron gate leading to Mrs. Adams's house. The front garden slumbered under the sizzling drone of bees. She walked up the steps and stood in front of a large door. Perhaps she should go around to the back. People like her didn't go to the front door of these kinds of houses. She turned to go when the door opened, and a maid in a starched cap scowled at her. "Yes?"

Eliza pulled herself up to her full height, still many inches short of the maid's. "I've come to see Mrs. Adams."

"Is she expecting you?"

"No."

"Name?"

"Mrs. Eliza Kingwell, but Mrs. Adams may remember me as Eliza Treleven."

"Wait here." The door shut, leaving Eliza to again stare at the elaborate door knocker. The intricately carved lion's face with the heavy ring passing through its nose likely cost more than Reg Kingwell brought home in a year. Eliza couldn't imagine living with such wealth, and she didn't suppose it would suit her. She'd be content running her own boarding house and bringing in a steady income to keep the girls in school with enough left over for decent clothes.

The door swung open. "This way," the maid said, her expression a mixture of surprise and disdain. "She'll see you in the conservatory."

Eliza followed the maid down a wide hallway flanked by an open staircase on one side and a row of closed doors on the other. Her entire downstairs room would fit in the entrance hall with plenty of space to spare. When she was ushered into the large, airy conservatory, Eliza stifled a gasp of wonder. Glass walls and a glass ceiling soared above her, high as the three stories of her house. A profusion of palm trees, ferns, and flowers filled the space with heat and color. Eliza had a sudden urge to turn and run.

"Mrs. Kingwell!"

The voice took Eliza back to the morning when she'd first sung for Mrs. Adams in the dusty schoolroom. At Miss Donahue's invitation, Mrs. Adams had come to pass judgement on whether Eliza was good enough to perform a solo at the Christmas bazaar, put on for the ladies and gentlemen of Briarstown.

Eliza had stood like a tattered statue, acutely conscious that the worn pinafore hanging from her thin frame made her look even poorer than she was. She remembered how Miss Donahue had looked frozen in place. The only sound in the schoolroom came from the carts rumbling past outside the window. Perhaps the older woman frightened Miss Donahue. Eliza almost laughed. As imposing as the woman was, she was nothing compared to Ma when she was in a mood.

Or Granny back in Devon, come to that.

Eliza shook off her fear as she walked past drooping ferns in the conservatory to where Mrs. Adams sat at a small table. She was no longer the ragged mill child begging for scraps. She was a mother with five children and the soloist of the choir that had just won first place in Whitby.

"Thank you for seeing me," Eliza said. "I wasn't sure if you'd remember me."

"Of course, I remember you. How could I forget your singing at the Christmas bazaar? That solo of yours was remarkable. I'm only sorry you couldn't do it again the following year."

"My mother made me leave school in the new year," Eliza said, needing all her resolve to keep her voice even. "I started working at the mill."

"You were far too young," Mrs. Adams said. "What were you? Eleven? Twelve?"

"Eleven, Ma'am."

"Humph. Well, I'm happy to say we've made some progress over the last decade. At least we've reduced the working hours for children under thirteen to just forty-eight hours a week."

"Yes, Ma'am," Eliza said. "My eldest turned twelve this past January. She wants to stay in school and be a teacher."

"Good for her. Well, what do you wish to ask me?"

"I, ah…" Eliza faltered.

"You haven't come to take tea with me," Mrs. Adams said, smiling at the absurdity, "but before you tell me what you've come for, I would be remiss if I didn't congratulate you. You and the choir are a credit to Briarstown. There were some among my acquaintance who didn't think it right for women such as yourselves to be putting themselves forward, but of course, I told them you are to be commended for your efforts. I only caution you not to let the success go to your heads."

"No, Ma'am. It be the choir that I've come…" She paused. "I mean, it *is* the choir that I'd like to speak with you about."

"Go on."

"You've perhaps heard that our conductor, Miss Donahue, is going to Canada?"

"Ah! Yes. Good for Adelaide. I'm surprised her mother's agreed to move to York, but it's to her credit. Adelaide deserves to have some joy in her life."

"Yes, Ma'am," Eliza said. "We, that is to say, all of us in the choir, would like to compete again."

"Oh?"

"At the festival in Morecambe. But we need a conductor."

"I see. And how do you suppose I can help with that? I flatter myself I'm not behindhand when it comes to appreciating music, but I do not have the skills, nor the time, to conduct a choir."

"I thought perhaps you could ask someone in the Choral Society?"

"You sang with them yourself for a time, did you not?"

Eliza was surprised that Mrs. Adams remembered. "Yes. I performed with them once."

"For a benefit that *I* organized. I remember your solo being much admired." She paused, regarding Eliza with calculating eyes. "And then you never sang with the Society again. May I ask why?"

"My father died, and I got married. Once my daughter was born, my husband wanted me home."

"Shame. I'd like to help you, Mrs. Kingwell, but the only choir conductor I know is Mr. Skinner and, well…"

"I understand." Dour Mr. Skinner, who conducted the society choir and had looked down his pointed nose at Eliza until she proved she could sing, was the last person she wanted to ask.

"I suppose I was hoping you could think of someone else," she said.

Mrs. Adams shook her head. "Regrettably, no." She stood and held out her hand to shake Eliza's. "I'm sorry I can't be of assistance."

The next morning, Eliza was sharper than usual with the girls. She tugged too hard while brushing Emily's hair and made the girl cry, and then Lily May wanted a ha'penny for something at school and even Annie was cranky. By the time she got them all out the door to school, leaving behind Bessie, Eliza felt worn down. She shouldn't have snapped at the girls and pulled poor Emily's hair.

"Ma?"

Eliza looked down at Bessie.

"What is it?"

"Don't be sad," she said, propping her doll on Eliza's knee. "You can hold Dolly."

Eliza couldn't stop her eyes closing over unshed tears as a shudder of anguish passed through her like a squall sweeping across the moor. She gathered Bessie and her doll into a hug, anchoring herself to the little girl like a lifeline.

"You're a good girl," she said, finally letting go of Bessie and handing her back the doll. "Off you go now. I need to write a letter."

She found a single sheet of cheap paper and a pencil and sat at the table.

Dear Ruth

I was happy to see you in Whitby, and I am sorry we did not speak further. I am home now, as I'm sure you have guessed. You know already the choir has been entered into the Morecambe Festival, but what you don't know is that Miss Donahue has left us to go on tour in Canada with a big city choir. I am sure she is very happy, so I can't be sorry, but without a conductor, we can't perform. There is no one here in Briarstown who can help us.

Can you come here for a few weeks to rehearse with us and then conduct us at the festival? I ask a lot, I know. We can offer you a place to stay with Josie. Do you

remember her from school? She lives with her mother and has a spare room.
If it is too much, I understand you must say no.

Eliza paused her writing. She hadn't written a letter or much of any-thing for years, and her fingers felt stiff, the action unfamiliar to hands more used to squeezing water from wet pinafores. Her letters were uneven; Miss Donahue would be mortified that a pupil of hers had such poor penmanship.

Ruth would never agree to come to Briarstown. She'd escaped, just as Eliza longed to escape. And why should she return, even to help an old friend? Ruth didn't owe Eliza anything, not anymore.

She should have stopped me from marrying Reg.

The old hurt surfaced for a moment, raising its scabbed head and sniff-ing the sour air. But if Ruth had tried to warn her, really tried, nothing would have changed. Eliza would still have married Reg to give Annie a father. *That* part she couldn't regret.

Eliza folded the letter and stood up. "Bessie! We're going out." She took the child by the hand and left the house to walk to the post office. Before she could change her mind, she handed the letter to the postmis-tress, a Miss Taylor. She was rumored to have gotten herself involved with some posh ladies from London who were banging on about women voting.

"I need to send this letter," Eliza said. "I don't have an envelope, and I'm not sure of the address."

"Let's see what I can do. Who is the letter to?"

"Mrs. Ruth Henton. She's an adjudicator with the association that puts on the music festivals?"

"Ah, like the one in Whitby. I've heard all about it, and may I say how pleased I am for you women? Some folk are saying it's a waste of time, that the lasses should be home with their bairns, but I don't think that. The world's changing and I'm all for it."

"Can you find an address for the Music Association?"

"I will most certainly try. I imagine their head office is in London. Leave it with me and I'll get it sorted." Miss Taylor leaned forward and lowered her voice. "We're looking for women to join us. Help with the cause, you know? Women like yourself who aren't afraid to be out in the world?"

"Oh, well, I don't know about that," Eliza said. She felt surprised, and a little flattered. "I'm not sure I'd be much use. I heard it's only for ladies."

"For now, maybe, but we must change that." Miss Taylor looked around Eliza to the next person in line. "Good day to you, Mrs. Kingwell. I'll make sure your letter gets to Mrs. Henton."

Chapter 48

En route to Manchester

Ruth

Ruth read the letter and then looked up at Silas. They sat knees to knees facing each other on the train from Liverpool back to Manchester.

"Who's it from?" Silas asked.

"My friend in Briarstown—Eliza? You'll remember her from Whitby."

"Mrs. Kingwell. Yes. What does she want?"

"She's asked me to come to Briarstown and work with the choir to prepare them for Morecambe. It appears their conductor has accepted an offer to lead a choir going on tour to Canada." She folded the letter and stared out at the passing landscape. She was happy for Miss Donahue. Her old teacher had always struck Ruth as someone longing to taste life but who had been denied the opportunity. Ruth marveled at the difference between herself and Miss Donahue. Ruth's life had been a whirlwind of fame, rich dinners, and adulation—and yet it wasn't enough.

"It may be for the best," Silas said.

Ruth regarded him with surprise. She hadn't expected Silas to agree so quickly. Her first feeling upon reading Eliza's letter was that she'd never set foot in Briarstown again. How could Eliza ask such a thing? She presumed Silas would immediately tell her that she couldn't possibly leave her duties with the Music Association.

"What about the association?" she asked. "Mr. Harrison was very clear that he expected me to stay. As a matter of fact, he lamented that the young women he hired often left to get married, but that he didn't suppose that would be a concern for me."

"He said that?" Silas looked so indignant that Ruth couldn't help smiling.

"Yes."

"Do you *want* to go help your friend?"

"When you put it that way, then yes, I do, but there are…reasons… why I'm hesitant to return to Briarstown."

"I won't pry," Silas said. He stayed silent for several moments, then seemed to come to a decision. He sat up straighter, squaring his shoulders. "Don't worry about the association. I'll deal with them."

"That's kind of you, but I haven't yet decided whether I'll go." Ruth suddenly realized that her reluctance to go to Briarstown had less to do with wanting to help Eliza and more to do with *not* wanting to leave Silas.

Silas shifted in his seat, then took a deep breath and reached for her hand. He held it loosely, like it was a precious object, and then gently let go.

"Forgive me," he said. "I'm too bold. The truth is I've been intending to ask the association to reassign you. This letter from your friend provides me with a perfect opportunity."

"You want to get rid of me? Why?"

"I wouldn't exactly put it that way," Silas said.

"Then how *would* you put it?"

Silas looked like a condemned man. His eyes behind his spectacles were bright with what appeared to be unshed tears. Ruth had a sudden impulse to reach out and touch his cheek, to close the distance between them. She crossed her arms across her chest and sat back in her seat.

"Well?"

"I don't think it's wise for us to continue working so closely together."

"You've said yourself, many times, that we make a good team."

"We do! Working with you has been wonderful!"

"But?"

He sighed. "You must know that I can no longer sit next to you day after day and not let you know how I feel."

"I don't understand…" she began, although she did.

"I care for you, Ruth," he said. Before she could reply, he rushed on. "I know you don't feel the same way about me. How could you? A beautiful woman like you with all your accomplishments? But since you came back, these past few weeks have been agony for me."

He loved her. No one except Mother—and Eliza for a time—had ever loved her. Ruth turned her gaze to the passing landscape, not daring to look at Silas. He was a good man, a man who'd never knowingly let her down. He'd never hurt her or ignore her or abandon her.

He loved her.

All she needed to do was look at him and tell him he was wrong, that she felt the same, and that she wanted to make a life with him. One glance, one touch… She thought back to the last time she'd seen her stepfather, Reg Kingwell. He'd dragged her small trunk out to the street and loaded it into the cart that he'd hired to take her to the station and from there to London.

"That's it then," he said, glancing down at her. "You'll be in plenty of time." He rested his broad hands on his hips. A gust of wind ruffled his luxuriant moustache that lifted and then settled over full lips. Ruth saw those lips kissing Eliza and those hands caressing her body.

Best friends. That's what she'd told Eliza they were when they were girls running and playing alongside the canal.

"Are you going to marry Eliza?" she asked.

"Maybe," he said. "What's it to you? You'll be long gone down in London. What Eliza does ain't no business of yours."

"Yes, but…"

Kingwell turned away to talk with the driver. She saw the flash of a coin as it passed from his hand to the driver's. He glanced back at her, nodding at the cart to indicate she should climb in. He didn't offer his hand to help.

"Off you go."

She wanted to call out, to *make* him promise that he'd never marry her friend, but she couldn't move.

"Ye gettin' in lass?" the driver asked twisting around in his seat. "I've not got all day."

Ruth climbed into the cart and stared straight ahead as it lurched forward, taking her away from Kingwell and her life in Briarstown forever.

Over the years, the guilt had lessened somewhat as Ruth came to terms with Eliza marrying Kingwell. She heard about the births of her daughters, one after another, so many that Ruth soon forgot their names. At Whitby, Eliza had made it clear she couldn't forgive Ruth.

As she looked at Silas, sitting so close to her, his expression hopeful, like the singers who stood on stage to await her judgement, she felt the old guilt return.

She didn't deserve a man like Silas, not after what she'd done to Eliza.

"I'm sorry, Silas. You're right. I can't be with you like that."

His breath caught, and for a moment she was sure he was about to cry. Then he mastered himself and inclined his head. "Of course," he said. "When we arrive in Manchester, I'll purchase your ticket to Briarstown."

"I shall see you in Morecambe?" she asked.

He bowed. "Of course."

Briarstown had changed little, Ruth reflected, as she rode through its grimy streets to Josie Smith's house. She was kindly received and installed in a small bedroom on the top floor of a neat terrace house. Josie's mother made tea and scones that she served in the damp front parlor. The house was identical to the one Ruth had lived in with Mother and Kingwell. She almost expected to see Mother's picture on the mantle.

After tea, she excused herself, saying she needed air. Josie offered to accompany her but, to Ruth's relief, was not at all offended when she told her she preferred to be alone.

"You'll be wanting to visit your ma, I'm guessing," Josie said.

Ruth looked at Josie in surprise, touched by her thoughtfulness. "I do. Thank you."

Her walk to the churchyard took her past many of the places she remembered from her childhood—the butcher's shop below the dusty room that housed the mill school, the court where Eliza had lived with her parents, the path leading down to the canal where she and Eliza had walked so many times.

Ruth knelt in the dry grass sprouting around Mother's untended gravestone. With one gloved hand, she brushed dust from the pitted surface.

Edith Kingwell

b. September 3, 1854 d. December 17, 1886, age 32

Rest in Peace

A sob caught in her throat. Mother had suffered so much in her brief life. Both Ruth's father and Kingwell had let her down—one taking her youth, the other her dignity. Ruth removed her glove and laid her palm over the words *Edith Kingwell.* The sun caught and glinted off the single ruby in the center of her mother's ring.

Red—the color of passion and of blood. Mother had loved Ruth without condition, without expectation of return.

Mother had loved her.

Something shifted inside Ruth's heart, like a fissure cracking apart to let in the light. Mother had loved her because of who she was, not for what she did or for the applause she commanded from strangers. Ruth deserved love because she was alive and she breathed and she'd once been a part of Mother.

She thought of Silas, of the soft look in his eyes when he spoke to her. He loved her so much that he'd not tried to stop her from going away. His was a love that gave and expected nothing in return. His was a love worth having and worth returning.

Ruth rose to her feet, brushed the specks of dirt from her skirt and gazed around the quiet churchyard. Mother was in the trees rustling above her and in the twittering of the birds and the softness of the summer air and the tolling of the church bells.

"Thank you, Mother," she whispered.

Chapter 49

Briarstown

Eliza

Eliza entered the church hall to find the women clustered around a table overflowing with piles of bright green fabric—silk by the look of it.

"See what Lottie's made for us!" Hannah exclaimed. She picked up a length of silk that shimmered in a shaft of light slanting in from a high window.

"We'll look sharp in these," Mary said. She picked up a length and draped it across her chest.

"You look just like one of them posh ladies at Whitby!" Josie said admiringly. "Eliza? What do you think?"

Eliza walked forward and picked up a sash, marveling at the feel of the silk between her fingers. "They're lovely," she said. "How did you get so many, Lottie?"

"When I was with the choir in Leeds, we wore sashes like this when we performed. I had a bit of money laid by, and my cousin who runs a haberdashery shop helped out."

"Please thank him for us," Eliza said. She draped the sash across her chest. "Come on, girls. Let's put them on!"

As the women laughed and preened, Eliza felt hope creeping back into her heart. Reg was very wrong if he thought he could prevent her from going to Morecambe. She'd just make very sure to keep out of his way when the girls weren't in the house.

"I must say, you all look very fine," said a voice behind them.

"Ruth Kingwell!" Hattie said. "You've come after all."

"It's Ruth Henton," Eliza said. "And of course she came." She wouldn't let on how worried she'd been that Ruth would turn down her plea.

To Eliza's relief, Ruth immediately put the choir at ease.

"Good afternoon, everyone," she began. "I'm honored you've asked me to conduct you. Your performance at Whitby was remarkable, and I feel confident you'll perform just as well in Morecambe."

"You think so?" Minnie asked. "I heard it's a much bigger festival. Are we really good enough?"

"There's only one way to find out," Ruth said. She raised her hands and nodded at Mrs. Walker. "Let's start with a warmup."

Over the two hours, Eliza discovered in Ruth a demanding taskmistress. She scowled, sighed, and demanded *again*. Every note, every pause, every nuance was repeated over and over again. Eliza's solo in the set piece was mercilessly picked apart, parsed, and found wanting. Eliza glanced at Hattie McKay and saw that even she was wincing with sympathy when Ruth demanded that she repeat a phrase for the tenth time.

"That's coming along," Ruth said at the end of the rehearsal. "You're wondering, I'm sure, why I'm being so hard on you. Take it as a compliment. I truly believe you can take first prize at Morecambe, but only if you continue to work very hard. Please practice your parts every chance you get, and I shall see you on Tuesday evening."

Eliza waited until all the women had left the hall, their tread weary. She touched Ruth's wide sleeve.

"Yes?"

"I'm entering the solo competition at Morecambe. After losing in Whitby, do you think I still have a chance?"

"I doesn't matter what I think, Eliza. If you don't believe you're good enough to compete, then nothing I can teach you will make any difference. Do *you* think you're good enough?"

Eliza thought of Reg's fists and the hurt, and of her girls, of Ma resenting her all these years, and of her little brother who had never got the chance to grow up.

"Yes," she said. "If you'll coach me, I'll work hard and do my best to win."

"Good. Come an hour before each rehearsal. And Eliza? Do you remember singing at the Christmas bazaar?"

"I don't suppose I'll ever forget it," Eliza said, taken aback by the question.

"I was so nervous for you when you walked onto the platform wearing those ridiculous red bows in your hair."

"Miss Donahue gave them to me."

"I'd never seen anyone look more frightened," Ruth said.

"I felt like I was standing on top of a mountain," Eliza said. "There was such a crowd! I'd never seen ladies' hats with so many feathers and ribbons and artificial flowers."

"I saw you open your mouth to start singing."

"And all that came out was a strangled croak. It was horrible," Eliza said, smiling now.

"And then people started talking," Ruth said. "I wanted to scream at them to be quiet and listen."

"The pianist had to play my introduction three times," Eliza said. "I remember thinking how I didn't belong in that fancy place with all the ladies and gentlemen. If Ma had known, she'd have put a stop to it." Eliza's smile faded. "I suppose, as things turned out, that would have been for the best."

"I can understand how you'd feel that way, considering what happened, but when you finally found your voice, you were remarkable," Ruth said. "You were only eleven years old, but your voice had such power!"

"All I wanted was to show all those posh people that I wasn't just some poor child who should keep out of the way and know my place."

"Keep hold of that feeling, Eliza," Ruth said. "In Morecambe, you'll have your chance to show them again."

On her way home, Eliza stopped at the bridge overlooking the canal. The mild June air was nothing like the sharpness of that December day when she'd experienced for the first time the sting of tragedy.

Ma had been sick the day of the Christmas bazaar with one of her headaches and insisted Eliza take care of little Ernie. Years later, Eliza still chided herself for not taking Ernie with her to the church hall. Miss Donahue would have minded him while she sang.

But instead, she'd waylaid her big brother Billy and thrust the little boy into his beefy arms.

Billy stared over the top of Ernie's head at Eliza. "You're jokin'!"

"Please, Billy! He won't be no trouble. Ma's got one of her headaches again and I got to be somewheres, and it will only be for an hour."

"What am I gonna do with a kiddy in the pub?"

"Take him for a walk down by the canal. It's a fine day."

"It's cold enough to freeze my balls off."

"Come on, Billy. I never ask anything of you."

"I be workin' since half six." At fifteen years old, stocky Billy Treleven had a bullish stare and large hands almost always curled into fists. Eliza wished it was her eldest brother Jack who had come by. Jack was slightly brighter than his younger brother and sometimes thanked Eliza when she gave him his packet of food in the morning. He even occasionally played with Ernie. He wouldn't have minded taking charge of his little brother for an hour.

"Where's Jack?" she asked.

Billy shrugged. "Off mooning over Milly Sparks, most likely. He's gone dotty for that girl. Can't figure what he sees in her. She's got a gob on her like a navvy."

Eliza wondered if it was possible to burst with frustration. She wanted to shake Billy. Would it kill him to be nice for once in his stupid life?

"Can you take him to Aunt Agnes for me?" she asked.

"All the way over there? You can't be serious."

"It won't take you more than half an hour and then you can go drink yourself silly all afternoon. Come on, Billy. Please!"

Billy's face clouded with confusion. "What's the big hurry? What you got to do that's so important?"

"I'm singin' at the bazaar over at the town hall," Eliza said. "It's a posh do being put on by the rich ladies. They're selling things to raise money for the school, and they want me to sing at it. Miss Donahue's arranged it, and I can't let her down."

"*You* singin'? What would you want to do that for?"

"I got to be there in fifteen minutes, Billy. I'll see you in an hour."

Eliza turned and ran back down the street. She heard Billy calling after her, but she didn't dare turn around. Her brother wasn't a bad sort, just slow and always in Jack's shadow. She was confident he wouldn't let little Ernie come to any harm. And if he was angry enough to tattle to Ma, well, so be it.

Hours later, flushed with triumph and with the sound of applause still ringing in her years, Eliza returned home to find everyone gone. Outside, a cacophony of bells, whistles, and sirens started up and dozens of grim-faced men streamed past. A cold hand closed around her heart. Something told her the noise had to do with Ernie.

Eliza ran into the street and tugged at the sleeve of one of the men, forcing him to stop. She recognized him as Jamie Burns who lived two doors down and was a friend of Dad's. "What's happened? What's going on?"

"There's been an accident." He looked at her, his face paling. "You're the daughter, ain't ye? Archie's daughter?"

"Yes."

"You'd best come along with me," he said.

"Where we goin'?" Eliza asked, barely keeping pace with the man's long legs.

"To the canal."

They arrived to find a small knot of people gathered on a bridge, all looking over the edge, some pointing and exclaiming. Eliza broke away from Jamie and ran forward. Several people stepped back from the railing. They were shaking their heads and muttering. One woman reached for Eliza's hand. "Come, pet. You don't want to see."

Eliza pulled away and threw herself at the railing. All she could see at first was the dark green water of the canal. And then she saw people gathered on the towpath and Billy on his knees next to a crumpled figure.

A man stepped off a barge carrying a sodden bundle. Carefully, he laid it next to the person lying on the ground who looked up, hatless in the cold.

"Ma!"

Eliza dashed across the bridge and down to the canal. Ma's hands, black with mud, reached for the bundle. A keening sound like the screeching of unoiled machinery razored the air. Eliza tugged at Billy's jacket. At first, he didn't seem to recognize his sister. He stared at her and then back at Ma, who was gathering Ernie to her breast. Her wailing became screams that sounded like they were being pulled from the deepest parts of her— ragged, gasping sounds that chilled Eliza's soul. Still holding Ernie, Ma fell back and was caught by Billy before her head hit the towpath.

"What happened?" Eliza screamed at her brother, overcome suddenly by the urge to slap him across his gormless face. "Billy!"

"You should never've asked me," Billy said, recognizing her finally. "I tried to hold him…"

"What happened?" she repeated.

"There now, lass," a deep male voice said behind her. "No use yelling at him. It were an accident. George here saw it."

"What?"

A tall boy loomed above her. Twisting his hat between his hands, he said, "The bairn broke away from Billy and then fell into the canal. I tried to help fish him out before it were too late, but he were beyond our reach." The boy's voice broke. "I'm that sorry."

"No!" Eliza threw herself at Billy, hitting him with all her strength, blind to everything but her need to hurt him, to make him pay. She wanted to send him into the icy waters of the canal and watch him sink into the blackness.

She felt hands on her—strong but also gentle. She tried shrugging them off, but the grip tightened, preventing her from shoving Billy until he teetered on the slick edge of the canal. She could do it. One big push and he'd go in, maybe even take her with him. But the hands holding her wouldn't let go.

"Get 'er off me!" Billy yelled. "Ma!"

She heard a grunt and a curse and then felt herself torn away from Billy. As if in slow motion, Billy's arms spread wide, flapping to help him keep his balance.

Eliza felt a terrible hatred well up inside her, a black, foul thing more terrifying than any monster. She turned her wrath onto George who was trying to hold on to her.

How dare he!

She pummeled his chest with her fists. Screams like needles scored her throat.

An hour earlier, she'd used her voice to fill a hall full of toffs with music. Now, she used it to scream with a rage too powerful for reason.

"Eliza."

Her father's deep voice reached her, and the strength drained out of her. George's grip on her loosened and he stepped back, and then Eliza felt Dad's thick arms wrapping around her, holding her tightly as her screams turned to wails that rose and fell with the rhythm of her breath. The agony would break her in two.

Ernie was only a baby.

"There, lass."

His coat felt rough against her cheek, his familiar smell soothing, like warm milk on a cold morning. Nothing could hurt her so long as she kept holding on to Dad.

But then his hold on her loosened, and she felt herself gently pushed away. She stood alone, as insubstantial as a reed against a stiff wind and watched Dad help Ma up from the ground. A heartbreaking mix of grief and pain twisted his usually placid features, making him look to Eliza like a stranger.

She felt lonelier than she ever had in her life—a shattering, all-consuming isolation that prevented her from reaching for Dad. All his attention was directed at Ma. He enfolded her in his arms and held her head with one large hand, his soft croons no match for Ma's wails.

The crumpled body of little Ernie was a white smudge against the mud. Eliza was to learn later that it was a miracle the child had been found. He'd floated downstream and been fished out by the pilot of a barge loaded with woven cotton bound for Liverpool.

Eliza dropped to her knees and placed her hand against the baby's cheek. It was a pale shade of blue and felt solid under her fingers, like polished stone.

"I'm so sorry, Ernie," she whispered, her voice hoarse from screaming. "I should never have left you."

A hand grabbed hold of her arm and yanked her to her feet. She stared into two black, dead eyes that had never looked upon her kindly, and now never would.

"You did this," Ma spat. "Because of *you*, our Ernie is dead."

Eliza peered down at the place by the canal where Ma had cradled Ernie's dead body. A clump of stinging nettles, the saw-toothed leaves brilliant green in the evening sun, grew there now. The hurt of Ma's words had never really left her.

Because if you, our Ernie is dead.

If only, Eliza thought. If only her brother Billy hadn't let go of Ernie's hand, if only Dad hadn't brought them to the North, if only she'd understood what Reg was doing to her and had squirmed away.

If only.

On the clear July evening, a perfect reflection of clouds and blue sky shone across the smooth waters of the canal. No barges passed to churn the waters, and the clanging mills were silent. A few birds chirped nearby, adding to the peacefulness of the scene.

If only.

Sometimes, Eliza wondered if Ma had ever looked at her the way she looked at her girls, felt for her what she felt for them. Had Ma ever held her close and kissed her hair and felt her heart burst with love? Even before Ernie's death, Ma had never been warm towards Eliza, always preferring the boys to her, always finding fault.

At least Dad had loved her. Of that Eliza was certain.

She leaned her elbows on the railing and breathed in the freshness of the summer air. Eliza knew she had a chance to do something truly special in Morecambe.

It wouldn't make Ma love her, but maybe that didn't matter anymore.

Chapter 50

Briarstown

Ruth

R uth was returning from an afternoon walk to the moor when she saw Kingwell coming towards her. She stopped walking so abruptly that she teetered forward and had to grasp hold of a lamppost to keep herself upright.

"Hello, Ruth."

"You!" She kept her grip on the lamppost, conscious of his eyes boring into her.

"I heard ye was back in town," he said. "Giving my wife notions and all."

"She has a beautiful voice. You should be proud of her."

Reg scoffed. "She's got responsibilities. She's not like you."

Ruth thought about contradicting him and then realized there was no point. He hadn't changed and never would. At least she was out in the open with people walking past on both sides of the street. He'd never dare come at her. If nothing else, Reg Kingwell was a coward.

"I've got to be getting on," Ruth said.

"That's all you've got to say to your old dad?"

"You're not my father."

"I kept you fed and clothed for a goodly number of years, which is more than your real father ever did."

"If you're waiting for me to thank you, you'll be waiting a long time."

Ruth started to walk past him. He stopped her with a hand on her arm and leaned close. The pressure was light, but she wasn't fooled. She stood very still. The sound of her wrist bone snapping all those years ago was still embedded in her soul like the sting of an enraged wasp.

"I'll thank ye to leave my wife be," he hissed.

Ruth shuddered at the smell of him—stale beer mixed with lye soap and sweat and a hint of the wax he used to stiffen his moustache.

"Let me go," she said between gritted teeth.

"I was good to you and your ma," he said. "Weren't my fault she got the pneumonia." His hand tightened for a second and then let go.

"You could have done more to help her," Ruth said, stepping away. Despite her desire to leave the past behind, the old hurt surfaced and with it all the pain and loneliness she'd endured for too many years. Reg Kingwell was still a handsome man, but there was a duplicity about him that repelled her. She thought of Silas—of his sincerity and his kindness.

"I loved your ma," Reg said. "You've got to believe that."

"Maybe you did," Ruth conceded. "But one thing I can say for sure is that she *never* loved you. She needed you to give us a home, but she never, ever loved you."

A spasm of pain crossed his face and Ruth knew, finally, that she'd hurt him—maybe not as much as he'd hurt her, but it was something.

"Goodbye, *Father*," she said, and then turned on her heel and walked away.

Chapter 51

Briarstown

Eliza

It was not yet twilight when Eliza left the church hall after the last rehearsal the choir would have before leaving for Morecambe in two days. She felt light and strong. Ruth had done an excellent job. Even if the choir didn't win at Morecambe, Eliza felt confident they'd be a credit to Briarstown and all the people who had helped send them.

The air was soft, the sky clear, slanting rays from the setting sun turning the dreary street into a stream of gold. Eliza detoured to the towpath, anxious for just a few more blessed minutes to herself to think about the choir and her solo. She heard Ruth's voice in her head—*breathe, come to the note from above, crescendo, diminuendo, don't forget the ritardando…*

Eliza remembered a time when all the foreign words had bewildered her. Now, they felt as much a part of her as the notes she'd learned to turn into music. Her new song for the solo competition was a stunning piece called *Ombra mai fu* by a man called Handel. The first long note was impossibly difficult to sing, but Ruth had worked with Eliza to master her breathing and pitch. She couldn't wait to sing it at the festival.

A slight figure standing by the canal caught her attention—a girl wearing a dark coat although the evening was warm. Eliza watched her walk to the edge and look down at the water. A barge slid past, pulled by horses plodding along the towpath on the opposite bank. Sensing that the girl wanted to be alone, Eliza was about to turn around when she noticed the swell of the girl's belly. A low moan competed with the lapping of the water against the sides of the canal. The girl stepped close to the edge and leaned forward.

"Stop!" Eliza called out. She started to run towards the girl. "No!"

She reached the girl just in time. Eliza wrapped her arms firmly around her and scrabbled backwards. The girl struggled and kicked, but memories of her brother Ernie turned Eliza's grip to iron. The canal was life and death in this town. She'd *never* let it take another soul if she could help it.

"Let me go!"

"No!"

The girl squirmed in Eliza's grasp.

"You can't be doing this," Eliza gasped. "It's wrong."

The girl suddenly went limp, dissolving into sobs that racked her small body. Eliza pulled her away from the edge and held her close.

Olive Grant—Reg's latest.

To her shame, Eliza remembered how relieved she'd been when Olive, like the other girls Reg had interfered with, was let go from the mill and Reg kept on. She'd convinced herself that Olive's family would take care of her, and that the whole affair would be hushed up.

"There, there, lass. Cry all you want. There's no one about to hear."

"I'm sorry, Missus," the girl finally gasped. "I don't mean no harm. It's just that…"

Eliza led the girl to the stone steps leading up to the street. "Sit here. You're Olive Grant, aren't you?"

"How did you know?"

"I'm Eliza Kingwell."

The girl reared back and started scrambling to her feet, but Eliza kept hold of her wrist and with gentle pressure coaxed her to sit down.

"I don't mean you any harm," Eliza said.

"You must hate me."

"Of course, I don't hate you. What's happened to you isn't your fault." Eliza felt like she was looking in a mirror. Olive's dark hair was scraped back in a bun, and she had a small, delicate face with wary eyes that made her look like a mouse caught in a trap.

"But it were your husband what did this." Olive looked down at her swollen belly and then back up at Eliza. "Ma said I were a disgrace. She told me I needn't darken her door ever again. Dad tried to reason with her, but she were 'avin' none of it." Olive's pale cheeks shone with tears.

"How old are you?"

"Seventeen, Ma'am. I been at t'mill five years. Mr. Kingwell were kind to me. He said he thought I were sweet. Called me his little bird."

Eliza felt the bile rising in her throat.

"I didn't know no better," Olive said. "He's such a fine-looking man, almost like a gentleman. He said he wanted to be wi' me, that the two of us could go away and live somewhere by the sea."

"You didn't know he had a wife and five daughters?"

"Not at first, Ma'am, and then he kept on saying such nice things over and over, and then, well..."

"You don't have to say anything more." Eliza's heart ached knowing that the poor girl must be feeling exactly as she had thirteen years earlier. At least Eliza hadn't been thrown out on the streets to fend for herself. "Do you have anywhere to go?" she asked.

"No." The girl sniffed. "Ma says I'm wicked. She told me there was a place for girls like me, but I went there, and it were horrible."

"You're not wicked," Eliza said. "Come with me. I know a place where you can stay. You'll be safe there."

Anger propelled Eliza home after leaving Olive Grant with Mary Denholm. To Eliza's relief, Mary had been sympathetic to Olive's plight. She lived alone and agreed to take Olive in until other arrangements could be made. Eliza had an idea of what those arrangements would be, but they would have to wait until she returned from Morecambe.

She slammed open the door to her house. Reg was at his usual place by the fire, unlit on the early July evening. She wanted to fly at him and make him pay for what he'd done to poor Olive. This time if she picked up the poker, she'd use it.

"What's with you?" he asked.

"Where are the girls?" Eliza asked.

"Out playing, which you'd know if you were home like you're supposed to be."

Eliza walked forward to stand directly in front of him. She knew she was taking a risk provoking him when the girls were out, but she was past caring.

"I just met Olive Grant," she said. "She was about to throw herself in the canal."

"What's she got to do with me?"

"You know perfectly well. She's carrying your child."

"She can't prove owt," he said with a shrug, but he was blinking rapidly.

"Oh please, Reg, spare me the lies. I don't expect you to be ashamed of yourself, but you should at least have the decency to own up to what you did."

Reg rested his hands on his knees, then curled them into fists. Eliza's throat tightened, but she'd not back down. Not this time.

She could not be broken.

"She were askin' for it," he said. "And I'm only human." He waved his hand dismissively and had the audacity to smile—charming Reg Kingwell whom everyone liked until they got to know him. "Happen I saw Ruth on my way home just now."

"You spoke with her?"

"'Course. She's my stepdaughter and all."

"What did you say to her?"

"Not much. I just told her to stay away from you." He looked up at her, his eyes slits. "You'd be well shot of her, the right bitch."

Eliza picked up the poker with both hands and pointed it at him. His eyes widened, but he didn't move. She started walking towards him.

"Ma?"

She turned to see Bessie standing in the open doorway. Eliza dropped the poker and lunged for her, but Reg was too quick.

He scooped Bessie into his arms. "There you are, my little one!" he crowed. "Give your old dad a kiss, there's a good girl."

Bessie squealed with delight, her blue eyes crinkling as she laughed. For the first time, Eliza realized how much her youngest resembled her little brother Ernie. Why had she never noticed? She'd always thought Bessie took after Reg, and it was true they had the same eyes, just like Gladys had. But there was something about the shape of Bessie's mouth, her red cheeks and plump hands that brought back Ernie.

Her baby brother was beyond help, but Bessie and the other girls were not.

Reg set Bessie down and glared at Eliza. "What did you think you'd do with that?" he asked indicating with his chin the dropped poker. "What if our Bessie had seen?"

Eliza was shaking so much that she gripped the edge of the table to steady herself. Had she really intended to go after Reg with the poker? She winced as she imagined the sharp tip lashing his handsome face. He'd have had it off her in seconds and then what? Did she want her girls to see her dead on the floor?

"Go call your sisters in," Eliza said to Bessie. "It's almost time for tea."

"Do as your ma says," he said. "When you're back, I'll give you a ride on my knee."

Eliza picked up the poker and returned it to its place next to the grate. She took the kettle to the sink and filled it from the bucket Gladys had brought from the pump. Her mind whirled with ideas about what she'd do next. Waiting was no longer an option. She had to get the girls and herself away as soon as possible.

"Yer not gonna talk now?" Reg growled.

"I've nothing to say. You'd best get washed up." She glanced over at him, noting with some satisfaction that his normally florid face was pale. "I'll get the fire lit and the kettle on, and then I'm going across the yard to talk to Hattie."

He didn't ask her why, and she wasn't about to say. Hattie would be furious about Eliza leaving the choir with so little time left before Morecambe, but what other choice did she have? Her girls came first. She still had her share of the money the choir won in Whitby. It wasn't much, but it would pay for a few weeks in a lodging house while she figured out her next steps.

The girls trooped in, and Eliza set them to work, then untied her apron and set off across the yard to knock on Hattie's door.

"What do you mean, you're not coming?" Hattie demanded. "You've got to come. We can't win without you."

"I can't come," Eliza said flatly. She debated about telling Hattie the truth. She supposed she owed it to her and the other women, but the humiliation would be too much.

Hattie narrowed her eyes. "Something's happened with that man of yours, hasn't it?"

Eliza nodded, appalled to feel tears springing to her eyes—and in front of Hattie McKay, of all people.

"Come with me," Hattie said. "We'll go get Minnie and some of the others and decide what to do. I'm guessing you don't want to leave your girls with him?"

Again, Eliza nodded, too humiliated to speak.

"Well, I'm sorry for it and all. But we'll get it sorted." Hattie took Eliza by the arm, then let it go, her expression aghast when Eliza winced.

"That bad, is it? You've never said."

"How could I?"

Hattie said nothing as she ushered Eliza down the passageway to the street-facing houses. She knocked on Minnie's door. "Can you get away a minute?" she asked.

"Aye. What's up?"

Eliza felt like she was sleepwalking as she followed Hattie and Minnie down the street to Gert's house and then Hannah's. Hattie then led them all down to the towpath.

"No one's likely to bother us here," she said. "So, Eliza here needs our help."

The other four women all began talking at once.

'course we'll help.

What can we do?

I'll do what I can.

What do you need?

Eliza bit the inside of her cheek to hold fast to her dignity. That Reg had brought her to this, beholden to women who, six months earlier, had barely given her the time of day. She corrected herself. It was *she* who had avoided *them*. Hadn't they invited her to join the choir in the first place?

"Eliza here needs a place for her girls to stay while we're off to Morecambe," Hattie said. She held up her hand. "Ain't no point asking why. Just knowin' she needs our help is enough. Now, who's got some extra room?"

"I can take Bessie and Emily," Gert said. "Your Emily's friends with my youngest. They'd think it a right treat to spend a few nights together. My Ma lives with us and will see to them."

"Your Annie's best friends with my Tilda," Minnie said. "She can stay with us. Frank won't mind."

"And I'll take Lily May and Gladys," Hannah said. "My Ma will spoil 'em rotten seein' as she don't have no grandchildren of her own."

Eliza knew she should volunteer her own mother, but the thought of asking her and enduring her cold looks and long-suffering sighs was too much. Besides, the house was near to bursting with Aunt Agnes, Uncle Bob and their four children in addition to Ma.

"Thank ye," Eliza said. "I'll bring the girls over first thing tomorrow before we go to the train." She paused, touched by the concerned expressions on the faces of the other women—her friends.

"You'd do the same for any of us," Hattie said. "Now, you'd best get off home. We'll see you bright and early tomorrow."

Chapter 52

Morecambe in Lancashire

Ruth

Hours after running into Reg, Ruth left for Morecambe, unwilling to wait a moment longer to get to Silas and tell him how she felt.

The festival venues were already humming with activity when she arrived. Established in 1893, the Morecambe Music Competition had already grown into one of the premier music competitions in northern England. Silas had told her that over fifteen hundred competitors would fill the town's theaters with music—from choral groups to brass bands.

A male quartet was performing when Ruth entered the newly built Victoria Pavilion on Morecambe's central promenade. The next afternoon, the ladies of Briarstown would compete there.

Her heart quickened when she saw Silas seated at the judges' table. He was leaning forward, his attention fixed on the men singing. A young woman wearing a neat shirtwaist and plain navy skirt sat to his right. Ruth judged her to be no more than nineteen. She nodded at something Silas said and then leaned close—too close. She had a light complexion and mousy brown hair swept into a simple bun at the base of her neck. She looked sensible and serious and very young.

"Ma'am?" A man behind her lifted his hat. "Are you looking for a seat?"

"Pardon me? Oh, no. Thank you."

He'd called her ma'am, not miss. Well, of course he had. She'd be thirty-one in August.

The male quartet concluded their performance and bowed to the applause. Silas wrote on his scorecard and then spoke to the other judge. He was smiling and looked relaxed. Ruth wondered if he already called the girl by her first name.

Ruth turned and left the hall. A warm breeze off the Irish Sea ruffled the feathers on the hats of the ladies walking past. Several carried black umbrellas to shield them from the sun. Two young boys ran around her, their voices shrill with excitement. Ruth sank onto a bench and gazed out at the lapping waves and at the people enjoying themselves, some strolling along the promenade, others sitting on blankets spread over the sand. A few were even wading in the shallow water at the shore. She heard shrieks of laughter when a wave broke too high, dampening skirt hems and rolled-up trouser cuffs.

She was being ridiculous. Silas could not have forgotten her so quickly. The young woman was a colleague, nothing more. But she couldn't rid her mind of the image of them smiling and chatting, their shoulders almost touching. There was an easiness about Silas's demeanor that she'd never seen when he was with her. He was always unfailingly polite, anxious for her comfort and frequently deferring to her opinion. But even when declaring that he loved her, he never seemed totally relaxed.

And whose fault is that?

Yes, she'd asked him to call her Ruth, but she'd also deliberately kept her distance from him. They never laughed together. They were friendly, but never friends.

Ruth closed her eyes against the glare of the summer sun. After Morecambe, she'd need to make her own way—a spinster on the wrong side of thirty with dwindling funds and a voice that no longer served her.

Chapter 53

Briarstown

Eliza

The next morning, Eliza rose at four and padded downstairs. In the pearlescent dawn, she packed four bags—one for herself, one for Annie, then another for Lily May and Gladys, and the fourth bag for Emily and Bessie. She climbed to the top floor and roused the four eldest girls. She'd told them the night before that they'd be going to stay with friends while she was at Morecambe, and they'd gone to bed in a flutter of excitement.

She'd made a bed for Bessie on the ground floor and had slept in Reg's chair. He'd stood by, glowering as she tucked in Bessie, but hadn't dared raise a hand to her before climbing to the second floor and sleeping alone for only the second time since they'd married. He seemed bewildered, and Eliza supposed she couldn't blame him. She'd never once left his bed, no matter how badly he hurt her. But this time was different, and it was high time he got used to sleeping alone forever.

Annie was already awake when Eliza emerged onto the top floor. She hopped out of bed and turned to gently shake her sisters.

"We'll be ready in no time, Ma," she whispered. "Is Dad up?"

"Not yet. Tell them they need to be very quiet on their way downstairs." She hated turning her daughters against Reg. He deserved no less, but she'd fondly hoped she could keep her girls from learning the truth for as long as possible. It wasn't right they should know.

"I'll leave you to it then," Eliza said. She turned away quickly to hide her flushed cheeks and descended to the second floor. To her dismay, Reg's bed was empty. She found him in the downstairs room, staring at the packed bags.

"You can't do this," he said.

"It's all arranged. The girls have places to stay while I'm away. You needn't worry about them." Eliza lifted Bessie from her makeshift bed. The child whimpered, still half asleep. "The girls will be down soon, and then we'll be off." She peered over Bessie's tousled head at her husband. "It's for the best."

"You can't do this," he said again. "I've done nothin' wrong."

Eliza bit back a laugh. She set Bessie down and knelt to help her into her dress. "There you go, pet," she said. She kissed the girl's silky cheek. "Play with Dolly, and I'll bring you a piece of bread."

She stood and took up the knife to cut slices of bread for the girls. "Your lunch pail's packed. Go get yourself dressed." She kept her voice steady, but every muscle tensed as she sensed him looming behind her. She'd never defied him so openly. Would Bessie playing at his feet be enough to keep him from coming at her? She regarded the knife sawing through the bread. Could she use it? She thought of her girls and knew she'd walk through fire to keep them safe.

She heard him climbing the stairs and let out a sigh of relief. Thirty minutes later, he came back down and without even a glance in her direction, left the house. Sighing with relief, she quickly gathered the girls and went out into the yard.

He stood a few feet away, his arms crossed.

"Yer not takin' my girls," he said. "I'll not allow it."

"How will you stop me?" she asked, keeping her voice down in a vain attempt to prevent the girls from hearing.

"I'm within me rights," he said. "You and the girls belong to me. Now, get back inside before I make a fuss. Do you want everyone to know?"

"Kingwell!" A deep voice cut through the early morning air. "Best get going t'mill."

Reg turned to see Andy McKay and Frank Jones closing in on him. Hattie and Minnie followed not far behind their husbands, each carrying a case.

"This ain't your business," Reg said.

"It is now," Andy said. "My Hattie's been looking forward to this Morecambe business for months. You're not going to ruin it for her."

"My Minnie as well," Frank said. "Your girls will be fine for a few days. When the lasses come back from Morecambe, you can sort things out."

"Seems Eliza thinks the girls would be safer away from you," Andy said, barely disguising his contempt.

"I've never laid a hand on them!" Reg sputtered. "Eliza's lying to you. She's too sharp for her own good."

Andy and Frank came to stand on either side of Reg, each taking an arm. For a moment, Eliza was afraid Reg would struggle. Then, Andy whispered something in Reg's ear and all the fight went out of him. He threw one last glare at Eliza and then let himself be led across the yard and into the passageway.

"All right, Eliza?" Hattie asked, grinning at the five girls standing behind Eliza. "We'd best get going. Your ma's going to make you proud."

Chapter 54

Morecambe

Ruth

Ruth's heart swelled as she regarded the choir—her choir. She'd agreed to conduct them as a way to make amends to Eliza, never expecting to become so invested in their success.

Behind her, Silas sat with his pencil at the ready to mark every nuance of the choir's performance. She hadn't spoken with him yet and wondered if she would. Basic civility required them to at least greet each other during the competition, but she dreaded coming face to face with him and his new partner. In her fashionable dress and precisely arranged pompadour, Ruth felt too showy next to the new judge's demure, no-nonsense appearance.

She also felt old.

Ruth dragged her attention back to the women standing in front of her. She couldn't let them down. Theirs was the last choir to perform, and the competition had been fierce. Ruth felt confident they could still win, but they'd need to be flawless, and nerves could pose a very real threat. Doris still occasionally sang a wrong note, and during their last rehearsal, Minnie had slurred a phrase in her solo. At least Eliza would perform her solo perfectly. Ruth could only hope it would be enough to take them to victory.

She smiled at the women and mouthed the words *Best of luck*. Most of them smiled back, cheeks flushed with anticipation. They looked so smart, each dressed in a plain black dress with a length of bright green silk draped across their chests.

The accompanist played the opening bars of *Ye Spotted Snakes*—the set piece in Morecambe as it had been in Whitby. The other choirs had done it justice, with the Leeds choir clearly the favorite to win. Ruth raised her baton.

Eliza sang the first few bars flawlessly. As she conducted, Ruth felt her jaw soften. It was going to be fine. The choir was as good as any performing that day. She sensed Silas's eyes on her back and fancied she could imagine his critique.

Clear tone, superb diction, full marks for expression.

The women sang with both passion and technical precision, with Eliza and Minnie performing their solos beautifully. Ruth barely managed to hold back tears. Their voices mingled and harmonized as though they'd been singing together for decades.

A few bars from the end of the piece, Eliza came in again with the refrain *hence away*. The notes were near the bottom of Eliza's range and sometimes during rehearsal, she'd struggled to deliver them with the same clarity with which she sang the higher notes. To her horror, Ruth saw Eliza's lips slacken and sing the lowest note with the tiniest crack in her voice. She recovered immediately and sang the last few notes brilliantly.

When the women finished the piece, the audience's applause was as loud and enthusiastic as it had been for the Leeds choir. Ruth caught Eliza's eye and smiled reassuringly. It was going to be fine. The error was so slight that even Silas would probably have missed it.

In every other respect, the Briarstown Ladies' Choir was faultless.

Ruth stood aside and gestured for the women to bow. She watched Silas lean towards the other judge, his expression serious.

Too serious.

Chapter 55

Morecambe

Eliza

"Third place is nothing to be ashamed of," Mary Denholm said. "Come on, girls. Cheer up! A few months ago, we'd have been lucky to get the odds of a lame horse."

"Mary's right," Lottie said. "I'm that chuffed. And remember that we won in Whitby, and we'll win again if we keep singin' together."

"We did our best," Josie said. She went over to Eliza and linked arms with her. "You sang so beautifully, Eliza, and Minnie too."

Eliza wanted to break free of Josie and run from the stifling hall. The women meant well, and no one could fault their performance, but they must know the loss was her fault.

"Well done, ladies!" Ruth said, coming over to join them. "I've just spoken with the Master of Ceremonies, and he told me only one mark separated you from the second-place choir. You should feel very proud of yourselves."

"Hear that, Eliza?" Hattie said. "Just one mark away from second place. That's a success in anyone's book."

"I say we celebrate!" Lottie said. "I don't know about the rest of you, but I'm starved."

"Aye, I could use a pie!" Doris said.

"That's settled then," Mary said. "Let's go find ourselves a bite to eat and then we'll come back and watch Eliza in the solo competition."

"Best of luck!" Josie exclaimed. She kissed Eliza's cheek. "We'll be cheering for you."

"Aye, that we will," said Hattie.

Eliza watched the women bustle off, their loud chatter in sharp contrast to the muted and refined tones of the women in most of the other choirs.

"I let them down," Eliza said. "You heard me."

"It was the tiniest crack," Ruth said. "I doubt the judges even noticed. Against the competition you women faced today, third place is a remarkable achievement. I couldn't be more pleased."

"We could have won."

"You can't know that, and you now need to put it behind you. The solo competition starts in an hour."

"I can't do it." The only other time Eliza could remember feeling so frightened was when she had seen Ernie's body lying in the black mud by the side of the canal. Even Reg had never scared her this much. With him, her primary emotion was usually more anger than terror.

"Nonsense. Of course you can."

"What if I lose again like I did at Whitby? I can't let that happen, Ruth. I need the prize money to take the girls away." It was the first time she'd told anyone about her Plan.

"You're going to leave him?"

Eliza nodded. She started for the door. There were too many people—hundreds and hundreds of them who would soon be looking only at her, judging her. She needed air and she needed to be alone. She should never have joined the choir and set herself up for failure. Ruth had been good to her, and Eliza had long since forgiven her for the past. How could she let her down? But it was too much. She'd have to find another way to get the money.

"Good for you," Ruth said quietly.

"What?" Eliza stopped and turned to look at her old friend.

"You heard me." Ruth sighed, her eyes brimming with sympathy and unshed tears. "I wish Mother had gotten us away."

"Oh Ruth, I'm so sorry! I didn't mean…"

"I know. And that's why you must win the prize money. Do it for yourself, Eliza, but also for me and for Mother. I've never told anyone this, but before she died…"

Her voice faltered and impulsively, Eliza reached for Ruth's hand. Compared to her own thin and calloused fingers, Ruth's plump fingers felt soft and smooth. "You can tell me," Eliza said softly. People were starting to return to their seats after the intermission following the Ladies' choir competition. She pulled Ruth to the side.

"Mother made me promise I'd never marry a man unless I loved him with all my heart. She'd married Kingwell only because she needed a home for us. She never loved him."

"You didn't love your husband in London?" Eliza asked.

Ruth shook her head. "I thought I did, but I soon found out I was wrong."

"My granny said much the same to me," Eliza said. "She told me to marry a man who was kind."

The two women looked at each other for several long moments and then at the same time began to laugh. The years fell away, and they were girls again, sharing their dreams at the edge of the moor.

"Well then," Ruth said finally. "That's settled. You *have* to perform now."

"For your mother," Eliza said, grinning.

"And for your granny," Ruth said. "Come on." She nodded toward the stage where the Master of Ceremonies was preparing to announce the start of the Ladies' solo competition.

Butterflies the size of bats swarmed Eliza's stomach as she took her seat. The Master of Ceremonies called up the first competitor—a large-bosomed woman of about forty who wore a purple dress that swished as she mounted the stairs to the stage.

She performed a Schubert song that earned her polite applause. One of the bats stopped flapping. Over the next hour, ten more women performed, only a handful of whom were applauded with any enthusiasm. A few more of the bats folded their wings and went back to sleep.

"You're next," Ruth whispered. "Good luck."

Eliza heard her name called. When she climbed to the stage and turned to face the packed hall, she saw the women from the choir seated several rows behind Ruth. All of them—even Doris—were smiling.

She nodded at the pianist to play the opening bars of her piece. A steely determination stiffened her spine as she raised her chin and fixed her gaze on the back of the elaborate hall. Everything in her life had led to this point. Win or lose, she'd earned her right to be here and to soothe her pain and her fear with music.

She opened her mouth and let the first glorious note of the Handel piece soar into the huge space.

Chapter 56

Morecambe

Ruth

Ruth threw her arms around Eliza. Even at the height of her fame in London, she'd never felt so elated. Against every obstacle thrown in her path, Eliza Kingwell had won first prize.

"I'm so happy for you!" she exclaimed. "I knew you could do it." She stepped back and peered into her friend's face. "How do you feel?"

"Flabbergasted, if you want to know the truth!" Eliza said. She looked at the envelope containing the prize money and then at Ruth, her gray eyes shining. "I really did it."

"Of course, you did! Come on! Let's go find the others. They'll want to congratulate you."

"Hold up," Eliza said. "There's someone coming to speak with you." She leaned forward and whispered. "It's that judge who's sweet on you."

"How do you know?"

"Oh, please, Ruth. I'm not blind. I saw the way he looked at you when we were in Whitby. He's head over heels." She grinned. "He looks nice."

"Mrs. Henton?"

"Mr. Gallagher," Ruth said, her voice tight.

Silas nodded at Eliza. "Congratulations on your win, Mrs. Kingwell."

"Thank you," Eliza said.

Silas turned to Ruth, his shoulders slightly hunched as if to make himself shorter. He looked nervous and unsure of himself. Keeping his eyes fixed on a point beyond Ruth's shoulder, he said, "May I introduce my colleague? This is Miss Sarah McNair."

"Pleased to meet you, Miss McNair," Ruth said. To her relief, her voice held just the right amount of polite warmth.

"Likewise! Mr. Gallagher has told me *so* much about you."

Miss McNair was positively bouncing with enthusiasm. A few strands of hair had escaped their pins and grazed her shoulders, giving her a charmingly tousled look which made her appear even younger.

"He has?" Ruth asked.

"Oh, dear me, yes! He keeps telling me that he hopes you'll come back to work for the association. I hope so, too. It would make me feel ever so less guilty."

"What do you mean?" Out of the corner of her eye, she saw Eliza smiling.

Miss McNair blushed. "I'm to be married in September. Mr. Harrison warned me not to get engaged when he took me on but…" She laughed and shrugged. "When Walter—he's my betrothed—asked me to be his wife, well, I couldn't *possibly* say no, could I?"

"She will be much missed," Silas said gallantly.

"Congratulations, Miss McNair," Ruth said. "I hope you will be very happy."

"I plan to be. Well, I'll leave you two to get caught up." She held out her hand to shake Ruth's. "It really is *so* wonderful to finally meet you."

"I'm off as well," Eliza said. "The choir's waiting for me outside." She nodded at Silas. "Good afternoon to ye." She turned so she was between Ruth and Silas and whispered, "He's a good'un."

The Ladies' Solo competition was the last event of the day. People streamed out of the auditorium, leaving only a few workers tidying up while Ruth and Silas stood alone next to the stage.

"I'm happy to see you again, Mrs. Henton," Silas said. "You've done wonders with the choir. I'm only sorry we couldn't award them first place."

"If I'd been judging, I would have awarded the same marks. The Leeds and Westmoreland choirs were superior." She paused. "Although not by much."

He inclined his head. "We agree completely."

They stared at each other, the silence lengthening.

"Silas?"

"Ruth?"

They both spoke at once and then laughed. Silas reached for her hand and brought it to his lips. She thrilled to the feel of them on her skin.

He dropped her hand, a horrified expression on his face. "Oh dear! Forgive me. I shouldn't have presumed."

She glanced around to be sure no one was watching them and then rose on her tiptoes and kissed his lips.

"There!" she said, lowering her heels back to the floor. "I should have done that months ago!"

"You mean you…?"

She nodded. "I'm a foolish woman, Silas, to have taken so long to see what was right in front of me. I know it's not seemly for me to be so bold, but I'm yours if you'll have me."

"Oh no!" he exclaimed. "No, no! Of course you're not too bold." He wrapped his arms around her and pulled her off her feet. "Oh, Ruth!"

Chapter 57

Briarstown

Eliza

Eliza closed her eyes against the chatter of the women filling the third-class train carriage. She wished everyone would stop talking so she could relive her win. She still couldn't believe it. Five guineas! The envelope containing the money was tucked under her bodice, snug between her breasts. She pressed her hand against it, smiling at the crackling sound of the paper.

Reg would try to get it off her, but she'd take the money to Ma for safe-keeping and tell her about the Plan. Now that some of the other men were on to Reg, he might think twice about making a fuss. If she had to, she'd go to Mr. Lewiston. The boss might take Reg's part, just as he had against poor Olive Grant, but there was a chance he'd listen to her. His patience with Reg must be wearing thin.

Eliza would write to Granny as soon as she got home and tell her to expect them by the end of the summer. It was already the middle of July. If Reg tried to stop her, she'd have the law on *him*. She wasn't exactly sure how, but she'd find a way. Maybe Miss Taylor at the post office would know something, what with her being so keen on women's rights. Hadn't she said that the world was changing?

When the train pulled into Briarstown station, Hattie was the first to jump off and announce to the large gathering of friends and family that the Briarstown Ladies' Choir had won third prize. To Eliza's relief, the whoops and yells that greeted this news drowned out any attempt that Hattie might have made to announce Eliza's win. She didn't want Reg to know until after she'd taken the prize money to Ma.

As the other women were surrounded by husbands and children and friends, Eliza searched for her brood. She planned to collect them all and go straight to a lodging house near the center of Briarstown. The girls would be confused and probably frightened, but she couldn't risk returning to her house.

Eliza couldn't see her girls anywhere. Panic gripped her. Had Reg taken them away? She pushed her way through the crowds to the exit and began to run.

"Mrs. Kingwell?" Jonas from the mill stepped in front of her.

"What is it?"

"It's your Reg. There's been an accident."

"A broken leg and a broken collarbone. He'll lose the leg, but he's lucky to be alive." Dr. Easton rubbed a patch of pink skin on his balding head, causing flecks of white to scatter across the shoulders of his black coat. His cravat was gray with overuse and under-washing, his general air one of exhaustion and neglect. He was the only doctor employed to tend to all the mill workers, and it was common knowledge he preferred drinking to practicing medicine.

"What happened?" Eliza asked.

"Your husband got himself caught in the rotating shaft. It's a bad business, to be sure."

"Will he work again?"

The doctor shook his head. "Not likely. A man with one leg's not much use at the mill." He stood. "Keep him quiet, feed him as well as you can, and…"

"What?"

"Pray?" He closed his bag and turned to descend the narrow staircase. "I'll see myself out, Missus."

She watched the doctor disappear down the stairwell, wondering if Reg had heard him. He'd been unconscious when they'd brought him home, but she'd seen his eyelids flutter while the doctor tended to him. Sighing, she turned to see him staring at her, his blue eyes clouded with pain and laudanum.

"Eliza?"

She walked forward and looked down at him, knowing as she did that her Plan again lay in ruins.

"Where's the money you won from Morecambe?" Reg asked a week later. He was sitting up in bed, his eyes bright, the old spark back.

"What money?"

"I know all about it, Eliza," Reg said. "It's no use lying. Andy told me that Hattie told *him* you won five guineas at that festival. Five guineas! That's more money than I'd see in God knows how many months. What are you up to, keeping it from me?"

Eliza almost wanted to laugh. Did he really not know how much she despised him? How much she wanted to leave? She contemplated the empty space on the bed where his right leg should be. The doctor had been by the day before and said the stump was healing nicely. What a terrible word that was, Eliza thought.

Stump. Stumped.

Like she was. Getting away had never seemed more impossible.

The doctor had also said that Reg could get around on crutches soon, and that he'd look into getting a pair made.

"Well? When were you going to tell me about the money? With me laid up like this, we'll be needing it."

Eliza glanced over at the bureau and remembered the time he'd pushed her into it, how her cheek had glanced off the corner. She remembered staying away from people for weeks as the bruise bloomed and then faded. She remembered the nights, the pain and the disgust, the staring into darkness, the feeling of being completely and utterly alone in a world that didn't want her.

That had been before the choir.

She made up her mind.

"As soon as you're up and about, the girls and I are leaving for good."

"What are you talking about? You can't leave me. I'll have the law on you."

Eliza shrugged. "You can try, but with no job, what are you going to use for money? Mr. Lewiston's got no use for a one-legged man." She patted the space next to Reg's good leg. "I'll get your tea now. Don't worry, I won't be going just yet. I'll wait until you can fend for yourself. Maybe there's a shopkeeper who won't object to his clerk hobbling around on a crutch."

"You can't do this!"

"I can, Reg. And I will."

Chapter 58

Whitby

Ruth

Ruth skeptically regarded the contraption. She knew it was called a bicycle, and she'd seen women ride them, but she never thought she'd be one of them. It didn't look safe.

"Are you sure?"

"Of course. Step over this middle part. That's it. Now put your hands on the handlebars. Like so." Silas stood behind her to the right of the bike, his arms stretched either side of her, his hands resting beside hers on the handlebars. She still marveled at how the heat of him felt so honest and good. It wasn't the perfumed touch of well-barbered, entitled men like William back in London or the applause of the boys crowding the stalls. This was different. Being close to Silas felt like coming home.

"Put your foot on this pedal. That's it." He leaned down and guided her boot, his forearm grazing her calf beneath the split skirt she was wearing for the first time. She'd felt very daring putting it on that morning in preparation for her first ride on a bicycle. When buttoned up, it appeared to be a proper skirt, but when she unbuttoned the front panel and wrapped it around herself, it revealed wide-legged trousers.

"I'm going to fall!" she said.

"I'm right here to catch you. Now, push forward on the right pedal and put your other foot on the left pedal."

"I can't!"

"Of course you can." Silas took hold of her left arm and lightly pushed her. "Put your foot on the pedal. That's it. Push down."

The contraption wobbled under her. Gravel crunched beneath the wheels, and the chain clinked. The front wheel skewed sideways and, just in time, she put her feet back on the ground to avoid falling. Silas came up behind her.

"You've almost got it. Come on. Try again."

"I can't!"

Silas walked around the bicycle to stand in front of her, holding the handlebars with both his hands and looking her in the eye. "You can do whatever you put your mind to, Ruth Gallagher."

"Do you think so?" She smiled at his earnest expression. How she loved him! They'd been married only a few weeks and had come to Whitby for their honeymoon. Silas had told her it was in Whitby when he'd first realized he was in love with her.

"Of course," he said. "Now, again."

"I… well." Ruth put her foot on the pedal and took in a ragged breath. Silas moved aside. She pressed down and hoisted herself onto the seat, then caught the left pedal with her left foot and pushed down, then again on the right, until suddenly the bicycle responded, and she was gliding down the narrow road. Waves lapped the pebble beach to her left, and the wind flowed like silk across her cheeks.

She kept pedalling.

Her heart opened, and she laughed into the wind.

Chapter 59

Briarstown

Eliza

“This letter's come for you, Ma,” Annie said. “Are you all right? You look pale.”

Eliza motioned impatiently. “I'm fine. I've been dealing with your dad. He's been that cranky all morning.”

“Is the letter from your granny? The return address says Devon.”

“It looks like a man's hand.” Eliza opened and read the letter, then let it fall to the table.

“What's wrong?”

“My Granny's gone,” she said. “This here's from Mr. Barton, the man she worked for. He says she died suddenly last week.” Eliza sat down hard. She'd intended to take the girls to Devon as soon as Reg was able to get around on crutches. Now, what was she going to do?

“I'm sorry, Ma.”

“Make a brew for your dad, will you? I'd best go tell your granny.”

“Yes, Ma.”

Eliza pulled on a coat and walked out into a misty September drizzle. Tiny drops caught in her hair and scattered across her cheeks, already wet with tears. She wasn't sure if she was crying for Granny or for herself, but what did it matter? It was all the same in the end. She headed towards Aunt Agnes's house. Ma would want to know, of course, and would likely be annoyed that the letter had come to Eliza instead of her.

“So, she's gone,” Ma said, her lined face impassive.

“I'm sorry, Ma,” Eliza said. “But at least she didn't suffer.”

“No, no. We can be glad of that.” Ma absently picked up her cup of tea, sipped it in silence, then put it down and stared at the grate. "I should have gone to her."

"You didn't know, Ma. She sounded fine in her last letter."

"Mr. Barton writes that he's got the money Ma left for Bob and me."

"I'd best fetch Bob," Agnes said, rising and leaving the room.

"How's your man?" Ma asked.

"He's learning to walk with the crutches."

"And you?"

"I get by."

"You deserve to do more than get by," Ma said.

Eliza stared at her mother. "What do you mean?"

"I've seen how miserable he's made you. For a while, I didn't think much about it. None of us have it easy. Some days my head pains me so much I wish I could die myself. But at least I had a good man who loved me."

"How did you know? About Reg?"

Ma shrugged. "A mother knows when her child's in pain," she said matter-of-factly. She took another sip of tea. "You need to take your prize money and leave him. And when the money comes from your granny, you shall have my half."

"What about Jack and Billy?"

"They needn't know nothin' about it."

"But, Ma…"

"No buts. My mind's been made up since your Gladys was born and I first saw bruises on ye. I knew then that I'd be giving you half of Granny's money when it came. I was blessed with a good man, but I saw what my dad did to your granny when I was growing up. Broke my heart to think you be suffering the same."

"Why didn't you say something?"

"What good would it have done?"

"I might have felt less alone."

Ma looked down at her clasped hands and said nothing.

"Ma?" Eliza wanted her to look up and meet her eyes, to see the hurt in them.

"The past is past," Ma said finally, a catch in her voice. "All you can do now is give your girls a future. And Eliza?" She looked up.

"Yes?"

Ma inhaled sharply, her thin lips quivering. "I should never have blamed you for our Ernie's death. It were wrong of me. I've been sorry for a long while now, but I didn't know how to tell you."

Eliza stared at the small woman who so closely resembled herself. For coming on eighteen years since Ernie's death, Eliza had lived with Ma's resentment, her sharp words and cutting looks. When he was alive, Dad had tried his best to smooth things over, but with little success. Ma was determined to hold Eliza responsible.

Eliza had learned to live with the certainty that Ma would never love her again. Suddenly, she wondered if that had been the real reason why she'd married Reg. She'd chosen a man who couldn't love her like she deserved to be loved. After all, if her own mother couldn't love her, then who could?

Ma was twisting her thin hands in her lap. With a start, Eliza realized she was no longer young. Hard lines scoured her pale cheeks, and her black hair was streaked with white.

"Thanks, Ma," she said finally. "That means a lot."

Ma nodded. "Aye. Go on with ye, now." She rose unsteadily to her feet and brushed Eliza's cheek with her lips. "You be worth a lot, my girl. Don't sell yerself short."

Eliza left her aunt's house and started for home, only to pass her street and keep walking until she reached the edge of town. The smoke from the mill chimneys blended into the mist so that the entire valley blurred and softened.

George's cottage looked warm and inviting. She knocked softly on his door.

He ushered her in, his smile wide. For several minutes, he fussed with the tea things, and then sat down across from her, his elbows on his knees.

"I'm leaving Briarstown," Eliza said. "I wanted to let you know because you've been so kind to me."

"I'll help you, lass. I want to."

"I know, but George?"

"Aye?"

"I need to do this on my own. Do you understand?"

"Can't say as I do, but if that's what you want, then I'll not stand in yer way."

When Eliza stood to leave, George came towards her and pulled her into his arms. She sighed and laid her head against his broad chest, and for the first time since Dad died, felt completely and utterly safe. George would take care of her and her daughters and see to it that none of them came to harm. They could have a life together. It wasn't too late.

She pulled back.

No.

"Goodbye, George."

Chapter 60

York

Ruth

"I can't do it!" Silas said. He turned to Ruth, his grey eyes wide with terror. "This was a mistake."

Ruth took his hand and squeezed it. "You *can* do it. I have complete faith in you."

They stood together at the front of one of the choir stalls at York Minster. Ruth nodded toward the nave, now filled with a large congregation waiting for the service to begin. "Think of how our singing will make people feel. That's what I do when I get nervous."

"I don't understand." Silas's tone was desperate, and he looked like he wanted to run and hide behind one of the massive pillars holding up the gothic arches on either side of the nave.

Ruth's heart swelled with love. She'd heard the term wedded bliss bandied about and had always thought it an exaggeration. It wasn't. These first months of her marriage to Silas were indeed blissful. She didn't know it was possible to love another human being with so much tenderness— and so much passion.

How much she had missed!

"Silas," she whispered. "Look at me." She held his gaze with soft eyes. "That's it. Now, breathe in slowly. Good. Hold it. Now, breathe out to the count of six. One, two, three, four, five, six."

His lips quivered with the effort, but she could see his shoulders retreat an inch or two from his ears.

"Again," she said. "We'll do it together."

He breathed in and out the way she directed several more times. Some color returned to his cheeks and the hand she held was no longer shaking.

"You really think I can do it?"

"Of course. You and I are a team, remember? Think about how beautifully our voices sound together. You've said yourself that singing with me is the most wonderful thing we've ever done together."

"I wouldn't say the *most* wonderful," he said.

"Silas!" She blushed and looked around, but they stood apart from the choir, and no one was paying attention to them. "Remember where we are."

"I doubt God is frowning upon us. We *are* married, after all."

"That we are." She grinned impishly.

The service began and they sat down to await their cue. When finally, the organist played the opening chords of *Ave Maria*, Ruth caught the eye of the choir master, who smiled. He'd competed with his choir at a recent festival and after winning, had invited Ruth to sing at York Minster.

She'd been happy to oblige, but only on the condition that her husband join her. Soon after their wedding, she'd persuaded Silas to sing for her, declaring that she didn't believe he could have won two of the prestigious Eisteddfods. How could she know he was telling the truth? She'd been teasing, of course, but Silas had cheerfully proved her wrong.

Ruth had been astounded by the quality and tone of Silas's voice and quickly decided it was a voice too wondrous to be heard only by her.

When she'd told Silas about the choirmaster's invitation, he'd flatly refused. Didn't she remember how he suffered from debilitating stage fright? How could she even think of making him perform in front of people. And at York Minster?

Out of the question.

Slowly, with patience and good humor, Ruth coaxed him into agreeing to share his gift with the world.

The organ swelled and Ruth prepared herself to sing. She looked over at Silas and nodded. He still looked frightened but also resolved. To her relief—and delight—when he opened his mouth and began to sing, his rich tenor voice soared through the great space.

Several bars later, she joined him, and together they made music fit for the angels.

Chapter 61

Briarstown

Eliza

"We'll miss you," Josie said.

"And I'll miss you," Eliza said. "I talked again with Mrs. Adams, and she's promised to find someone from the Choral Society to lead you. She'll not leave you in the lurch."

"It won't be the same without you," Hannah said.

"You'll do fine."

"Maybe we'll compete again in Whitby," Mary said. "I heard that's where you're going."

"I am and that would be wonderful. I'll be cheering you on."

"Or more likely competing against us in a new choir," Hattie said.

"We'll see about that." Eliza nodded at Mary Denholm. "Is she ready?"

"Oh, aye, and excited as all get out." Mary stood aside and ushered forward Olive Grant. She wore a shawl over her head and carried her newborn baby.

"I'm so glad you want to go with us," Eliza said.

"Oh yes! Thank *you*! I'll work hard for you, I promise."

"Don't worry about that. You take care of your wee one. I've got plenty of girls to help me."

"So, I guess this is goodbye," Doris said, scowling to hide the wobbling of her bottom lip.

Minnie was openly crying as she stepped forward to hug Eliza. "Take care of yourself, luv," she said.

Lottie and Hannah and Josie also hugged her, while Hattie stood to one side, her eyes suspiciously red.

"Right, then," Eliza said finally. "I'll see you lot in the spring."

Autumn leaves skittered across her path as she walked with Olive from Mary Denholm's house to Court Four. She was relieved to discover in Olive a quiet-spoken girl who was content to croon quietly to her baby and didn't need Eliza to make conversation. The girls would love having the baby to fuss over.

"You can wait here," Eliza said, when they reached the passageway. I'll fetch the girls and we'll be off. I'm guessing you don't want to risk seeing Reg."

Olive shook her head. "No, Mrs. Kingwell. That I don't."

"Call me Eliza, please. Think of me as a sister. I've only had brothers, and I've always wanted a sister."

"Oh, aye, me too. You're too good to me."

"No less than you deserve."

Eliza found her daughters already out in the yard standing guard over the pile of their belongings—two battered suitcases, three boxes, and an assortment of small bags. She put her arm around Bessie, who had started to cry.

"Our new place is near the sea," she said. "You'll like it there."

"I don't want to go to the sea."

"Aye, well, you'll be all right." Eliza looked over Bessie's head at Annie. "See as she's occupied for the journey. I'll just go have a word with your dad."

"Yes, Ma." Annie had also cried when Eliza first told her they'd be leaving Briarstown, but she'd recovered quickly enough. That she'd understood *why* they were leaving broke Eliza's heart, but there was nothing for it. She'd made her decision, and the girls would need to accept it, just as she'd accepted Dad's decision to move the family to the North all those years ago.

"What's it like in Whitby?" Annie had asked.

"It's a lovely little town," Eliza said. "There's a wind blowing all the time and the air's that fresh."

"Can we come back here to visit?"

"We'll see."

Eliza mounted the stairs to the second floor. Reg was sitting on the edge of the bed, the new crutches next to him.

"Why Whitby?" he asked.

"I'm to help out at Mrs. Sheridan's boarding house," Eliza said. "She's got plenty of room for us."

"Who's Mrs. Sheridan?"

"I told you already. I stayed with her when I went to Whitby for the competition last June. She's getting on in years and so I wrote to her asking if we could come stay and help her run the place."

"Why would she want a stranger helping her?"

"Because, Reg, we met and we talked, and she liked me. It's not so much of a mystery."

"So, you're abandoning me."

"I've asked Mrs. Harris to check in on you every day and gave her a pound for her trouble. Has Mr. Lewiston found something at the mill you can do?"

Reg shrugged.

"Ah, well, something's bound to come up." Eliza stood at the foot of the bed as far away as she could get from him in the small room. "In case you're interested, I'm taking Olive Grant with me. She had her baby three weeks ago. A son. She's called him Paul."

Eliza had the satisfaction of seeing a look of anguish pass over his face.

Serves him right.

"I'll come after ye," he croaked. "You'll not be takin' my children from me."

Eliza managed to restrain herself from laughing. Reg would never change, still full of bluster, even in the face of defeat. "And if you do, I'll have you up on charges for abusing your wife."

"You can't do that."

"There's a law about it. Been on the books for a while now. Miss Taylor who runs the post office told me."

"Nonsense."

"It's not."

"Will you at least let me see them now and then? The girls?" He paused. "And the boy? You owe me that much. They're *my* children."

Owe him? Eliza took a deep breath, filling her lungs with the smell of him for the last time, and then let it out slowly and with relief. He'd never be sorry. He didn't know the meaning of the word.

She walked to the top of the stairs and paused. The darkness inside her would never go away on its own. She turned to face him again and then reached into her bag and pulled out the framed photograph that Mr. Grayson had taken almost a year earlier. "Here." She placed it on the bed next to him.

"What's this?"

"It's me with the girls. So as you don't forget what they look like."

Eliza felt a lump in her throat as she watched Reg study the photograph, his eyes passing over her and resting on each of his girls in turn. He had been a good father, she couldn't deny him that.

But it wasn't enough.

"I forgive you," she said.

"For what?" He looked up, his eyes wet.

Eliza laughed out loud, and then, shaking her head, ran lightly down the stairs and out the door. "Come on, girls," she said when she reached the yard. "Time to go."

Chapter 62

Whitby

Eliza

Eliza and Mrs. Sheridan found seats near the front of the hall at the Third Annual Whitby Music Festival a few rows behind Ruth and Silas, who sat at the judges' table. Eliza had been so pleased to hear that they intended to continue judging music competitions—at least for awhile.

As she settled herself next to Mrs. Sheridan, Eliza thought back to how she'd felt standing on the stage a year earlier. Her disappointment that she wasn't competing at this year's festival was quickly replaced by excitement for her daughters.

The Master of Ceremonies strode onstage and announced the first category—children's choirs.

"Are ye nervous?" Mrs. Sheridan asked. The older woman wore her best dress—a rust brown silk that had been fashionable two decades earlier.

"A little, although not as much as if I were competing myself."

The first two school choirs sang well. Eliza hoped her girls wouldn't be too disappointed if they didn't bring home a trophy. After all, it was their first time singing with a choir. Miracles couldn't be expected.

That wasn't quite true, Eliza thought, smiling to herself. Wasn't she living proof that miracles were possible?

"Here they are!" Mrs. Sheridan said. "Them hair ribbons I bought look right nice."

"They do."

The thirty children in the school choir ranged in age from five to thirteen. Bessie stood in the middle of the front row next to two children her age. The other four Kingwell girls stood among the older children on two rows of risers. Each of her daughters wore a blue ribbon tied near the crowns of their heads. Eliza beamed with pride.

The teacher raised her arm, the pianist struck a chord, and the children began to sing. When Annie stepped forward to perform her solo, Eliza's heart soared. The past six months since they'd come to Whitby had been challenging, to say the least. The girls hadn't always behaved themselves, and Bessie still cried for her dad almost every night.

But Eliza was determined, and slowly, week by week and month by month, the clean salt air blowing in from the North Sea began to dull the years of pain so that now she woke up every morning with a smile on her face.

"I'm happy to see you, Eliza," Ruth said after all the children's choirs had performed and the winners announced. The Whitby school had placed second.

"Married life agrees with you," Eliza said.

"It does. And you'll never guess, but we've decided to settle here in Whitby now that I can't work anymore."

"Oh?"

Blushing, Ruth put her hand on her belly. "The Music Association didn't mind me working as a married lady so long as it was with Silas, but they draw the line at accepting mothers."

"Oh, Ruth! I'm so happy for you." Eliza folded her friend into a long hug.

"And what about you?" Ruth asked as she stepped back. "I hope you're still singing, although I see you're not competing in the festival."

"Not this year. I've been busy helping Mrs. Sheridan here in her boarding house." She waved one hand toward Mrs. Sheridan.

"Pleased to meet you, Ma'am," Mrs. Sheridan said. "Your friend's been a godsend."

"Eliza is the most capable person I've ever known," Ruth said.

"So, we're to be neighbors again. I'm glad of it."

Ruth grinned. "Maybe we could even sing together."

"Funny you should say that," Eliza said, returning the grin.

"Eliza's already started getting together some women around here for a choir," Mrs. Sheridan said. "They plan to compete in next year's festival."

"Why does that not surprise me? And I'd be honored to join." Ruth paused. "As your conductor?"

"Of course!"

At that moment, Eliza's daughters ran up, hair ribbons dancing, faces alight with smiles. "What did you reckon, Ma?" Lily May demanded. "Weren't Annie good?"

"Annie did very well," Eliza said. "You go on now with Mrs. Sheridan. I'll catch up with you."

"Yes, Ma!"

The girls followed Mrs. Sheridan from the hall, and Eliza turned back to Ruth. "I never knew being happy felt like this," she said.

"Like what?"

"Like I'm exactly where I should be in the world. Like I have everything I'll ever need."

"Everything?" Ruth's eyes danced. "Leave some room in your heart for love, Eliza. I highly recommend it."

Eliza was up to her elbows in dirty water. Running a boarding house meant scrubbing sheets two days out of every seven, but she didn't mind the hard work. She sang as she squeezed and twisted and mangled.

Now that it was June and the weather fine, she'd hang the wet sheets outside in the large back garden. In no time at all, the sun and wind would dry them. When she gathered them back into her basket at the end of the day, she'd stop a moment and inhale their sweet, clean scent.

The front doorbell rang. All the girls were at school, Olive was walking with the baby along the seafront, and Mrs. Sheridan was lying down. Sighing, Eliza reached for a clean cloth to dry her hands and then climbed the steps from the kitchen to the main hallway. Perhaps Ruth had come to call. She sometimes did, especially on sunny days. They'd stroll to the beach or climb the steps up to the ruined abbey on East Cliff.

"Och, Missus?" Mr. O'Malley, one of the boarders, met her at the top of the steps. "There's a man at the door askin' fer ye."

"What man?"

"Didn't ask, Missus. He's a fine tall fella is all's I can tell ye."

"Thank you." Eliza patted her hair. She knew she looked a mess, but there was nothing to be done about it. She'd wondered for months if this day would come, and now that it had, she wasn't sure what she'd do.

George Ledbetter stood on the front steps. He scrunched his cloth cap between his hands, and his broad forehead shone with sweat.

"I don't expect nowt'," he said before she had a chance to speak. "I love you. And I want to be with you. Will you and your girls have me?"

"I don't…" Eliza paused, searching for words. She hadn't dared hope he might still want her after she'd said goodbye to him in Briarstown. But as the months flew by in her new life, she'd thought about him more and more often. Her heart warmed, knowing he'd waited for her to settle herself before seeking her out.

Only a man who truly cared for her would do such a thing.

"I can't go back to Briarstown," Eliza said.

"I know that."

"My girls have opportunities here. Annie's going to be a teacher and Lily May's top of her class."

"Aye, so's I've heard." George grinned. "Your Annie writes to her friend Tilda who lives next door to my sister. I know all about your doings here in Whitby. I'm not asking you to come back to Briarstown, Eliza. I'm asking if you'll have me."

"But…"

"Here. Now. I can't say nowt else except to say it again, will ye have me?" He gripped the doorframe with one hand, his knuckles white. "I don't want to live another moment without ye, Eliza."

Eliza stared up at George, at the kindness in his eyes and the strength in his large hands. She knew as well as she knew her own name that those hands would never touch her in anger.

But was she ready to share her life with another man?

She didn't need him, not like she'd needed Reg to give her a name and a home. She'd proved to herself that she could manage on her own. Mrs. Sheridan had promised to leave the boarding house to her when she died, seeing as she hadn't any family of her own.

Eliza was proud of how she'd made a comfortable home for herself and the girls and Olive and the baby. They were fed and clothed respectably, and her days were full.

But the nights…

"Well then," Eliza said briskly. "You'd best come in. I've not got all day to be standing on the doorstep in this wind."

The End

Author's Note

The Choir, perhaps more than any of my previous novels, is a labor of love. As a child, I remember my granny talking about how my great-great-grandmother Eliza had two men in her life: my great-great-grandfather with whom she had six children and then another man with whom she had seven more children. Why did she leave the first man for the second? This was the 1870s, and Eliza was a working-class woman living in a mill town in Yorkshire. Nothing was ever said, but I knew from the records that Eliza and her first husband did not divorce for many years after their split and long after the second family was in existence.

Since I didn't know the real story, I needed to invent one because I wanted to delve into the lives of the women who had come before me—strong, capable women who ran boarding houses, emigrated to Canada on a ship dodging U-Boats during World War I, and in the case of my granny, never took guff from anyone. Granny also had a beautiful singing voice, and so I decided that my Eliza would use her voice to escape an unhappy marriage.

In the 1880s and 1890s, the music competition movement was sweeping Great Britain. Choirs were formed at all levels of society to compete, particularly in cities such as Blackpool, Leeds, and Sheffield in the North. Mary Wakefield, who makes a cameo appearance in *The Choir*, really was responsible for the growth and success of the music competition movement. Her legacy lives on. I well remember performing in many choir competitions (usually as the piano accompanist because singing is not my gift) when I was in school in Vancouver, Canada.

Although based on family stories, the plot and characters in *The Choir* are fictional, with times and places changed to suit the story. The town of Briarstown is also fictional.

Acknowledgments

My amazing mother, Ruby Cram nee Scott, played an integral role in helping me research and write *The Choir*. She passed in 2021, but I know she'd be so proud to read the finished novel.

I'd also like to thank the two brilliant choir directors who live on Bowen Island in Vancouver, BC, where I live. Ellen MacIntosh, who leads the Bowen Island Community Choir, patiently gave me singing lessons and taught me so much about breathing and performing. Lynn Williams, who runs the Penrhyn Academy of Singing and directs the Ladies Madrigal Singers, was generous with her time helping me determine a repertoire for Eliza, sharing her insights about choir conducting, and letting me sit in on choir rehearsals.

Stephanie Williams, my friend forever and an amazing editor, was a tremendous help to me while I was writing the many drafts of *The Choir*. Her comments and advice are always spot on! Thank you also to my four long-time friends, Cathy Hamre, Selinde Krayenhoff, Jean Leckie, and dear Elizabeth Wilson whom we lost in 2024, for their ongoing encouragement. When we meet for our annual get-together, they are always a supportive audience when I read from my latest work-in-progress. I feel very blessed to have them in my life.

Thanks also to Clare Bamber, a writing mentor and novelist based in Yorkshire, who read early drafts of *The Choir* and helped me with the Yorkshire dialect. Clare also very kindly took me to visit Quarry Bank Mill, a preserved cotton mill, similar to the one my Eliza would have worked in. Hearing all the looms turned on at once was a visceral experience I'll never forget.

I'm also very grateful to Robin Henry for her intelligent editing and to Colin Mustful and the team at History Through Fiction for an excellent publishing experience.

And finally, as always, I owe everything to my wonderful family—my awesome daughter, Julia Simpson, and my partner, support and love for over forty years, Gregg Simpson.

About the Author

Carol M. Cram is the award-winning author of the Women in the Arts Trilogy (*The Towers of Tuscany*, *A Woman of Note*, and *The Muse of Fire*), the contemporary novel *Love Among the Recipes* (which received a *Publishers Weekly* Starred Review), and her forthcoming historical novel *The Choir*. She also hosts the *Art In Fiction Podcast*, where she interviews authors who write novels inspired by the arts, and writes a travel blog called *The Artsy Traveler*.

Before becoming a full-time novelist, podcaster, and blogger, Carol authored over sixty bestselling textbooks in computer applications and business communications for Cengage Learning and Houghton Mifflin. She holds an MA in Drama and an MBA, and taught for many years on the faculty at Capilano University. She lives on Bowen Island near Vancouver, Canada with her husband, visual artist Gregg Simpson.

About HTF Publishing

Founded in 2023 as an imprint of History Through Fiction, HTF Publishing is hybrid publisher of compelling, high-quality historical novels. Following in the tradition of History Through Fiction, HTF Publishing seeks to provide readers with engaging historical narratives that are rooted in detailed and accurate historical research. As a hybrid press, we want to work with authors who are serious about their craft and aspire to share imaginative, important, and well-researched, historical narratives with the world.

If you enjoyed this novel, please consider leaving a review. It's the best way to support us and our authors. Plus, you'll be helping other readers discover this great story.

Thank you!

www.HistoryThroughFiction.com